Echoes from Afar

Tamara McKinley

Echoes from Afar

Quercus

First published in Great Britain in 2015 by

Quercus Publishing Ltd
Carmelite House
50 Victoria Embankment
London EC4Y 0DZ

An Hachette UK company

A CIP catalogue record for this book is available
from the British Library

TPB ISBN 978 1 78429 696 4
EBOOK ISBN 978 1 78429 542 4

10 9 8 7 6 5 4 3 2 1

Typeset by CC Book Production

Printed and bound in Great Britain by Clays Ltd, St Ives plc

PROLOGUE

Paris, 1956

Despite the passing of the years, he'd hoped that by some miracle he would see her there once more, so when she finally appeared, he wondered if it was the sheer force of his longing that had somehow conjured her up.

His breath caught and his pulse quickened as he sat forward in his wheelchair by the third-floor balcony windows, the glass of wine and cigarette forgotten as he tried to believe it was really her. Two decades had passed, and his eyes were not as reliable as they had once been. Could they be playing a cruel trick on him? Was his imagination running riot? Yet as she stood on the Pont Neuf and gazed down the swift-flowing Seine towards the distant Eiffel Tower and the rooftops of Paris, it was as if those years had been swept away and she had returned to him.

He eased further forward, confident she couldn't see him in the rapidly darkening room, but still not trusting what his eyes were telling him. Her hair was longer than he remembered, flowing over her narrow shoulders in a tumble of silken curls, but her slender figure still retained the delicate grace that belied the fierce energy and determination she'd always possessed. And even in her relaxed state, there was an almost defiant tilt to her chin that he remembered so very well. Dressed in narrow slacks and a sweater, there were suitcases at her feet and she carried an artist's portfolio, and a coat over her arm.

'Belle?' he breathed in wonder. 'Can it really be you?'

As if she'd heard him, she turned from the river, her gaze sweeping beyond the bridge to the cobbled Quai de la Mégisserie, and the tall grey houses whose balconies and windows overlooked the Seine.

His breath caught again as her face was illuminated by a nearby street lamp, and her eyes seemed to find his momentarily before she looked away. The disappointment was sharp. It wasn't Belle, couldn't possibly be Belle. Too many years had passed, and this girl was younger than Belle had been on that fateful day when they'd met on the bridge. And yet there was something about her that held echoes of the past . . .

'Are you all right, Patron?'

The light was switched on, startling him, and he blinked in its sudden glare. 'Turn that off and come here,' he ordered the young man as he turned once more towards the window. 'See that girl? Go and find out who she is and where she's come from. Now, quickly, before she leaves the bridge.'

The look was quizzical, the smile wry. 'She's a bit young, even for you, isn't she, Patron?' he drawled.

His impatience made him sharp. 'Just do as I ask, Max,' he rasped. 'I'll explain later.'

As Max left the room, he turned once more towards the window. She was looking up now, her gaze drifting over the wrought-iron balconies, perhaps drawn by the sudden glare of light which had just as swiftly been extinguished. Her eyes seemed to hold him there for a second, and he could sense her unease as she broke the spell and hurriedly looked away.

He touched the glass in the window as if by doing so he could keep her there, but before Max had even reached the street, she'd picked up her cases, turned her back and was immediately lost amongst the stream of homeward-bound office workers and strolling tourists.

He slumped back into the chair, the moment lost, his pain raw. He closed his eyes to try to dispel some of his anguish, but all he could see was the young, vibrant Belle who had stood on the Pont Neuf so many years before, and the memories and deep regrets over what had happened to tear them apart now threatened to overwhelm him.

1

London, 1936

Annabelle Blake padded across the cold linoleum and pulled back the thin curtains to discover it was raining heavily, and the sight of water gushing from blocked gutters, pooling on dirty cobbles and swirling in the clogged drains seemed to emphasise the hopelessness of her situation. Her unfair dismissal from the hospital two weeks before, and the far from glowing reference they'd eventually sent, meant it was proving impossible to find another nursing post – and her money was fast running out.

Annabelle was twenty-three, with very little to show for all the years of training and hard work at the hospital. She had no family to turn to after her father had banished her from home, and her mother was too frightened to defy him by staying in touch; she was living in a run-down boarding house in a poor part of London where she had little in common with the other tenants. Her sense of isolation was compounded by the fact that her closest friend, Caroline Howden, had left to nurse in Spain's civil war, and there had been no sign of the usually

4

dependable and supportive George Ashton after she'd turned down his proposal.

She moved away from the bed-sitting-room window and dragged her fingers through her tangled hair as she tried to see the positive side of things. At least she now had a reference – however double-edged it was; George was intelligent enough to eventually understand why she'd had to turn him down; and although it might not be the sort of day that encouraged being out of doors, she was meeting her mother, Camille, for coffee. As this was a rare and unexpected occurrence – made so because they had to keep their infrequent meetings secret from her father – she should at least try to put a brave face on things and concentrate on healing the breach between them that had widened over the past five years.

Annabelle mourned the fact that she and her mother had never been close, and although she knew Camille held some affection for her, it was carefully guarded beneath a veneer of coolness. As Annabelle had grown up in that great gloomy house in Fulham there had been little opportunity for her to get to know her mother – her father even less, although that proved to be a blessing because she was frightened of his hard grey eyes and his inflexible rules.

She had spent her youngest years upstairs in the nursery with a succession of nannies and saw her mother only briefly when she came up to say goodnight. Even then there was no hug or warm kiss, just a rather distracted pat on the head or shoulder. Camille had never been a tactile person, choosing rather to remain almost aloof, and as Annabelle had matured she'd begun to understand that Camille's whole existence centred around Edwin – even though it was clear that he terrified her.

Annabelle snapped from her thoughts, checked the time and got quickly dressed in her best tweed skirt and woollen sweater. With barely enough money for food, let alone new clothes, there was little she could do about her lisle stockings which were heavily darned, or the gaberdine raincoat and black shoes which had certainly seen better days.

She put on a defiant slash of lipstick and a few sweeps of mascara and then brushed her dark blonde curls into some sort of order. Regarding her reflection in the fly-spotted mirror, she noted the shadows of sleepless nights beneath her violet-blue eyes, and the lacklustre tone of her once creamy skin. She swiftly dusted on some face powder, rammed on her oldest felt hat and wrapped a scarf round her neck before picking up her umbrella. It would have to do, even though Camille would no doubt throw up her hands in horror, for she was very particular about appearances.

Deciding to take the bicycle as it would make the journey quicker, she put her handbag and umbrella in the basket and lugged it down the stairs. Slamming the front door behind her, she opened her umbrella and attempted to steer the bike one-handed as she pedalled over the lumpy cobbles and through the puddles.

By the time she'd reached the Copper Kettle she knew she must look a fright. The umbrella had blown inside out, her coat was sodden and her stockings were splashed with water and muck from the roads. She managed to get the umbrella sorted and left it in the basket as she tucked her straggly wet hair behind her ears and made a dash for the tea room.

The Copper Kettle was situated in a narrow cobbled street in a part of town that her father never visited. It was warm and welcoming after being outside in the chill rain and the tables were bright with white linen and flowery china. There were three other women enjoying their morning coffee and they didn't give her a second glance as they carried on gossiping.

There was no sign of Camille, and Annabelle hoped desperately that she hadn't taken one look at the weather and changed her mind. She had sixpence in her purse, and she doubted very much that it would cover the cost of a cup of coffee in this rather pretentious little place. 'I'm meeting someone,' she said firmly to the waitress. 'As I'm early, may I use the powder room to tidy up?'

She was shown into a small room which had been painted bright pink and glaring white. But there was hot water, soap and a towel. Annabelle grimaced when she saw herself in the mirror, for her felt hat drooped sullenly over her mass of bedraggled wet hair, her mascara and lipstick were smudged and her scarf and coat were so wet they could have been wrung out through a mangle.

She found a handkerchief to remove the mascara smears and tidy up the lipstick, and then used the tea room's hand towel to rub her hair dry and dab at her stained stockings. It didn't make much difference, so she just ran a comb through the tangled curls and hoped for the best.

Having shaken the water from her raincoat and stuffed her

sodden scarf in the pocket, she prayed Camille had arrived. It would be horribly embarrassing to ask for a glass of water after using their facilities. She picked up her things and returned to the main room.

'*Mon dieu*,' gasped Camille as she paused in the act of shrugging off her mink coat. '*Tu fais peur a voir! Qu'est-ce qui est arrivée?*'

As on their previous meeting in the café, Camille had obviously decided to conduct their conversation in French so the other customers couldn't eavesdrop. 'I know I look a fright,' Annabelle replied in the same language – she'd been fluent since childhood. 'But this is what happens when one has to bicycle through the rain.' She smiled at her mother, who was looking dry and composed in her veiled black hat, dark grey two-piece suit and high patent leather heels. 'I see you didn't get caught in the downpour.'

Camille pouted and adjusted her fur over her shoulders as she sat down. 'I have always found that the London Hackney Carriage people are most helpful when it is raining. You should have called one instead of cycling.'

Annabelle was stung by the realisation that her mother hadn't a clue as to the depth of her straightened circumstances, or the extent of her situation. But then Camille had never known poverty so it wouldn't have occurred to her that taxis were beyond the reach of most people, let alone unemployed nurses.

She hung up her coat and hat and joined her at the table. 'I would hire one if I could afford it,' she said mildly. 'Especially on a day like this.'

Camille regarded her evenly and was then distracted by the waitress. Having ordered, she turned back to Annabelle. 'I don't usually have cake,' she murmured as she regarded Annabelle more intently. 'But I thought you might like a little treat. You look far too thin, and rather down-at-heel in those awful shoes.'

Annabelle didn't need reminding, but was determined to keep the conversation light and friendly. 'Cake would be a lovely treat, thank you, Maman.'

Camille was silent for a while, her eyes thoughtful behind the veil of her black hat. 'Caroline's mother told me what happened before I received your letter,' she said eventually. 'Is it very hard for you?'

'I lost the job I love, Maman, and my reputation. It seems that none of the other hospitals will give me an interview, and even the factory managers have turned me down for the most menial of jobs. Of course it's hard.' She shook back her damp curls, immediately regretting her bitter tone. 'But I'll survive, don't worry.'

Camille was silent as the waitress served them, and when she'd gone again, took her time to pour the fragrant coffee into the small cups. Once she'd taken a sip and approved of it, she leant forward. 'I'm sorry you find yourself in this predicament,' she said softly. 'But perhaps you should now reconsider Dr Ashton's proposal. After all, you're no spring chick, Annabelle, and he can offer you respectability and a far steadier sort of life.'

Annabelle stared at her in bemusement. 'I'm twenty-three, Maman, hardly ready for the shelf just yet. And I'm not going to marry someone just for the sake of escaping the situation I find myself in,' she said firmly. 'George is a friend – a very good friend – but I'm not in love with him, and it would be wrong to accept his proposal when I can't give him the sort of love he should have from a wife.'

'*Poof.* Love has very little to do with it,' she replied with an impatient wave of her hand. 'If you love him as a friend and have things in common, then that's a sound basis for any marriage. You shouldn't be so fussy, Annabelle. George Ashton might be Irish, which is rather unfortunate, but he's a solid, reliable young man with a respectable career and excellent prospects. What more could you want?'

She bridled at her mother's snooty dismissal of George's heritage, but to keep the peace let it pass. 'To be in love with the man I marry,' she replied. 'You're beginning to sound like Father,' she said in a softer tone. 'Please, Maman, allow me to make my own choices, and to find a way out of this situation without resorting to compromise. Marriage isn't the answer; it never was. I'm a nurse – one who's out of a job – and I need desperately to clear my reputation and do what I was born to do. That's all I care about at the moment.'

Camille gave a deep sigh. 'I suspected as much, so I would like to help.'

'I can't come home, Maman, if that's what you're suggesting.'

'No, no, that is not it at all.' She opened her expensive leather handbag and pulled out an envelope. 'I want you to have this.'

Annabelle gasped as she realised it was full of banknotes. 'Maman! I can't take this. If Father found out you'd given me your allowance, he'd be furious – and we both know what he'd do.'

Camille gave a secretive little smile and selected a small iced cake which she placed on Annabelle's plate and chose a slice of Madeira for herself. 'Eat your cake, Annabelle.'

Annabelle realised Camille would say nothing more about this mysterious money until she'd eaten the cake, and although she was hungry and it was a real treat, she was so pent-up she hardly tasted any of it.

Camille nodded her approval, popped a morsel of Madeira into her mouth and sighed with pleasure. 'It's almost as good as French cake,' she murmured. 'Would you like another?'

Annabelle was getting fretful, and the envelope seemed to be growing heavier in her lap with every passing minute. 'No, Maman,'she said evenly. 'I would like you to tell me how you think you can get away with giving me that much money without Father finding out.'

Camille savoured another morsel of cake. 'Edwin doesn't know that I have it,' she said airily.

'But you have no money of your own,' Annabelle replied distractedly. 'And I know for a fact he counts every penny you spend of your allowance.'

Camille's demeanour was unruffled as she continued to enjoy her cake, and Annabelle wondered what she was up to – and more importantly, where the money had come from. She had never seen Camille like this before and it worried her.

'I have for some time been saving a *sou* here and there from the housekeeping and my allowance.' Camille's tone was casual.

Annabelle shook her head. 'It would have taken years to save all that, Maman. Where did it really come from?'

Camille gave a deep sigh. 'I have a little hobby which provides me with some extra capital now and again,' she said with irritating vagueness.

'What sort of hobby?'

Camille shrugged and then smiled quite impishly. 'Just a few games of bezique, piquet or bridge. They can be quite profitable when one is playing with women who prefer gossip to paying attention to the game.'

'I never knew you played cards for money.' She stared at her mother, who was now looking decidedly pleased with herself, and wondered if her card-playing was completely honest to have made so much money. But it was an impertinent thought and not to be voiced. 'You obviously play very well,' she said carefully. 'But why hoard your winnings? Why not splash out on little treats for yourself?'

She dipped her chin and dug about in her handbag. 'Your father does not approve of gambling, so of course I couldn't spend it on new clothes or a nice hat – he would have questioned me about where the money had come from.'

Annabelle waited impatiently while she drew out a gold cigarette case and selected a pink Sobranie.

'At one time I thought I might use it as security for when I finally had the courage to leave him,' Camille admitted. 'But I enjoyed seeing it mount up, and when he was out of the house I used to count it and dream of how I might spend it if I had the chance.'

Annabelle stared at her in amazement, for she'd never heard her mother talk like this. She gathered her wits and pushed the envelope across the table. 'Then take it back, Maman,' she said urgently. 'Your need is far greater than mine. You can get to Paris and Tante Aline's with this much and I'm sure she can find you some kind of employment or . . .'

She tailed off as Camille's expression told her how ridiculous she was being to even think about her living with her sister in that crowded Parisian house, let alone having a job.

Camille concentrated on fitting the cigarette into her long ebony holder. As the flame from her gold lighter caught the tobacco, she drew in the smoke and released it almost impatiently. 'The money is for you,' she said firmly. 'I'm too old and set in my ways to run off to my sister in Paris. But you, Annabelle, are still young, and it is you who must find a new life with Aline.'

'But I don't want to go to Paris,' she protested. 'I'm English and my life is here.'

'You have the blood of the French in you, *ma chère*, and it's time you discovered a world beyond all this.' Her hand waved dismissively at the rain, the teashop and London in general.

'But my work is here,' she said firmly. 'And now I've got a reference, I'm sure to get at least one interview.'

Camille's gaze drifted down to the table as she tapped her cigarette against the glass ashtray. 'Sometimes it's better to walk away and begin in a different place,' she said quietly.

'I'm not ready to give in and run away to Paris,' said Annabelle fiercely. 'I need to clear my name and get another nursing post here in London.'

As Camille lifted her chin her eyes betrayed her sadness. 'You have always been strong, Annabelle, although some might call it wilful and disobedient. I admire your courage, but in this instance it's misguided.' She reached across the table for Annabelle's hand. 'Don't waste time fighting a battle you cannot win. Not here. Not in London.'

She felt a chill of foreboding. 'What do you mean by that?'

Camille gave a deep sigh and left the cigarette to smoulder in the ashtray as she placed both hands over Annabelle's. 'I wish that for once you would simply take my advice and not badger me with questions, Annabelle. Take the money, go to Paris and start again. There is nothing for you here.'

'How can you be so certain of that?' she asked quietly.

Camille threw up her hands. '*Zut alors*, more questions. You try my patience, Annabelle.'

Annabelle noted how she avoided her gaze, and that her hand trembled as she toyed once again with the cigarette. 'What are you hiding from me, Maman?'

She gave a Gallic shrug and pursed her lips. 'Why should I know anything? After all, I am just a housewife, and of little importance.'

'Stop it, Mother,' snapped Annabelle in English. 'Stop prevaricating and tell me what all this is really about.' She pushed the envelope towards her.

Camille stubbed out her cigarette, noted the curious glances from the other customers, and leant forward, her voice low as she spoke in rapid French. 'You might have managed to get a reference because of Caroline's father's persistence, but you will not get another nursing post in a London hospital. And I suspect it was your father who has seen to that.'

Annabelle rocked back in her chair, her gaze fixed on her mother, her thoughts in turmoil. 'Father? But how? I don't understand.'

'Of course you don't, why should you? I have no proof that it was him, but it's the sort of thing he would do out of spite. He's a vengeful man, and has never forgiven you for disobeying him by going to nursing school.'

'But it's been five years,' she gasped. 'Why wait until now?'

Camille moved her shoulders beneath her fur coat. 'He has the patience to wait, and he knew that sooner or later you would make a mistake – and when someone slips up, that is when he is at his most ruthless.'

Annabelle knew that Edwin Blake was one of the most feared barristers in England, and therefore the man to have on your side when prosecuting a case – but God help the person in the dock. The long list of defendants that were now serving prison sentences was testament to his Machiavellian skills, and Annabelle hadn't even suspected he might use them on his own daughter to get his revenge for her defiance.

'You are such a foolish girl,' Camille said on a sigh. 'Why did you get involved in those riots in Cable Street and then break the hospital rule by tending that Jarrow marcher in the park? Couldn't you, for once, have thought about the consequences of your actions?'

Annabelle had a clear memory of that day in Hyde Park. It had come only a few days after she and George had been caught up in the terrifying riots on Tower Hill and Cable Street between the fascists, unionists and communists. The police had protected the hated Black Shirts, charging their horses into the crowd, trampling women and children and forcing them through the back streets. She'd gone to see the men from Jarrow complete their long, peaceful protest march, and after listening to the speeches, had seen one of the men fall and hit his head. Having checked he wasn't badly hurt, she'd given him some water and a couple of coppers so he could catch a bus to the next rallying point.

'I didn't purposely get involved in the riots,' she protested. 'George and I were simply in the wrong place at the wrong time. As for the hospital ruling against helping marchers, it goes against everything I believe in as a nurse, and I only did what any decent person would have done in the circumstances. How was I to know someone would report me to the hospital board, or that I would be so severely punished?'

She looked at her mother and saw something in her expression that told her Camille knew exactly who it was who'd informed on her, but was reluctant – perhaps even afraid – to actually admit it. 'It *was* father at the bottom of all this, wasn't it?'

'I can't prove it, not really,' she admitted with reluctance. 'But I do rely on my instinct, and I've spent many years watching your father conduct his vendettas. I don't know how he was aware of what happened in the park – perhaps he was passing and saw you. But I do know he has powerful friends in high places, and has made it his business to know their secrets.'

Camille lit another cigarette. 'I too have become adept at discovering secrets,' she said with the ghost of a wry smile. 'I listen at doors and on the extension telephone. It is good to be armed with knowledge. I've learnt that much since I married him,' she said bitterly.

Annabelle regarded her mother with growing awe, for this was yet another side to Camille that she'd never suspected existed. This Camille had learnt to survive Edwin's harsh regime and bullying tactics, and now was strong and clever and sly – not the cowering, dutiful mouse Annabelle had known.

'Of course, I cannot do this all on my own,' continued Camille. 'My cleaner, Mabel Watkins, has proved to be an excellent co-conspirator. She tells me who is coming to visit, what she overhears when I am not there, and keeps me abreast of his daily schedules.'

She paused to sip from her second cup of coffee. 'It was she who informed me of the unexpected visitor a couple of weeks ago, and neither of us could understand why the hospital chief administrator should be calling.'

Annabelle's stomach churned and the coffee she'd drunk earlier suddenly left a bitter taste.

'It seems that the man had been having difficulties in finding a sponsor to attain membership at some pompous club where your father serves on the committee. I don't think he was considered quite the thing despite being on the hospital board, but your father promised to get his application passed if he would see to it that your position at the hospital was made untenable.'

'But surely he was shocked to be asked such a thing? And his word wouldn't have been enough anyway. Everything has to go through the chairman.'

Camille stubbed out her cigarette. 'It seems the chairman has a nephew who's a bit of a tearaway. The young man had been arrested several months before and, despite the strong evidence against him, Edwin discovered a point of law and got him off.' She shrugged. 'A favour for a favour. The chairman avoided family scandal and the administrator got his club membership. You became the sacrifice when you played right into their hands by helping that man from Jarrow.'

'What about the other hospitals? Surely my father's influence isn't so great he could manipulate them too?'

'A word here or there about your unreliability; a hint that there might have been more to your dismissal; Chinese whispers amongst a closed society. They can all have a devastating effect, Annabelle.' Camille gave a deep sigh.

The evidence against Edwin was too compelling to argue against and Annabelle closed her eyes and buried her face in her hands. Edwin Blake might show the world his intelligent, successful and respectable side, but beneath that veneer was a bully who liked to make his wife and daughter cower and bend them to his will. He'd proved before that he would go to any length to get his own way, which was why he'd banished Annabelle from home when she'd refused to marry the man he'd chosen for her and had used her small inheritance from a great-aunt to finance her tuition at nursing school. She'd never understood why he'd been so against her becoming a nurse – and he'd never explained – so she'd come to the conclusion that it didn't matter what career she might have chosen, he'd have disapproved simply because it was his way of controlling her.

'I'm sorry, Annabelle, I didn't want to tell you this shameful thing. But now you know what is against you, it would be wise to take the money and get as far from here as possible.' Camille slid the envelope back across the table. 'There's a ticket in there which will get you to Paris in comfort. The night ferry leaves London at nine.'

Annabelle gasped. 'Tonight?'

'At nine o'clock.'

'But I—'

'Annabelle,' she hissed. 'For once in your life, take advice and be sensible. Your father has ruined your career and is trying to bring you to heel. He knows how you live, and what your circumstances are, and knowing him so well, I wouldn't be at all surprised if he doesn't do something else which will leave you no alternative but to come home.'

'I'll never go back there,' she breathed.

'Then go to Aline. You'll be safe there, and with your fluent French you will soon find a good nursing post.' She delved into her handbag and drew out Annabelle's passport and another envelope.

'I managed to find your passport in a locked drawer in your father's study – Mabel has proved quite adept at picking locks,' she added with a brief smile. 'This is a letter to Aline that explains the situation. I've written her address on the front just in case you had forgotten it.'

She handed the envelope and passport over. 'You will love Paris, Annabelle. It is a city for the young at heart, and so beautiful. I almost envy you.'

'Then come with me, Maman. We can both start again and—'

'Non, *ma chère*,' she interrupted. 'It is too late for me. But you . . . you are young and beautiful and have so much more life to live.' She softly patted Annabelle's cheek. 'Go to Paris, become the woman you were always meant to be, and make me proud.'

Annabelle nestled her cheek into the soft, delicate hand and blinked back the tears. 'I love you, Maman,' she whispered.

'And I love you,' Camille replied softly. The touching moment was fleeting and she became businesslike again. 'Now we must part. I have to be at home for my afternoon bridge party, and you must pack and prepare for your journey.' She waved to the waitress for the bill and asked her to telephone for a taxi as she pulled on her coat and gloves.

Annabelle fetched her coat, still reeling from everything she'd learnt today. The thought that in just a few hours she would be heading for Paris was simply breathtaking, and yet she knew that her mother's advice was wise and should be heeded. Edwin had now shown how vengeful and cruel he could be and she knew he wouldn't be satisfied until she was completely broken and living under his roof again – and that must never happen.

The taxi arrived and they stepped outside to discover it had stopped raining. As Camille put her arms about her, Annabelle breathed in her familiar French perfume and was taken back momentarily to her childhood. 'Will I ever see you again, Maman?'

'Perhaps one day,' she murmured. 'For now we must write many, many letters. Send them to Caroline's mother, *ma chère*. She will see that I get them.'

Annabelle could barely see through her tears as her mother climbed into the taxi and the driver slammed the door. 'Goodbye, Maman,' she managed.

'Not goodbye, my darling: *au revoir*,' she replied through the open window.

The taxi sped away and Annabelle blinked back the tears as she watched it disappear around the corner. When the sound of it faded, she slowly rode the bicycle back to her lodgings, her mind whirling with thoughts of all she had to do before she caught the train.

Dr George Ashton had gone to her lodgings because he'd heard that morning that Angus Fraser had changed his mind and agreed to sell him the general practice in Dartford, and had been eager to share his good fortune with her. Now the pleasure and excitement he'd felt had been swamped by an impotent fury that he'd left it all far too late to make amends.

He strode down the street, furious with himself, and with Annabelle. What the hell was she playing at, running off like that without a word or a note? And why had he virtually ignored her these past weeks, when he'd known how difficult things were for her at the moment? He knew, of course, that it was because he'd made a fool of himself by proposing to her at the most inopportune time, and his pride simply couldn't withstand the awful embarrassment. But that didn't excuse his appalling lack of care for her just when she'd needed it the most.

He snapped from his thoughts as he saw a taxi and flagged it down. 'Victoria station,' he said tersely. 'And there's an extra bob if you can get there in five minutes.'

As the driver hurtled the taxi through the crowded streets, George swept back the lock of dark hair that always drooped over his forehead, and tried to remain calm. Annabelle had left her lodgings with two suitcases and by all accounts was heading for Victoria – which meant she wasn't returning to her family home in Fulham. Something must have happened to make her leave so suddenly, and his great fear was that she'd taken leave of her senses and decided to join Caroline in Spain.

Of all the hare-brained ideas, that about capped it, he thought furiously. A civil war was no place for a girl like Annabelle – or any girl for that matter – and he could only pray that he was in time to stop her.

As the taxi screeched to a halt outside the station George virtually threw the fare at the driver before hurrying onto the concourse. He looked up anxiously at the departure board, noted that the boat-train was about to depart and began to run.

Coming to a skidding halt at the gate, he saw the final carriage disappear down the line. 'Damn, damn, damn and blast it,' he hissed.

'You've missed it, sir,' said the porter unnecessarily.

'I do realise that,' he snapped.

'There's another one tomorrow night,' he replied almost complacently.

George just about held on to his patience. 'Did you see a pretty, fair-haired young woman go on board? You couldn't miss her. She has the most extraordinary violet eyes.'

'I don't take much notice after twenty years in this job. But there was a pretty girl booked into first class.'

George knew she couldn't afford such luxurious travel arrangements, so having thanked the man, he walked away. He returned to the concourse, hoping beyond all reason that he'd see her, and when it became clear that he'd set himself an impossible task, he admitted defeat and headed for the station hotel bar and a double Irish whiskey.

Staring at his reflection in the mirrors behind the bar, his anger and impatience slowly dwindled to an aching sense of loss. He'd fallen in love with Annabelle the first moment he'd looked into her amazing eyes, and he'd spent the past five years hoping that one day he'd be in a position to propose. He knew he could be taciturn and impatient; knew that he wore this veneer of irreproachable confidence in who he was and what he'd achieved because it was expected of him. Yet beneath all that he was a man in love – albeit a man who found it difficult to express his innermost feelings – and he was cross with himself for letting her get so deeply under his skin.

He took a drink of the whiskey and felt it burn its way down his throat. His proposal had been rejected, which was hardly surprising, but what on earth had possessed her to run off like that without a word? Didn't she care for him at all?

He drained the glass, placed it on the bar and strode out of the hotel. He had no option but to get on with his life in the hope she'd see sense and come back to him. The thought that she might not was something he didn't dare contemplate.

2

Annabelle had gone through customs without a hitch and the porter had taken her two cases to the first-class sleeping compartment which would be hers until she arrived in Paris. She couldn't think how this would happen as she was going on a boat, but didn't quite have the nerve to ask him. Having tipped him, she unpacked her nightwear and washbag, admired the cosy and surprisingly comfortable sleeping quarters and then went to explore.

The dining room was as beautifully appointed as any in the grand London hotels. The tables were covered in starched white linen; crystal glasses and silver cutlery winked in the diffused light of small table lamps, and the menus were tucked away in frames fixed to the walls between the wide, curtained windows. As she explored further, she discovered a comfortable lounge with a well-stocked bar presided over by smartly dressed stewards. There were daily newspapers and the latest glossy magazines stacked on the low tables, and as she sat down a steward came to ask if she'd like a drink.

Annabelle felt slightly intimidated by her surroundings as she sipped from a glass of sherry and watched the other passengers.

She was still catching her breath after the mad rush to prepare for this journey, and as everything had happened at such a pace she couldn't quite believe she wasn't dreaming. But the shouts of the guards and porters were real enough, as was the luxury of the first-class lounge, and the ticket in her handbag was the proof that she really was going to Paris.

The two small suitcases she'd brought contained everything she owned of value, and it wasn't a lot to show for five years, but at least she looked respectable enough in her best clothes. The cream straw hat with the red velvet ribbon around the brim and crown had been a parting gift from Caroline and was very chic, and although her navy-blue overcoat wouldn't have stood close inspection, it was well made, as was her good black leather bag. She could do nothing to disguise the fact that her shoes were shabby even though she'd polished them, so she folded her feet beneath the seat hoping no one would see them.

As the compartment began to fill and grow noisy, she heard the sound of French voices intermingle with the English ones. Drinks orders were made, cigarettes lit and curtains pulled across the windows as people fussed over newspapers and travelling rugs and the steward passed along the carriage to ask which sitting was preferred for dinner in the dining car.

Annabelle sat there in a haze of excitement and terror. She'd never travelled first class, had never been to Paris, and had certainly never taken the packet-steamer across the Channel. And yet there could be no turning back, not now she knew about her father.

Her thoughts turned distractedly from wondering if she was expected to change for dinner to her abandoned bedsitter in Goose Lane. It had been a shabby place, with badly fitting windows, damp in the walls and the all-pervading smell of other people's cooking, but she'd made the room her own with bits of junk shop furniture and second-hand curtains and rugs, and had been quite sad to leave it. It had probably already been stripped bare by the other tenants and she didn't begrudge them, yet she would miss London and George.

She gasped as she realised that in all the rush and excitement she hadn't given George Ashton a single thought. But how could she have done that? How awful of her to abandon him after he'd been turned down by the general practice he'd interviewed for and she'd rejected his heartfelt but badly timed proposal. He might have been avoiding her of late, but he'd still be very hurt to discover she'd left without a word, and would rightly think of her as being utterly self-absorbed and uncaring.

She stared out of the window in a lather of indecision as the last few passengers rushed along the platform. She should go and find him, or at least telephone the hospital and leave him a message. But did she dare to leave her cases and jump off, thereby not only possibly losing everything she owned but wasting her train ticket and missing her boat? She shifted to the edge of her seat, poised to make a move, but unable to come to a decision.

She and George had met at the hospital during her nursing training, and although there was six years' age difference, they'd become close friends. They'd spent their precious leisure time together walking in London's parks or visiting the Crystal Palace, and she'd helped him choose his suit when he qualified as a doctor, while he'd taken her out to supper when she passed her nursing exams.

Annabelle loved him dearly as a friend, but hadn't realised George was in love with her until Caroline had pointed it out, and his sudden, ill-timed proposal had perhaps made her rather harsher with him than she'd intended. But she'd been reeling from her dismissal the previous day, was torn between Caroline's urging to join her in Spain and her need to clear her name in London, and beleaguered by thoughts of what the future might hold if she couldn't nurse. How could she possibly have made any sensible decisions at such a time?

She snapped from her thoughts and saw the guard was raising his flag as the last door was slammed. The piercing whistle echoed through the station and smoke and steam billowed past the window as the wheels began to turn. She sank back into her seat with mixed emotions. It was too late.

With an inward sigh of distress she silently promised George she would write to him the minute she reached Paris. Their friendship meant too much to her to simply run out on him without explanation.

During the three-hour train journey to Dover, Annabelle discovered she was travelling with people like her parents, who took such luxury in their stride and were quite blasé about everything that she found so exciting. She ate a delicious dinner – the cheapest meal on the menu – stuck to drinking water, and after sitting in the crowded, smoky lounge for a while, went to her sleeping compartment. There were few on board of her age, and she'd felt rather out of things as they talked amongst themselves and made no effort to include her.

It was lovely and peaceful in her couchette, and as she sat at the window and tried to make out the details of the passing scenery, she realised that it was almost midnight and soon they would be arriving in Dover. She was still intrigued as to how the train would go on the ship, for that seemed to be the only way in which she could sleep in here.

Annabelle's thoughts turned to Caroline and her brothers as the train chuffed its way through the darkness. They had made a similar journey only the day before, but their destination had been Madrid, not Paris, and she wondered if they'd arrived yet, and what the conditions were like in a country ravaged by civil war.

Caroline Howden had been her friend since childhood, and her older brothers, Bertram and Arthur, had accepted her as just another annoying little girl who followed them about. Annabelle had had a fearsome crush on Arthur at one time, but thankfully he hadn't seemed to notice, so there was no awkwardness between them. Now her childhood friends were heading into a war zone despite their parents' best efforts to dissuade them, and Annabelle could only pray that they came through everything unscathed.

Annabelle stared out into the darkness, remembering the night, several weeks ago, when they'd all sat down to dinner at the Howdens'. Robert and Philippa had been as welcoming as ever, but the pleasant evening had been ruined by an innocent remark Annabelle had made about the amount of cheese and butter Arthur was using on his biscuits. He'd replied that he had to feed himself up in case there weren't decent rations in Spain, and from then on the atmosphere had grown tense.

When Caroline announced that she too would be going to Spain, her mother had burst into tears and Robert had had great difficulty in keeping his temper. He'd made a powerful and embittered speech which had shocked them all and still resonated in Annabelle's memory.

'I have no doubt your nursing skills will be needed,' he'd said, 'but you won't be working in a pristine hospital with beds and clean sheets, or even the most basic of equipment or medicines.' His brown eyes had regarded his daughter with unflinching steadiness. 'At best, you'll be in a tent in the middle of a muddy field. Surgeons will be operating without anaesthetic on men ripped apart by shellfire and bullets. You'll see men with their limbs blown off, half their faces gone and their innards in their hands while they scream for their mothers. And those screams will live with you day and night, Caroline – and long after you return home.'

Caroline had tried to argue with him, but he'd been adamant that things hadn't changed since he'd been a soldier in the First World War. He'd gone on to talk about the endless barrage of gunfire, the attacks by enemy planes, the stench of death and the tragic futility of using men as cannon fodder to take a scrap of land which would be lost again within hours.

He'd become impassioned when his sons tried to silence him, and had slammed his hand on the table. 'War is bloody and vicious and a terrible waste of young lives,' he'd roared. 'And there's no such thing as the glorious dead. The dead are dead, and the sacrifices they made will soon be forgotten when the graveyards begin to fill again.'

Annabelle shivered at the memory, for his words still rang in her head and conjured up the most terrible images. She had been contemplating going to Spain with Caroline, but after that speech she'd had second thoughts, and begun to doubt that she would ever be brave enough to face such horrors. And yet Caroline and her brothers had stood firm. They wanted a chance to do their bit to fight fascism and put a stop to the very real threat of another world war, and for that Annabelle admired them.

A light tap on the door startled her from her thoughts. 'Yes?'

'It's your steward, miss.' He opened the door. 'All passengers will be alighting at Dover to walk on board the SS Hampton Ferry. I would advise you to wrap up warmly, miss. It can get very cold being this close to the Channel.'

'But I thought I was to have this sleeping carriage right through to Paris?'

He smiled back at her. 'Indeed you do, miss. The first-class sleeping carriages will go onto the ship, so you won't have long to wait until you can retire.'

He closed the door before she could question him further. 'Goodness,' she breathed. 'I can scarcely believe it.' Not wanting to miss a moment of this rather baffling arrangement, she pulled on her coat and hat again, found her gloves, scarf and bag and shoved her feet back into her shoes. It might be almost midnight after a long, traumatic day, but she was wide awake.

Returning to the lounge area, she discovered that it was almost deserted in the rush to prepare for the arrival at the port. She sat at the window and through the smoke coming from the train's funnel she could see the harbour, and the white cliffs of Dover in the distance. As the wheels slowed and the train chuffed into the station and came to a standstill with a sigh, the lounge area was suddenly filled with people who babbled in excitement as they determinedly edged towards the carriage doors.

Annabelle held back from the initial rush and then followed them down to the platform where the second- and third-class passengers were already heading for their waiting room. The wind was sharp as it blew in from the sea, its salty tang quite refreshing after the heated carriages, and she took a deep, restorative breath.

The enormous steamship was anchored at the end of the railway lines, and she could hear the rush of water above the still panting engine and the screeching gulls. She followed the others to the first-class waiting room, where they were greeted by stewards serving cups of hot chocolate, and went to warm her hands at the welcoming fire blazing in the hearth. Yet she was intrigued to see what would happen next, so she moved to the window, and was soon joined by others who hadn't made this trip before.

Ghostly-white seagulls swooped and mewled in the beams of the strong harbour lights as they shone down onto the ship, which seemed to be floating within some sort of lock system.

As the water filled the second enclosure and the ferry began to slowly lower, Annabelle could finally see the tracks on both decks.

The sluice gates opened and the ferry edged closer to the end of the platform until the tracks were aligned. There was a sudden rush by the stevedors and dockers who quickly wound thick ropes round the capstans to secure the ferry firmly.

As Annabelle and the others crowded at the windows to watch, the engine chuffed off onto a smaller branch line and the first-class carriages were uncoupled from the rest of the train. Then the carriages were shunted one by one along the lines and onto the decks.

There was a lot of shouting and toing and froing by the dock workers, but finally the carriages were considered to be correctly aligned and evenly weighted on either side of the ship. Once they'd been chained firmly into place the lock gates closed again and the ferry slowly rose back to sea level.

'All aboard,' shouted the guard some time later. 'Mind your step, ladies and gents. Steady as you go up the gangway.'

There was a great deal of chatter and excitement as they trooped back into the cold, salty air and carefully made their way up the sloping gangway to midships. More stewards were waiting to take the lucky few to their sleeping carriages, and Annabelle had only a fleeting glimpse of the public rooms as she passed through them. It seemed that those less fortunate would have to sleep in their seats, but there was a dining room of sorts and somewhere they could buy a sandwich or a cup of tea.

As the steward closed Annabelle's door quietly behind him,

she looked nervously out of her window into the black night pierced by the harbour lights. The sea appeared to be calm, but as they were still within the harbour walls that didn't mean much, and she had no idea whether she would prove to be a good sailor or not.

It seemed an awfully long way down to the water, and in a moment of sudden panic, she searched for and found the life jacket neatly stowed away beneath her bunk. She didn't really feel very safe, and surely, if it was rough, the carriages would rock alarmingly even though they'd been tethered by heavy chains?

She pulled the blind down and determinedly prepared for bed. If she thought about all the things that could go wrong, she'd never get to sleep. Besides, she reasoned, these ferries had been going back and forth for years with no mishap.

As she lay in the narrow bed she heard the shouts of the men on the dockside and the rumble of the great steam engines below deck. With a blast from the funnel, the ship began to move, smoothly at first, and as it began to dip and rise, she realised they had passed through the arms of the harbour walls and were ploughing through the choppy waters of the Channel.

Annabelle slowly relaxed and allowed the movement of the ship to soothe away her fears, and as she snuggled beneath the warm blankets the arduous, emotional day took its toll and she fell asleep.

She was woken by the sounds of people moving along the narrow corridor of the carriage. Sitting up and stretching luxuriously, she was amazed to find that it was only five in the morning, and yet in those few hours she'd had a refreshing sleep and was now ready for the next part of her journey.

She pulled on her dressing gown and lifted the blinds, squinting into the brightness of a rising sun which sparkled on the sea. The water was clear and as smooth as glass, the white wake made by the ship curling languorously across the blue.

A discreet tap on the door was followed by a stewardess bearing a large tray, which she placed on the small table beneath the window. 'We shall be docking in an hour,' she said, smiling warmly, 'so there's no need to rush your breakfast.'

Annabelle returned her smile and then sat down at the table. As she lifted the silver covers on the chaffing dishes she discovered scrambled eggs, grilled bacon, toast and warm croissants. There was a pot of tea with milk, sugar and slices of lemon, and small dishes containing marmalade and thick strawberry jam. Her mouth watered and she realised she was ravenous as she tucked in. The eggs were fluffy, the bacon crisp – just the way she liked it – and the croissant was so light and flaky that it melted in her mouth.

Having eaten her fill, she washed and dressed for her onward journey, and went up on deck to catch her first glimpse of the French coastline. As it became clearer she could see the long stretch of beach, the sand dunes and little houses perched by the shore where fishing boats were already setting sail in search of an early catch.

As it was high tide, there was no rigmarole of going into the lock system and waiting for the water levels to adjust, and the ferry edged directly to the quay. Annabelle and the other passengers followed the instructions to debark, and stood watching as the first-class carriages were efficiently removed from the ship and carefully hooked onto the waiting engine. Once all the carriages were in place everyone climbed aboard.

Many of the passengers returned to their sleeping compartments, but Annabelle was far too excited to sleep, and was determined not to miss a minute of this extraordinary adventure. She managed to get a window seat in the salon, and as the great iron wheels turned and the smoke billowed from the engine's funnel, she gazed out at the French countryside.

The scenery reminded her of the southern counties of England, for there were a few hills on the horizon, but mostly it was flat farmland, with tiny villages and hamlets scattered across it. Now and again she was forcibly reminded that this was France, for they passed through a town with the inevitable belltowers and steeples of churches rising above the clustered red-tiled roofs. There were great sweeps of tilled fields and solitary barns and farmhouses made of a light-coloured stone; lines of tall slender poplars marking boundaries, and dark mysterious forests that looked impenetrable.

Annabelle was charmed by it all, and waved cheerfully back to the children who came out of their houses to watch them pass. She saw more children walking to school, nuns emerging from a church doorway, their wimples gleaming white like great wings, and housewives hurrying back from the bakery clutching their long batons of bread. It was all so quintessentially French, and the land felt foreign with its endless horizons and wide sky, but Annabelle had a feeling she would like it here.

As the train drew nearer to Paris there was a quickening in the atmosphere, and people began to talk just that bit louder as they hunted for lost gloves and spectacles and prepared for their arrival. Annabelle went back to her sleeping compartment and packed away her nightwear and washbag, remembering to leave a tip for the stewards. With only two light cases, it didn't seem at all necessary to ask for help, so she carried them back to the salon and placed them at her feet.

The guard came through to tell them they would be arriving in five minutes, and Annabelle's heart began to thud with excitement as well as anxiety. She had heard a great deal about Tante Aline, but had never met her. Widowed after just three years of marriage, she was still only forty years old, and according to Camille, led a rather disgraceful life as an artist. Was she as bohemian as her mother had said? Did she really have a house full of writers, poets, musicians and artists – and would Annabelle be welcome there?

She dug in her handbag for the letter Camille had written to her sister and memorised the address before consulting the map she'd bought while waiting for the carriages to be unloaded from the ferry. Aline lived at number four, rue de l'Arbre, which was a small cul-de-sac off the Boulevard de Strasbourg on the borders of the third and fourth arrondisements. As Annabelle's finger traced the long boulevard down to the River Seine, she realised that this map wasn't detailed enough to show every small street. But at least she knew where to look for it, so it shouldn't pose too great a problem.

The train slowly chuffed and puffed into the station, and there was a rush to alight. Picking up her cases, Annabelle waited impatiently and then stepped down onto the platform. The great glass ceiling of the Gare du Nord echoed with the sound of train engines and iron wheels on tracks, the confusing reverberating voice of the station announcer almost lost in the excitable chatter of the people surrounding her and the sharp whistles of the guards.

Annabelle showed her passport at customs and was waved through without her cases being checked. She stood on the bustling concourse watching the milling crowd and listening to the rapid French of those passing by. It wouldn't be long, she realised, before she began thinking and dreaming in French, and it certainly would make her life easier, for she hadn't really spoken it much for five years and knew she was rusty.

Clutching her cases, she headed for the exit and emerged into a bright, crisp, sunny Parisian morning. The noise of the endless stream of traffic that rumbled over the cobbled streets was quite a shock, but above the tooting horns and the high-pitched whistle of the gendarme attempting to direct the traffic could be heard the clear chimes of a church clock striking the quarter hour.

Women hurried past, looking chic even though they were dressed for the cold weather. Men walked quickly by, the brims of their hats at a jaunty angle, their suits and overcoats of finer cut and quality than any seen in London. The smell of French cigarettes, garlic and olive oil wafted to her from a nearby café and she was tempted to stop and buy a cup of coffee. But sitting at a café and watching the world go by was a joy to be savoured at another time, for she needed to find her aunt's house first.

Annabelle eyed the ranks of taxis waiting at the kerb, but decided her cases were light enough to carry; she didn't have far to go and it would save money to walk. It was a beautiful day, perfect to get her bearings and absorb the atmosphere of this famous city. She checked the map, then tucked it into her coat pocket before setting off along the rather unfortunately named rue de l'Abattoir to cross into rue de Saint-Quintin, which would lead into the broad Boulevard de Strasbourg.

As she strolled along enjoying the sights and sounds of this vibrant city, she was struck by how clean and ordered it was. There was no litter in the streets, no graffiti on the walls; small cafés had bright awnings to shelter the tables set out on the pavements, shops tempted with colourful window displays, and the myriad of wrought-iron balconies that graced the tall grey-stone buildings were made even more attractive with potted herbs and winter pansies. There was the vague hint of drains amidst the more pleasant smells, but as she was used to the overflowing gutters of the East End, she accepted it as part of city life.

Despite her awe and excitement at being here, it wasn't long before Annabelle began to regret not taking a taxi. Her cases seemed to have become heavier as she'd walked, and the distance felt much further than the map suggested. But it was when she saw the banks of the Seine ahead of her that she realised she'd somehow missed her turning.

With a sigh of frustration she crossed the narrow street and walked along the broad embankment to the Pont Neuf – the New Bridge – which Annabelle knew from her mother was in fact the oldest bridge in Paris. Drawn to it, she slowly walked along until she was at its centre. Putting down her cases, she flexed her numbed fingers as she admired the bronze statue of Henry VI on horseback, and then leant on the ancient stone parapet to take in the view.

The two graceful arches of the Pont Neuf spanned the Île de la Cité, on which stood the Place Dauphine and the sprawling building of the Sainte Chapelle. As she looked downriver she could see the magnificent Louvre museum, and far off to her left, the top of the Eiffel Tower. There were five more bridges spanning the river before it turned west, and looking back, she could see many more beyond the towers and spire of Notre-Dame Cathedral.

So this is Paris, she thought in awe. Spread out before her beneath a clear blue sky, its river running dark and swift beneath bridges that had been here for centuries, it was like a precious gift after the smog and filth of London. She could almost feel the history surrounding her, could almost discern the city's heartbeat beneath her feet as she gazed along the boulevard of lovely trees and admired the timeless grace of the tall grey buildings whose windows reflected the sun. No wonder it was called the city of love, and regarded as one of the most romantic places in the world.

She felt a flutter of excitement that was laced with hope as well as doubt. Would she find romance – or would she simply love being here? She suspected she would fall in love, but it would be this beautiful city that would capture her heart.

3

Henri-Pascal Baptiste and Etienne Benoît had known each other since they were toddlers, growing up in an isolated farming community close to the French town of Bayonne and the Spanish border. They were of the Basque people who lived in the region and could speak Spanish, French and their own Basque patois. With their black hair and olive skin they were as alike as brothers, but for Henri's bright blue eyes. Henri was twenty-six and older by a month, but it was always the more adventurous, hot-headed Etienne who led them into trouble – and Henri's cheeky grin and blue eyes which got them out of it.

They'd had little interest in farming, even as boys, and although they helped their fathers and uncles in the fields, they preferred the silence and solitude of the wide open spaces that sprawled between the shadow of the Pyrenees mountains and the wild surf of the Bay of Biscay. As boys, they'd built a hideaway formed of driftwood and stones they'd gathered from the shore, and had made a rough thatched roof from grass and turf and bits of old tin they'd found lying around. It was here that Henri drew and painted pictures, and where Etienne would write wild adventure stories and keep a diary.

'Do you remember our little hut?' asked Henri as they strolled back along the embankment from their early-morning meander through the galleries of the Louvre.

'Of course, but what made you think of that today?'

He shrugged and paused to look around him as the traffic thundered over the cobbles. 'I don't know,' he confessed, 'but now and again I long for the peace and solitude we found there. I'd paint and you'd write, and somehow we were lost to the rest of the world, whereas here there is always noise and bustle and people demanding things of you.'

Etienne came to stand beside him and leant his back against the parapet to light a cigarette. 'We came to Paris to make our fortune,' he said as the smoke dribbled from his mouth. 'You're not having regrets at this late stage, are you?'

Henri shoved his hands into his trouser pockets and breathed deeply of the clean, green watery scent of the Seine. 'Not really. But I had hoped I could have found a patron to support me by now. It's been almost seven years, Etienne, and I still have to sell my soul to the tourists in Montmartre to keep a roof over my head. After looking at those great paintings in the Louvre, I'm beginning to wonder if I should just throw it all in and go home.'

Etienne raised a dark eyebrow, his almost black eyes widening in surprise. 'You're sounding very sorry for yourself all of a sudden.' His handsome face lit up in a broad smile. 'Has little

Amélie thrown you over for someone richer and more dashing? Is that what this is all about?'

Henri laughed as he leant against the balustrade. 'Amélie's a free spirit with an eye on the main chance. She'll never be tied down to someone as poor as me. But she was a good model – and cheap.'

Etienne laughed with him. 'There are plenty of pretty girls in Paris who would model for you, Henri. And most of them will come cheap if you flash those eyes and give them your most beguiling smile.'

He turned to lean against the balustrade, shoulder to shoulder with Henri, his expression suddenly far more serious. 'As you're feeling so restless, have you given any more thought to what we discussed last night?'

Henri lit his own Gauloise and turned his thoughts from the luscious but unreliable Amélie to the darker subject of the Spanish Civil War. The Basque people had always suffered at the hands of both the French and the Spanish, but now that the fascists were threatening to overrun Spain and cause havoc throughout Europe, his natural patriotism was beginning to stir a hitherto dormant fighting spirit.

'I feel the same as you, that we must do something,' he said eventually. 'But neither of us are fighting men. What good could we do by getting involved?'

'You can handle a rifle, as can I. Our fathers taught us as soon as we were big enough to hold one. And we can ride as well as anyone, should there be horses involved.' Etienne regarded his friend thoughtfully and then nudged him with his elbow. 'You're not afraid, are you?' he teased.

'Yes, I am,' Henri said flatly. 'I'm an artist, not a soldier, and any sensible man would admit as much.' His rather stern expression melted into a grin. 'But then you never were sensible, Etienne. And neither was I to let you persuade me to come to Paris in the first place.'

'We've had some adventures, though, haven't we?' Etienne replied with a smile. 'Remember when we were about five or six and we packed food in a feed bag and went off into the mountains looking for the legendary chimera? And when we were eight we made a raft out of tree branches and tried to set sail for America.'

Henri flung his arm around his friend's shoulder and gave him a hearty squeeze. 'I remember our fathers giving us a strapping after we disappeared for four days and came home half-starved and scared witless, and how our raft sank and we almost drowned. It was just lucky that old fisherman hauled us out in time otherwise we wouldn't be standing here today. You're a liability, Etienne, and always will be.'

Etienne smiled back for he'd known Henri for too long to read any insult into his words. He finished his cigarette and watched it float away on the swiftly flowing river. 'So,' he said as he turned to look at Henri, 'are you coming with me or not?'

'I suppose I'll have to,' he replied with a sigh. 'Someone's got to be there to get you out of the trouble you're bound to fall into.'

They grinned at each other like schoolboys and began to walk towards the Pont Neuf. 'One day,' said Etienne as he regarded the elegant houses that overlooked the Seine, 'I'll be rich and famous and own one of those. I'll fill it with artists and writers and poets and spend my last years just sitting and gazing down at the Seine remembering the adventures I've had and the women I've loved.'

'And will there be a place for me in that fine house?'

'You'll have your own,' said Etienne cheerfully. 'In fact, we could be neighbours.'

'Then we need to start doing rather better than we are at the moment,' Henri said. 'I've sold very few paintings over the past months, and although the quick sketches I do of the tourists bring in enough to keep the wolf from the door, they don't pay enough to afford more than an attic room, let alone a house like that.'

'Well, I'm not doing badly,' said Etienne with his usual lack of humility. 'My book of poetry is selling rather well; there's a second one due out in the new year, and the publishers have asked me to write a diary while we're in Spain. I also had the genius idea of speaking to the editor of *Le Monde*, and he's commissioned me to write a monthly article concerning the progress of the civil war as I witness it.'

Henri glanced across at the rather smug face and thought how typical it was of Etienne to promote himself even in the midst of war – but then his friend had never been backward when it had come to seizing the smallest chance of making money and advertising his skills. 'That's all very well for you, Etienne, but I have no savings at all, so what am I supposed to do for money while we're away?'

Etienne's arm swung over Henri's shoulder. 'Have no fear, my friend. I mentioned you to the editor, and he's very interested in you doing quick on-the-spot sketches to illustrate my articles. He'll pay you well. I arranged it all.'

Henri roared with laughter. 'You really are impossible,' he spluttered. 'How did you know that I'd agree to such a thing?'

He gave a shrug. 'Because I know you, and you'll be drawing like a demon anyway, so why not get paid while you're at it?'

They carried on walking and Henri pulled his pocket watch from his waistcoat and sighed heavily when he saw how late it was getting.

'That's the third time you've checked that thing,' said Etienne with a knowing glint in his eye. 'Who's the lucky girl?'

'No girl this time, my friend. But I have someone interested in my latest painting and I need to put the finishing touches to it before he comes for a second viewing tomorrow. If I leave it too late, the light will be all wrong.'

'That's splendid news. Is he serious about buying it, do you think, or just another time-waster who thinks he knows everything there is about art, but actually knows nothing?'

'Serious enough. He's a rich merchant and a regular at the coffee house – and has quite a growing art collection.'

He realised Etienne wasn't really listening for his gaze had drifted off and his mind was clearly focused elsewhere – which could only mean one thing. As Etienne slowed to a halt and gave a low whistle of appreciation, Henri knew he was right and followed his gaze to the young woman who'd caught his friend's roving eye.

'Look at her, Henri,' he breathed. 'Look at the girl with the suitcases and the tourist map. Do you think she's lost?'

'Quite possibly,' he replied dryly as he admired the slender figure of the fair-haired girl on the bridge. 'But she's hardly your sort – not enough curves.'

'Oh, I don't know.' Etienne cocked his head and regarded her thoughtfully. 'Girls don't have to have curves to be attractive. The hat is very chic, and so is the handbag, but it's a shame about the lack of style in the coat and shoes.' He turned to look at Henri with a grin. 'I wager you a *sou* that she's English and has lost her way.'

'I'm not betting anything,' he said lightly. 'You always seem to win, especially when it's something to do with a woman.'

'Then let's find out if I'm right this time, shall we?'

As they approached the bridge and he could see her profile more clearly, Henri noted how creamy her skin was, and how delicately her nose and chin were formed. Her hair was curly beneath the hat, a mixture of flaxen gold and shades of brown, and her figure was slight in that awful dowdy coat. But her legs were shapely, the ankles slender, and there was a certain grace in the way she studied the tourist map and looked at her surroundings.

Etienne was already striding ahead and Henri hurried to catch him up. It was always interesting to watch his friend use his charm offensive on girls, and he wondered how this one would react – especially if she was English.

'*Bonjour, mam'selle*,' said Etienne as he swept off his beret and dazzled her with his brightest smile. 'Are you a visitor to our city?' he asked in rapid French designed to confuse and intrigue her. 'Can we help you find the way?'

As she turned towards them Henri was struck dumb by the colour of her extraordinary eyes, her perfect skin and the way her lovely mouth moved so delightfully into a warm smile. She was absolutely stunning and as her eyes met his he experienced a jolt of shock that set his heart racing.

'Thank you. I have to confess that I am lost,' she replied in perfect Parisian French. 'Could you possibly show me where rue de l'Arbre is? I can't find it on this map, and must have walked straight past it.'

Henri could see that Etienne was just as taken aback by her eyes and her fluent French for, most unusually, he seemed to have lost his senses and was simply standing there and staring. 'You must excuse my friend,' Henri said quickly. 'He's from the provinces and his manners are still a little rough around the edges.'

She laughed then and Henri smiled. She was perfect, utterly perfect, and he wanted to whisk her away to his studio and capture her in a painting . . . or better still, gather her in his arms and feel the softness of her lips against his. He cleared his throat. 'My name is Henri-Pascal Baptiste, and my dumb friend here is Etienne Benoît.'

'Annabelle Blake,' she replied as she shook their hands.

'So, you are English,' breathed Henri.

She smiled into his eyes which made his heart thud even faster. 'Yes, but my mother is French and she taught me to speak her language from the moment I could talk.' She looked from one young man to the other in amusement, no doubt puzzled by the effect she was having on them.

'So,' she continued in her flawless French, 'can you show me the way to rue de l'Arbre?'

Etienne pulled himself together. 'We know it well,' he said. 'Are you visiting someone there?'

'My aunt, Aline Fournier.'

'Aline is your aunt? But we are great friends with her, aren't we, Henri?'

'Indeed we are,' he replied, happy to be able to help this lovely creature. He looked at her cases. 'Are you an artist too?'

She shook her head. 'I haven't an artistic bone in my body,' she said and smiled. 'I'm a nurse.'

Henri looked at her with keen interest, imagining her in a uniform, her lovely hair almost hidden by a starched winged cap. He realised she was watching him, perhaps reading his thoughts, and he quickly gathered his sensibilities. 'Well, you're lucky to have such an aunt, for her home is open to all of us poor artists and writers, and her evening salon is one of the most prestigious in all Paris.'

He saw Etienne's glance of mockery, realised he'd been babbling and shut up before he made even more of a fool of himself.

She didn't seem to have noticed. 'Goodness, I didn't realise she was so well known.' She regarded Henri steadily. 'So you are both artists?'

'I am an artist,' he replied. 'Etienne is a writer and poet.'

'A *published* writer and poet,' corrected Etienne rather pointedly.

'How very commendable,' she replied mildly before turning back to Henri. 'I'm a little worried that Tante Aline isn't expecting me to turn up out of the blue like this,' she said hesitantly. 'With her being so popular, do you think she'll have room for me?'

'Aline has room for everyone,' said Etienne rather extravagantly. 'Henri, why don't you carry the lady's cases?' he said as he offered Annabelle his arm. 'The cobbles can be hard to walk on when one isn't used to them, so it's best if you lean on me,' he said to her conspiratorially.

Henri was once more at the mercy of Etienne's wicked ability to push himself to the forefront of any situation and sighed as he gathered up the cases and kept pace with them. 'It's only a short walk from here, but easy to miss,' he said as he walked on the other side of her. 'There is a short narrow lane with no name and the rue de l'Arbre leads off it in a sharp dog-leg.'

'Are you planning a holiday with your aunt?' asked Etienne, determined to draw the focus back on himself. 'If so, I would be delighted to show you the city before I leave for Spain next month.'

Henri saw her look of surprise. 'We are both going,' he said hurriedly so Etienne didn't steal all his thunder. 'It's important to us to show the fascists that they will not be tolerated in either France or Spain.'

'Yes, I've heard all the arguments back in England,' she replied. 'In fact, a friend of mine, another nurse, is in Spain now with her brothers.'

'Are you planning to meet her there?' asked Henri as they

reached the short alleyway that led into the rue de l'Arbre. 'If so, you could travel down with us.'

'That's very kind of you, but I really haven't made my mind up about anything as yet. I need some time to settle in and get my bearings.'

'Of course, of course,' murmured Etienne as he guided her down the alley towards the sound of someone practising the violin, and turned the sharp corner into Aline Fournier's cul-de-sac.

The two short rows of tall terraced houses faced each other, the front steps leading from the doors to the cobbled square and overshadowing the basements. Each window of the three storeys possessed a pair of wooden shutters in varying colours and states of repair; there were window boxes displaying herbs and winter flowers, and the knotted, entwined branches of a very old wisteria traced their way across the white-painted walls on the left. At the end of this small enclave was an ornate iron fence and gate which marked a boundary for the peaceful park beyond. The violin music seemed to be coming from one of the attic rooms.

'Oh, how simply lovely,' Annabelle breathed as she saw the gnarled and ancient tree guarded by more iron railings at the end of the cul-de-sac. 'Does it flower in the spring?'

'Indeed it does,' said Henri, who'd sketched and painted it many times over the years. 'It's a very old magnolia, and the white blossoms are quite magnificent.' He carried her cases up the steps of the house with bright blue shutters and, with only a fleeting rap of the knocker, opened the door.

'Madame Fournier,' he shouted. 'It's me, Henri-Pascal, and I've brought you a surprise visitor.'

Annabelle was rather alarmed at the cavalier manner in which Henri had gone into her aunt's house, although it did mean that he knew her well, and yet she still felt a little uneasy that her unexpected arrival might not be welcome.

'It's all right. Aline won't bite you,' said Etienne with a gentle smile as they climbed the steps. 'She might hug you to death or feed you until you think you will burst, but she is never unkind.'

Annabelle was about to reply when a voice came from within the house. 'What are you up to, you naughty boy? Some mischief, I'll be bound, and I bet a *sou* to a franc that Etienne is part of it.'

She emerged from the gloom at the back of the house into the light-filled hallway, a waiflike vision in loosely draped layers of jersey silk and vermillion chiffon and bedecked in numerous strings of pearls and colourful beads. Her hair was a fiery, untamed mop of impossible red which was held back from her face by a scarf of orange silk; her lips and nails were painted scarlet to match her exotic slippers, her fingers were covered in enormous rings, bracelets rattled on her wrists, and long pendants of red and gold swung from her ears. For a woman of forty she looked amazingly young and carefree.

'You're a scallywag,' she said as she gave Henri a smacking kiss on each cheek. 'You always arrive just in time for coffee and pastries. Now, where's your partner in crime, and who is this mysterious visitor?'

Annabelle stepped up to the door rather nervously. 'It's me, Tante Aline. Camille's daughter, Annabelle.'

The big dark eyes widened and the mouth opened, and then she broke into a wide, glorious smile. 'Annabelle? I cannot believe it. Oh, what a joy!'

Before Annabelle could answer, she was swamped in an all-encompassing embrace of whispering fabric, jangling beads and bracelets and the scent of gardenias.

'What a heavenly surprise,' Aline breathed as she finally stepped back and regarded her more closely. 'But why didn't you warn me you were coming? I would have cleared out the spare room properly and prepared a good meal and—'

'Please, Tante Aline, I didn't want you to fuss, or to put you to any inconvenience. But would it be possible to stay for a while until I can find somewhere else?'

The lively eyes widened again. 'But of course you must stay here with me for as long as you wish. Where else would you go but to your Aunt Aline?' She turned to Henri and Etienne. 'Shoo, the pair of you, and leave me to my niece. You may come back this evening for supper.'

Annabelle would have thanked them, but Aline had closed the door on them before they'd reached the bottom step.

She took Annabelle's hand. 'You don't want to take either of them too seriously,' she said confidentially. 'They're good-looking, pleasant young men and very talented, but they like the girls too much and cannot be trusted – especially Henri. You should hear what he gets up to with his models.'

She rolled her eyes and then winked. '*Ooh là là*. I have such stories to tell, and you will hear them all, my little one, but first you must have coffee and pastry. You are far too thin.'

4

The house in rue de l'Arbre held the delicious, heady aromas of cinnamon and coffee, French cigarettes, gardenia perfume and garlic, with an underlay of the sharper tangs of oil paint and turpentine. Aline took Annabelle's coat and after an askance look at it, placed it and her hat haphazardly amongst the others on the overloaded rack before watching in amusement as her niece took in her surroundings.

All of Annabelle's senses were assaulted and overwhelmed as her gaze scanned the random and chaotic décor. Tiny bells on red silken ropes hung from the scarlet banister rail. The treads and risers of the steep wooden staircase had been given thick coats of dark green gloss and decorated with painted vines and grapes which meandered up to the landing. Vivid paintings of Mediterranean scenes crowded the cerulean-blue walls beneath the billowing white clouds and duck-egg sky of the painted ceiling.

Plaster cherubs peeked out from the cornices, and paper flowers gathered dust in glass bowls that glowed like gems on the dark hall table. Shoes, slippers and galoshes were piled haphazardly beneath the staircase alongside mops and brooms and hat boxes, and at the end of the hall was a curtain of spar-kling beads which glittered from the coloured rays of sun that poured through the fanlight above the door.

Annabelle was left reeling by so much colour and vibrancy after the shabbiness of her room in Goose Lane, and the dour-ness of her family home, and she knew that it would take time to absorb even a fraction of this glorious, hectic house.

'So, you approve of my home?' Aline's smile was soft.

'It's breathtaking, and unlike anything I've ever seen.' Annabelle grinned back at her. 'It certainly bears little resem-blance to Maman's overly ordered house. Are those your paintings, Tante Aline?'

'You must call me, Aline. Being an aunt makes me feel far too old,' she said with an impish pout. 'And yes, they are my paintings. I go to the south of France every summer because the light there is remarkable, and it seems that people like to have some sunshine in their rather dreary lives, for they sell very well here.'

Annabelle thought they were beautiful and wondered if the south of France really was as vibrant as Aline had depicted.

'Now, come, Annabelle. I want to show you a little more of my home and then we must have our coffee. Leave your cases there; we'll take them up later.' She led the way through the curtain of bright glass beads, which rattled and clicked in their wake, into a cluttered room lit only by various small lamps that had been draped in exotic jewel-coloured chiffon.

'It's always dark in here in the mornings,' Aline declared as she wound her way through the mess to the French windows. 'But look, in the afternoon the garden will be full of sunlight.'

She flung open the doors to reveal an oasis of lush green plants, a fountain where a stone angel trickled water into a large shell, a sizeable table and eight wicker chairs and numerous terracotta pots positively stuffed with greenery. The rear wall of the garden had been artfully turned into a mosaic of turquoise and glass chippings depicting a sea monster rising from the deep, and a huge ginger-and-white cat was sprawled luxuriously in the only sliver of sunlight to fall on the stone patio.

'That's Cicero – he's very vocal when he's not sleeping – and this is my sanctuary,' she explained. 'Life can be hectic, and there are times when I enjoy just being on my own.' She smiled as the violin music began again. 'That's Miriam. You'll meet her later.'

'Come in. Come in. Mind the cat,' screeched a raucous voice.

Annabelle started and Aline laughed. 'Don't take any notice of Napoleon,' she said as she closed the doors and turned back into the room. 'He's just a naughty old bird, aren't you?' she crooned.

As Annabelle's eyes adjusted to the gloom she saw the large ornate cage in the corner of the room, and the exotic blue and red parrot which sat on the perch watching her with bright, beady yellow-ringed eyes. He was quite magnificent, but his beak looked cruelly sharp as he delicately pecked seeds from Aline's hand.

'I wouldn't advise you try this,' said Aline. 'Bonaparte is inclined to bite if he's feeling out of sorts – which he often is unfortunately.' She closed the door on the cage and began to throw things from one of the chairs onto the floor. 'Sit down and I'll fetch the coffee and pastries from the kitchen.'

As she bustled out, Annabelle sank into the over-stuffed chair and tried to catch her breath and prepare her senses for another onslaught as she began to absorb her surroundings at a more leisurely pace.

The proportions of the ornately plastered ceiling showed that it was actually quite a large room, but with so many pieces of furniture, and so much clutter, it appeared at first glance to be much smaller. There was an unfinished landscape painting on an easel in one corner, the parrot cage in another, two low armchairs and three sagging couches arranged by the fire, and a jardinier holding a rather dusty and drooping aspidistra. The walls were covered in framed pictures and paintings, the dark red-and-gold striped paper almost hidden from view. The red-and-gold theme continued in the heavy velvet curtains and draped pelmet, which were richly fringed and held back by tasselled silk ropes.

The fireplace looked old and sturdy, with blue-and-white tiles, a black hearth and a tall brass fender that had a strip of padded leather on top. The mantelpiece and surround were made from intricately carved dark wood, and above it was an ornate mirror framed in gold ormolu and decorated with fat gold cherubs perched on what looked like grapevines. Photographs in pretty frames jostled for space on the mantelpiece amongst cards, invitations, discarded letters and interesting bits of dusty pottery and porcelain.

There was a lovely crystal chandelier hanging from the plaster ceiling, and lots of small tables dotted about to trip up the unwary. But it was the many and varied collections of things scattered on every surface and hiding the rugs that really made it feel more like an antiquarian shop than someone's drawing room. Shawls and scarves were draped over the back of the couches, where cushions and blankets vied for space with numerous sketchbooks, discarded handbags and a pile of newspapers. There were more newspapers and magazines piled beside them along with precariously stacked books.

Annabelle regarded the chaos and was strangely warmed by it. This room was welcoming in the soft light from the lamps – like an Aladdin's cave filled with treasures, that drew you in and made you want to stay and be a part of the love that seemed to imbue each and every corner.

'I keep meaning to tidy up,' said Aline as she came into the room carrying a tray of coffee and pastries. She nudged a nearby small table with her knee to clear it of magazines and put down the tray. 'But life is too exciting for housework, and I never seem to find the time,' she said as she stepped over the spilled magazines and plumped down into a nearby couch.

There was a furious yowl and a hiss which made them both jump and Aline shot to her feet. 'My poor babies,' she wailed. 'Did I sit on you?' She hoisted two very large, fluffy cats from the depths of the blankets and cushions and made a fuss of them as their tails flicked and their green eyes regarded Annabelle with disdain.

Annabelle liked cats, but she didn't think either of those two would appreciate her stroking them now they were disgruntled. 'They're very beautiful,' she said. 'What are their names?'

'This is Claudette,' she replied, indicating the one with the green collar. 'And this is Mignonette in the blue. I have six in all, but I suspect the other three are asleep on my bed.' She carefully put them on the floor and sat down again as they stalked off with their plumed tails stiffly to attention.

'Who's a naughty boy? Mind the cat. Come in. Come in.'

'Silence, Napoleon, or I'll put the cover over your cage,' Aline said sternly. 'You must excuse him, my dear, he's an old rogue, but I do so love him.'

'He's very exotic,' said Annabelle, who was now thoroughly enjoying herself. 'Where does he come from?'

Aline gave a Gallic shrug and poured the coffee. 'I inherited him from a lover five years ago,' she said airily. She laughed in delight and clapped her hands. 'Oh, my dear, your face! You look just as disapproving as your mother. But it's nothing to be ashamed of,' she added with a wave of dismissal. 'Everyone has lovers here. Life would be far too dull otherwise.'

Annabelle was rather taken aback by the matter-of-fact way her aunt talked of such things, so she took the tiny cup of fragrant coffee and sipped it to give her time to recover. She was having trouble trying to absorb the fact that this colourful, vivacious woman was related in any way to the stiff and very formal Camille. 'It must be nice to have something to remember him by,' she said awkwardly.

Aline sipped her coffee and then passed the plate of pastries. 'Don't worry about crumbs, the cats will soon clean them up.' She smiled at Annabelle. 'It will take time for you to get used to my funny ways, my dear. I am not at all like my sister, thank goodness, and live my life very differently.'

'Yes, I think I've already realised that,' Annabelle said, and chuckled. 'It's very good of you to take me in at all. Are you sure I won't be a nuisance?'

'*Poof*, of course not. This house is large and I can always find a corner for someone so special.'

Annabelle ate the sweet fruit pastry that melted in her mouth and dropped crumbs into her lap. She was still intrigued about Aline's lover who'd left her the parrot. 'You were saying about Napoleon,' she reminded her.

'Ah, yes. Well, I wasn't at all pleased that Jean-Michel left me with just his parrot. After all, we'd been lovers for some time and he was a wealthy man. I thought I had meant more to him than just a squawking bunch of feathers and claws.' She grinned and brushed crumbs from her lap onto the floor. 'But I soon found that I had done him an injustice, for when I cleaned out the cage and took the tray from the bottom, there was a box. And in that box was a suite of emerald and diamond necklace, earrings and bracelet.'

'How wonderful. You must have been thrilled that he thought of you so highly.'

'Oh, I was,' Aline said with a happy smile. 'But of course I never wear them, for they are a perfect match for the set he bought his wife.' She grinned wickedly at Annabelle, knowing she'd shocked her further. 'I regard them as my pension,' she continued, 'and they're locked in a safe at the bank in case I need to sell them one day when I am old. This place takes a lot to keep, and with all my friends coming and going and the young ones who lodge with me needing things, it's surprising how expensive life can be.'

Annabelle felt a pang of guilt for not realising that amid all the glamour and chaos, the widowed Aline could very well be struggling financially. 'I do have a little money that Mother gave me. You're very welcome to it, of course. And once I've found a nursing post, I can pay you a proper rent.'

'I will not hear of it,' Aline said sharply. 'You are family. Keep your money, Annabelle, and use it on yourself.' She sipped her coffee and eyed her over the lip of the cup. 'Camille didn't write to me about you coming,' she murmured thoughtfully. 'So I'm guessing that this was all very last minute. What are you running away from, Annabelle? Or should I ask from whom?'

Annabelle suddenly remembered the letter and scooped it out of her bag. Having given her aunt a potted version of everything that had happened over the past few weeks, she handed the letter over. 'Maman explains everything in more detail in this.'

Beneath the distant refrain of the violin there was silence but for the rattle of the cage as the parrot edged back and forth along the perch and the clatter of Aline's bracelets as she read the long letter. It was a good few minutes later before she folded the pages and returned them to the envelope.

'My heart aches to think he could be so cruel to his own flesh and blood,' she said sadly. 'I never liked your father,' she continued thoughtfully as she played with the beads around her neck. 'I met him only the once, but that was enough.' She gave a deep sigh. 'Poor Camille, I tried to warn her that he would make her a ghost and take away her life – and sadly I was proven right.'

Annabelle knew very little of her mother's life before she'd married Edwin, for it was a subject Camille refused to discuss. 'What was Maman like before she met him?'

'Oh, she was full of life; pretty and very chic, even as a little girl. She could wear the plainest things and look quite wonderful – unlike me, who prefers colour and frou-frou,' Aline said with a self-deprecating shrug. 'She was more like our father with her love of books and poetry, and although she could draw quite well, it was only a hobby to her. She was a solitary, rather studious girl, who loved taking long walks and seemed so at home in the countryside.'

Annabelle frowned. 'I thought you were both born here in Paris?'

Aline shook her head, the long earrings swinging. 'No, no. We lived near Rouen in a large house with many acres of farmland that backed onto forests. Our father was the mayor, and we were quite well off. I came to Paris shortly after Camille went to learn English at the academy in London. I knew that if I wanted to succeed in art, I had to be here and not stuck in the back of beyond. She met and married Edwin, and a short while later I met Daniel Fournier and we moved into this house. We write regularly but I haven't seen her since her wedding, and although we live very different lives, I do miss her,' she admitted sadly.

'I was sorry to learn that your husband died so young. That must have been terribly hard for you.'

'Yes, it was,' Aline said softly. 'We had only been married for such a short while when he was struck down by that runaway horse and carriage. And he was just beginning to get commissions for his paintings, too.' She looked across the room at the unfinished canvas on the easel. 'That was his last work, and I was offered a great deal of money for it; but I couldn't let it go, for all the while I have it, he is still with me.'

Annabelle heard the poignancy in her voice, and realised with some sadness that her aunt's *joie de vivre* and hectic lifestyle masked the loneliness and heartache of a lost future with the man she had loved so well.

Aline made a visible effort to banish the gloom and her expression brightened. 'At least Camille had the sense to send you to me, and now you're here, I will show you how wonderful life can really be. You will see such things, my dear, and learn so much, and I will teach you how to dress cheaply but with Parisian style. That dreadful old coat will have to go, you realise that, don't you?'

Annabelle was still trying to get used to the bewilderingly swift changes in her aunt's conversations. 'But it's a good coat and from an expensive shop,' she protested.

Aline pursed her lips. 'It might have been passable some time ago; now it is tired and shabby and does not suit you at all.' She cocked her head and regarded the rest of Annabelle's outfit. 'The skirt and sweater are surprisingly chic, but your shoes and those awful thick stockings . . .' She threw up her hands in dramatic

Gallic despair. '*Ooh là là.* I can see you have much to learn, but I will teach you, my dear.'

Annabelle wasn't at all sure that layers of chiffon and clashing colours were quite her style and was rather alarmed at the thought of her aunt taking her in hand. Aline had the personality to carry off such a style and did it with aplomb, but Annabelle feared she would simply look ridiculous.

They talked for an hour or more and Annabelle learnt of the young Jewish couple from Poland who lived in the basement apartment and played violin and cello in one of the most prestigious Parisian symphony orchestras; and of the poet who lived on the first floor next to the struggling writer; and the three artists who had the top rooms and shared the attic studio with Aline.

Annabelle was fascinated by the tales she told about her lodgers and the gossip of the evening salons she held once a week. She listened as Aline talked of the coffee houses and bars where like-minded people met to discuss their work and anything that had fired up their imagination, while they hoped for an introduction to someone who might become their sponsor and patron.

As Mignonette returned to climb on her lap and settle down to sleep, Aline stroked her fur and described the streets of Montmartre where young artists like Henri made enough to keep body and soul together with their quick charcoal sketches of the tourists. She spoke fondly of the leisurely Sundays spent around her laden kitchen table talking about everything as the newspapers were studied from cover to cover, the wine flowed, and the meal stretched from noon to early evening.

Mignonette purred loudly as she explained how she tried to help the struggling artists by holding poetry readings, and sessions in which aspiring authors could come and read out their latest work so it could be critiqued. And without a hint of egotism, she mentioned the fact that she was well known in the artistic circles of Paris, so could invite those best placed to offer guidance and perhaps even sponsorship.

'You seem to have a full and exciting life,' said Annabelle, who'd been completely absorbed by her vivid descriptions.

Aline glanced at the mantelpiece cluttered with invitations. 'There is always somewhere to go, to be seen, and to meet interesting people,' she said in her matter-of-fact way. 'I'm very lucky.'

Annabelle was about to ask if she had a patron when they heard the toll of a nearby church bell.

'*Ooh là là*,' Aline exclaimed as she dumped Mignonette unceremoniously on the floor and hauled herself out of the couch. 'It's lunchtime and I haven't even started to prepare myself. Quick, quick,' she said impatiently as she grabbed Annabelle's hand and hurried her through the beaded curtain. 'We are having lunch at the Lafayette with my patron, and I cannot possibly allow you to wear that coat and those shoes.'

Annabelle was laughing as she grabbed her cases and followed Aline up the stairs. Her aunt was quite wonderful, but if every day was like this, then she'd have trouble keeping up with her.

As Aline flung open a door on the first landing, Annabelle gasped in awe and disbelief. 'Is this your bedroom?' she breathed.

'Of course. Quick, quick, come in.'

Annabelle could only stare at the vast, sunlit room in complete astonishment. The enormous four-poster bed took up much of the space, and was draped in the finest and most exotic silks of every hue. The canopy was of yet more silk that had been exquisitely pleated and topped off with a crown of fabric roses; the frame was a perch for yet more plump cherubs, and strung with numerous tasselled ropes of silk; feathered and lacy fans; glittering beads and embroidered hangings.

The bedspread was gloriously embroidered with gold birds and sequined flowers, which the three Siamese cats obviously found very comfortable to sleep on; the fat pillows were edged with thick white lace and there was a full-length mink coat sprawled across the foot of the bed. The walls had been painted black with ibis, herons and flamingos wading through delicate streams of silver and beds of lotus water lilies.

Feeling overwhelmed by such an extraordinary room, she tore her gaze from the bed and saw that clothes in every colour of the rainbow spilled from a wardrobe and chest of drawers, shoes were scattered about the floor and the large Siamese cats were eyeing her belligerently as they stretched and yawned and made it clear they didn't appreciate being disturbed.

Aline shooed them out and shut the door. 'Now, we must find a coat and shoes,' she said as she returned to rummaging in the wardrobe. 'We are not the same height, but hemlines are shorter this year.'

She stopped suddenly and gave Annabelle a critical look. 'A jacket would be better,' she decided, and went to the tightly packed rail fixed to the wall. Selecting a beautifully tailored, fitted jacket of lavender-coloured tweed, she ordered Annabelle to try it on while she went in search of shoes.

Annabelle managed to see her reflection in the peer-glass around the belts, scarves, feather boas and long gloves that had been draped over it. The jacket fitted like a dream, went with the skirt perfectly, and the row of tiny pleats at the back were very flattering to the waistline.

'You will need this, this . . . and this,' said Aline bossily as she draped a scarf artistically around Annabelle's neck, fastened a narrow belt over the waist of her cream sweater and firmly pinned a very chic dark purple velvet hat into her hair. 'And of course you must have proper gloves. Those others are too thick and clumsy.' She produced butter-soft kid gloves and stood back to admire the effect.

'Good,' she said decisively before giving a dramatic sigh. 'But the shoes and stockings I cannot do anything about. My feet are smaller and narrow, and I only have one decent pair of stockings left, which I'm wearing. We'll go shopping in the market tomorrow and find some.'

'I can't really afford—'

'*Poof*, you will by the time I've finished bartering.' Aline whipped off the orange scarf she'd used to tie back her hair and reached for a black, broad-brimmed hat which had a cluster of drooping red silk roses at the crown. Having secured it to her satisfaction, she slipped on a black velvet cape. With a jaunty scarlet scarf draped around her neck, she added another dash of lipstick, sprayed them both liberally with her heady gardenia perfume and then picked up black gloves, a small clutch bag and kicked off her slippers.

'We don't have to walk far, so I'll wear my heels,' she declared as she headed back out of the room and went downstairs in her stockinged feet. The heels proved to be at least three inches high and were bright red leather with a black butterfly stitched just above the peep-toes. They set off her slender legs and ankles perfectly.

'That is a lovely hat,' said Aline as she caught sight of the one Annabelle had worn on her journey from England abandoned on the hall clothes rack. 'Is it French?'

'I have no idea,' Annabelle admitted. 'It was a gift from a friend of mine.'

'Your friend has good taste for an Englishwoman. You must tell me about her on our way to the Lafayette.' Aline put her arm through Annabelle's. 'I never had children, but now it's as if I have a daughter at last,' she murmured as she patted her cheek. '*Ooh là là*, we'll have such fun, my little Belle.'

Henri was having no fun at all as he paced the attic studio and tried to decide if he'd done enough to his painting to impress Monsieur Marcel. The man was a wealthy entrepreneur who collected art as a hobby, had strong opinions about what he did and didn't like and wasn't afraid to speak his mind. Was this good enough to add to his vast collection?

There had been so many times that he'd been disappointed by people who'd expressed their liking for his work and then not backed it up by opening their wallets, and if he was about to go to Spain with Etienne, he would need money to support himself.

Henri turned the easel so that the midday sun fell directly onto the painting from the large skylight windows. Amélie had been a joy to paint, for she was not only a natural beauty, but a lazy piece who would quite happily sit for hours doing nothing more than staring dreamily into space. What went on in her head, he had no idea, but their brief affair had been fun, and he would miss her.

Amélie lay dreamily in a hammock strung between two trees, the leaves of which were green and gold and amber from the sunlight that peeked through them. One arm was resting above her head, the fingers curving towards the wild violets she'd pinned in her dark hair; the other was languid as it draped from the hammock to rest on the violet-strewn grass, a forgotten book lying open at her fingertips.

Her straw hat lay discarded on the ground, the colour of its ribbons echoing the same soft green of her simple dress. One sleeve had slipped to reveal the exquisite curve of her naked shoulder and a single tendril of her long black hair curled tenderly over it and nestled between the suggested sweet plumpness of breasts which pushed at the delicate fabric.

Amélie's heart-shaped face was beautiful in repose, her eyelids as delicate as rose petals beneath the fine arch of her brows. Her nose was short and straight with just a hint of hauteur. Yet it was her mouth that told of her sensuality, of her lust for life and all she meant to take from it; and in the slightly parted lips there was a hint of a smile as if she were remembering a secret tryst with a special lover.

Henri was experienced enough to know that it was finished; that it was now as perfect as he could get it, and any more fiddling would only ruin it. He carefully carried the painting out of the sun and propped it on another easel in the far corner so the oils he'd added today would dry properly.

Then he whistled cheerfully as he cleaned his brushes and tried to bring a bit of order to his untidy studio. It was the large attic room of a house he shared with a dozen other lodgers, and he knew he was lucky to be the only artist, for it meant he could shut himself away in here and work to his heart's content knowing he wouldn't be interrupted.

The light was excellent in the mornings, but by mid-afternoon – especially in winter – it had disappeared below the rooftops, making it impossible to carry on working in the faint flickering of the ancient gas lamps. It was always cold up here, even though there was a fireplace which he tried to keep alight with scraps of wood and coal. But it gave out little heat, and like today, he was often forced to work in several layers of clothing and a pair of fingerless gloves to ward off hypothermia as his breath misted in the frigid atmosphere.

There were finished canvases stacked against three of the walls and a dark red chaise longue he'd picked up in a flea market took up the other. He'd draped a colourfully embroidered fringed shawl over the arm to hide the stuffing that was bursting through, and had placed cushions over the exposed springs to appease the girls who modelled for him and make it more comfortable when he made love to them. If that chaise longue could talk, he thought wryly, it could certainly tell a tale or two.

A scarred table and wooden chair sat beneath one window, and this was where he kept his paints, brushes, pencils and sticks of charcoal and pastels, alongside the bottles of turpentine and oil, and several discarded palettes and palette knives of varying widths. Three clean canvases had been stretched over frames and had been carefully placed far from where they might have been splattered as he worked.

Henri finished cleaning everything and hunted out a sketch-book and a piece of charcoal, eager now to do what he'd wanted to since he'd first caught sight of Annabelle. He sat down at the table and swiftly drew her face and the sweep of her hair from memory.

She was a lovely girl, and those extraordinary eyes and that beautiful hair would make her a perfect model, but he had the feeling she'd be shocked if he proposed such an idea. Indeed, she would probably be shocked if she saw most of his canvases, he thought with a smile as he carefully tried to capture the memory of the bow of her top lip and the swell of the lower one.

He fully admitted that he was lusty; he had enjoyed learning the secrets of a woman's body and how much pleasure it could give when he was just fifteen. She'd been much older, the married sister of one of his friends, but she'd taught him well and enthusiastically and he would always be grateful to her.

He enjoyed women, loved their curves and their soft skin, the way they teased with their eyes and promised so much with their mouths, and how their long hair acted as a temptation as it barely veiled the swell of a breast or the delicious peachy roundness of a bottom. Annabelle was slender, but even beneath that awful coat he could see the thrust of her breasts and imagine what she would look like naked on the chaise longue.

Henri chuckled as he realised he was letting his thoughts carry him off into realms he had no business exploring. Annabelle had struck him as a girl who would keep herself pure until the right man came along, not the sort to strip off in a freezing attic and lie wantonly on his couch as he painted her.

He laughed out loud and tossed the sketchbook onto the table. 'Henri, you should be ashamed of yourself,' he softly chided as he wrapped his scarf more firmly round his neck and adjusted his black beret. 'At least get to know the girl before you try to seduce her.'

Checking that the meagre fire had gone out, he locked the studio, shoved the keys into his coat pocket and clattered down the stairs. 'Etienne,' he yelled as he thudded his fist on the door. 'It's time to go to Aline's.'

'There's no need to shout,' he replied as he opened the door. 'I'm well aware of the time, and anyway, what's the rush? I thought we could go to Bar Rousseau for a Pernod first.'

'Only if you're buying,' said Henri. 'I've barely got enough money for the rent at the end of the week.'

Etienne grinned and slapped his shoulder. 'You worry too much, my friend. That painting of Amélie is the best you've ever done, and old Marcel is certain to buy it. But I'll pay for a Pernod or a Ricard or two, because there was a rather nice royalty cheque waiting for me when I got home.'

Henri congratulated him enthusiastically and they ran down the next flight of stairs, ignored the yelled insults thrown at them by the harridan who lived on the ground floor and managed the house for the landlord, and set off for the bar.

Rousseau was a small bar and *tabac* wedged between a butcher's shop and the entrance to a large block of apartments. Due to the inclement weather the outside tables were empty, so the atmosphere inside was smoky, the voices of the men standing at the bar rising to be heard above the music coming from the wireless.

The owner was a thickset middle-aged man with a dour expression, a bald head and a walrus moustache. He regarded the two young men suspiciously as he wiped down the highly polished copper sheeting of his counter. As they ordered their drinks, he held out his hand for the money – their credit had long since run out. Once the coins had been dropped into his palm, he poured two shots of Pernod into tumblers and set a jug of water beside it.

They carried their drinks to a table at the back, poured a little water into the aniseed-flavoured spirit and waited for it to cloud over before they took an appreciative sip. 'So,' said Etienne, 'I suppose you're in a mad rush to see that English girl again.'

'Not at all,' Henri lied. 'And she's not English – her mother is French.'

'Oh dear, you have got it bad,' sighed Etienne with a wicked sparkle in his dark eyes. 'You realise, of course, that she's probably a virgin, and because she is very English despite her mother and her good French, she more than likely regards sex as something to be stoically borne as she closes her eyes and thinks of England and Empire.'

'That's not a nice thing to say about a girl you hardly know,' protested Henri.

Etienne gave a shrug and sipped his drink before lighting a Gauloise. 'We are both experienced in the ways of women, my friend, and I wager that one is not the sort of girl who will tumble into bed at the first kiss.'

'Well, I like her,' he replied stubbornly. 'And as it's obvious that she's a lady, I really don't appreciate you talking about her like that. If you can't be civil, then stay away from her.'

Etienne raised a dark eyebrow. 'That sounds like a challenge, Henri.'

'It wasn't meant to be.'

'Well, I will take it as one,' he said decisively. 'We will both get to know the lovely Annabelle, and see whose charm gets him into her oh-so-refined drawers.'

'I'm not wagering with you over something like that,' said Henri crossly. 'She's a nice girl and I won't be a part of such a challenge.' He lit his own cigarette and was alarmed to discover that he was so angry with Etienne his hand was shaking.

Etienne sipped his drink and regarded Henri through the smoke of their cigarettes. 'As you seem so defensive of the girl I apologise,' he said quietly. 'We have never fallen out over a woman, and I hope we never will.' He shot a wicked grin at his childhood friend. 'Let us see who she favours, shall we, and take it from there?'

Henri eyed him distrustfully. Etienne was a sly dog at times, and although he hadn't expressed an attraction to Annabelle, he suspected that his friend had been as taken with her as he – and was testing the waters to see how Henri felt.

'I doubt she'll favour either of us,' he replied with deliberate lightness. 'After all, we have nothing to offer her, and as she's related to Aline, she must come from a well-to-do family.'

A sly smile played at the corners of Etienne's mouth. 'Well, we shall soon find out, won't we?' he murmured.

5

As Annabelle lay in the downy bed that night and watched the moon sailing across the chimney pots and tiled roofs of Paris, she felt as if she'd been living in a dream for the past two days. So much had happened that she'd barely had the time to absorb it all, and here she was, in France with Aline, and feeling overwhelmed by all she'd seen and experienced.

This wonderful house, her aunt's welcome and the sumptuous lunch at the Lafayette had gone a long way towards helping her to set aside the shock of her father's betrayal, but the hurt still lingered, and with it the regret that she hadn't spoken to George, or given him a thought before she'd left. She'd rectified that by sitting down this afternoon and writing him a long letter in which she explained her reasons for leaving so suddenly, and gave her heartfelt apology for not telling him.

Having assuaged her guilt somewhat, she'd then written to her mother and to Philippa Howden, asking that Philippa send on her address to Caroline and keep an eye on Camille. There was always the chance that Edwin would discover what Camille had done, and now that Annabelle could think more clearly, she'd begun to fret over the consequences. If Edwin could seek revenge so bitterly on his daughter, then God only knew what he might do to Camille.

Annabelle's thoughts skittered back and forth, the worries and regrets tangled up in the knowledge that she couldn't go back – the die had been cast, her future was here on the other side of the Channel – and that whatever it might bring, she had to make the best of this chance her mother had given her. Camille now had Philippa to confide in, perhaps even to run to if things got very bad, and Annabelle realised that her mother had known what she was doing, but had been prepared to take the risk. The knowledge that she'd loved her enough to do such a thing warmed Annabelle, but the regret that she hadn't known of this love was great and she wished with all her heart that Camille had shown some sign of it earlier.

She determinedly put aside her troubled thoughts, snuggled beneath the downy quilt and regarded her room in the glow from the moon. It was larger than the one she'd rented in Goose Lane and a world away from its austerity. The walls had been painted a deep blue and there was a frieze of hand-painted cherry blossom running below the picture rail, but compared to the rest of the house it was soberly decorated and tidy.

The bed was huge beneath a canopy of pale blue silk, the pillows soft and plump, and the rest of the furniture was dark and aged, but of good quality. Aline had used this room to keep yet more clothes and she'd bundled them up and carried them away to add to the chaos of her own bedroom so that Annabelle had a bit of space to move about. The few clothes Annabelle had brought with her had been examined with Aline's sharp eye and mostly approved of; now they'd been placed in the large wardrobe where they looked rather drab and uninteresting after the zinging colours she'd been surrounded by all day.

She lay there unable to sleep with her mind going over all that had happened since her arrival in Paris. Aline's patron, Monsieur Montand, had proved to be an excellent host and not at all put out that Aline had brought her along uninvited. He reminded Annabelle of Caroline's father in a way, for he had a definite presence, and put her at ease immediately, helping her to choose from the menu and asking her opinion of the different wines which came with every course, even though he must have realised she was naive when it came to such things.

He and Aline had flirted with each other outrageously all through lunch and Annabelle had a suspicion that perhaps they were rather closer than just artist and patron, and was surprised that she could so swiftly accept this. Paris was definitely having an effect on her.

After the lunch, which had gone on for over two hours, he'd taken them both in his car for a short tour of Paris to show her the sights. Annabelle had delighted in seeing the famous buildings, boulevards, palaces and parks that she'd only known through the pages of schoolbooks and her mother's descriptions. Yet throughout the day she'd become aware of something that she hadn't given a thought to before: her French wasn't as good as she'd imagined.

There had been times, both during lunch and the tour, and again in the evening when Etienne and Henri had joined the rest of the household for supper, that she found she couldn't understand the idioms and modern phrases, and often made them laugh with her dated language. The French her mother had taught her was clearly old-fashioned, which was hardly surprising, for Camille had left France over twenty years ago. And Annabelle had experienced some difficulty in keeping up with the rapid and sometimes bewildering conversations.

She turned over in bed and nestled into the wonderfully soft bank of pillows. The confusion wouldn't last long, she decided, for she was a quick learner, had an excellent grasp of the basics, and would soon get the hang of it.

Annabelle dismissed this minor niggle and turned her thoughts to the evening gathering around Aline's vast kitchen table. It had been lively, to say the least, with wine and bread and delicious slices of tasty sausage and cheese. She'd met the artists, writers and musicians that lived in the house, and felt the vibrancy of so many talented people all in one place.

She'd also had the chance to get to know Etienne and Henri a little more when they'd finally arrived armed with bottles of wine to celebrate Etienne's royalty cheque. They obviously felt at home here and knew everyone in the house very well, and Etienne had regaled them with several scandalous tales about Henri's adventures with his models, which had had them all in stitches.

As she lay there in the comfort of her bed, Annabelle smiled. They were both entertaining, but she'd felt drawn to Henri more than his friend, for he was quieter and thoughtful and not half as flamboyant. He was also quite relaxed at Etienne's teasing, taking it all in good part, even though Annabelle sensed that some of it bordered on spitefulness. She wondered if Etienne was perhaps a little jealous of his childhood friend – though why that should be, she had no idea.

Etienne was a terrible flirt and clearly considered himself to be irresistible to women, his black eyes flashing with intensity as he wholly focused on the woman in question, his white, even teeth showing in his broad smile as he revelled in becoming the centre of attention. Annabelle had been flattered and a little embarrassed as he'd teased her about her old-fashioned French and her Englishness, and although she'd laughed at his stories and enjoyed his company, there was a lingering sense that he wasn't quite all he made himself out to be, and it made her wary.

Deciding that she was being oversensitive after a long and quite overwhelming forty-eight hours, she closed her eyes. This was Paris and all the men openly flirted and flattered. She'd just have to take it in her stride and get used to it. But she did wish Caroline was here, for she was far more sophisticated and would know instinctively how best to handle men like Etienne.

'You'll wear the floor out pacing like that,' said Etienne as he sat on the chaise longue in Henri's attic studio and lit a cigarette.

Henri came to a standstill in the pool of early morning light that poured through the skylight; he stared at his painting. Monsieur Marcel was due to arrive at any minute and the nervous tension that had been building over the last two days was making him feel slightly sick.

'It's all right for you,' he said mildly. 'You have money in your pocket. But if I don't sell this today, I'll be penniless and unable to go to Spain.'

Etienne slowly got to his feet and adjusted his jacket and cravat. 'You worry too much, my friend,' he said as he squeezed his shoulder. 'And if the worst comes to the worst, then I'll bankroll you in Spain until the money comes through from the newspaper.'

He picked up his beret and admired himself in the mirror as he placed it fussily on his head. With a nod of satisfaction, he turned back to Henri. 'I thought I'd stroll round to Aline's for coffee,' he said casually.

Henri eyed him sharply. 'We've already agreed to take Annabelle on a walking tour of the city this afternoon. There's no need to bother Aline twice in one day.'

He raised one dark eyebrow, his black eyes sparkling with mischief. 'What's the matter, Henri? Afraid the English girl will be dazzled by my charms and put you out of the running?'

'We're not in some sort of competition, Etienne,' Henri replied as he fought to keep his impatience at bay. 'If you wish to have coffee with Aline, then that is not my concern. But if you're hoping to get your wicked way with Annabelle, then don't be sly about it. Declare your interest in her, and I'll step aside.'

'That's very noble of you, Henri,' Etienne drawled with a hint of sarcasm.

'It's not noble at all. It's simply how things have always been between us when a girl catches our eye. If you're serious about Annabelle, then so be it. But be careful with her, Etienne,' Henri warned softly. 'She's not like Amélie and the others, and with all that's happened to her over the past few days, she needs time to adjust to her new life and the way things are done here before you bombard her with your dubious charm.'

Etienne laughed and stubbed out his cigarette. 'You sound like a ruffled papa protecting his virginal daughter. Lighten up, Henri. A bit of flirting never hurt anyone and it might even loosen the girl up and get rid of that English starch.'

'She doesn't need loosening up,' Henri said crossly. 'For goodness' sake, Etienne, if you're going to pursue her, then do it seriously or not at all.'

'You know me, Henri,' Etienne said with a wink.

Henri certainly did. His friend saw women as an amusement, and enjoyed the thrill of the chase. But he knew too that Etienne soon grew bored once the chase was over and the girl was his, and he didn't like the thought of the rather naive and innocent Annabelle falling into his trap.

He stared at the painting on the easel. Girls had come and gone in their lives, and there had never been any sense of competitive jealousy between them. And yet he sensed that Etienne's interest in Annabelle had been piqued, not merely because of her beauty, but because of her very difference from all the others – and perhaps even because Henri had foolishly shown his hand by defending her when Etienne had spoken of her so scathingly.

'What if I were to tell you that I like Annabelle very much and would enjoy getting to know her better?' Henri asked solemnly.

Etienne regarded him thoughtfully for a long moment. 'I would tell you that you should go ahead and get to know her, if that's what you want. We've never fallen out over a woman and although this English girl is intriguing and very pretty, she's hardly worth arguing over. Enjoy the chase, my friend.'

He grinned and slapped Henri's arm. 'I hear footsteps on the stairs. Good luck. I'll wait for you in the coffee house.' He opened the door to the portly entrepreneur, who was wheezing after climbing all those stairs, and gestured for him to enter before he clattered off and out of sight.

Annabelle left the house early that morning to go to the nearby *tabac* to fetch the newspapers and a packet of Aline's favourite Disque Bleu cigarettes. It was a sunny day, but the wind was chill, and she was glad of the fox fur wrap Aline had insisted upon her wearing.

She took her time and spent some lazy minutes in the park at the end of the rue de l'Arbre before strolling down to watch the Seine rushing beneath the bridge. Paris looked lovely in the early sunshine: the elegant towers and turrets of the ancient buildings rising above the rooftops and smoking chimneys, the many windows glinting above the balconies as the Saturday morning traffic rumbled over the cobbles and the icy wind made the bare branches of the trees shiver and sway.

She was about to leave the bridge and head for the *tabac* when she heard her name being called. Turning, she felt a strange sort of thrill as she saw Henri running towards her, his face alight with happiness.

'He bought three paintings!' he yelled as he grabbed her hands and swung her round in a mad sort of dance. 'Can you believe it?'

She laughed with him, charmed by his boyish joy, and delighted that he wished to share this moment of triumph with her. 'That's wonderful,' she breathed as they finally came to a halt from their hectic dance. 'And there you were full of gloom last night and so certain he wouldn't like any of them.'

He suddenly looked bashful and couldn't meet her eye. 'I'm sorry I grabbed you like that,' he said. 'You must think me very foolish.'

'Not at all,' she assured him quickly. 'Why shouldn't you be excited when something like that happens?' She smiled back at him, admiring the way his happiness and the cold sunshine had brought colour to his face and made his eyes an even brighter blue. He really was very attractive.

'He's already given me the money and asked me to keep them until tomorrow when he will send his man to collect them. Would you like . . . ? I mean, do you have the time . . . ?' He cleared his throat. 'Would you like to come and see them?' he said in a rush.

'I'd love to,' she enthused. 'Although I can't stay long. I'm supposed to be buying the papers and then Aline is taking me to the market.'

His answering smile was mischievous. 'And I'm supposed to be meeting Etienne at the coffee house. But it's not far, and won't take long.'

With a sense of playing truant, she placed her hand in the crook of his proffered arm and they walked over the bridge to the Left Bank and into the winding, narrow streets where the old houses seemed to lean towards one another as if exchanging secret confidences.

She soon lost her bearings as Henri led her through a confusion of tiny lanes and squares and eventually came to a halt outside an ugly building which looked as if it were about to fall down. The front door and many shutters needed repairing and painting; one of the downpipes had come loose from the guttering and the plaster on the walls had fallen away in large chunks to expose naked bricks and crumbling mortar.

'It might not look much,' he said, shooting her a hesitant smile, 'but at least the roof doesn't leak. Just don't take any notice of Madame Léon. She's the caretaker and never in a good mood,' he added quietly as he held the door open for her.

Annabelle stepped inside a vast, echoing hallway and came face to face with a no-nonsense battleaxe who glared at both of them as she stood guard at her doorway, arms akimbo.

'Good morning, madame,' he said as he neatly sidestepped her. 'Looking as lovely as ever, I see,' he added as he hurried Annabelle up the ugly, rickety stairs.

'You're an insult!' she yelled back. 'And if you don't pay your rent on Monday, I'll take great pleasure in throwing you and your disgusting daubs out of the door!'

Annabelle glanced at Henri to see how he took this awful threat, but as he was still grinning and seemed utterly unconcerned, she supposed this sort of badinage was quite usual. By the time she'd run up four flights of stairs, she was out of breath. 'Goodness,' she panted. 'I didn't realise how unfit I was.'

'I've got used to it,' he said as he unlocked his studio door and opened it with a flourish. 'Welcome to my *atélier*.'

Annabelle stepped into a light-filled room that was almost bare of furniture. Her sense of smell was assailed by scents of oils and turpentine, of dust, mice, damp and the distant memories of many smoky fires. The studio was freezing and she could see the mist of her breath as she caught sight of the beautiful painting on the easel.

'Oh,' she sighed as she walked towards it. 'Oh, Henri, it's no wonder he bought it.'

His smile broadened at her praise, and he quickly told her the story behind the painting. 'We'd gone to a friend's house in the country and after a long, rather heavy lunch, we lazed in the garden. Amélie fell asleep and so I sketched her there and then, knowing it would make a good painting. She always had a way of settling herself into the perfect composition, and of course the setting was ideal.'

Annabelle studied the sensuous, languid girl sleeping in the hammock and envied her complete composure and natural elegance. 'She's beautiful,' she murmured.

'She's also very irritating and unreliable,' he replied as he moved about the room. 'But she was an excellent model, and I shall have a tough task to find another like her.' He set up the other two canvases on easels. 'As you can see, she figures in all three paintings Monsieur Marcel favoured.'

Annabelle moved from the first painting and saw Amélie again, but this time she was artistically draped over the chaise longue, her naked body barely covered by the artfully placed length of red velvet as she thoughtfully admired herself in an ornate hand mirror. The third painting was of Amélie sitting at a window, staring wistfully out, the neckline of her peasant blouse drooping from her lovely shoulders, the full peasant skirt hoisted up to reveal a shapely thigh, a long leg and a neat ankle.

Annabelle felt rather uncomfortable in the presence of such sensual and intimate portrayals, for they spoke all too clearly of the relationship between the artist and his model, and with Henri standing so closely beside her, she felt suddenly awkward and far too aware of him.

Henri must have felt it too, for he quickly steered her away from the paintings and tidied away his sketchbook while offering to make a pot of coffee on the small spirit stove.

'I really must go and fetch the newspapers,' she said shyly. 'Aline will wonder where I've got to, and Etienne will be waiting to hear your news.' She dared to look up at him and shot him a nervous smile. 'I think your paintings are wonderful,' she said quietly. 'And I'm so glad that someone has recognised your amazing talent.'

He grinned back as he pulled the key out of his trouser pocket. 'At least now I won't have to rely on Etienne to fund my trip to Spain. Come on, it's freezing in here and we're both in danger of getting frostbite.'

Madame Léon berated them as they reached the hallway and they ran laughing down the narrow lane as her shouts of derision echoed after them. She linked arms with him, feeling more relaxed now that Amélie was not a silent bystander, and they talked about his proposed trip to Spain.

'Do you really have to go?' she asked, as they began to walk across the Pont Neuf.

'We are Basque, and our ancestors share the blood of the Spanish and French. It's our duty to see that these fascists are put to the run. We both have cousins and brothers who are already fighting, and it's a matter of pride to us that we should take part.'

'As I mentioned before, I have friends who've gone out there too,' she replied before going on to tell him about Caroline, her brothers and colleagues from the hospital. 'They asked me to go with them, and I might have done if I hadn't come here first,' she said with a sigh. 'But now I'm here and feel so at home, I can't think of anywhere I'd rather be.'

'So you will stay?'

'If I can get a nursing post here, then of course.'

They drew to a halt at the end of the bridge, reluctant to go their separate ways. 'I can't see there would be anything stopping you from finding work here,' he said. 'There are plenty of hospitals, and there is always a need for good nurses. But those who fight against the fascists need nurses too.'

Annabelle took a deep breath and let it out on a sigh. 'I realise that, Henri, but although the idea is tempting, I don't know if I have the courage to go into a war zone. I don't feel the same urgent need as you and the others to immerse myself in something that I know so little about.' She smiled back at him. 'There, you see, I'm a coward at heart, and I'll be quite content to stay here far from any conflict.'

He smiled and she felt the attraction between them draw her like a magnet until their surroundings faded, the bustle around them died, and it seemed as if they were alone on the bridge. It was a heady moment – like nothing she'd ever experienced before – and she was too innocent to know how to identify and understand this sudden thrilling onrush of emotion that surged through her.

'I don't think of you as cowardly,' he said, his voice soft as he looked deep into her eyes. 'You wouldn't have made that long journey here on your own otherwise.'

She found she couldn't speak or even think of anything other than the colour of his eyes and the way his nose sloped so delightfully towards the curve of his lips.

'Perhaps,' he said as he drew even nearer, 'on my return, we can meet here again on the Pont Neuf, so we can exchange tales of adventures?' His finger traced the line of her jawbone where the fox fur nestled against it.

His light touch sent shock waves through her and made her sway towards him. 'Yes,' she breathed. 'That's a lovely idea.' She tried desperately to control the overwhelming sensations that were teeming through her, for surely he could tell from her demeanour the effect he was having on her?

She finally managed to step back from him before she dared to look at his face. 'But you aren't leaving just yet, are you?' She heard the wistfulness in her voice and blushed as she dropped her gaze.

He reached for her hand, drawing her close again, forcing her to look at him. 'Not until after Christmas,' he replied, his blue eyes holding her for perhaps a second or two too long. 'We'll have plenty of time to get to know one another.'

As he released her hand and stepped back the spell was broken, and Annabelle suddenly felt as if she'd been cast adrift.

'But for now I must go and find Etienne,' he said, as if unaware of the turmoil he'd wrought within her. 'We will come to pick you up at two for your walking tour of Paris, and I'd advise you to wear comfortable shoes: these cobbles aren't easy to walk on.'

Annabelle watched him hurry away, and once he was out of sight she leant against the parapet and stared into the water. She was breathless, her heart hammering as if she'd just run a marathon, the memory of the electricity of his light touch on her face and the warmth of his hand surrounding her fingers lingering still. How could she feel like this when she hardly knew him? Was she drawn to him because his dark hair and blue eyes reminded her so much of George? But George had never made her feel like this – it was the reason she'd turned down his proposal.

Confused and still trembling from the effects of that brief moment with Henri, she wondered how she would feel when he left for Spain. Was this a momentary aberration, or something deeper and more meaningful? Either way, it could have no future if she was here and he was in the south fighting a war.

The thought of him risking his life was sobering and she felt the prick of tears as she looked out across the river. Surely such strong emotions had to mean something? Surely something that felt so special couldn't just end before it had even begun?

The chimes of the nearby clock tower snatched her from her dark thoughts. She hadn't realised how late it was and Aline would be waiting for her. She sniffed back her tears, but her thoughts and emotions were in turmoil as she headed for the *tabac*.

*

Etienne enjoyed the camaraderie of the coffee house, for it was where he could boast about his royalty cheque, his new deal with the newspaper editor and his cleverness at also getting Henri involved in his reports from the Civil War.

The atmosphere beneath the low-beamed roof was smoky, not only from the many pipes and cigarettes but from the fire in the large hearth. The delicious aroma of coffee cut through it to mingle with that of wine and brandy; the conversation was lively and the customers a fair and widespread example of the artistic people who lived in this part of Paris. It was a place to make new friends, to debate important issues over a glass of wine and discuss the furthering of careers, and somewhere to keep warm during the bitter winter days.

Etienne was in a deep discussion with a fellow writer about a rival's latest book, which they both agreed was pure rubbish and fit only for the fire, despite the fact it was selling extremely well and getting marvellous reviews.

He reached for his glass of wine and glanced up towards the door just as Henri burst through it. He knew in an instant that he had good news to tell. 'Over here, Henri,' he shouted through the babble as he edged along the settle and made room for him.

'I've done it,' panted Henri as he unwound his scarf and pulled off his beret. 'Marcel bought three – and gave me the money there and then.'

Etienne was delighted for him and he gave him an extravagant and none too gentle thump on the back. 'Well done, my friend,' he said as he raised his almost empty glass. 'The next round is on you, then.'

Henri laughed and after digging in his pockets, placed a few coins on the table. 'That's it until I clear the cheque,' he said.

There was a general cheerful groan from the others around the table and Etienne shouted across at the owner for another round. 'You can pay me back next week,' he said. 'This is a cause for celebration.'

As the pitchers of wine were placed in front of them and glasses were filled, everyone made a toast to Henri's success before returning to their previous discussions. Henri took a deep draught of the wine and rested back in the settle, his expression dreamy, his gaze distant as if he could see beyond the crowded coffee house to somewhere even more pleasurable.

Etienne eyed his friend sharply, for there was something different about him, and he had a suspicion it had nothing to do with selling his work. 'Marcel must have taken his time to decide on which ones he wanted,' he said with studied casualness. 'We were supposed to meet at least an hour ago.'

'Actually, he didn't take long at all,' Henri replied, clearly lost in thought.

Etienne was immediately curious. 'So what kept you? Amélie didn't come back to distract you with her luscious body, did she?'

Henri seemed to come out of his wool-gathering as he shook his head. 'No, I bumped into Annabelle and took her to see my paintings. We got talking and the time just seemed to fly past.'

Etienne recognised the silly look he always got on his face when he'd fallen for some girl. 'You're a dark horse, Henri,' he said jovially. 'I didn't expect you to get to her first.'

'It was nothing like that,' Henri protested. 'We just talked, that's all.'

'You mean you were alone with her in your studio and you didn't get her nicely tucked beneath you on your infamous chaise longue?' he asked incredulously. 'Henri, my friend, you're losing your touch.'

Henri's face flared with heat. 'I care about her, Etienne. She's different to all the others, and I want to get to know her properly.'

'*Mon dieu*, Henri, how many times have I heard that before?' he said and laughed uproariously. 'You fall in and out of love at the drop of a hat, and by the time we leave for Spain she'll be forgotten.'

Henri regarded him thoughtfully. 'But I really do feel something for her,' he said firmly, 'and I think she feels the same way.'

'Of course she does,' Etienne replied. 'What woman could fail to fall for your charms when you flash those eyes at her?' He thumped Henri's back again. 'The only thing you're feeling is randy, my friend, but you'll get over that once she's dropped her drawers. You always do.'

Henri flushed scarlet and his lips thinned as he looked away. 'If you're going to talk about her like that, then I'm leaving,' he said tightly.

Etienne experienced a pang of unease as he realised he'd gone too far and that this girl obviously did mean something to his friend. 'Come, come, Henri, don't be like that. I was only teasing. You're not usually that sensitive.'

'I know you were,' he said gruffly, 'but I don't appreciate you denigrating Annabelle like that.'

He watched as Henri took a sip of his wine and settled back to light a cigarette before he once more drifted off into a daydream. No woman had ever separated them before, and he doubted the rather prim little English girl would be the one to break the strong bond of brotherhood that they'd forged since childhood. But he was wise enough to know that sooner or later one of them would be ensnared by real love – they were of an age for it, after all – and if Henri was serious about this girl, then it was a good thing they were leaving soon for Spain. There was nothing like a good fight to pull a man to his senses, and as he and Etienne had shared so many other adventures, he didn't want some stupid girl to get in the way of this one.

Etienne drank some wine and silently toasted the Civil War that would inevitably sever all ties between Henri and Annabelle. *Let him have his fun*, he decided. *There are plenty of dark-eyed señoritas waiting for us over the border and Henri will soon forget her as we carouse our way through Spain and perhaps even earn some battle honours along the way.* It was the way it should be – the way it had always been – and no woman would ever change that for as long as he could draw breath.

Aline didn't seem at all concerned at the length of time she'd been away, but if she noticed Annabelle's heightened colour and rather distracted demeanour, she said nothing. She was dressed and ready for their trip to the market as Napoleon shouted a welcome to Annabelle from his cage and the sounds of someone practising the violin drifted up from the basement.

Whether it was Annabelle's heightened senses that made it so, or whether it was always a heady experience, the market proved to be another sensual delight, and as Annabelle let Aline do the bartering on the shoes and stockings they'd found, she breathed in the varying scents and tried to take in the colour and energy of the place. The French was rapid and colloquial, the bartering carried out with good humour as accordion music drifted towards them from the busker who stood in the shadows of the nearby church with his dog and cap at his feet.

The farmers and market traders had come into the city very early that morning to set up their stalls, and the number of people jostling through the narrow passages between those kiosks was a testament to the bargains that could be had. Fruit of every colour and shape was piled high on barrows; glossy onions and pure white fat bulbs of garlic had been strung together and hung from the bright canopies; scarlet tomatoes and hot green and red chilli peppers jostled for space next to pale fingers of celery, knobbly brown ginger and bunches of rosemary, thyme and parsley.

Numerous buckets held bunches of glorious flowers, pots contained brightly coloured exotic plants Annabelle had never seen before; and there were packets of seeds and bags of compost. Gardening tools were stacked in ranks alongside wheelbarrows, rustic wooden furniture and doormats. Great carcases of fresh meat hung beneath their muslin sheets from hooks at the butchers' stalls, where spicy sausages, ham and bacon were displayed next to chops, pigeon, tiny yellow *poussin* and minced meat. There were chicks and ducklings in pens, canaries in cages, stalls selling everything from underwear to fur coats and dungarees, and tempting tables laden with *brocante* – jumble – which begged to be rummaged through.

And through it all wafted the delicious scents of freshly cooking stew that was sold for a few sous in rough earthenware dishes, – and chickens stuffed with butter and garlic and herbs, roasting on a rotisserie turned by a young boy. There was *vin chaud* – hot spiced wine – bread and golden pats of butter, and so many cheeses it made it hard to choose. If you weren't hungry before you got here, Annabelle thought, you certainly soon were.

Entranced by it all, she followed Aline from stall to stall, and when the shopping was complete, they sat at an outside table of a nearby bar and watched the world go by as they drank cups of thick, rich chocolate that had been topped with a swirl of cream.

'I've spoken to some friends of mine about your wish to return to nursing,' Aline said eventually. 'There are vacancies, and I've been reliably informed that you must go to a nursing agency to make your applications.' She smoked her cigarette and adjusted the fur around her neck, just as Camille used to. 'I should warn you, though, that these agencies will need copies of your qualification certificates and, of course, references. They'll also charge you for their services.'

'Oh. I didn't realise . . .'

'Don't worry, my dear,' Aline said comfortably. 'Their fees will be taken from your first month's wages. Your qualifications should be enough to get you a very good posting, and the letter from your Matron is excellent.'

Annabelle's delight in the day was overshadowed by doubt. 'Well, I hope it's enough,' she murmured. 'The one from the chairman was a stinker.'

Aline shrugged and pursed her lips. 'Then it's probably best if you don't show it to them.' She smiled and patted her hand. 'Now, you must put all that aside and enjoy yourself while you can. You're on holiday, Annabelle, and I will not allow anything to spoil it.'

As Aline turned her attention back to the market, Annabelle tried hard to recapture the happiness of the day. Yet it seemed that the harder she tried, the more difficult it became and the tighter the knot of anxiety grew. A life without nursing was something she couldn't even contemplate, and she knew her fear of not finding a post was making her anxious. But more than that, she recognised why she was really in turmoil – she couldn't stop thinking about Henri going off to war.

She stared into the cup of hot chocolate, knowing there was a very real possibility that once he left, she might never see him again – and that would be as impossible to bear as losing her nursing career.

6

Annabelle had now been in France for two weeks. She had gone to the agency with Aline and filled in the numerous forms and applications they required, but was still waiting to hear from them. They had taken Matron's reference without comment and placed it alongside copies of her certificates and applications in a folder. Aline had been right about the French love for paperwork.

There had been letters from home which had brought some relief from the worry over Camille. Philippa had written to say that they met at least once a week, and that Camille was beginning to trust her enough to confide in her. Edwin was his usual unpleasant self by all accounts, but he seemed to have no knowledge of what Camille had done for their daughter; in fact, he was furious that Annabelle had given him the slip, and that no one appeared to know where she'd gone.

Camille's letters were long and informative, describing the outings she had with Philippa. She even expressed her regret that they hadn't had the chance to form a closer relationship, hoped that she was settled and happy in Paris, and that Aline had finally learnt to conduct herself with more restraint.

When Annabelle read this out, Aline had laughed and pulled a face. She and Camille were unalike in so many ways, and they were both far too old and set in their habits to change now.

Caroline had written from Spain where she was nursing in a field hospital that was rather too close to the front line for comfort. Her letter was disjointed and hurried, the dates above each paragraph telling of the many days it had taken her to find time to write it.

She hadn't seen her brothers since they'd parted at Victoria station, and knew only that they had joined a battalion of volunteers under the leadership of the communists who supported Spain's ousted government. Caroline had been moved from camp to camp, and it was the same with her brothers, so it could take some time for any letters to find them.

She envied Annabelle, for she adored Paris, and promised that if she ever got any leave, she would try to catch a train up there so they could spend time together. This sentiment was soon lost in the description of the endless bombing raids which shook the earth; the surprise raids by the fascists who came from nowhere with their guns and mortars and killed indiscriminately; and the dirt and squalor surrounding the makeshift hospital which made it almost impossible to keep anything clean.

She cursed the lack of morphine and proper medicines, and the slow delivery of the most basic of needs to the camp. Death was all around her, but the doctors and nursing staff were wonderfully brave and totally dedicated, and she was proud to work alongside them. She didn't go into too much detail about the injuries she'd seen or the long, weary hours she was expected to put in, but after Robert Howden's impassioned speech at the dinner table on that fateful night, Annabelle could imagine it all too well.

Caroline had finished her scrawled letter by saying that the need for more nurses was as urgent as the need for fresh supplies, and she begged Annabelle to change her mind and travel down to Spain. She warned that it was frightening, and unlike anything she had ever experienced, but explained that the work was vital, the wounded needed as much help as possible and Annabelle's skills and calm nature would be a godsend.

Caroline's spirit came through in her letter, but Annabelle could tell she was living the hell her father had predicted; was experiencing things and seeing sights that no young woman should ever witness. And yet, through it all she was still a fervent believer in the cause, and there hadn't been a single word of regret.

Annabelle had read the letter many times, and was beginning to wonder if perhaps she should go to Spain where her nursing skills would be needed and her past forgotten. Yet she hesitated to reply in such a vein, for she felt it would be running away, and she had to prove herself here first. With that done, she could go to Spain later the next year if the war still continued, with her head held high and her reputation restored.

The most difficult letter to read had arrived from George, and although she'd read it many times in the past few days, it still made her feel horribly guilty, for beneath the rather stiff and formal words was an underlying bitter hurt which he'd been unable to disguise.

He'd received her letter on his last day at St Swithin's, and although he'd been shocked that she could leave so suddenly without a word, he was relieved to discover that she hadn't fled to Spain. He told her about the practice in Dartford, and said that by the time she received his letter, he would already have settled in. He described his dash through the city to tell her his news, and his thwarted attempt to find her at Victoria station, and admitted that he'd been furious with her for running out on him like that after all their years of friendship. He'd apologised rather stiffly for distancing himself after his proposal, which he realised had been inappropriate, and hoped they could stay friends.

Annabelle had written back immediately, assuring him that of course she still regarded him as a dear friend and looked forward to hearing from him again. She made the letter chatty and light-hearted, full of the sights and sounds of the Paris she had come to love, and the riotous, warm and loving home Aline had provided – although she was careful not to mention Henri, for their friendship was blossoming into a sweet romance. George was clearly still smarting, his pride knocked sideways, and it would only make things harder for him.

To keep her occupied during the interminable wait to hear from the agency – and to assuage her guilt over the hurt she'd caused George – she'd filled her days by walking the city, often alone while Aline painted in her studio, and sometimes hand in hand with Henri. After that first tour, when they'd walked all the way up the steps to Montmartre and explored the magnificent basilica of the Sacré-Cœur, she'd been inspired to explore further, and now felt so at ease with the city she would often put the tourist map in her pocket and hardly consult it.

She explored the galleries, palaces and museums, walked in the beautiful Bois de Boulogne and down the length of the magnificent Champs-Elysées to the Arc de Triomphe, looking through the windows of the frighteningly expensive shops on the way. She found tiny boutiques tucked away that sold cheap copies of the latest designs, and many more which were positively stuffed with second-hand garments discarded by wealthy women who refused to contemplate wearing last year's fashions. Shoes, handbags, hats, gloves and underwear all proudly announced their Parisian chic, and Annabelle came to accept that Parisian women had far more choice than those living in London.

The air was cleaner too, although the traffic was constant and the rumble of car tyres over cobbles, which she barely noticed now, only fell silent in the very early hours of morning. There was poverty here, which showed in the run-down buildings of quarters where it wasn't safe to walk alone; in the number of prostitutes plying their trade, and the beggars and buskers in the streets; and although there had been one or two minor skirmishes during student protest rallies, Annabelle certainly didn't get the same sense of anger that she'd experienced in the Tower Hill and Cable Street riots.

At night when the city was lit up and the shops remained open, Paris really came to life. Pavement cafés were popular places to meet friends; bars and restaurants did a roaring trade well into the night – the French ate very late – and there was always music coming from the nightclubs and hotel ballrooms and bars.

When Henri couldn't escort her because of his work commitments at a nearby art school, Annabelle didn't find it too hard to persuade Aline to go with her on a stroll after supper, and they nearly always bumped into someone she knew, so it made for a lively evening. Neither of them had the money to eat in the restaurants, or sit in the nightclubs to watch a show, but a glass of wine or a cup of coffee cost very little, and the ever-changing parade passing by the crowded pavement cafés was as good as any cabaret.

Annabelle's delight in Paris continued to grow, and soon she felt more at home here than she ever had in London. And yet the frustration of having to wait for replies to her applications was beginning to take its toll. Christmas was barely two weeks away, her money was swiftly running out, and she didn't want to begin the new year of 1937 without a job to help pay for her keep. Aline had assured her she didn't want payment, but Annabelle had realised some time ago that her aunt often struggled to cover her bills and so felt horribly guilty about taking advantage of her kindness.

And then, of course, there was Henri and the knowledge that he would soon be leaving for Spain. They had stolen a few kisses as they'd walked along the Seine or through the tiny backstreets of Montmartre, and held hands as they'd wandered through the Saturday morning markets, but they both felt the weight of each passing day that drew them nearer to his departure.

Annabelle was in love for the first time and she saw the world in fresh bright colours – the sky seemed bluer, the Seine clearer, each veined leaf and blade of grass fresher than before – and every time Henri kissed her she wanted to melt and fuse into him, her body aching and yearning to be loved by him. And yet the ghost of his leaving remained between them and in the light of a clearer mind, she knew she daren't risk loving him completely.

She rose early that cold winter morning so she could have a bath before everyone else began to stir. The bathroom was freezing, but the water was piping hot and the scented crystals Aline had given her smelt wonderful. Having dressed for the day, she made her bed and tidied her room before going downstairs to prepare breakfast. Aline usually slept late, for she was a night owl and rarely went to bed before two in the morning, but this gave Annabelle the chance to do something for her for a change.

'Come in,' shouted Napoleon from his covered cage. 'Mind the cat. Have a drink.'

'Good morning,' she said as she took off the cover and added more seed and water to his bowls. 'And what sort of mood are you in today, Napoleon?'

He eyed her balefully and edged towards her on his perch. 'Pretty boy,' he rasped.

Annabelle made no attempt to stroke his bright feathers. She'd been bitten once before, and didn't relish a repeat per-formance. She turned her back on him, and the chaos of the lounge, and made a start on tidying up the kitchen.

It was a pleasant room that led off the lounge, with another set of doors opening onto the rear garden, which was white with frost and still in shadow. There was a square stone sink set between wooden draining boards, and chunky brass taps, one of which had to be hit with a mallet before the hot water ran freely. Lines of shelves had been placed above the ancient and rather fierce black range, and these were laden with mismatched crockery and cooking pots. Copper pots and pans hung from butcher's hooks, utensils had been stuffed into brightly painted metal jugs, and herbs grew in earthenware pots on the windowsill.

The enormous scrubbed pine table sat in the middle of the room beneath yet another decorative chandelier, with an assortment of chairs surrounding it. This was the actual heart of Aline's home, for it was here that everyone met to eat, talk and discuss their day – but at the moment it looked as if a bomb had hit it.

Annabelle ignored the mess as she hunted out food for the six cats which were already purring and winding themselves round her legs in eager anticipation. She placed the saucers on the floor and watched them gobble the food, tails flicking, bright eyes keeping watch that none of the others had something tastier. Having stroked each of them, she began to clear away the dirty plates and glasses.

Once the kitchen was straight and the freshly washed crockery and glasses had been left to dry in the rack above the sink, she prepared the coffee percolator so she could place it on the stove when she returned, and went to get her coat.

She stepped outside to find that everything was frosted with ice that glittered like diamonds in the early sunlight. The magnificent old tree at the end of the street looked quite festive, but the duck pond in the park had frozen over and the pavement was like glass.

Annabelle had come to love these quiet, deserted early hours, and she tucked her chin into her coat collar, pulled down her hat and carefully negotiated the slippery ground until she reached the main road. The street cleaners were already out and sweeping sand onto the pavements and along the road.

She opened the door to the bakery and was immediately wrapped in the heavenly smell of fresh bread and the warmth from the enormous ovens at the back of the shop. She greeted Madame Cecile and chatted to her as the bread for the day was placed in Annabelle's basket, and then with a cheery wave, carefully made her way to the newsagent's for the daily paper and Aline's packet of cigarettes. Having completed her purchases, she returned home to find an excited Aline waiting for her on the stairs.

'You've got a letter,' she said before Annabelle could close the door behind her. 'It's from the agency.'

Annabelle handed her the basket of bread in exchange for the letter, and opened it with trembling fingers.

'Dear Miss Blake,' she read out breathlessly. 'We are delighted to inform you that we have arranged an interview for the post of staff nurse at l'hôpital Laennec in the seventh district. The interview will take place on the fourteenth of December at 8.30 a.m., in the chief administrator's office at the hospital.'

She looked up from the letter and grinned delightedly at Aline. 'But that's the day after tomorrow,' she said excitedly. 'Oh, how wonderful it would be if I got a job before Christmas.'

Yet, as she read the rest of the letter out to Aline her smile faded and her spirits plummeted. 'Prior to this interview it is a requirement of the French government that all foreign nationals must sit a written and oral examination. This examination is to be held at 8.30 on the twelfth December in the School of Medicine, which is attached to Laennec hospital. Should you fail this most important examination, the offer of an interview will be withdrawn, and no other will be sought until you gain the pass mark of 75 per cent.

'We realise that this comes at very short notice, and if it is not possible for you to attend, please telephone us immediately. If this should be the case, your application will have to be resubmitted, and a further date in the new year arranged for your examination.'

'Oh, Aline,' she gasped. 'The test is tomorrow and they never warned me. It never occurred to me that I'd have to do such a thing, and it's far too late now to try and get hold of a medical dictionary to swot up on the words I may need.'

'The French love red tape even more than the English,' she soothed, 'but I'm sure you'll sail through the exam.'

'But I qualified at one of the best hospitals in the world. Surely that should be enough?'

Aline pursed her lips and gave a Gallic shrug. 'I would have thought so, but the hospital probably wants to make certain that your French is good enough to be able to understand everything you might come across on the wards. And it is, Annabelle, really it is.'

'I wonder if that's so,' she murmured. 'It's vital work and

people's lives are at stake. One slip or misunderstanding and . . .' She fell silent as she imagined the harm she could do if she wasn't completely prepared. 'They've given me such short notice, Aline,' she said in despair, 'and I really don't know if I can do it.'

She pulled off her hat, gloves and scarf and hung her coat on the rack. 'I can't afford to fail, Aline,' she said, blinking back the tears. 'I owe you so much already and—'

Aline put her arm around her waist and steered her through the beaded curtain and into the kitchen. 'Let us not think about failure before you've even tried, my dear,' she said firmly. 'Your French is a little outdated, but absolutely good enough to pass any of their silly old tests. Now, you sit down here, and I'll pour you some lovely warming coffee.'

Annabelle slumped into a kitchen chair and stared gloomily into the garden as the doubts crowded in and her confidence dwindled. She couldn't fail – simply couldn't even contemplate such a disaster after everything she'd been through.

George watched the taxi take Angus Fraser to the station and his retirement. He'd appreciated his help and advice over the past week, and although he'd quite enjoyed the old boy's company, he was relieved that his settling-in period was over and he could make the home and practice his own.

The house was a rambling Victorian semi in a quiet tree-lined street, with the surgery laid out in what had once been a drawing room and dining room. Apart from the downstairs kitchen, the living quarters were on the top two floors, and as he closed the front door and turned to look along the hallway, he felt a sense of achievement and pride. He'd come a long way since he'd left the family home outside Dublin to take up his scholarship at medical school, and having dealt with prejudice, ungodly hours of study and hard work, he'd finally made it.

As he wandered through the silent house he determinedly refused to think about Annabelle and all the plans he'd had for their future together. She'd turned him down, run off to Paris and would no doubt make a new life for herself there. He consoled himself by remembering how stubborn she could be, how impossibly independent she was at times, and how she was so fiercely focused on her career to the point where she hardly noticed what was going on around her. She could be wilful and wayward and utterly infuriating. But despite all this he missed her, loved her and wished that things had turned out differently.

George stomped back down the stairs. His appalling weakness for Annabelle was something he had to learn to stifle, and in time it would probably be no more than an irritating niggle, but for now he had his afternoon rounds to deal with.

He unlocked the side door to the surgery and was startled to be faced by a small raised fist and a pair of sparkling brown eyes.

'Oh, hello,' she said and laughed. 'I was about to knock. I'm Felicity Jenkins and I realise I don't have an appointment, but I've come about the receptionist job.'

George liked the look of her, for she was pretty, in her mid-twenties, well-spoken and suitably dressed. She seemed very eager and if she could take shorthand and type as well as keep his appointment book in order, then the job was hers. He waited until she'd settled in a chair and began to question her about her previous experience.

He read through the glowing reference from the practice in Surrey, discussed her rate of pay and then smiled. 'Welcome to Morpeth Road surgery, Miss Jenkins. When can you start?'

'Today, if that's all right. I'm bored rigid at home and can't wait to get stuck in.'

George's smile widened as she took off her hat and coat and began to tidy the desk. 'I can see we're going to get along just fine,' he said as he reached for his medical bag. 'I'm off on my rounds now, but I'll be back in good time for evening surgery.'

As he left the house he was still smiling. The efficient and rather attractive Miss Jenkins would be a definite asset to the practice.

The morning of the examination dawned grey and cold and there was a murky drizzle that fogged the horizon. Annabelle had barely slept, and as she prepared for the day, she wondered how she would ever get through it. Aline had discovered a medical book amongst the hundreds that were stacked all over the house, but it was an ancient tome, and probably had no bearing on today's modern medicine.

Aline was up early too, and as Annabelle came into the kitchen, she placed a deep bowl of milky coffee before her. 'I've put in some sugar to give you energy,' she said, 'and there are *pains au chocolat* fresh from the bakery. You cannot possibly face the day on an empty stomach.'

Annabelle tried her best to do justice to the delicious flaky chocolate treat, but she was so nervous she could barely taste it. Sipping the sweet milky coffee only made her feel nauseous, and she gave up on it halfway through. 'Do you have any tea?' she asked a frowning Aline. 'Only it's what I'm used to and—'

'*Ooh là là*, Annabelle, you should have said. Of course I have tea.' She rushed to the cupboard for the tea caddy and placed the kettle on the hob. 'How do you like it? With lemon and sugar, or with milk?'

'With milk, please, and only a tiny bit of sugar.'

The tea was a real boost and Annabelle drank two cups of it, and even managed to finish the pastry. As she left the table and pulled on her coat, Aline pinned a sprig of heather to the lapel. 'It's for luck,' she murmured. 'Now, would you like me to come with you?'

Annabelle shook her head. 'Henri and I walked the route yesterday, so I shouldn't get lost. It's actually quite close to where he lives and has his studio.'

Aline's gaze sharpened momentarily. 'So, you've been to his house?'

'To see his paintings, Aline,' she replied with a nervous smile. 'There's nothing more sinister going on, believe me.'

Aline folded the scarf neatly around Annabelle's neck and then patted her cheek. 'Be careful, my Belle, that boy's in love with you, and I think you also are a little in love with him.' She kissed both her cheeks. 'But today you must concentrate on practical things, not the affairs of the heart. Good luck, my sweet girl.'

Annabelle left the house, her umbrella shielding her from the increasingly heavy drizzle. As she turned the corner into the narrow alleyway she bumped headlong into someone coming the other way. '*Pardon*,' she said as they untangled their umbrellas.

'That's all right,' said Henri cheerfully. 'I wasn't looking where I was going either.'

They laughed and sheltered beneath both umbrellas as they looked into one another's eyes. 'I've come to escort you to your torture chamber,' he joked as he lightly kissed her lips and offered her his arm.

'You really don't have to, but I am glad you're here. I'm so nervous my legs are threatening to give way on me.'

Henri made a show of inspecting her legs. 'And very nice legs they are too,' he teased. 'But if they fail you, I have a sturdy arm to keep you from falling.'

They walked in companionable silence and as they reached the Pont Neuf and began to head for the Left Bank, they felt the knife of the wind and heard the sharp daggers of the sleet rattle against the umbrellas.

'This is as bad as London,' she said with brittle brightness. 'I thought Paris was always supposed to be sunny.'

He chuckled and pressed her hand to his side as she held on to his arm. 'It's always sunny when one is in love,' he teased. 'There, can't you see the sun trying to come through those clouds?'

She giggled as she looked up at the lowering skies and the smog of chimney smoke. 'You have a vivid imagination, Henri.'

'That's why I'm such a good artist.'

They walked on for a few minutes and Henri finally broke the silence. 'I suppose you heard the news that your king abdicated two days ago?' At her doleful expression he smiled. 'A man in love will do crazy things, Annabelle. But not many would give up his crown so easily. She's a strange woman, isn't she? Very chic, but hard – brittle somehow. I wonder if she really did expect to be your queen?'

'I'm sorry, Henri, I can't concentrate on Wallis Simpson and her ambitions right this minute. I've got a nightmare morning ahead of me and it's all I can do to keep my breakfast down.'

'Oh, my darling Belle, how thoughtless of me.' He came to a halt and put his arm round her waist. 'I thought it would ease your worries by talking of such things. But I can see how nervous you are.' He drew her close and rested his chin on the top of her head. 'You'll be absolutely fine, I promise,' he murmured. 'And I'll be waiting for you outside when you're finished.'

'But I don't have any idea of how long I'll be,' she protested. 'And you have a painting to finish. Please don't stand about in the rain waiting for me.'

'There is a small café on a nearby corner. I'll sit in there and wait.'

He smiled and his blue eyes looked into hers with such tenderness that she felt as if her insides were melting. 'Oh, Henri,' she sighed.

He kissed her passionately and then placed her hand back into the crook of his arm so he could keep her close as they approached the hospital.

The main building was set in large grounds off the rue de Sèvres and surrounded by ancient walls. It was a bit of a maze inside those walls, and the buildings, especially the eleventh-century chapel, looked quite forbidding, and Annabelle had to force herself to remain calm.

'You can do this,' he said firmly. 'Now go, and I'll see you here when you're done.'

She shot him a tremulous smile, tilted up her chin and walked determinedly through the gate, past the fountain, and made her way to the School of Medicine, which stood on the far side of the main buildings. Shaking the rain from her umbrella, she walked towards the reception desk.

'I'm Miss Annabelle Blake,' she said to the rather sour-looking woman behind the imposing desk. 'I'm here to take the examination.'

'Go through that door and take the third one on your left. You'll find someone there who will tell you what you have to do.'

Annabelle would have liked to question her further, but her expression didn't encourage it. She went through the double swing doors and found her way to the correct room where she discovered six other girls were already waiting.

'Hello, I'm Annabelle,' she said as she joined the group huddled around a huge iron radiator. 'Are you all here for the test?'

It turned out they were, and as they chatted Annabelle discovered that two were English, one was Spanish, there was a Canadian, a girl from Persia and an Australian. They may have come from all corners of the world, but each of them had a French background of some sort, whether it be a parent or grandparent, or simply time spent living in France.

'Silence, please.'

They turned to look at the woman who had entered the room and it was as if they were all back in the schoolroom again.

'You will take your seats while the papers are handed out,' the woman said as she drew sheaves of papers from her large briefcase and gave them to her colleague, who looked equally fierce. 'The examination will take one hour. There is to be no talking and if for any reason you have to leave the room before the time is up, you will be escorted by my colleague.'

Annabelle sat down on the hard wooden chair and slowly unbuttoned her coat. The papers had been placed face down on the desk, but there seemed to be an awful lot of them and she was beginning to panic. She hated exams at the best of times, and this one was so important she could feel a knot of anxiety tighten in her stomach.

Tucking her beret, scarf and gloves into the pocket of her coat, she hung it over the back of her chair and tried not to show how nervous she was as she waited for the hands on the clock to show the half hour.

'You may now begin,' said the woman into the deathly silence. 'You have one hour precisely.'

Annabelle's hand was trembling as she turned over the pages and swiftly read the first paragraph. The words blurred before her, and she had to take a deep breath to steady herself to take it all in. As she realised it was just a simple story from which she had to answer ten questions, she quickly set to work.

The next two questions were just as easy, but as she turned the page, she realised the questions became more complicated, the French more medically specialised. She took a long time trying to translate it, and only got half a sense of it before she realised she was wasting time. She wrote down what she thought had been asked of her, but it was technical and the phrasing gave no clue as to the meaning of the unfamiliar words that kept leaping out at her.

The anxiety heightened as she turned the next page to discover it was more of the same. This time it was about the use of medical equipment, and what she would use when faced with a series of different injuries. She did her best with that, for a lot of the words were similar in English, so she could make some sort of educated guess at it all.

The last page was a complete stinker, with idioms and modern phrases dotted here and there as she was asked to discuss the dangers of anaesthesia for the asthmatic patient, and to suggest other ways in which such a patient could be operated on.

At the very end of the paper was a long list of instruments that were used in theatre nursing, and although some were easy, there were others that flummoxed her completely.

'Time.'

Annabelle sank back into her chair. She was drained of energy and certain she must have failed. And yet there was still hope that the oral test would count towards the incredibly high pass mark required. She had a nasty feeling she would need all the help she could get, for she hadn't managed to complete every question to her satisfaction.

Following a short break in which they were served coffee and biscuits, each girl was called into a side room. As they all waited and counted the minutes before the next one was called, the tension grew, for none of the girls who'd gone in had come back out again, so there was no way of discovering the sort of things that would be asked.

She had been almost the last to be called into the oral test, and she'd thought she'd done very well, so when she left the building and discovered Henri waiting for her in the sunlight, she felt it was a good omen.

'How did it go?'

'I honestly don't know,' she admitted. 'But I think I did all right. The woman said they'd telephone later this afternoon with the results, so now all I can do is wait.'

'There's time for some lunch and a glass of wine,' said Henri as he firmly steered her into the tiny café he'd been sitting in all morning. 'A bowl of warming vegetable soup sprinkled with cheese and some hot, crusty bread to dip in it is just the thing on this miserable day.'

To her surprise, Annabelle was ravenous. She let him order their lunch and began to relax as the hot soup and gorgeous crusty bread restored her spirits. The red wine was a little rough and sour for her taste, but after living with Aline she was beginning to appreciate wine and had found that she preferred red to white, which she found too acidic.

'Thank you, Henri,' she said fondly as the empty bowls were carried away. 'I didn't realise I was so hungry.'

His smile was warm and affectionate. 'I want to spoil you in the short time we have left together,' he said softly as he tucked one of her curls behind her ear.

The thought that he would be leaving straight after Christmas made her want to weep, but she put on a brave face and smiled back at him. There had been no passionate declarations of love between them, just a tacit agreement that they felt deeply about each other and that if circumstances had been different their feelings might have had a chance to grow and mature into something very special.

'Then I shall let you spoil me,' she said. 'But for now, I must go back home. Aline will want to know how I got on, and I don't want to miss that telephone call.'

'Then I will walk with you. And tonight I will come to Aline's to help you celebrate.' He placed some coins on the table and helped her on with her coat and scarf before fleetingly kissing her lips and escorting her outside.

They walked in silence through the streets where the rain-water shone between the cobbles and gurgled along the deep gutters. When they reached the midway point on the bridge he drew to a halt and pulled her to him. 'I have decided that every time we cross this bridge your toll is a kiss,' he said with a smile.

'It's a toll I'm delighted to pay,' she replied with a lightness she didn't feel, for soon he would be gone and there would be no more kisses. She clung to him and tried to convey the depths of her feelings in her kiss, wondering how something so powerful could be doomed before she'd had the chance to fully understand it.

He walked her back to the rue de l'Arbre and kissed her again. 'I will see you tonight, my sweet Belle.'

She felt warm and loved and happy as she slotted the key in the door and stepped into the hall.

'Annabelle, where have you been?' asked Aline frantically as she came rushing through the beaded curtain. 'The hospital has telephoned and you must ring them back at once.'

She could feel the colour drain from her face and the light meal she'd just eaten began to churn in her stomach. 'What did they say? Why do I have to ring them?'

'I don't know, *ma chère*. They just said they had to speak to you in person.'

'When was this?'

'Ten minutes ago – not long. Quick, quick, before they think you have no interest.'

Annabelle reached for the telephone on the hall wall. The wait for the operator to put her through was agonising, and when the woman's voice came down the line, her mouth was so dry it was difficult to speak. 'This is Annabelle Blake,' she croaked. 'I am returning your call.'

She listened as the woman spoke, and then asked a few questions before thanking her and replacing the receiver.

'Well? Did you pass? Have you got the job?'

Annabelle was fighting back the tears and could barely speak for the lump in her throat. 'I did pass, but only by a half mark,' she finally managed. 'The post has gone to another girl who got a hundred per cent. They say I must wait three months and take the test again before they will consider me for another post.'

'But if you passed, you passed,' stormed Aline. 'How could they do that to you?'

'My technical French wasn't good enough,' she said brokenly as she plumped down onto the stairs. 'And I misinterpreted a couple of things which would have been disastrous if I'd been in theatre.'

'*Ma pauvre petite*,' crooned Aline as she perched beside her and took her in her arms. 'You will pass next time, you'll see.'

The tension of the day and the bitter disappointment were too much. 'I can't wait all that time, Aline,' she sobbed. 'I need to nurse now, and not have the agony of not knowing if I'll pass their next test to their satisfaction or not.'

She finally withdrew from her embrace and pulled herself together. The tears and the outcome of that telephone conversation had focused her mind and suddenly she felt strangely calm and determined. 'As I can't nurse here, then I'll go to Spain with Henri and Etienne,' she said firmly. 'They won't care if I speak the language or have a proper reference, and at least my skills will be appreciated.'

'But you mustn't,' gasped Aline. 'Your mother would never forgive me if I allowed you to do such a thing.' She grabbed Annabelle's shoulders and forced her to look her in the eye. 'I know you're disappointed; that you feel you've failed. But please don't make such a serious decision in the heat of the moment.'

Annabelle kissed her cheek and because she couldn't bear to see Aline so upset, she turned her back and stared at the telephone. 'I'm not taking this decision lightly,' she said. 'It's one that really has been inevitable ever since I was dismissed from St Swithin's.'

'But why? I don't understand.'

'I'd planned to find a job for a while, get my reputation back and a decent reference and then go to Spain to join Caroline. Now it seems to be not just the right option, but the *only* option. I will travel with Henri and Etienne after Christmas, and see if I can discover where Caroline has been posted and join her there.'

'*Mon dieu.* Your mother will kill me,' breathed Aline as she regarded her with wide brown eyes filled with tears.

'I doubt it,' she replied with a gentle smile. 'But I'll write to her and tell her my decision wasn't influenced by you in any way.'

Aline lit a cigarette and regarded her through the smoke. 'I hope this decision hasn't been made because of the way you feel about Henri,' she said. 'If it has, then you really do have to think very seriously about the consequences. You are both young, and I suspect this is the first time you have fallen in love, but—'

'It's nothing like that,' Annabelle interrupted. 'I admit that Henri and my feelings for him do play a minor part in my decision, but he isn't the main reason for my going.'

'Your nursing is very important to you, isn't it?'

'Yes,' she replied simply. 'And as Henri and Etienne are going anyway, it feels as if it's meant to be. It will be safer and easier to travel with them – they speak Spanish fluently and if there are any problems they'll be able to take care of them.'

'Oh, Annabelle,' Aline sighed in defeat. 'I do wish you'd reconsider. I can't bear the thought of you putting your life at risk down there.'

'I'm sorry I've upset you,' she said as she took her hand, 'but I really do have to do this, Aline.'

'So be it,' Aline replied, patting her cheek. 'But you are to write to me as often as you can so that I know you're all right.' She gave Annabelle a soft smile and became suddenly business-like. 'According to your friend Caroline, they are in desperate need of medical supplies, so I will telephone a few people I know who could be persuaded to organise such things. If you are determined to go to Spain, then you must not go empty-handed.'

There were tears of gratitude and relief in Annabelle's eyes, and now that her mind had been made up, she felt strangely at peace for the first time in weeks.

7

Etienne was feeling very pleased with himself as he strode towards Aline's house that evening, for he'd not only spent most of the afternoon tucked up in bed with the delicious and very willing little poppet he'd met the day before, he'd followed this up with a successful meeting with his publisher who'd been full of praise. His book of poetry was selling far better than even he had expected, and with another book about to be released and a generous advance offered for a third, he knew that finally he was making his mark in the literary world.

He was whistling as he opened the front door and his spirits rose even higher as he heard the sounds of celebration coming from Aline's kitchen. Annabelle must have passed her test and been given the nursing post, so she would soon be out of the equation, and he and Henri could get back to the way they'd always been.

His friend had been so occupied with the wretched girl lately that Etienne had hardly seen him – and when he did, she seemed to be the only topic of Henri's conversation. He was heartily sick of hearing how wonderful she was, how lovely her eyes were, how soft her skin . . . And with every lovesick declaration, Etienne grew to resent Annabelle's intrusion into their lives even more.

He checked his appearance in the hall mirror, smoothed back his thick black hair and winked at his handsome reflection. Life was good and it was about to get even better.

'Etienne,' called Aline as he entered the crowded kitchen. 'We thought you'd deserted us! But you've brought wine, so we can forgive you.'

He kissed her cheeks and placed the two bottles on the table with a flourish. 'I've been with my publisher discussing a very generous advance on my next poetry book,' he said rather grandly.

There was a chorus of congratulations as he sat down and tried not to preen. He noted the flushed excitement on the English girl's face, and the possessive pride on Henri's. The musicians, Malachi and Miriam, were sitting close together as they always did; the three bearded young artists were already feeling the effects of too much wine as they sprawled in their chairs; and the writers were stuffing bread, cheese, olives and salami into their mouths as if they hadn't eaten for a week – which they probably hadn't, for in Etienne's opinion neither of them wrote anything worth publishing.

'I take it we're celebrating Annabelle's success in passing her test and getting a nursing post,' he said as he poured a generous slug of wine into a glass. There was a sudden silence and as he noted how they all looked to Annabelle, his previous good spirits began to waver.

'She didn't get the post,' said Henri flatly. 'Her technical French let her down.'

'Oh dear,' he sighed with just the right nuance of regret. 'I am sorry. So what will you do now? Go back to England?'

'She's coming with us to Spain.'

Etienne felt a stab of fury and had to struggle to maintain his smile. 'That's rather a hasty decision,' he said with studied calm. 'Personally, if she was my girl, I would forbid such a thing. A war is no place for women.'

'I don't appreciate you talking as if I'm not here,' said Annabelle rather crossly. 'And it's not up to you or Henri to forbid me to do anything.'

His gaze slid away from her to Henri. 'And how do you feel about that, my friend?'

'I think she's being very brave,' he said stoutly as he took her hand. 'Of course I'm afraid for her safety, but as she's determined to go, then I will support her in any way I can.'

Etienne was furious, but didn't dare let it show. 'That's very noble of you, Henri,' he said smoothly, 'but don't forget that once we arrive in Albacete to join the International Brigade and begin our training, she'll be posted elsewhere and you probably won't see her again until it's all over.'

'I do realise that,' Henri said with a worried frown as he clasped Annabelle's hand more tightly. 'But Belle knows what she's letting herself in for – probably more than we do – and nurses are desperately needed down there.'

Etienne could see the set look on both their faces and knew he had to tread carefully if he wasn't going to show how infuriated he was by this change of plan. 'I admire your bravery, Annabelle,' he said silkily. 'Not many women would risk their lives in such a way. But are you sure you're doing this for the right reasons? After all, you have never shown much interest in the cause before now.'

'I'm not changing my mind, Etienne,' she said firmly. 'I know it's dangerous and the conditions I'll be working under will be fraught with difficulty, but as a nurse, I must go where I'm needed the most.'

'But forgive me, my dear, you don't speak Spanish,' he said with all the kindness he could muster. 'And if your French wasn't considered good enough for the post at the hospital here, how on earth do you think you'll cope with Spanish?'

He saw the doubt flicker briefly in her eyes and pressed his point. 'There won't be time to translate everything in the heat of the moment, and surely it's vital you fully understand what is needed of you?'

The doubt was dismissed as quickly as it had come and she met his gaze squarely. 'There are other English nurses out there,' she retorted, 'and several hundred American ones. If they can manage, then so can I.'

Etienne could see he was getting nowhere, so he looked to Henri. 'Have you explained how we're planning to get to Albacete?'

'I only arrived a short while ago and haven't really had much time to explain anything,' he replied fretfully.

'Then don't you think you should? After all, crossing the Pyrenees at night to avoid enemy forces is not for the faint-hearted.'

Annabelle was clearly shocked by this – just as he'd intended. 'But I thought we would catch a train straight to Madrid,' she breathed.

'Madrid is a battleground and too far north for us,' said Etienne. 'We're going by train to Perpignon, and will cross over the mountains into Spain. There will be transport from Figueres to the Brigade training centre at Albacete.' He saw her blanch and knew he'd shaken her confidence.

'There are boats leaving for Spain every few days,' said Henri. 'Perhaps we should consider taking one instead of what we'd planned. It would be safer for Annabelle, and—'

'Our tickets have already been paid for and the onward transport arranged,' interrupted Etienne, furious that things were already being changed because of the damned girl. He took a sip of wine to calm himself. 'I think the wisest thing would be for Annabelle to stay here and wait for the next hospital ship,' he said in a reasonable tone. 'She'll have the company of other medics and by the time she's sent to her posting, she'll have made friends and feel more settled.'

Annabelle was about to speak when Aline interrupted. 'I think that's a very good idea, Etienne,' she said. 'The journey will be dangerous enough without Belle having to risk crossing mountains in the middle of the night. I'll telephone the authorities tomorrow and find out when the next hospital ship will be leaving.'

Etienne smiled his most charming smile and happily sipped his wine. With Annabelle on a boat, he and Henri would be unhampered by her presence and could fulfil their carefully made plans.

As the conversations went on around him he savoured the thought of the two of them returning to old haunts, of climbing the steep and rugged mountainside as they had as boys, and drinking from the icy cold waters when they camped. It would be like the good days of their youth, and by the time they'd reached the training camp, Henri would have forgotten all about the silly girl and come to his senses.

It seemed the argument had been settled and the conversation turned to other topics as they drank wine and ate the delicious cheese and bread. Annabelle sat close to Henri all evening, exchanging private smiles and unspoken feelings as they held hands and tried not to think about their imminent parting.

As the evening progressed, Annabelle silently acknowledged that she'd been shocked by Etienne's talk of crossing mountains, and could only pray that Aline would be able to get her onto a ship instead. It would mean not being able to travel with Henri, which she'd been looking forward to, but it certainly would be easier.

Aline's series of telephone calls the next morning had come to nothing. There wasn't another hospital ship leaving for Spain until February, and as she wasn't prepared to wait that long, Annabelle took matters into her own hands.

Yet, having contacted the local communist organisation which arranged for medics to travel to Spain, she discovered that there would be no more special trains going into Madrid because of the fierce fighting there, but if she could make her own way to the hospital at Tarragona, she would be welcomed with open arms.

It seemed the only option she had now was to travel to Perpignon with Henri and Etienne, and although the idea of going across the Pyrenees still filled her with dread, she was determined to get to that hospital where at last she would be allowed to use her skills. Having discussed it with Henri, she spent the last of her mother's money on the train ticket.

Christmas was spent eating and drinking in Aline's cosy kitchen, but the knowledge that Annabelle would soon be leaving with the others for a war zone meant there was a solemn air hanging over the festivities.

Two weeks later, as the sun began to rise above the smoking chimneys and frosty rooftops of Paris on her last morning, she threw open the shutters and leant out to take in the view. She would miss this lovely city and the routine of her day which had become so familiar, but this was the beginning of the next chapter of her life and she was eager to embark upon it.

She turned from the window and eyed the rucksack Aline had unearthed from her accumulated clutter. It was now tightly packed with thick socks and a sweater, warm trousers and shirts, and even a pair of sturdy boots which they'd found in the market. The clothes had belonged to Aline's late husband, and although she'd been tearful about giving them away, she was determined Annabelle should have them. Everything had been taken in to fit her by Miriam, who had proved to be handy with a sewing machine, and stout new laces had been purchased for the boots.

In a side pocket of the rucksack she'd tucked her passport and the identity papers Aline had managed to get through a friend at the Bureau des Etrangers, and alongside a box of precious syringes was nestled another of morphine and a Spanish dictionary – Etienne's jibe about her language skills had hit home and she'd been studying the little dictionary ever since. At the bottom of the rucksack were her nursing dresses, buckle and badge, copies of her certificates, and the letters from home.

Camille had been horrified to learn of her plans at first, but Philippa had managed to talk her round and her last letter had included five crisp green-and-white pound notes which she'd taken to the bank to exchange for francs. Philippa's letter was full of her fundraising to send a fleet of ambulances and more medical supplies, which would have to be sent from France as England had placed an embargo on any supplies going to Spain for the duration of the war. Aline, bless her, had leapt at the chance to do something and had tirelessly trawled her network of influential friends to put the funds to good use and get the arrangements for a convoy in place. It would probably leave in March, and carry both nursing staff and much-needed medical supplies.

Annabelle washed and dressed quickly in her warm woollen skirt, cotton blouse and sweater, and then packed her hairbrush and washbag. She had left most of her things behind for Aline to look after, for if she was to carry this rucksack over a mountain range, then it would necessarily have to be as light as possible.

The house was quiet at this early hour, for the farewell party had gone on until well after midnight, and Annabelle had insisted they didn't make it harder for her by coming down to say yet more tearful goodbyes. She slowly went down the stairs, taking in the bright colours and the lovely paintings on the wall for the last time. Leaving the rucksack in the hall, she was greeted by a sullen Napoleon.

'Mind the cat,' he yelled as she placed his seed into his bowl.

'You mind the cat, you old grouch,' she murmured fondly as she dared to stroke his feathers.

His beak darted down and missed her finger by a hair's breadth. 'Pretty boy, pretty boy. Arrgh!'

'He's got no manners,' said Aline from the kitchen. 'Put the cover back on and come and have your breakfast.'

Aline was resplendent in a silk dressing gown of scarlet and gold which should have clashed horribly with her halo of russet hair, but somehow didn't. 'You're looking remarkably lively considering you've had hardly any sleep,' said Annabelle as she gave her a hug.

'And so are you,' she replied warmly. 'Now, sit down. You have half an hour before you have to leave, and we must make the most of it.' She poured coffee and hot milk into a china bowl and pushed it towards her. 'I haven't had time to fetch fresh bread, but I've warmed yesterday's and the croissants are still edible.' She placed a string bag on the table. 'There is bread, cheese, sausage and wine in there and a flask of tea.' Her smile was wan. 'I know how you like your tea.'

Annabelle was touched by her thoughtfulness, and after thanking her profusely, she petted the cats who were winding sinuously round her legs, then sat down to drink the sweet, milky coffee and eat the *pain au chocolat*. Mignonette jumped onto her lap and curled into a purring ball, and Annabelle stroked her soft fur. She would miss Aline and the cats and this lovely kitchen – the love and happiness that she'd found here – and the thought of leaving it all behind made her quite emotional.

'Are you having second thoughts?' Aline reached across the table for her hand. 'If so, it's not too late, Annabelle.'

She blinked back her tears and shook her head. 'It's far too late for second thoughts,' she replied, 'and actually, I'm very much looking forward to it. Just think, Aline, this will be the experience of a lifetime, and what tales I'll have to tell my children and grandchildren after this.'

'I think you're crazy,' Aline muttered. Then she shrugged. 'But you're still very young and I'm too old and set in my ways to be having adventures. Just be careful, Annabelle. I'd hate anything to happen to you.'

'I'm going to miss you, Aline,' she sighed. 'You've been so kind, done so much, and I want you to know how very grateful I am.'

'I've loved having you here, Annabelle, and from now on you must think of it as your home.' She shot her a tear-bright smile and then busied herself lighting a cigarette. 'There is something I wish to say to you before you leave,' she began hesitantly.

'You're looking very serious, Aline. Please don't worry about me. I'll be fine, really I will. And with Henri and Etienne with me—'

'It's Etienne I wish to speak to you about,' Aline interrupted. At Annabelle's frown, she shifted on the chair as if uncomfortable with what she had to say. 'Darling, you must be careful not to make an enemy of Etienne. He is very jealous of your closeness to Henri.'

Annabelle blinked in astonishment. 'What's made you think that?'

'I have an artist's eye and I notice things others miss. He might seem affable and fun, but I sense his resentment of you coming between him and Henri.'

She waved away Annabelle's protest with a flick of her fingers. 'It is important that you understand how long they have been friends, and how tight the bond is between them. In the past they have shared many things and the blood of the Basque people runs hot, deep and swift. Women have come and gone in their lives, and until now, it has been a game – another one of their little adventures that is not taken seriously. But it's clear that Henri loves you as much as you love him, and it is driving a wedge between them.'

'I didn't realise,' Annabelle murmured. 'But surely, if Etienne is truly Henri's friend, he should accept that this would happen sometime.'

'Etienne thinks only of himself,' Aline said almost dismissively. 'He is vain and self-seeking, and brave only when he has someone to show off to. He and Henri are like two sides of a coin – they balance each other out – and in his mind there is no room for someone else.'

'But that's terrible,' Annabelle breathed. 'I wish you hadn't said anything, Aline. Now I shall be always on edge.'

'Oh, my dear, he'll do you no harm, believe me. But he will try and come between you, I can promise you that. Just be aware, that's all I'm saying.'

Annabelle was about to reply when they heard the chime of the mantel clock. 'I must go,' she said suddenly all in a dither. She pushed back from the table and dumped Mignonette from her lap as she reached to embrace Aline.

'Thank you, Aline,' she breathed into the fragrant mop of red hair. 'Thank you for everything and I promise to heed what you've said and write as often as I can.' She held her for a long moment, breathing in the scent of gardenias, hoping its memory would linger with her long after she'd left this loving sanctuary. And then she picked up the string bag, went into the hall, pulled on her coat, hat and scarf and hoisted up the rucksack.

Blinking back her tears, she opened the front door and stepped outside into the bitter cold of early morning. Turning on the step, she embraced Aline again. 'I'll be back before you know it,' she said hoarsely. 'I love you, Aline. I love you very much.'

Then, before she made a complete fool of herself by bursting into tears, she hooked the rucksack over one shoulder and ran down the steps. Her shoes tapped on the cobbles of rue de l'Arbre for the last time, and as she reached the sharp bend that would take her to the main street, she couldn't resist one last look back.

Aline was still standing in the doorway, her hair blowing in the chill wind, the red-and-gold silk fluttering round her ankles as she wrapped an arm about her waist and blew her a kiss. And then she was gone, the front door closed behind her, the windows reflecting only the early sunshine.

*

'We must hurry,' urged Henri as they crossed the bridge. 'It's bitterly cold and I don't want Annabelle hanging about waiting for us.'

Etienne hitched the straps of his rucksack to a more comfortable position and lengthened his stride. He'd decided he could afford to be pleasant to Annabelle and to ignore Henri's almost constant concern over her. After all, he'd reasoned, they would go their separate ways once they reached Tarragona, and there was little profit in alienating his friend by being boorish.

'There she is,' breathed Henri. 'Doesn't she look wonderful?' He didn't wait for a reply and rushed ahead to sweep her into his arms for a long, passionate kiss.

Etienne affected a smile as he strode towards them, and had to admit reluctantly that Annabelle did indeed look very lovely this morning. Her eyes were shining and there was a glow in her face that brought colour to her cheeks. It was probably because she was overexcited and cold, he thought sourly, but it certainly enhanced her extraordinary eyes.

'Good morning,' he said cheerfully as he kissed the air by her rosy cheeks. 'Are you all ready, Annabelle?'

'As ready as I'll ever be,' she said breathlessly as she struggled to get the straps of her rucksack over her shoulders.

Etienne moved swiftly before Henri had the chance. 'Here, let me help with that.' He could feel the tension in her as he adjusted the straps and set the rucksack squarely so the weight was distributed evenly. 'There we are.'

'Thank you,' she replied. 'That feels much more comfortable.'

He smiled down at her, his eyes twinkling. 'It's my pleasure,

Belle,' he said softly. 'We are about to make a long journey, and it's important to me and to Henri that you are not in any discomfort.' He tested the straps again. 'It's not too heavy?'

'It's fine, really.'

Etienne was about to turn away when she placed her hand on his arm. 'I realise I'm being a nuisance by travelling with you and messing up your plans,' she said quickly. 'But I'll do my best not to hold you up in any way.'

He looked into her beautiful eyes and felt suddenly quite drawn to her. 'My dear girl,' he said gruffly, 'the thought never occurred to me.' He gathered his wits, aware that she was regarding him with some amusement. 'We're both delighted to have your charming company on what will probably prove to be a long and very tedious journey. Now, come along, we must get to the Metro.'

Annabelle wondered if perhaps Aline's lively imagination had played her false, for Etienne was being charming and helpful, and as they travelled the two stops on the underground to the Gare de Lyon there was a heady sense of camaraderie between the three of them.

As they came up the steps into the enormous station, they were bombarded with the noise of steam trains, echoing announcements and the ever-present babble of the commuters who were pouring through the barriers and scurrying for their city offices.

Annabelle held tightly to Henri's hand as they searched for the correct platform and wound their way through the melée.

Her heart began to beat a little faster as her ticket was inspected, and she gripped Henri's arm as they walked down the long platform to find their carriage.

Etienne helped her up the very high step while Henri took charge of her rucksack, and before long they were comfortably ensconced in their seats, their bags in the racks above their heads. Annabelle's pulse was racing now, the excitement for the journey far outweighing the fear of what might lie ahead.

The last passengers settled down and the slam of the doors was like a volley of echoing rifle shots before the guard blew his whistle. Annabelle sat on the edge of her seat as the rolling cloud of steam and smoke obliterated her view from the window and the great iron wheels began to turn. The future was a blank page yet to be written upon, but this was her first step on an adventure which she knew would remain with her for the rest of her life.

8

Spain

The journey would have been interminable had it not been for the magnificent scenery and the camaraderie amongst the passengers. Unlike travellers in England, they talked to one another as bottles of wine were opened at lunchtime and shared along with baguettes filled with cheese and ham, and tasty little pastries and bonbons. Following this makeshift meal people settled down to read, sleep, chat or play cards and Annabelle was content just to sit and dreamily look out of the window at the passing scenery.

Etienne sat opposite with a notebook on his knee, fully concentrating on a poem he was trying to write, while Henri sat beside her and sketched him on a pad. The train chugged its way busily along the tracks, stopping at tiny villages and little towns as well as the large, sprawling cities of Orléans and Limoges. Eventually the excitement of the day got the better of her and she leant back into her seat and drifted off to sleep.

She was woken by the sound of singing and discovered that her head had been resting on Henri's shoulder; that they had now been travelling for almost ten hours and it was close to nightfall. Blinking away the drowsiness, she sat up and drank the refreshing tea from Aline's flask and listened to the lusty English voices belting out a song from the next carriage.

'We're coming to sunny Spain, to make the people smile again,
And drive the fascist bastards from the hill and from the plain.
Oh, the ri, oh, the ri, oh, the rio, rio, rio, ha, ha, ha.'

This last line was roared with great enthusiasm and accompanied by the clapping of hands and the stamping of feet. Annabelle grinned. 'It sounds as if they're having fun. Are they volunteers, do you think?'

Henri nodded, but he wasn't smiling. 'Stupid idiots,' he muttered. 'If they go on like that, they'll be arrested the minute they try and leave the train.'

'But why? I thought the Spanish people wanted us to help them fight?'

'Keep your voice down,' hissed Etienne. 'You never know who might be listening, and there are fascist spies everywhere.'

'They do want our help,' murmured Henri, 'but we'll be leaving the train where the fascists are already taking over the towns and villages. They'll be looking for people just like that, so their enthusiasm will soon get them into dire trouble.'

Annabelle hadn't realised the fascists had broken through into France. 'What if we get stopped?' she asked fretfully.

He hurried to assure her. 'Etienne and I have a story prepared,' he said quietly, 'and as long as you hide that British passport and use only your French identity papers, no one will suspect you.'

'So, what's this story you've prepared?'

Henri's gaze slid away from her as colour rushed into his face. 'We're returning home to attend an important family celebration, and you have been invited along as my fiancée.'

She looked at him askance and then giggled. 'You're jumping the gun a bit, aren't you, Henri?'

His cheeks were still rather pink as he reached for her hand. 'It's the only thing Etienne and I could think of should you get stopped. As long as you remember you're a French woman, and stick to the story, it should be fine.'

He rummaged about in his pocket. 'But just in case, I thought you should wear this.' He opened his hand and revealed a small silver ring embedded with a single garnet. 'I know it's cheap and that this isn't the time or place to propose, but would you wear it for me until we can do things properly?'

Annabelle's heart swelled as he placed the small ring on her engagement finger. 'Oh, Henri, I'll treasure it always,' she sighed before she kissed him. 'But I won't hold you to your promise when this is all over. You might feel differently about me by then.'

His expression was very solemn as he looked deeply into her eyes. 'Never in a million years will I stop loving you, my beautiful Belle. You're in my heart until it beats its last.'

Etienne gave a snort of derision. 'For goodness' sake, you two, will you stop all this silly talk and concentrate. We'll be arriving soon, and we need to make sure we don't get off the train anywhere near that rowdy lot. If the guards think we're a part of their group, we'll be stopped and searched for certain.'

'They could actually make an excellent shield,' said Annabelle quietly. 'If we wait for them to go through the barrier first, the guards will be so occupied they probably won't even notice us.'

'That's a good idea,' Etienne replied with some surprise. 'And may I suggest you take off that hat and tie a scarf around your head instead? It will help you to blend in better with the other women.'

'If we're going over the mountains tonight, I need to change my clothes,' she murmured, aware that others could be listening to their conversation.

'We'll find somewhere between Perpignon and the lower slopes,' he muttered.

Annabelle had a sudden thought and turned to Henri. 'Would they really search us if we were stopped? Only I've got syringes and morphine in my bag.'

'Are they well hidden?'

'Not really,' she admitted. 'They're in a side pocket of my rucksack.'

Etienne leapt to his feet and pulled down her bag. Rummaging about, he found the small boxes and the tin and regarded them thoughtfully. 'If they stop you, they'll definitely search your bag, but I doubt they'll search you too thoroughly. You'd better hide them under your clothes.'

Annabelle nodded, took the boxes and tin and hurried into the vile-smelling lavatory that rocked and swayed alarmingly as the train juddered over the tracks. The tin fitted snugly between her breasts, held there by her brassiere and flannelette vest, but the boxes of morphine phials were too big. She stood in an agony of frustration as she tried to think how best to hide them – and then had a brainwave. She slipped one into each of her stocking tops, pushing them down so they were well tethered. It felt odd having them there, and she'd have to remember not to cross her legs when she sat down.

She returned to her seat and smiled. 'Mission accomplished.' Pulling out the silk square she'd worn at her neck, she tied it over her hair and knotted it under her chin. 'There we are, all ready for inspection.' She sat back, was about to cross her legs when she remembered the precious cargo in her stockings and crossed her ankles instead.

'Exactly where have you hidden everything, Belle?' asked Henri with a glint of naughtiness in his dark blue eyes.

'Never you mind,' she giggled.

Minutes later the train pulled to a slow halt with a long exhalation of steam and smoke. As this was the end of the line everyone stood and gathered their things together. The singing, Annabelle noted, had lost none of its vigour, and as she stepped down from the train she saw the group of young Englishmen perform a ragged march towards the barrier where there were armed soldiers as well as the usual railway guards.

Henri and Etienne saw them too, and with a silent glance of agreement, the three of them weaved carefully through the other passengers so they were a little nearer, but far enough away not to be taken as part of their group.

Annabelle's heart was racing as they slowly approached the barrier. The soldiers had stopped the Englishmen, and the singing had petered out. Their papers were closely examined with aching slowness, and then they were taken aside to be thoroughly searched and questioned. The scowling guard waved everyone else through impatiently and didn't even notice when Annabelle, Etienne and Henri slipped by and hurried through the large concourse, past great stacks of sandbags guarded by yet more soldiers, and out into the street.

Annabelle found she'd been holding her breath, and she let it out with a sigh of relief. That was too close for comfort. Yet this was only the beginning of her journey into Spain. How much worse would it get? And would her nerves stand it?

As she walked nervously between Henri and Etienne she imagined they were being watched from every street corner and window, but then decided she was being paranoid and began to take in her new surroundings. Her first impression of Perpignon was of its shabbiness, and that it seemed dwarfed by the backdrop of the towering, snow-covered peaks of the Pyrenees that lay in deep shadow against the rapidly darkening sky. They looked terrifying, and the thought that soon she would be trekking through them dried her mouth and made her heart beat that bit faster.

'They aren't as frightening as they appear,' said Henri, as he took her hand. 'We know a way through that won't involve scaling the higher peaks.'

She nodded and adjusted the rucksack over her shoulders as a way of hiding the doubts that were flooding through her. She could only pray she possessed the mental and physical stamina to climb such a fearsome-looking mountain, and that she didn't let either of the men down or hold them up.

'We'll go to a café we know at the other end of the old town, and wait until it's truly dark before we start the climb,' murmured Etienne as they walked down the main street and entered a labyrinth of twisting, narrow lanes.

Annabelle wasn't the least bit hungry, and the thought of food made her stomach knot. Yet, as they went further and further into the maze of tiny cobbled streets, she became fascinated by her surroundings. The houses were ancient and in varying states of disrepair, but many had been painted a soft peach, yellow or green and the twisted branches of brightly coloured bougainvillea gave the downtrodden area a sense of quiet, almost exotic beauty. There were still remnants of the invading Moors in the murals and mosaics, and in the towers and domes of the mosque that stood next to a crumbling church. She could smell the tang of the sea, although it was several miles to the south, and the scent of pine trees which mingled with that of coffee and spices.

As the three of them walked through the narrow streets of the old part of Perpignon, Annabelle saw Arabs in white flowing robes and dark-skinned men wearing army uniform. The language they spoke was utterly foreign to her and she looked to Henri for an explanation.

'France and Spain have strong ties with Algeria and Morocco,' he said, 'and if we're to beat the fascists, we must use our foreign troops. The Moors, of course, have been here for many years, and the language they speak is a mixture of French and Spanish, with a smattering of Catalan and even Basque.' He smiled at her. 'They're an ambitious people who do a very good trade in beaten copper, tooled leather, spices and silks; but they are also fierce fighters and good to have on one's side.'

They looked rather frightening to Annabelle, and she stayed close to Henri as they headed even further into the dark mass of the old quarter.

'Here we are,' said Etienne as they came to a stall that had been set up in one of the narrow alleyways. A few rusting tables and chairs had been placed beneath an awning, and a brazier was tended by a dark-skinned man who grinned at them, showing rotten teeth capped with gold. Despite her misgivings, Annabelle's mouth watered at the delicious smells coming from the roasting meat and vegetables on skewers, and the great pot of rice scented with spices and yellow with saffron.

Henri and Etienne greeted the man warmly as if they were old friends, and then, disconcertingly, disappeared with him behind the sacking sheet that shielded the interior of this makeshift café.

Annabelle shifted uneasily on the chair, aware that she'd become the focus of attention from the men who passed by and were regarding her with dark, curious, almost insolent eyes. She was about to go and find Henri when he and Etienne suddenly appeared from behind the sacking. They were both carrying rifles, and pistols were tucked into the waistbands of their trousers.

'There's no need to look so startled,' drawled Etienne as he sat down. 'We have to be armed and ready for any ambush, and Ali can always be relied upon to have decent weapons.'

Annabelle felt the blood drain from her face. 'Ambush?' she breathed.

'It's unlikely,' said Henri quickly. 'But it would be foolish in the extreme to go into the mountains unarmed.' He placed the two rifles on the ground and pulled his jacket over the pistol before taking her hand. 'Please don't fret, Belle. They are for your protection.'

Annabelle realised he was talking sense, but she still felt uneasy at the thought that they might be ambushed up in those terrifying mountains. 'I know you must think me very foolish,' she murmured, 'but I've never seen a gun before.'

'You'll get used to it,' said Etienne, as Ali placed bowls of food on the table. 'This is a war, Belle, and you'll witness far more frightening things than a couple of rifles.'

Annabelle knew then that she couldn't afford to be terrified of her own shadow. She had to pull herself together, accept where she was and what she was heading into and get on with it. She breathed in the delicious aroma of scented rice and roasted meat Ali brought to the table along with a battered teapot, a bowl of sugar lumps and three tiny glasses. Even the tea smelt fragrant as he poured the pale gold liquid into the glasses.

Henri and Etienne placed a sugar lump between their teeth and slurped the tea through it as Ali nodded with approval and showed his gold teeth in a beaming smile.

'It's the way to drink tea here,' said Henri apologetically as he noted the surprised look on her face. 'The tea is jasmine-scented and if you put the sugar in the glass, it will destroy its purity.'

He grinned. 'Well, that's what the Arabs say, but too much sugar rots the teeth, as you can see by our friend's example.'

Annabelle decided she would drink the tea without sugar, and in fact found it very refreshing. Without further hesitation, she tucked in to the delicious meal. The meat was tender, the peppers and onions charred just right to release their full flavour, and the rice was fluffy and rich with butter. She finished her meal, drank some more tea and with a sigh of pleasure, rested back in her chair. 'That was wonderful,' she murmured.

'It will have to last you until tomorrow,' said Henri as he scraped the last of the rice from his bowl. 'So if you want anything more, you'd better have it now.'

Annabelle shook her head and smiled. If she ate another morsel, she wouldn't be able to walk, let alone climb a mountain.

The two men lit cigarettes and took their time finishing the tea. The night was velvet soft, perfumed with exotic scents. Lanterns had been lit, and lights shone from behind shutters and in open doorways. The alleyways were quieter now, with only a few scavenging dogs and cats slinking in and out of the deep shadows as they hunted for scraps.

'It's time,' murmured Henri. He paid the bill and spoke to Ali, then hoisted his rucksack over his shoulders before helping Annabelle with hers. 'We'll get out of the old town and find you somewhere to change your clothes in the foothills.'

Etienne said his own goodbyes to the Arab man, and they hurried through the streets until they came to the western edge of the town. The plain stretched before them until it reached the foothills of the towering mountain range where the snow-dusted peaks glimmered in the pale moonlight.

Annabelle's pulse was racing as she followed Henri's instructions and went behind a jumble of boulders to get changed. The grass was tough, and there were prickly shrubs which could have hidden all manner of creeping, biting, stinging things, but she gritted her teeth, refused to panic and got on with it.

She carefully removed the phials and the tin box, and then pulled on the heavy trousers, thick shirt, socks and jumper. With the boxes and tin now in the pockets of her rucksack, she tied the laces on her boots, drew the knitted skiing hat over her ears, and reached for her coat. It wouldn't fasten over the bulk of her shirt and sweater, but it was another layer against the cold, so she grabbed the rucksack and emerged from behind the boulders.

Henri helped her with the rucksack and gave her a kiss. 'We must walk fast across the plain and get amongst the shadows of the mountain while the moon is still low,' he murmured as he slung the straps of his rifle across his shoulder. 'Are you ready?'

At her nod, he adjusted his own rucksack, glanced across at Etienne and strode out.

It was rough underfoot, with scattered boulders, winding streams and clumps of thorny bushes hampering her progress, but Annabelle was determined not to lag behind, and after a while her eyes adjusted to the gloom and she got into a rhythm that kept her between the two men. The boots proved to be comfortable as well as sturdy, and by the time they reached the deep black shadows at the foot of the mountain, she was hardly out of breath.

'We'll go this way,' said Henri. 'The path will lead us through the lowest pass, which will be much easier for Annabelle.'

'If we go that way, we'll be asking for trouble,' hissed Etienne. 'It's the easiest path used by the volunteers who come this way, and the one the fascists will be guarding. We should go that way.'

'She'll never be able to negotiate that. It's a tough climb and will take too long.'

Annabelle looked from one to the other and came to a decision. 'We'll go Etienne's way,' she said firmly. 'Better a tough climb than to be caught in a fascist trap.' She didn't wait for the arguments to break out again, but began to walk up the steep, winding slope where a narrow trail led deep into the mountains.

The trail had once been the route for the traders with their laden horses and mules, and it crawled and twisted through the dark, jagged rocks, falling away here and there to a precipitous drop.

Annabelle slowed to let Etienne lead the way and Henri was behind her as they negotiated the track in silence. She could feel her calf and thigh muscles begin to tighten as her lungs ached and her heart pounded with the effort, but she was damned if she was going to falter or panic.

They had been climbing for some time and were now high up, the trail crumbling beneath their boots as they edged along the precariously narrow ledge that was the only remnant of the original trail.

Annabelle's rucksack bumped against the unyielding wall of the mountainside, making each step a battle to keep her balance. She didn't dare look down at the endless drop beneath her, or break her concentration, for there was no rope binding them together and one false move, one moment of inattention could bring tragedy.

She gritted her teeth and blinked away the sweat that stung her eyes as she shuffled inch by inch towards what she hoped would be firmer footing. She could no longer see Etienne, for he'd rounded the smooth curve of rock she now had to negotiate.

'Turn and face the rock, it's the only way,' said Henri softly. 'You can do it, Belle.'

She slowly faced the rock, sliding her hand over the smooth surface in search of something to grip. She dug the tips of her fingers into a narrow cleft and slowly edged round the bulge of rock, feeling the weight of her rucksack threatening to pull her backwards. Her breath was a sob and her leg muscles burnt as she shuffled tentatively along, the scrape of her boots sending stones and clumps of dried mud clattering into the void beneath her.

And then she was on the other side. She closed her eyes and clung to the black rock of the mountain as she tried to steady her breathing and quell the terrible, debilitating panic that threatened to overwhelm her. She was trembling so badly, she doubted she'd ever move again, and it was only Etienne's harsh voice that drew her out of her frozen stupor.

'You can't stay there. I can hear enemy planes. Come on, Belle. Don't fail us now.'

She opened her eyes, saw the gap in the trail between them and the abyss of darkness below her. 'I can't,' she stammered. 'Really, I can't.'

'If you don't, you'll die,' he said fiercely. He leant towards her and held out his hand. 'It's one step, Belle. Take my hand and trust me.'

She looked away from the endless darkness beneath her and back to Henri, who was just emerging from the other side of the rock. She could hear the distant drone of many planes now and knew she had no choice but to do as Etienne said.

She wet her lips, let go of the rock and tentatively reached for his hand. She felt his firm, strong clasp and before she could have second thoughts, stepped over the chasm and into his arms.

He held her close until she'd stopped trembling and was steadier on her feet. 'Well done,' he murmured. 'The way is a little easier now, and soon you'll be able to rest.'

Annabelle watched as Henri reached for Etienne's hand and almost casually stepped across the gap. It seemed he didn't share her fear of falling from great heights.

'Well done, Belle,' he said softly. 'Now we must hurry if we're to avoid being seen by the planes.'

They set off again, walking in single file along the broader, much trampled trail. It was still steep and unforgiving, and Annabelle's calf muscles were tight and painful as the air became thinner and she had to fight for breath. She could see the snow-capped peaks much more clearly now, and feel the bite of the wind on her face as the sweat grew cold and clammy beneath the layers of clothing.

Etienne came to a sudden halt, his head cocked. 'They're coming this way. Quick, quick, we mustn't get caught out here in the open.'

'Hurry, hurry,' hissed Henri. 'We're too exposed here.' He grabbed Annabelle's hand and roughly pulled her along the path until they reached the mouth of a cave.

She stumbled inside, gasping for breath, her skin crawling with dread. She could hear rustling and squeaks coming from the depths of the cave, and the raw smell of wild animal stung her nose and made her eyes water. Whatever was living in here was lurking in the inky darkness behind her.

'It's just bats,' said Henri not unkindly. 'They won't hurt you.'

Annabelle cowered against the rocky wall of the entrance, the fear of the creatures behind her at war with her fear of the advancing enemy planes. She looked out to the sky as the menacing roar grew louder, and then she saw them: twelve small, bright planes glinting in the moonlight as they roared in formation high above the mountain peaks and headed north. 'What are they?'

'Italian Fiat Fighters,' muttered Henri, 'and they won't be alone.'

Annabelle heard the deeper bass of much heavier planes and realised that the Fiats must be escorting bombers. She hunkered down deeper into the shadow of the cave, fear crawling across her skin as the bats left their roosts and swarmed out into the night sky.

'Heinkel one-elevens,' shouted Henri as he crouched beside her and put his arm round her waist. 'Don't worry, Belle. They won't be able to see us in here.'

Annabelle shivered as an even deeper, more menacing roar approached and filled the very air with a pounding, ear-shattering noise until the cave rang with it and the ground vibrated beneath her feet. The dozen Heinkels came in tight formation, flying so low their wings seemed to skim the mountain peaks, and as their deafening roar reached an unbearable crescendo, Annabelle covered her ears and closed her eyes.

The silence they left behind was no less deafening, and she could hear it ringing in her head for many minutes as they huddled at the mouth of the cave and watched the skies. More bombers came from the west, to be followed by the higher-pitched whine and rattle of at least fifteen Fiats, which flew in a tightly formed V as if emulating the flight of wild geese.

They waited and watched in the numbing silence, and when it was judged to be safe, they crept out of the cave and continued their journey along the narrow shelf of the ancient trail.

Annabelle was still trying to come to terms with her first enemy encounter, and despite the fact the noise of the bombers and fighter planes had been all-consuming, the sight of such power and aggression had somehow imbued her with a quiet courage and a profound sense that they had to be defeated at all costs. She might only play a very small part in the fight for democracy, but she knew without doubt that she was doing the right thing.

The trail petered out for a while and they had to climb and scramble through the jagged rocks where scree slipped from beneath their boots and fell with an echoing clatter into the void far beneath them. And then, close to one in the morning, they turned a torturous bend in the path and saw the glitter of the sea beneath the moon and the distant beam from a lighthouse.

'That's the beacon on the cliffs at Cap de Creus,' said Henri. 'Welcome to Spain, Annabelle.'

She eased the weight of her rucksack as she flexed her shoulders and tried to ignore the deep ache in her back and neck, and the burn of overstretched muscles in her legs. The plain before them looked much like the one they'd left behind in Perpignon, but in the moonlight she could see the many coves and long stretches of sand that ran along the coastline, and in the distance that looked like the huddled outline of islands.

'Those are the Balearic Islands,' explained Etienne. 'All this area was once the kingdom of the King of Mallorca.' He looked at Annabelle and smiled. 'I know you must be tired, but we'll rest when we get down there.'

'But I thought you said we would be met?'

'And we will, but not until next nightfall. Don't worry, Annabelle, there are plenty of nice dry caves to sleep in, and Henri and I will make sure they don't have any other inhabitants lurking about inside.'

Annabelle said nothing as they began the steep descent to the valley. She was almost numb with exhaustion, moving like a mechanical toy, never breaking the rhythm and always with her gaze set on the next obstacle. Yet despite this, she doubted very much if she'd sleep in a cave where unknown terrors might be lurking amidst the reek of guano.

They reached the final shelf of mountain above the plain just as the sky was beginning to turn pearly grey and pink on the horizon. It was just after four, which meant they'd taken over twelve hours to traverse the Pyrenees; but the knowledge that she'd achieved such a feat gave Annabelle an enormous thrill, and despite her almost debilitating weariness, she scrambled over the rocks with vigour.

Her enthusiasm waned as she saw the cave, and even though the early sun showed it to be quite shallow, she was loath to enter it.

'You are a silly girl,' said Henri affectionately. 'You've survived the terrors of enemy planes and crevasses, and yet you're frightened of caves.' He kissed her forehead. 'Never mind, Etienne and I will search it thoroughly before you have to sleep in it.'

She felt rather foolish as they went deeper inside and then returned grinning to declare that it was free of man-eating wild beasts and bats. She smiled weakly back at them and gratefully sat down with her back pressed against the wall.

While Etienne sat in the shadows at the mouth of the cave with his rifle across his knee, Henri began to unpack the remains of their food and drink. 'We can't have a fire,' he explained. 'The smoke could be seen in the valley.'

He spread Annabelle's scarf on the rough cave floor and laid out their meal. 'The bread is stale, and the cheese and sausage are a little sweaty, but it's better than nothing,' he said apologetically.

Annabelle fidgeted as the need to empty her bladder became quite urgent. 'Is there anywhere I can . . . um . . . you know . . . wash my hands?'

Henri grinned. 'You can be very English at times, my Belle. If you need the toilet, then why not say so?' He pointed left.

'There's a mountain stream running nearby, with plenty of scrub cover. You can wash your hands to your heart's content there and not be disturbed.'

Her face was hot with embarrassment as she passed a grinning Etienne, clambered round the cave entrance and followed the small stream up to where it bubbled out of the mountainside amidst a large patch of scrub and wiry grass. The view was so magnificent in the rising sun that she forgot to fret over any creatures that might be lurking nearby as she dropped her trousers.

Comfortable again, she returned to the others and after the unappetising breakfast and a cup of lukewarm tea from the flask, she laid her coat on the floor and settled down, her head pillowed by her rucksack, her eyelids already heavy with sleep.

She woke to the sound of strange bird calls, and as she opened her eyes she realised she must have slept for a long time, for the sun was now setting to the west, throwing the cave into deeper shadow. She stretched her stiff, cold limbs and rubbed some life into them before getting to her feet. The floor of a cave wasn't the most comfortable of beds, but she'd obviously been so exhausted she'd hardly noticed.

As she approached the entrance to the cave she realised it was no birdsong that had awoken her, but the soft whistles and trills from Henri who was crouched low and maintaining a watchful eye through his binoculars on something below him. He turned sharply as her boot scraped a pebble against the stone floor, and pressed a warning finger to his lips.

Annabelle froze and attempted to melt into the shadows. Were they about to be discovered by the fascists? And where was Etienne?

Henri cupped his hands around his mouth and made a soft warbling noise, similar to that of a nesting pigeon. It was answered by another, and then a dark head appeared around the side of the cave to be swiftly followed by a long, lean body. 'Hola, Henri,' he said, his tanned face splitting into a beaming smile.

The two men embraced with much back-slapping and jocular laughter. They could have been brothers, for they shared the same black hair and olive skin, the same well-defined nose, high cheekbones and strong chin.

Annabelle tried to understand what they were saying, but it bore little resemblance to the Spanish she'd learnt from the dictionary and had to assume it was their native patois.

Etienne then clambered into the cave, swiftly followed by a stocky older man whose face was as rugged as the surrounding rocks. Like his companion, he was dressed in peasant clothes of rough twill, and was armed with a rifle. A bandolier of bullets was slung across his broad chest, and several handguns were tucked into a sash at his waist.

There were more hearty greetings and back-slapping before Henri turned back to Annabelle. 'This is Joaquim and Pedro. They are providing the transport to get you to Tarragona and us to Albacete.'

Annabelle shook the older man's hand. It was rough and calloused, but warm and strong. Joaquim's was just as warm and firm, but his hand had clearly not done as much rough labour, and there was a critical look in his dark eyes as he regarded her.

'So, you are nurse,' he said in broken English. 'Is good you help. We need much for many is wounded.'

'How long will it take to get me to Tarragona hospital?'

He gave an elegant shrug and flashed a beaming smile that exposed perfectly aligned white teeth. 'If the *fascisti* do not bother us, perhaps three hours.'

Three hours wasn't very long at all when every minute counted and the time to part loomed ahead of them. Annabelle glanced across at Henri and knew he was thinking the same. Yet there was no time to say anything, for Etienne was already gathering up the rucksacks and the last scraps of food, and Henri was checking the rifles.

She moved back into the cave and snatched up her own rucksack. Dragging on her coat, she thought longingly of the last bit of tea in her flask, and wondered if she'd have time to drink it before they had to leave.

'Come, come. We must descend quickly before the *fascisti* find the horses,' said Pablo impatiently.

Annabelle recognised the word for horse and all thoughts of tea fled. 'Horses? But I can't ride,' she whispered urgently to Henri.

'Then you'll have to learn, my love,' he replied as he took her hand and helped her down the steep decline. 'They can't risk the sound of an engine out here, and horses are much quieter.'

'Does that mean we'll have to travel all the way to Tarragona on horseback?' she asked fearfully. 'Just how far is that?'

'It's over a hundred miles,' he replied, and then grinned. 'I'm only teasing. We'll do the first part on horseback and then go on in a truck.'

Her heart was hammering at the thought of facing yet another challenge, and she could only pray that she didn't make a complete fool of herself in front of everyone by falling off. She didn't know anything about horses, except they were big and she didn't trust them.

As they reached the valley floor and she saw the string of dusty and rather shaggy horses tethered between a stand of trees, their hooves muffled in thick strips of sacking and cloth, her confidence plunged further. They looked half wild, but well muscled and tough – rather like the Spaniards who owned them, she thought distractedly.

Some were carrying loaded packs, whilst others had been saddled and carried only water bags and spare rifles. They milled about and snorted softly as the two Spaniards quickly swung into the saddles and gathered up the leading reins.

Annabelle dithered. She didn't know the first thing about horses, let alone how to get on one.

'Put your left foot in the stirrup and grab the pommel – that's the knob on the saddle – and I'll hand you up,' said Henri. 'When you sit, grip with your knees and don't pull on the reins. These horses will follow the others without question, so there's no need for you to do anything but stay on board.'

Annabelle put her foot in the stirrup and grabbed the pommel, and before she had time to think about it, Henri had hoisted her into the ornately tooled and surprisingly comfortable saddle.

Henri handed her the reins and she sat there staring between the beast's ears as she gripped its sides with her knees. It was a long way down if she fell, and the ground was as hard as iron and strewn with cacti and sharp rocks.

The horse fidgeted and shook its head, no doubt realising it had a complete novice on board, and she gripped even tighter.

'Ease off a little bit,' Henri warned as he brought his horse alongside. 'If you grip too hard, he'll think you want to go for a gallop.'

Annabelle quickly relaxed her thighs and tried to settle firmly into the saddle, just as the ladies who rode in Rotten Row used to do. They'd made it look very easy, and she was beginning to wish she'd taken the lessons her mother had suggested all those years ago. But it was too late now, and whatever happened next was up to God and fate, and her ability to stay on the horse.

Pablo was already leading the way out of the copse on a fine but dusty chestnut, with Etienne following. Henri clicked his tongue at Annabelle's horse so it moved on next and then he followed on, with Joaquim bringing up the rear.

Annabelle was as tense as a violin string as she tried to get used to the strange dip and roll of the horse beneath her, but as they eventually emerged from the trees into the final blazing glow of the dying sun, she got into the rhythm and began to relax and appreciate her surroundings.

The Mediterranean sparkled in the distance, and she could see tiny stone villages dotted across the plain where goats, sheep and cattle grazed. The sky was wide, the horizon stretching away into infinity beneath the pink- and orange-streaked blue as the sun sank.

They rode in silence, the horses' muffled hooves making no sound as they crossed the stony ground, and Annabelle was feeling much more confident until she heard the now all-too-familiar sound of aircraft.

The horse seemed to sense the urgent need to get under cover and picked up his pace as the others trotted towards a stand of trees and scrub.

Annabelle clung on, her knees gripping as she bounced up and down, and when the animal mercifully came to a sudden halt, she slid out of the saddle and fell to the ground in an untidy heap.

She saw the grins exchanged between the two Spaniards and her face was fiery with shame as she lay sprawled there, winded and covered in dust.

Henri jumped from his saddle, scooped her up into his arms and carried her into the trees. 'Are you all right?' he asked anxiously.

'Only my pride's been hurt really,' she replied wryly as she dusted herself down and tried to ignore the pain in her buttocks, which had taken the full brunt of her fall.

There was no time for further talk, and they crowded with the horses beneath the trees as the first wave of Fiats flew overhead. As before, these were followed by at least half a dozen Heinkels; but then came the much heavier Junkers with their fighter escort in tight formation behind them.

Pablo spat his disgust and waved a gnarled fist at the departing planes as Joaquim muttered under his breath, and Annabelle needed no translation to understand their hatred for this fascist enemy who was tearing their country apart.

Once they were certain it was all clear, Annabelle was helped back into the saddle and they resumed their trek south in the grey light of dusk. She felt easier now, and if she hadn't been aching from the mountain climbing and bruised from her fall, she would have actually enjoyed the steady plod of the sturdy horse beneath her as they passed through streams and followed tracks that were barely discernible in the ever-growing darkness.

They eventually came to a deserted stone village, but Pedro and Joaquim told them to stay back while they did a quick check for any hidden fascists who might by lying in wait for them.

As the two Spaniards tentatively explored the remains of the village, Annabelle could see that the outer wall that had once protected it had been blasted into rubble, and the shattered remains of the little houses were standing open to the elements amongst the debris of their village church and market square. The surrounding farmland that had once supported the village was now covered in weeds and thistles.

'The fascists bombed it,' explained Etienne as he translated what Joaquim had told him earlier. 'Those that didn't die in the bombing were slaughtered for their allegiance to the Republicans. There were none spared, not even the women and children.'

Annabelle felt sick at the thought of such barbarity, and as the men returned from their reconnaissance, she wearily slid from the horse's back and stretched her aching spine. Man's cruelty and inhumanity had been widely recorded in history books over the centuries, and from the Boer war in Africa to the conflicts in India and the Crimea, and even during the Great War, it seemed man's thirst for savagery could not be slaked, so why should this Spanish war be any different?

'How are you holding up?' asked Henri as he filled a tin cup with water from the leather bladder slung across his saddle.

She drank the warm, leather-tainted water and grimaced, but she was so thirsty she didn't care what it tasted like, and as it washed the dust and grit from her throat she felt immediately refreshed. 'Better than I expected,' she replied. 'How much further is it?'

He put his arm around her shoulder. 'We pick up the truck from here, so it won't be long now,' he murmured.

She gripped the front of his jacket and looked up into his face. 'Promise you won't do anything stupid,' she begged. 'Don't be a hero and get yourself hurt or killed. I couldn't bear it.'

He pulled her to him and rested his chin on the top of her head. 'I have no intention of getting killed or injured,' he murmured. 'And when this is all over and we can be together again, we will walk onto the Pont Neuf and I will claim my kiss.'

'We must move on now,' said Etienne, as he stepped out of the nearby shadows of a shattered house. 'It's still an hour to Tarragona and then another three before we'll even get close to Albacete.'

Henri kissed her passionately. 'I love you, Belle. Never forget that,' he said gruffly.

She nodded, her emotions so overwhelming that she couldn't find the words to express her feelings. She planted a light kiss on his cheek and quickly turned away to find the other men waiting for them by a rusting, dust-laden truck which didn't look as if it would make it out of the village let alone another two hundred miles to Albacete.

Pedro had gathered up the horses from the drinking trough and was once more in the saddle, the others tethered on leading reins. He would ride with them to the outskirts of Tarragona and then meet them on the way to Albacete. Etienne was already sitting beside Joaquim who was at the wheel of the dilapidated truck, and Henri quickly handed Annabelle up and into the back seat.

Despite the lateness of the hour and the chill of the night, the atmosphere in the cab was stifling after having being out in the sun all day, and as Joaquim set off they opened all the windows to try to lighten it. Despite its age and the rust that threatened to destroy the truck, the engine had been carefully maintained and it ran quite well.

Annabelle held Henri's hand as the truck bounced and rattled over the rough ground, the gears clashing, the engine whining as it strained up the hills to the west of Barcelona. They could see the glow of fires where no doubt there had been an enemy attack, and heard the distant rumble and thunder of many planes; but Joaquim knew the countryside well, keeping the truck away from the villages and towns where they might be stopped by enemy patrols and avoiding the heavily wooded areas where they could come under attack.

Henri slipped his arm round her shoulders and held her close, for the truck was slowing and Pablo had disappeared with his horses into the dark wilderness.

'Roadblock,' muttered Etienne. 'They'll need to see everyone's papers, and as Tarragona is still in Republican hands at the moment, it'll be safe for you to tell the truth as to why you're here, Annabelle.'

The truck ground to a rumbling halt and a uniformed guard pushed the butt of his rifle through the passenger window as his colleague demanded their papers. They sat in an agony of suspense as Joaquim was rigorously questioned, and then breathed a sigh of relief as the papers were handed back and the barrier was lifted.

They drove through the almost deserted streets of Tarragona and finally turned into an entrance heavily guarded by soldiers and piles of sandbags. They'd reached the hospital.

As the truck came to a grinding halt in front of the steps, she felt a moment of panic and turned to Henri. 'Take care, my love,' she whispered urgently, 'and let us pray that we'll see one another soon.'

'Just remember that I love you,' he replied, as Etienne opened the door and reached for Annabelle's rucksack.

She kissed Henri swiftly and climbed out to give Etienne a fond hug. 'Thank you, Etienne, you've been a true and patient friend. Look after yourself.'

'I'll see you back in Paris,' he said cheerfully.

She watched as he climbed back into the truck and slammed the door. Joaquim shot her a wink and floored the accelerator and before she knew it, the truck was disappearing out of the gateway.

She sniffed back her tears, hoisted the rucksack over her shoulder and climbed the steps to the grand entrance. There was some damage to the walls and pillars from shellfire and bullets, she noted, but the marble floor was polished to a high shine and she could hear the echoes of many voices coming from beyond the ornate set of wooden doors at the end of the hall.

Annabelle hesitated, and then strode towards them, but as she pushed them open she was met by a wall of noise and the sight of wounded men, women and children crammed together on mattresses, blankets and stretchers which covered the floor. Nurses moved back and forth, while voluntary aid workers carried bowls and towels and tried to clean up spilled blood and vomit as the doctors treated their patients.

'Hello, love. You come to help then?'

Annabelle looked into a pair of bright blue eyes above a freckled nose and cheerful smile. A riot of ginger hair was escaping from her volunteer's cap and her apron was smeared with blood.

'I'm Annabelle Blake,' she said above the awful noise of men moaning and women screeching. 'I'm from London.'

'Then I hopes you're a proper nurse, and not one of them hoity-toity lot what think they knows it all and knows nuffink,' the girl replied with a grimace.

'I worked at St Swithin's as a staff nurse,' Annabelle said firmly.

'Right, well, get yer coat off and wash yer 'ands. There's no time to be standing about 'cos there was a raid and we got a lot of casualties.'

'Who's in charge?' Annabelle asked as she shed her coat and rucksack, quickly found a bowl of water and scrubbed at her filthy hands and arms.

'Gawd knows. We all get moved about that much, it's anyone's guess. You'd better talk to Dr Quemada. He's the top surgeon 'ere.'

Annabelle followed the girl's pointing finger and saw a tall man in his forties with the same dark Spanish good looks of Joaquim. 'Does he speak English?'

'Better than what I do,' she said with a weary smile. 'He's Spanish all right, but he was born in America.' She shifted from foot to foot and glanced down at the pile of towels she was holding. 'Look, I'd better get on. Me name's Sal, by the way. Sal Piper.'

'Good to meet you, Sal, and thanks for your help.'

As the little Cockney shot off with her towels, Annabelle dried her hands carefully and wended her way through the chaos to the doctor. 'Excuse me, sir,' she said. 'I'm Staff Nurse Blake and I was wondering what you'd like me to do first.'

He paused in the act of inspecting a deep wound in his patient's chest and looked at her with thickly lashed eyes the colour of molten chocolate. A slow smile revealed white teeth and crinkled the corner of his eyes in a most attractive way. 'You look as if you've been through the wars yourself,' he drawled in his American accent as his gaze travelled from her heavy boots to the tangle of her dusty hair and grubby face. 'Are you sure you're not too tired to go straight to work?'

'I crossed the Pyrenees, slept in a cave; rode horseback for the first time and got here in a rusty old truck. If I can do all that, I can do anything. I'll rest later.'

He chuckled. 'Welcome to the madhouse, Staff Nurse Blake,' he said warmly as he shook her hand. 'We need young women like you. Now go and find an apron so you can re-dress this wound. You'll soon get the hang of how we do things around here.'

Warmed by his welcome and thrilled to be wanted and needed, Annabelle's grief at parting from Henri was banished, and she shot off to change into her uniform dress and find a clean apron.

9

April 1937

George had thrown himself into his work over the past few months, and had eased the financial burden of running such a large house by renting out the top floor to two medical students. He'd joined the golf club and had even begun to play rugby again when time allowed, and amidst all that he'd managed to organise a rota to encompass the other Dartford practices so that absences could be covered and a respite could be had at least one weekend a month. The golf kept him sane, the rugby left him aching and bruised, but the aggression of the game was cathartic and he'd been delighted to discover he was still fit and agile at thirty and able to play an important role on the front row.

Apart from missing Annabelle – which he did all the time – there was little to overshadow this new life he'd made for himself. Felicity Jenkins was efficient and the patients liked her – although she would insist upon bringing him casseroles and milk puddings, which he usually gave to his lodgers. It seemed she worried about him not eating properly – as did the district nurse, the midwife and even some of his women patients, who donated cakes, biscuits, pies and stews to the cause. Being a bachelor was a bit of a liability, he'd discovered, and if it hadn't been for the rounds of golf and the occasional game of rugby, he would have put on some considerable weight.

He eyed his reflection critically in the mirror, patted his still flat stomach and finished dressing. Knotting the rugby club tie, he then brushed back his dark hair and pulled on the tweed jacket which fitted perfectly over his broad shoulders. He wasn't quite six feet tall, but he was sturdily built and useful in the front row, just as his father had been. And although he wasn't a vain man, he did realise he could cut quite a dashing figure when he put his mind to it. Satisfied that he'd pass muster, he strode along the landing and went into the sitting room to fetch his pipe and matches and then ran down the stairs, eager to get to the club for their annual luncheon.

There was a letter on the mat and as he picked it up, he realised it was from Annabelle. All thoughts of the club lunch disappeared as he carried it into the kitchen, his mind on the other hurried notes he'd received from her. Although he was still rather put out by her running off – and furious that she'd endangered herself by going to Spain – his admiration for her courage had grown. Not many women would take such a dangerous journey to prove their worth, and yet Annabelle seemed to be thriving.

Taking the thin, crumpled pages from the envelope, he noted the date, which was three months ago, and that Annabelle was no longer in Tarragona but in some place called Cañete, which

was approximately seventy miles north of Valencia. He began
to read.

15th February
My dearest George,

*I write this in haste as we are once more about to be evacuated
and moved on, and I don't know when I shall have time to write
again. We are being constantly attacked by enemy planes, and
it seems the fascist brutes are determined to target hospitals
and unprotected villages known to be loyal to the Republicans.
Considering the number of bombs they drop, there is surprisingly
little damage done, but when they're followed up by a raiding
party of overzealous louts, no one is safe.*

*An Italian division attacked us earlier, and although they
were pushed back by the Republican guards who protect us,
there is talk of an even larger raid to come from Franco's Spanish
Nationalists, who have already laid nearby towns to waste with
their looting and mindless destruction.*

*We have spent the day packing everything and arranging
for the more seriously wounded patients to be taken to another
hospital. Some of the walking wounded have been discharged, but
there are still many more who will have to come with us in the
few ambulances Rafael Quemada has managed to beg, borrow or
steal from the American Medical Corps, who seem to be far better
equipped than us.*

*The bombing has disturbed the rats, which now plague us even
more than before. They seem to be immune to the poison we lay
down and steal or infect what little food we have. We exist on*

rice, bread and almonds, and a strange concoction that is neither
tea nor coffee, but a fusion of both mixed with hot water – there's
no milk or sugar to be had – but at least it's warm and wet and
fools our stomachs into thinking they're full.

The rain's been unrelenting and our clothes are now rotting
from the damp and mould. We are surrounded by a lake of mud,
and can only pray that the ambulances will be able to get us out
of here. Now I must go. I will finish this later.

Love as always,
Annabelle xx

George could only imagine the hardships and terrors she was going through, but it seemed that her spirit remained undaunted, and that she and the others had survived their perilous escape from Cañete, for her letter continued.

26 February
Aragon Province
We have had to say farewell to our beloved Rafael Quemada,
as he's been seconded to an American unit near Madrid, and
it has been difficult to get used to his replacement, who is an
arrogant Englishman called Cyril Beecham. But any surgeon
is better than none, and I suspect the arrogance will soon get
knocked out of him once the shelling begins again and the number
of casualties increases.

We have been at the Santa Rosa mission hospital for over
ten days now, but because it was little more than a ruin, we've
spent all that time cleaning and repairing and trying to make

at least two rooms clean enough for our patients. Yet it's proved impossible to have a sterile theatre, and Beecham has to operate beneath freshly washed sheets that we suspend on a series of pulleys above him and the operating table like a tent.

We have to boil our drinking water and wash all the linen as well as any bandages we can salvage, so it comes hard after a long day on the ward, but we manage somehow. There are few beds here, but we've managed to find a local carpenter who's proved to be ingenious with whatever bits of scrap he can find, and finally we have blocks to raise the beds he made, backrests, pulleys, stretchers, back-boards, and numerous other things which all help to comfort our poor patients.

We care for both civilians and the military, and the barbarity shown towards innocent women and children is quite, quite shocking, George. I've seen so many terrible things here, and the only way any of us can bear it is to just keep on working and doing the best we can to help ease their suffering. I have nothing but praise for the volunteer aides who work tirelessly and without complaint as they do the dirtiest, most menial jobs. Little Sal Piper, who's from the East End, is a particular ray of sunshine, and no matter how tough the day has been, she's always got a smile and a giggle that is infectious.

News is filtering through of terrible fighting in the north between the Nationalists and the International Brigade. The battle has been going on for days, with neither side able to claim a victory as yet, but already the death toll is simply unbearable, and I wait in agony to hear word of Henri, Etienne, Bertram and Arthur. But, as you can imagine, communication is difficult and *frustratingly slow, and I received only a short note from Henri back in January, which told me very little.*

But there is some good news. I've heard from Caroline at last. She's nursing in a field hospital close to Albacete. True to form, she's not suffering the same deprivations as the rest of us, for she's working with an American medical unit, and apart from the usual lack of good food, seems to have no difficulty in getting decent medical supplies. I'm hoping that we will somehow manage to be in the same place at the same time, but we are at the mercy of our superiors and enemy raids, so I doubt it will ever happen. At the time of her writing, her brothers, Arthur and Bertram, were still alive and uninjured, so that is a huge relief and I'm sure their parents cling to the hope they'll all come through this terrible war unscathed.

And yet, despite the hardships and the horrors, I am happy, George. This is real nursing, and I feel at last that I'm making a difference, and that whatever the future may hold, I've been given the chance to do what I was born to do.

I hope that you are settled in your home. From your letters – which do eventually reach me – it sounds wonderful, and I can just imagine sitting in your lovely garden on an English summer's day, perhaps with a bowl of strawberries and cream! Oh, how simple life was when we would take our picnics to the park and spread a blanket on the lush green grass, and how I miss the signs of spring in this barren, red and dusty land. But the memories of those times we spent together still sustain me when things get tough here.

I hear trucks approaching, so must go. Will finish this later. xx

George was gratified she hadn't forgotten their times together and still held them dear. He turned the page, hoping to see more reminiscences and discovered there was only a single, tear-stained paragraph to end her letter.

> *The trucks came from the front line. Some of the injured had died on the way, whilst others survived for less than the time it took us to clean their wounds and comfort them. My dear childhood friend, Arthur Howden, passed away in my arms at two o'clock this morning, and I weep not only for my loss, but for the heartbreaking grief this will bring to his parents and siblings. In deep sorrow,*
> *Annabelle xx*

The June sun blazed mercilessly down as the dust filtered into every sweating pore and clogged throats, eyes and ears. Etienne was so exhausted he couldn't dredge up the energy to put pen to paper. The heat, the dust and the great clouds of irritating black flies were driving him mad, but he lay in the shallow defile of rock beside Henri and let the damned things crawl all over him.

They were both filthy, not having washed for days, and their eyes were sore and weeping, the lids swollen from the bright light and constant dust. They could no longer smell their own stench, or that of the rotting corpses of their comrades nearby, for they'd become immune to it – just as they'd almost become inured to the ever-present flies.

The fierce fighting over the small village to the north-east of Madrid had gone on for days, and not even the three weeks of hard training back at headquarters had prepared them for what they'd encountered since. They'd experienced a baptism of fire within days of finishing their training, and the onslaught had continued over the past six months with little respite.

The bombing and almost complete destruction of Guernica had imbued them with a fierce determination to defeat this enemy at any cost. Guernica was the spiritual heart of the Basque people, and although their own families had not attended the farmers' market on that fateful Monday, many of their neighbours had, and the death toll was still rising as the injured succumbed and more bodies were found in the rubble.

The small farming community they were now trying to capture had been virtually demolished when it was taken by the combined forces of the fascist splinter of Moroccans and Spanish Legionnaires. The International Brigade had joined forces with the Thaelmann Brigade, which was made up of French and Canadian volunteers, to oust them and try to rescue the inhabitants. However, the Fiats were constantly strafing them, the Heinkel one-elevens dropped bombs all round them and the Hotchkiss machine gun hidden behind the turrets of the church tower cut them to ribbons if they so much as put their heads above the stony outcrops in which they hid.

The major in charge of the International Brigade was a vicious bastard who would harangue the men and threaten to shoot them if he considered their injuries were not enough to stop them from fighting, or suspected they were malingering. He saw cowardice in the slightest waver of confidence, in the stumble of an exhausted man, or the moan of someone who carried an injury – and had no compunction in executing any man under his command that he considered to be a weak link. There wasn't a man amongst them who didn't loathe and fear him, and Etienne suspected that given the chance, someone would eventually give him a taste of his own medicine and put a bullet through his head.

This was not the glorious, hero-making, adventurous war Etienne had envisaged, but brutal, unremitting slaughter played out beneath a torturous Spanish sun for a worthless few yards of land which would be lost again before the day ended. They'd seen their comrades cut down, had heard the bewildered cries of men so badly injured they were numbed by it and didn't even know they were dying. The nightmares came not only in the few moments of snatched sleep, but in the villages and towns where they'd arrived too late and found the hacked corpses of women and children festering where they lay, and in the shallow pits that revealed the piled bodies of those who'd been forced to dig them before being shot.

'*Merde!*' Etienne spat in disgust as a fly crawled into his mouth. 'I swear to God, Henri,' he rasped. 'If I survive this, I'll invent something to wipe these bastards off the face of the earth.'

'Do that, and you'll make your fortune,' he murmured as he continued to sketch the magnificent hills and mountains of the Sierra de Guadarrama, where the highest peaks were still capped in snow despite the heat of the sun.

Etienne's leg muscles were cramping and he tried to ease them as he huddled behind the rocks in search of shade. They'd been stuck here since mid-morning, pinned down by the machine gun and the snipers that were hidden around the village. Shifting awkwardly in the tight space, he made a conscious effort to relax, but hunger gnawed at his belly, the heat of midday was intolerable and there were only a few sips of brackish water left in his leather bottle. If they didn't retreat soon, none of them would get out of here alive.

He watched Henri for a moment and wondered how he could remain so calm in the light of their situation. And yet he turned over the page in his sketchbook and with sweeping strokes began to draw the ruins of the village that lay close to the fertile plain where rivers and lakes shimmered beneath the bleached sky.

Etienne adjusted his sunglasses and looked beyond his friend to the scene of destruction. The fields had been trampled; farming machinery was abandoned and the livestock had been quickly rounded up and slaughtered to feed the invading army. The houses were made of adobe – a mixture of mud, manure and straw – with chimneys and buttresses of stone that had been gleaned from the foothills of the mountains. Bombs and rifle fire had crumbled them to dust, the roofs of slate and corrugated iron collapsing onto the dirt floors and crushing those trapped inside. Some of the locals had managed to flee when the fighting began, but many more had been mown down by that machine gun, and now there was no movement in the village square or its surrounds.

'Why the hell don't we just leave them to it?' he hissed crossly. 'It's worthless anyway.'

Henri finished his sketch, closed the book and tucked it back into his satchel. 'Ours is not to reason why,' he murmured as he began to clean his rifle, 'but I agree that this particular venture seems pointless.'

Etienne heard a whisper coming down the line and his stomach clenched. They were being ordered to prepare to advance. It was suicidal. Nevertheless, he checked his rifle and handgun, both of which constantly jammed because of the damned dust, and rolled onto his side. 'If I don't make it out of here, will you tell my parents?'

'Of course,' whispered Henri. 'And will you tell mine and Annabelle if I don't come through? I'd hate to think of her finding out through the rumour mill.'

Etienne nodded, his mind already on the course of direction to take when the order came to advance. The priority had to be wiping out that machine gun. He narrowed his eyes and followed the path least likely to draw the snipers. There were two ruined houses nearby, and if—

'Advance! Advance!'

With a barrage of gunfire, and a bellow of defiance, the men of the combined brigades rose from their hiding-places and were met by a lethal line of fire from the machine gun.

'Follow me!' yelled Etienne. He ducked low and instead of following the others into the square where certain death awaited, he ran towards the first ruined wall as bullets slammed into the soft ground at his feet and whined past his head.

He reached the wall and pressed hard against it as Henri joined him. The adrenalin had wiped away his hunger and exhaustion; now he was focused. He sneaked a peek around the corner, felt the wind of the sniper's bullet whistle past his nose, then threw himself into the lee of the next house.

The deathly rattle of the machine gun echoed across the plain as the crump of grenades and whine and ricochet of bullets mingled with shouts and screams. Etienne judged the distance he would have to run to reach the tumbledown barn – he realised he'd be out in the open too long – and decided to make for the animal pens instead. He pointed them out to Henri, and at his nod, threw himself onto the ground and rolled swiftly into the shadow of the sturdy wooden fencing.

As Henri joined him they both grimaced. They were caked in the churned-up muck of a pigsty. 'We have to get to that bastard on the machine gun,' yelled Etienne. 'If we can reach the barn, and climb into the rafters, we should get a clear shot. Are you with me?'

Henri nodded, his expression determined as he surveyed the barn. 'Sniper,' he warned as he took aim at the man lying on the roof and shot him down.

They crawled through the stinking muck of the sty as bullets thudded into the fence panels and zipped over their heads. Someone had clearly spotted them, so it wasn't safe to stay there any longer. Etienne and Henri reached the last bit of cover, shared a glance and hurled themselves across the open ground, the bullets thudding at their feet and tearing at their clothes.

'We made it,' panted Henri as they huddled behind the high bales of straw in the barn. They grinned at each other like schoolboys as they caught their breath.

The machine gun bullets zipped a tight line of holes into the barn wall just inches above their heads. 'Time to deal with him once and for all,' muttered Henri, as he surveyed the bales and began to climb.

The rafters formed a cathedral arch high above the cobbled floor of the barn, and as Henri reached the top of the bales, he grasped one of the sturdy beams and shinned up it. Etienne reached the same cross-beam moments later and they both jabbed their rifles into the adobe walls to make holes big enough to see through.

'He's got our men pinned down in the grain store,' muttered Henri as he eased the point of his rifle through the hole and squinted through the sight, his index finger resting lightly on the trigger. Adjusting it slightly so the cross hairs were fixed on the gunner's head, he squeezed the trigger. The man went down like a felled tree and the machine gun was silenced.

Etienne picked off the second man who suddenly emerged to take over the big gun, and then a third.

With the machine gun out of action their men found new courage and surged across the village square shooting at anything that moved. A sniper picked off several before Henri managed to get him in his sight and finish him off. With a grunt of satisfaction, he saw another fall from his hiding-place as Etienne's bullet found him.

The gunfire was sporadic now, and they decided it was safe to emerge from their hiding-place. They reached the entrance to the barn, their rifles primed and ready should they come under attack. However, the few surviving enemy soldiers had been rounded up and placed under guard in the grain store with their wounded, while their own men were either tending to their injured comrades or looting the village wine store.

Henri and Etienne grinned as they shook hands and stepped out into the square, unaware of the gunman hiding on the roof of the grain store.

Henri heard the crack of the rifle seconds after he felt the punch of something hit him low in the shoulder. He staggered as the second blow threw him off balance, and fell to the ground in a heap as a third narrowly missed his head. He lay there in shock as he heard the answering report of Etienne's rifle and the alarmed cries of his comrades. There was no pain, only a strange numbness which seemed to be spreading through him.

'It's all right, Henri. I'll get you help. Just stay awake. Do you hear me? Stay awake, Henri.'

Etienne's voice sounded distant, and there seemed to be an edge of fear to it, which was most puzzling. And now a hot, white agony rolled through him as he felt himself being lifted up. Talons of unbearable torment threatened to rip him apart as they dug into his flesh and sent shock waves through him.

So this is what death feels like, he thought fleetingly as a great darkness began to surround him.

'Don't you dare die, Henri,' Etienne said fiercely.

He wasn't ready to die – couldn't die before he saw Annabelle again. But the agony was all-consuming and the darkness was thick and heavy with the promise to relieve the pain. And ultimately, it was irresistible.

10

The Catholic mission stood squarely at the end of the village, the iron cross at the apex of its bell tower proclaiming its purpose, which was to oversee the spiritual care of the small farming community of Santa Rosa. It had been abandoned after a lightning strike by a rogue band of Franco's thugs in search of food and treasure. Thwarted by the lack of either, they'd killed the priest and his housekeeper, and terrorised the village before they were rounded up by a brigade of Republicans and taken off to prison. As the mission was a fairly large building in an area that was not considered worth fighting over by either side, it had been decided by those in charge of such things that it would make a perfect hospital.

The young men of the village had gone to fight, but the women and the older men had helped to repair the roof and the crumbling walls that had been shot to pieces by the band of marauders during their drunken spree, and the ageing carpenter had done a sterling job with what he could lay his hands on to make beds for the thirty or more patients.

Water had to be drawn from the village well; there had been no electricity until a generator had arrived from Tarragona, and the range oven was so ancient, there was a very real fear that one day it would either explode, or collapse into a rusted heap and set fire to the place.

There were two wards in what had been the priest's living quarters, and once two inner walls had been knocked down to make a better space, the operating theatre had been set up in the housekeeper's bed-sitting room. The six nurses, two VADs and the surgeon lived in what had been the schoolroom which was at the back of the main house. Flimsy partitions gave them a degree of privacy, and although they slept on thin mattresses in unyielding bunk beds, they were usually so tired, they didn't notice the discomfort.

There was no plumbing, so the two baths had to be filled with water from the well that had been heated on the range. The outside lavatories were on a par with those in the East End according to Sal Piper – only more terrifying at night, for there were scorpions, snakes and lizards as well as huge hairy spiders to contend with in the darkness.

Annabelle dropped the scrubbing brush into the bucket of dirty water, tucked her limp hair back into its bun, and eased her back. The sweat was pouring down her face, her light cotton uniform dress was sticking to her, and the boiling hot water and carbolic soap had reddened her hands. Yet it was the mindless sort of work she needed to dispel the ache of grief that still lingered after Arthur's death.

She consoled herself by knowing he hadn't died alone amongst strangers; that he'd realised, even through his debilitating pain and delirium, that she was there, holding him as he struggled to take his last breath. Yet his passing had touched her deeply and even after all these months there were moments when she felt the deep pang of sorrow and loss.

'That looks better, don't it?' Sal Piper sat back on her heels with a sigh of pleasure as she surveyed the scrubbed floor of the smallest ward.

'It certainly does,' agreed Annabelle as she wearily got to her feet. 'But it's a never-ending job while the dust blows in.' She eyed the shuttered windows, which were so badly fitted they were almost useless. 'I've asked Emanuel to fix those windows, but I think they're beyond even his carpentry skills.'

They collected their buckets and tramped outside to the fledgling vegetable garden, which looked wilted despite being in the shade of a canvas tarpaulin that had been strung from hooks in the mission wall and fixed to two sturdy posts. Having trickled the dirty water over the thirsty peppers, tomatoes, onions and potatoes, they watched it drain swiftly away to leave the pale ochre soil as dry and crumbling as ever.

'It was a good idea of yours to have the garden,' said Sal, 'but I don't reckon much will survive – certainly not enough to feed everyone proper.'

Annabelle had known it was probably a doomed project when she'd first sown the seedlings she'd bought from a local farmer, and although she'd followed his instructions to the letter and added plenty of manure, the crop didn't look at all promising. 'At least the food supplies arrived today,' she said, 'and by the smell of it Marge and Cybil are cooking something delicious.'

'They're a couple of diamonds, aren't they? Still, I suppose, coming from Australia, they're used to the heat. But you won't catch me in that kitchen. It's a bleedin' furnace.'

'They're both from some town near Alice Springs, and according to Marge, this is nothing compared to the heat they get there.'

'Well, I ain't looking forward to summer, and that's a fact,' said Sal. 'Emanuel's wife told me this is just the flaming start, and if it wasn't for this blooming war, the whole village would make their yearly trek up into the mountains for July and August.'

Annabelle eyed the thin cap of snow that stubbornly remained on the highest peak. She wiped her sweating face on her apron and pushed back another lock of lank hair. *The villagers had it right*, she thought, as she imagined the cool air and the cold water in the streams that ran through the rich mountain pastures. *If I had half a chance, I'd be up there too.*

It would soon be nightfall, but the heat was still sibilant in the rocks that lay scattered across the barren, dusty valley floor, the watery haze of it shimmering on the horizon, while the sky remained bleached of colour as the sun began its descent to the peak of the Caimodorro mountain. It was a dramatic landscape, with earth the colour of crushed chilli peppers, slashed by thin silver ribbons of shallow rivers, sprawling at the foot of the Serrania de Cuenca range, which lay in deep indigo shadows as the sun slowly sank behind it. Tall cacti, clumps of tough yellow grass and the dark, twisted trunks of olive trees grew out of the stony landscape, and beyond the small village of adobe houses and farm shacks which stretched out from the mission, Annabelle could see the blur of eau de Nil pastures.

'It ain't much like home, is it?' said Sal with a sigh. 'What I wouldn't give fer a bit of cold wind and rain.'

'You'd soon moan about it,' Annabelle laughed. 'Remember the floods and the mud we had to endure before?'

Sal nodded and grimaced. 'They don't do fings by 'alves out here, do they? If it ain't frying yer, it's drowning yer.'

Annabelle looked out at the parched earth, the wilting olive trees and the swirls of dust that eddied through the deserted village square, remembering the lush grass in the London parks, the tinkle of fountains and the citrus green of new leaves on the trees. There were times when she too longed for the misty, cold mornings, the light drizzle and the friendly summer sun that was so much kinder than this blazing inferno.

'I'd better get on. I promised to read Sergeant Smith's letter to 'im before tea, and 'e'll think I've forgotten 'im.'

As Sal bustled off, Annabelle remained in the shade of the tarpaulin and sank down onto the bench the carpenter had made to light a cigarette. It was a habit she'd taken to some weeks ago, and although they were rough on her throat and didn't taste very nice, they were cheap, seemed to relax her and make her forget momentarily how hungry she was. Yet as the delicious aromas of frying onions and meat wafted out to her from the kitchen, her stomach rumbled in expectation.

Supplies had been dangerously low, and the staff had been forced to ration everything in order to ensure that their patients got the lion's share. A crust of bread or a handful of rice in a watery soup was slowly savoured, washed down with more boiled water or the strange coffee and tea combination. When the convoy had finally arrived bringing fresh supplies, the boxes of canned food and sacks of flour and rice had been eagerly fallen upon and cooed over. The atmosphere had become quite festive, and even the patients had perked up at the thought of getting something more interesting for supper that night rather than the usual hotchpotch of rice and vegetables.

Annabelle leant back, her fingers automatically reaching for Henri's garnet ring that always hung round her neck from a thin strip of leather. She regarded the scenery beyond the shade of the tarpaulin, her thoughts turning to home and loved ones. George was clearly settled and happy in his new life, and she wondered if he even realised that Felicity Jenkins had set her cap at him. The thought that his affections could turn to someone else bothered her, strangely enough, and although she'd tried to analyse why, the answer still eluded her.

There had been letters from Camille expressing her concern over Annabelle's safety after the news of Arthur's death. Yet it appeared that she was finding some purpose to her life as she and Philippa Howden raised funds for medical supplies to be bought by Aline in France and then sent to Spain. It seemed that Edwin approved of her charitable causes, for it meant socialising with the great and the good of English society, though Annabelle suspected he didn't realise what they were actually raising money for.

The death of Arthur had hit Philippa and Richard hard, and Caroline's irregular letters to Annabelle had proved how badly she'd taken the news, for she was now seriously considering her position here, and even thinking of returning home to be with her grieving parents. They still hadn't had the chance to meet, and Annabelle doubted she'd see her again until they were both back in England. How long that would be was anyone's guess for the fighting was still just as fierce, and neither side was willing to surrender.

Aline had sent chatty letters about her own fundraising, and the comings and goings of her tenants. Her exhibition had been a tremendous success, and she was delighted to report that she'd managed to pay off most of her debts and have some repairs done to the roof. However, despite the cheerfulness, there was an underlying concern that Annabelle was in great danger, and that now she'd proved herself, perhaps it was time to return home to Paris.

And then there was the post she waited most anxiously for. Henri's letters and notes, however short, were treasured, as were the little cartoon sketches he enclosed with them of him and Etienne making the best of bad situations. His endearments clearly came from the heart, and although they were miles apart, those loving words brought him nearer and she treasured them.

And yet Annabelle knew that between the lines of his hastily scribbled letters lay hardship, horror and fear, and the memory of atrocities that had been seared into his mind as if by branding irons. She'd heard the stories from her patients, had witnessed the aftermath of the traumas they'd gone through in their desperate nightmares, and she knew that Henri must be experiencing the same.

Etienne's two letters had been a surprise, for he usually just added a jocular note at the bottom of Henri's. His tone was just as light and he'd included several lines of doggerel which poked cruel fun at his commanding officer who was clearly loathed by all. The fall of Guernica had obviously affected both of them, but at least they'd had news from their families that they were all right.

She'd been saddened to learn that both Joaquim and Pablo had been killed during a night raid on their camp. The knowledge that Pablo's courage and strength, and Joaquim's vibrancy, and almost devil-may-care joy of life, had been snuffed out so indiscriminately had made her weep, and she'd lit a candle and prayed for both of them in the tiny village chapel.

She looked across at the chapel as she ground the butt of her cigarette under her shoe. She wasn't particularly religious, and the sights she'd witnessed and the stories she'd heard had shaken what little faith she had in a loving, all-seeing God, but there had been times when she'd found solace within those walls.

Knowing that she wasn't expected back on the wards for a while, she headed across the village square. Darkness had fallen swiftly, as it usually did, and her way was guided by the few lanterns that had been lit in the tumbledown houses. She returned the soft greetings as men and women came out to fetch water from the well and go about their work now the sun was gone, and sidestepped a herd of goats which were being driven out to the pastures, their bells tinkling and jangling from their collars.

The thick adobe walls and narrow windows of the chapel kept

it cool, and her rubber-soled shoes squeaked on the marble floor
as she went up the aisle past the rough-hewn pews. Unlike some
of the churches she'd seen in Tarragona, this had no gold taber-
nacle or candlesticks; no richly embroidered altar cloth, gilded
pictures of the Stations of the Cross, or exquisitely carved pulpit.
The altar was a simple table covered with handmade lace, the
crucifix carved from the wood of an olive tree; candles flickered
in glass jars beneath the plaster statue of the Madonna, and the
faded frescoes which decorated the walls had succumbed to the
damp of centuries.

Annabelle dropped a peseta into the collecting box, lit a candle
and sat down. The extraordinary sense of peace enfolded her,
quenching and renewing her weary spirit in a way that was unique
to this place. She could feel it reaching out to her, gathering her
in with sacred warmth and tenderness, and could almost hear the
murmured prayers of the generations who'd come before. This
simple, ancient sanctuary had the power to heal and restore, and
she closed her eyes and gave herself up to it.

The light tap on her shoulder made her start, for she'd been so
deeply immersed in the essence of her surroundings, she hadn't
heard anyone approach.

'Sorry, Annabelle,' drawled Marge in her Australian accent,
'but we've had word over the radio that there's an emergency
convoy coming in, and by the sound of the size of it, it's going
to be all hands on deck.'

Annabelle gathered her wits and quickly followed her out of
the church. The rumble of heavy trucks could be heard in the

distance and the locals were already fearfully coming out of their homes to see what was going on, whilst the entire medical staff was waiting at the front door of the hospital with stretchers.

'It's all right,' Annabelle assured the locals in her halting Spanish. 'The trucks are bringing in the wounded.'

Once they knew it wasn't an enemy attack, the women hurried over to join the rest of the medical staff so they could help.

'Do you know where the convoy's come from?'

'Fair go, Annabelle, it could be from anywhere. But I reckon it's the fallout from that fighting outside Madrid.'

'If that's the case, then why not take the injured to Madrid? They've got better facilities there.'

Marjory shrugged good-naturedly. 'It's too late to worry about that now, mate. They're here.'

The convoy of trucks and ambulances came out of the darkness, their headlights heavily shaded to avoid being spotted from above by an enemy plane, the dust rising in a great thick cloud behind them. The leading truck screeched to a halt outside the mission house and the driver, a swarthy man in peasant clothing, jumped down to open the back doors.

As the stretchers were unloaded and the walking wounded helped into the hospital, Annabelle and Dr Beecham quickly assessed the injuries. They were mostly gunshot wounds, and several were deemed to be fatal and beyond the most skilled surgeon.

'That long journey here couldn't have done any of them much good,' said Annabelle as the two ambulances roared away to their next consignment.

'At least most of them survived it,' said Marge who was helping a man on crutches.

Annabelle glanced across at the five stretchers which had been laid on the hall floor. The bodies had been covered by blankets, a tragic reminder that not all had come through that tortuous journey.

Her heart was heavy as she walked alongside the stretcher bearing a young man who was close to death and softly calling for his mother. He'd been given a shot of morphine before he'd arrived, so at least he wasn't in any pain. She gripped his hand as he was gently transferred to a bed. 'It's all right,' she murmured. 'You're safe now.'

He turned his bandaged head towards her, his eyes unfocused with the morphine. 'Mother? Is that you?'

'Yes, my dear. I'm here,' she whispered as she stroked the soft cheek that had barely known a razor.

'I'm sorry, mother. I . . . I . . .' His head rolled on the pillow and with a sigh, he was gone.

Annabelle kissed the back of his grubby hand and tucked it under the sheet. She gently searched his pockets and found his identity papers, which she placed on his chest before drawing the sheet over the boy. He was barely sixteen, and although she'd seen so many young men die, and had told the same white lie to give them that last moment of comfort, it still affected her, and she had to blink back her tears as she headed for the next patient.

Dr Beecham barked orders as he went from bed to bed and sent the nurses and volunteer aides scurrying. It was an orderly chaos as lesser wounds were cleaned and bandaged, tiny splinters of shrapnel were removed and eyes were bathed in warm water. The discomfort of sand blight could bring about blindness if not treated, and Annabelle and her colleagues had seen to it that the village children were treated regularly.

As the peasants brought in more stretchers, and the walking wounded slumped onto the floor and waited patiently, Annabelle realised they'd run out of beds. 'You'll have to put the stretchers on the floor. Just leave enough room between them so we can get through,' she said as she bustled past, her focus on another patient.

'Annabelle?'

She stopped mid-stride and looked back at the grubby-faced man and her heart thudded with shock. Thin and aged by experience and hardship, Etienne was almost unrecognisable. 'Etienne? Are you hurt?'

He shook his head. 'It's Henri. He's taken a couple of bullets.'

With a cry of distress, Annabelle sank to her knees beside the stretcher and reached out a trembling hand to the figure cocooned in blankets. Drawing them back from his face she gasped in horror. Henri was ashen beneath the grime, his pulse was thready and rapid and he was burning with fever. She threw back the blankets and saw that his shirt was thickly bloodstained beneath the bandaging.

'Has anyone tried to get the bullets out?' she demanded as she removed the blood-soaked bandage and saw the gaping, jagged hole in Henri's shoulder.

'One went straight through him, but the other's too deeply embedded. He's not going to die, is he?'

'Not if I have anything to do with it,' she muttered fiercely. 'Has he had any morphine?'

'In the ambulance on the way here.'

'Dr Beecham,' Annabelle called across the room. 'I need this man in theatre now.' She looked at Etienne. 'Help me get the stretcher into that room over there.'

The stretcher was heavy, for Henri was a dead weight, but they managed between them to get him into the theatre and onto the table beneath the tent of sheets. Turning on all the lights, Annabelle began to cut away the shirt, her voice soft and soothing although she knew he couldn't hear her.

The wound was now fully exposed, but there was no sign of Beecham. 'Dr Beecham,' she yelled. 'I need you in here now!' She began to clean the wound and pluck out the threads of fabric, dust and grit that had become embedded into it.

Beecham was scowling as he marched into the room. 'I do not appreciate—'

'I don't care,' snapped Annabelle. 'This man needs help before the infection really sets in.'

He glanced at Henri's wound. 'There are more urgent cases than this,' he muttered. 'He'll have to wait.'

'No. He won't. This is Henri-Pascal and we're engaged,' she snapped. 'And if you don't try and get that bullet out, then I will.'

He raised an eyebrow and folded his arms. 'Go on then. You've had practice enough.'

She stared at him in disbelief. It was true she'd performed this operation many times, but this was Henri, and if he died because of her she would never forgive herself. 'I . . . I . . .'

He sniffed in derision. 'Not so cocky and bossy now, are you? Step aside, staff nurse, and go and tend your other patients.'

'But—'

'You're too involved, and overwrought,' he barked. 'Get me Cybil, and while you're at it, take him with you.' He glared at Etienne. 'Get out, the pair of you.'

Annabelle hurried to find Cybil and one of the nursing aides to go and help Beecham, and then turned to Etienne, who was pale and shaking with distress. 'Beecham might be an arrogant so-and-so, but he knows what he's doing,' she said firmly.

'He will pull through, won't he, Belle? I have to get the truck back to HQ in the morning, but I need to know he's all right before I leave.'

'We won't know until the doctor's finished.' She put a consoling hand on his arm. 'Try not to worry, Etienne, he's in very good hands.' She caught a glimpse of Marge struggling to quieten a patient who was lashing out in his delirium. 'I'm needed. See you later.'

Annabelle helped Marge to settle the poor man, and with an anxious glance towards the theatre, hurried off to clean a thigh wound which looked worse than it was and just needed a few stitches and fresh bandaging. She'd just finished suturing when the theatre door opened and Cybil appeared carrying one end of the stretcher with Beecham at the other.

'He'll live,' he said gruffly. 'The bullet was embedded in the soft tissue beneath his shoulder, but there were no other fragments and the second bullet made a clean exit. I've given him something to fight the infection, so just keep up his fluids, and remember you have other patients more in need of your attention.'

Annabelle was stung by his accusation and she could feel the colour rise in her face. She turned to Henri who was now lying so still upon the bed. His colour was a little better, she noted, and his pulse was definitely stronger and more even. Knowing that she was being watched keenly by Beecham, she stroked back Henri's hair, kissed his forehead and left him in the very capable hands of Sal Piper, who would undress and wash him and settle him in.

The next two hours flew by, but at last the more serious injuries had been operated upon, the other wounds cleaned, stitched and dressed. The twenty men were now sleeping fairly peacefully but for the occasional groan or mutter, and the two not expected to last what was left of the night had been wheeled into the corner of the ward where curtains had been strung across washing-line cord to give them privacy. One of the nurses would stay with them until the end.

Annabelle tiptoed through the sleeping ward and stood by Henri's bed. He was deeply asleep, probably because of the morphine, but his breathing was much easier and although his temperature was still a little high, he was definitely improving.

Taking his hand from where it lay on top of the sheet, she held it to her heart. 'Thank God you're safe, my love,' she whispered. 'Sleep well, my darling, and I'll come back to sit with you later.'

She slowly made her way out of the ward and into the corridor where there were now seven bodies awaiting burial. They would be interred in the plot behind the chapel just after daybreak while it was still cool, their passing marked by the crude crosses that Emanuel had made, their names carved into the olive wood.

Stumbling in her weariness, she went outside into the still, warm night and looked up at the stars that shone so clear and bright above the sleeping earth. It was an awesome sight, and the cooler air was like a balm on her skin, but she was almost asleep on her feet.

'You look exhausted.' Etienne emerged out of the gloom. 'Come and sit down for a while.'

She needed no pressing, and sank onto the bench. 'He's sleeping peacefully and the signs are good that he'll make a full recovery,' she said as she lit a cigarette. 'But it'll be a while before he's well enough to be discharged.'

'Yes, I know. I looked in on him earlier and had a word with the doctor.' Etienne regarded the cigarette with amusement. 'I see you've succumbed at last.'

'We all smoke,' she said matter-of-factly. 'It keeps us awake and makes us forget we're hungry.' She gasped. 'Good grief. I've been so preoccupied that I forgot we've actually got proper food this evening.'

'And very nice it is too,' he replied and smiled. 'There's plenty left. We didn't eat it all.'

'Thank goodness for that.'

'I must go, Annabelle, but I just wanted to say that I think you're doing a marvellous job here, you and all the other girls.'

'It's what we're trained for,' she replied with a light shrug.

Etienne stood and mangled his cap between his grubby hands. 'Thanks for what you did for Henri,' he said almost shyly. 'I didn't realise you could be such a fierce little tiger.'

Annabelle laughed. 'I'm not usually that rude and bossy – it was exceptional circumstances.'

He took her hand and softly kissed the palm. 'You're an exceptional woman, Belle. Henri is a very lucky man.' He looked deeply into her eyes for a moment and then sauntered off.

Startled by his actions, Annabelle stared after him, and as she heard the rumble of the truck engine she left the bench so she could watch him drive away. Etienne really was the most enigmatic man she'd ever met. He could be a braggart and an outrageous flirt; could be coolly sophisticated, yet amusing and sharp-witted; and he had proved during the past months to be brave and fully dedicated to his cause and his friendship to Henri. Yet tonight he'd shown a softer, gentler side which she suspected he rarely revealed to anyone, and for the first time since meeting him, she found she really liked and admired him.

Annabelle's stomach reminded her that she hadn't eaten since breakfast, and she put all thoughts of Etienne behind her as she headed for the kitchen and the first decent meal she'd had in weeks.

11

It was the end of July now, and almost a month since Henri had been brought in. Annabelle had ensured that the wards were running smoothly before she told Marge she was taking a break. 'I'll only be outside, so if you need me . . .'

'Don't worry, Annabelle. You go and spend some time with that lovely bloke of yours, and don't fret about us.'

Annabelle hurried outside and found Henri sitting by the vegetable patch, his arm still in a sling as he tried to make Sal understand what he wanted her to do to the tomatoes.

'It's no use you gabbling away like that. I can't understand a blooming word you're saying,' she said crossly.

'He wants you to prick out the flowers and budding fruit at the top of the plant to encourage the growth of the ripening fruit at the bottom,' translated Annabelle. She smiled at Henri and switched effortlessly back to French. 'I didn't realise you were a gardening expert.'

'We had a farm, so of course I know how to grow fruit and vegetables, and if you want a decent crop, then you have to conserve the best bits.'

'It's too flaming hot to do anything,' grumbled Sal as she got to her feet and brushed the dirt off her hands. 'I'll leave you lovebirds to it.'

'Oh dear, have we frightened her away?'

Annabelle laughed. 'I doubt it. Sal's a tough Cockney sparrow, and nothing much daunts her.' She kissed him softly on the lips. 'How are you feeling this afternoon?'

'Much better, although my shoulder's still a bit stiff and sore. But at least my fingers are working properly again, which is a huge relief. I don't know what I'd have done if I couldn't draw or paint any more.'

'You'd have found a way,' she said fondly.

He lit cigarettes for them both and they sat in companionable silence in the shade of the tarpaulin, looking through the shimmering heat-haze at the village square where a few boys were kicking a football about without much enthusiasm.

'Dr Beecham thinks I'll be fit enough to go back to the Brigade in a week,' he said some time later.

Annabelle felt her spirits ebb and the dread return. 'Do you have to go back, Henri? I can't bear the thought of you getting hurt again, and it would be so much more sensible to go home to France. After all, your art is now becoming more recognised through those newspaper articles and you could easily—'

He silenced her with a light kiss. 'I'm not a deserter, Belle. And I'm not about to leave Etienne and all those other brave men to fight my cause while I paint pictures in Paris.' He kissed her again. 'We'll both get through this, you'll see.'

Annabelle was about to press her argument when they heard someone approaching.

'Ah, there you are,' said Dr Beecham as he rounded the corner and stepped out of the glare into the shade. 'I've been looking through your notes, Henri,' he said in halting schoolboy French, 'and it seems to me that you're making a splendid recovery at last. As we're so short of beds, I was wondering if you'd mind if I discharged you a little earlier than planned.'

'But he can't go back to the fighting,' gasped Annabelle. 'His shoulder wound won't withstand the kickback of a rifle, and he's still weak from the fever.'

'I am well aware of that, Staff Nurse Blake, which is why I propose to send him to a small place on the south coast where he can recuperate in the comfort of a cooler climate. It's fairly basic accommodation close to the beach, but my wife and I have enjoyed many summers down there over the years.'

Annabelle stemmed any further protest, for although she didn't want to be parted from Henri, it would certainly do him good to rest and recuperate out of the awful heat.

'There's no need to be stoic, Staff Nurse Blake,' the doctor continued with the hint of a smile. 'I couldn't possibly allow my patient to go off on his own without a capable nurse to look after him. And as you've been working tirelessly without a break for months, I think it's only right that you should accompany him.'

Annabelle stared at him, the hope and excitement rising, only to be dashed by the knowledge that her absence would put a greater strain on the others. 'But I have work here,' she began.

'There's always work here,' he said and gave her a broad grin.

'There's a truck coming from Zaragoza tomorrow morning with medical supplies and two more nurses. It will be yours for ten days, by which time you will return it to the hospital in Belchite. I've squared it with Henri's commanding officer – although he wasn't best pleased – and he will send transport to collect him. I'll also arrange for someone to pick you up, Annabelle, and bring you back here.'

Annabelle shot to her feet and threw her arms around him. 'Oh, thank you, thank you,' she said through her tears. 'You have no idea what this means to us.'

He cleared his throat and looked rather bashful. 'Oh, I think I do,' he replied gruffly. 'I was young once, you know.' He eased back from her embrace. 'I'll write down the directions and let you have them after supper.' He turned on his heel and stomped off.

'Henri,' she breathed. 'Can you believe it?'

'I would if I knew what you've been talking about,' he said with a frown. 'And why did you hug him like that? I thought you didn't like him.'

'He's a wonderful, kind, thoughtful man and I won't have a word said against him,' she said joyously, and then went on to explain what he'd done for them.

As realisation dawned, Henri's wan face broke into a broad smile. '*Ooh là là*, Miss Annabelle,' he teased. 'Are you seriously suggesting that we spend a whole ten days together . . . alone? Does that mean you trust me not to take advantage of you?'

Annabelle blushed furiously and giggled. 'If you don't take advantage of me, I'll be most upset. In fact, I might even make the first move on you, so watch out.'

'Miss Blake,' he gasped in feigned shock. 'I never realised you were that kind of girl.' They broke into happy laughter and shared a kiss before settling down to speculate on where the house might be and how long it would take to get there.

The truck arrived just after dawn, and as it drew to a halt and backfired, the girl at the wheel cheerfully hooted the horn. Turning off the engine, she and her companion climbed down to reveal sweat-stained shirts, grubby trousers and sturdy boots.

'Phew,' she said. 'I'm glad that's over.' She stuck out her hand to Dr Beecham. 'Nurse Alice Frobisher reporting for duty, sir,' she said in a Home Counties accent. 'And this is Nurse Caroline Howden.'

Annabelle heard the name as she was carrying her case up the hall. 'Caroline?' she yelled as she dropped the case and broke into a run. 'Caro? Is that really you?'

'It definitely is,' she replied as they hugged in delight. 'Though I must say, I do rather feel as if I've been dragged through a hedge backwards.'

Annabelle laughed as she took in the wild hair and the filthy clothes. Caroline's creamy complexion had been darkened by the sun, and although she was dishevelled and sweat-stained, she looked leaner and fitter than ever before. 'Oh, Caro,' she said fretfully. 'This is awful timing. I'm about to leave for the coast.'

'So it's you who's taking my truck, is it?' she laughed. 'Well, you be careful with her. I've had to baby her all the way from Zaragoza, and she can be a little temperamental.'

'I promise we'll take great care of your truck, Caro.'

Caroline's dark eyes glinted with humour as she raised a questioning brow. 'We? Who's we?'

Annabelle blushed. 'Me and Henri. We've got ten days' leave,' she replied.

Caroline looked over Annabelle's shoulder as a rather puzzled Henri appeared in the doorway carrying Annabelle's abandoned suitcase. 'Goodness,' she breathed, 'you never said anything in your letters about how dashing and handsome he is. Well *done*, Annabelle.'

Annabelle was flustered as she made the introductions and the aides were sent to help Nurse Frobisher and Dr Beecham unpack the medical supplies from the truck.

Henri greeted Caroline with his most charming smile and then carried the case and his satchel to the truck where he settled patiently into the passenger seat to wait.

'Oh, you lucky, lucky girl,' breathed Caroline.

Annabelle giggled. Caroline hadn't changed a bit. 'I know I'm lucky, but then it's about time, isn't it?' At Caroline's nod, she continued, 'But I do wish you and I could have spent more time together.' Annabelle took Caroline's grubby hand. 'I feel awful running out on you like this.'

'Don't be daft. If the boot was on the other foot, and I had someone as gorgeous as that waiting to whisk me off, you wouldn't see me for dust.' She shot Annabelle a naughty grin. 'Just promise me you'll have a wonderful time, and that you'll tell me all about it when you get back.'

Annabelle had absolutely no intention of telling her anything, for what she and Henri were planning was strictly private. 'So you're staying on here?'

Caroline giggled. 'Well, I can't go anywhere without my truck, can I?' She swept her up in a hug. 'I've missed you horribly, and it's lovely to see you looking so well and happy and fulfilled.' She drew back. 'I'll be here when you get back and we can catch up then. Now get out of here so I can go and have a wash and something to eat.'

Annabelle said goodbye to the others as the medical supplies were replaced by a canister of water and a spare can of petrol. She climbed into the truck and put on her sunglasses. 'I'm sorry about keeping you waiting, but Caro and I haven't seen each other in ages.'

He shifted on the seat, his shorts riding up a little to reveal sturdy brown knees. 'You'll see her when we get back,' he said comfortably. 'Dr Beecham told me she's here on a six-month secondment.'

Annabelle was delighted to hear this, but she too wriggled on the leather upholstery, for it was cracked and worn, the heat from it penetrating her thin dress and cotton underwear. She turned the key in the ignition and the engine coughed before it rumbled to life, making the framework rattle. 'Have you got the instructions on how to get there? And the salt tablets?'

'Yes, my darling. Now, can we go before we fry to death in this tin can?'

Annabelle grinned, eased off the handbrake, and with a happy wave to Caroline and the others who were watching from the hospital entrance, she put her foot down on the accelerator and headed along the rough track which would lead them to the main highway and eventually the blue waters of the Mediterranean.

Annabelle climbed back into the truck and fleetingly admired Henri's tanned and muscled legs as she placed the bag of provisions on the floor by his booted feet. The small shop and wine store had been very well stocked considering how out of the way it was, and it meant they wouldn't have to shop again for at least another few days.

She turned the key, adjusted her sunglasses, and set off once more. She was tired and her eyes felt gritty after staring through the scratched windscreen at the bright landscape, but it would be worth it, she just knew. She had been driving all day and her dress was sticking to her from the heat, but despite her weariness and discomfort, she couldn't quell the nervous excitement that kept bubbling up inside her.

'Are you sure you don't want me to take over the driving?' said Henri for the umpteenth time. 'I feel so bad, not to be doing something useful.'

'You can't drive,' she reminded him yet again. 'Your shoulder's too stiff and it will give you pain. Besides, you've kept me awake and amused with your stories, so you've been very useful.'

'I wonder how the fighting's going,' he murmured as he tried to find the military waveband through the heavy static on the radio. 'The news that the Nationalists regained Brunete will mean the Republicans will be looking for another Basque target.'

Annabelle reached over and switched the radio off. 'We agreed there'd be no talk of war in the next ten days,' she said over the rattle and roar of the engine. 'This is to be our time away from the rest of the world and all its troubles.'

'Yes, you're right.' He settled back in the seat with a sigh of contentment and reached for the roughly drawn map and list of instructions Dr Beecham had given him that morning. 'We'll need to turn left at the next crossroads, and that will lead us through a small forest and straight down to the coast.'

They travelled in companionable silence as they followed the turning and headed through the pine and eucalyptus trees that formed a dappled archway over the narrow road. The temperature was already several degrees cooler and the tang of the sea was heavy in the air.

As the road became a dirt track and wound its way up a gentle incline, Annabelle's pulse began to race. And then, as they crested the hill, she gasped with pleasure and brought the truck to a halt.

There, spread before them in a sparkling blaze of azure blue, was the Mediterranean, and on the horizon were the hazy blue smudges of islands. Trees bordered an arc of golden sand where plovers and gulls fished in the shallows of the gently rippling waves; headlands on either side of the horseshoe bay were green with pines and covered in vibrantly coloured wild flowers, the tumbled red rocks forming a natural sheltering harbour.

They were in awe as they climbed out of the truck and silently linked hands to walk slowly down the gentle slope to discover the small, white wooden cabin nestled in amongst the trees, scarlet bougainvillea spilling over the roof and down the walls.

As Annabelle regarded the bright blue shutters at the windows, and the startlingly orange terracotta tiles on the roof, she heard the birdsong and the soft hiss of the waves against the sand. 'It's perfect,' she breathed.

Henri fished the key out of his pocket and shot her a rueful smile. 'I feel I should carry you over the threshold,' he said, 'but I don't think it's possible.'

She kissed his cheek and laughed. 'Just get the door open, I want to explore.'

On closer inspection the paint on the walls and shutters was weathered, the bougainvillea was pushing tendrils through gaps in the woodwork and, as they opened the door, they could smell the trapped heat and mustiness of a place that hadn't been used in a while. And yet everything was so delightful they could ignore these minor problems.

They grinned at one another and hurried inside to throw open the windows and shutters to let in the clean salty air and bright sunlight. They excitedly explored the main room, with its sturdy stone hearth and chimney breast, the faded couches and sun-bleached curtains. Double doors led out to a narrow veranda where a jumble of deckchairs, fishing nets and rods and beach balls were stacked beneath a weathered awning. A shallow step led to the makeshift boardwalk, which lay partially covered by sand and reached almost to the high-tide mark.

The kitchen was basic, with just a sink, a cold tap, two gas rings, and a few shelves lining the walls. There were a table and chairs, some pots, cutlery and china stacked onto a wooden draining board, and the real luxury of a gas fridge. Beyond the kitchen door was a square walled area open to the sky where a cold water shower had been rigged up. The outside lavatory bore only a momentary inspection and they hurried back in to see what else there was.

The one bedroom was quaintly furnished with a large, ornate brass bedstead, on which sat a thick horsehair mattress and two rather lumpy pillows. There was a small dressing table and stool, a faded Spanish rug on the dusty floor, a chest of drawers and an amateurish picture of a flamenco dancer on the wall above a clothing rail.

They stood, hand in hand, looking at the bed, both suddenly shy and awkward in the knowledge that this was where they would sleep tonight.

Annabelle was the first to break the spell by releasing Henri's hand and searching through the small chest of drawers. 'Oh, look, swimsuits,' she said as she held them up. 'One each, thank goodness. I thought we'd have to bathe in our underwear.'

Blushing furiously, she opened the large cedar chest that stood at the end of the bed and discovered it was full of linen and towels. 'Why don't you go and fetch our provisions while I sort this room out and make us both something to drink?' she said, unable to look him in the eye.

Henri nodded and his hasty retreat told her he was feeling just as awkward.

She quickly opened the windows and threw back the shutters to let the fresh air in, and then made the bed and covered it with the handmade lace spread. The linen was good quality, and surprisingly still dry and crisp, and the lace-edged pillowcases added a touch of luxury.

She stood and regarded the bed, her heart beating rapidly. Henri would be the first man she'd slept with, and she felt a tiny thrill shoot through her as her imagination took flight.

Her pleasant and rather erotic thoughts were dispelled by the sound of the front door slamming, and she hurried out to find that he'd taken off the sling and was putting the food away in the kitchen.

'Shall I try and make us a cup of tea?' she asked, sure that he could tell from her flushed face what she'd recently been thinking.

'I've got a much better idea,' he replied, turning away from the gas fridge and holding up a bottle of wine, a corkscrew and two glasses. 'Let's go down to the beach and celebrate the start of our holiday.'

She gathered up a blanket from the back of a couch as they passed through the main room. Stepping through the doors, they walked over the strips of planed wood which formed the sandy boardwalk, and then sat down on the blanket to take off their footwear and plant the bottle in the sand.

The warm sand trickled deliciously between her toes as they held hands and moved away from the shade of the trees into the bright, hot sunlight that was tempered by a cooling sea breeze. The crystal-clear water was just cool enough to be refreshing, and they paddled and splashed and foolishly grinned at one another as they found pretty shells and pieces of driftwood, or spotted a crab making a quick getaway from his hole in the sand.

As they stood in the water and looked back at the little house, they could see that the beach was hidden from prying eyes on all sides, the sand smooth and marked only by the tracks of birds as the waves gently lapped around their feet. Birds sang in the trees, the sea sparkled beneath a bleached sky, and the salty breeze was a caress. It was their private paradise.

'It's perfect, isn't it?' she breathed.

'It's you who is perfect,' he replied as he smiled into her eyes and softly kissed her cheek. 'Come on, let's have some of that wine before the sun goes down.'

They strolled slowly back to the blanket, and Henri opened the wine expertly and poured some into the glasses. 'I hope it's not too rough,' he said almost shyly.

She was equally as bashful as she smiled back at him. 'It was very cheap, but it doesn't matter.' She took a sip and found it was fruity and velvety on her tongue.

'Mmm. Not bad,' said Henri. 'Though I wish we could have found some champagne.'

The wine was rich and red and, with dappled sunlight making patterns on the blanket, the sea sighing on the sand, and the scent of mimosa drifting from the surrounding forest, it was perfect. They had no need for champagne.

Annabelle took another sip and set the glass aside. Looking across at him, she noted how blue his eyes were in his tanned face, and how their steady gaze made her insides tighten with wanting.

He set aside his own glass and reached out to softly trace the line of her cheekbones and chin with his fingers.

Annabelle sat very still, afraid to break the spell he was weaving.

He ran his hand over her hair and captured a curl, which he coiled around his finger before tucking it behind her ear. 'My beautiful Belle,' he breathed as he tenderly ran his fingers down her throat and followed the arch of her neck.

Annabelle's heart was thudding as spirals of delight prickled her skin and made her languid at the hypnotic touch of his fingers. She closed her eyes as his caress moved to her collarbone, tracing its path beneath her skin to the hollow at the base of her throat.

'Look at me, Belle,' he whispered.

Her breath was shallow and uneven, her reflection was in his eyes, and as his gentle fingers once more followed the curve of her throat she saw his pupils widen and heard the rasp of his breath.

She was trembling now, the yearning spiralling through her as she touched his beloved face and followed its strong contours. There was a cleft in his chin beneath the dark six o'clock shadow, and a small scar marred one of his high cheekbones. His brows were dark and silky beneath her fingers, and she traced the laughter lines around his eyes and softly brushed her finger against the thick black lashes.

Henri's dark blue eyes mesmerised her as he softly traced the curve and swell of her lips and explored the tender flesh inside.

Annabelle placed her hand over his heart and could feel the heat of his skin through the thin shirt. She was weak with longing, her senses swirling in the heady, unfamiliar desire that was threatening to take her to the very edge of something she knew would be wonderful. She moaned softly and arched her back, her whole being crying out for him to hold her, to love and possess her.

He gently slid his arm round her, bent his head and, after a breathless moment, kissed her deeply.

She melted into him, pressing against him, her yearning body demanding to become one with him, and as they slowly lay back on the blanket she could feel herself opening up to him like a flower to the sun.

12

Etienne had survived the brutal attack on Brunete, and although he'd suffered a bullet wound to his thigh, it hadn't been considered serious enough by his commanding officer to warrant a stay in hospital. He'd had the bullet removed and the wound cleaned and stitched at a field hospital and within hours was sent straight back into the fighting. When it was over and the Nationalists had claimed a surprising victory, the men of the Brigade were given a few days' leave and he'd managed to hitch a lift to his family home which lay just north of San Sebastián in the French Basque region.

His family had been delighted and relieved to see him, for although their part of the Basque region hadn't been badly hit by Franco's fascists, they had heard of the ferocious fighting and suspected that he'd taken part in it. He spent a pleasant three days with them, visiting Henri's family and assuring them that their son was recovering well from his injuries, and that he was due back from his respite by the sea very soon.

He packed his bag on the last day as the sun was beginning to sink behind the Pyrenees to the west. His mother was tearful as she cupped his face in her work-worn hands. 'Go back to Paris,' she begged. 'This war is taking too many young men, and I don't want you to come to any more harm.'

'I'd be shot as a deserter,' he said as he pulled her into his arms. Her head reached only to his midriff, and he bent over to kiss her hair, which he noticed had more silver in it than he'd remembered – somehow this made their parting more poignant. 'We'll help to win this war, Henri and I, and when it's over, we'll come home for a long visit. I promise.'

She looked up at him, her dark eyes swimming with tears, her face lined with grief. 'We're proud of you both,' she managed. 'God be with you, my son.'

He hugged her to himself fiercely and then quickly stepped outside to join his father, Xabier, who was waiting with the horses. They would ride to San Sebastián, where someone from the Brigade had arranged to meet Etienne to take him by truck to the camp at Logroño, and then his father would make the long journey back with both horses.

'Your mother has one son,' Xabier said gruffly. 'You must forgive her tears.' His weathered face and black eyes held a determined pride. 'I am proud of you, Etienne. Never forget that.' He clamped a heavy, gnarled hand on Etienne's shoulder for a moment, and then swung up into the saddle. 'We have a long ride ahead of us,' he muttered. 'No point in wasting the last of the light.'

Etienne sat on the back of his horse and looked once more at the adobe house that had been his childhood home, smiled encouragingly at his tearful mother who was standing in the doorway, and gazed longingly at the fields where his sisters and cousins were harvesting the last of the summer crops and tilling the soil for autumn planting. This was home, and he had no idea when he would see it again, and although it was tempting to remain in the French part of the Basque region and make his way back to Paris, his homeland was worth fighting for – perhaps even dying for – and he knew he couldn't live with the shame of abandoning the cause and his comrades, or disappointing his father.

He turned the horse's head away from the pastures of France towards the coastal route that would take him back into Spain.

They had left the idyllic beachside house very early that morning, and as Henri drove the truck along the main highway, and their moment of parting drew nearer, Annabelle rested her hand on his knee and began jealously to hoard all the precious memories of their days together.

The swimsuits had never been used during those long, hot days that had drifted by in a haze of love and languor. They'd swum naked in the sea, made love on the beach and in the big brass bed; had cooked food on fires of driftwood they'd foraged from the beach, and drunk wine as they lay on the blanket and looked up at the stars.

He'd made her a necklace of shells, and carved their names in the bark of a gnarled tree that dipped its branches close to the water's edge, and when she was still sated and drowsy from their lovemaking, had painted watercolours of her in his sketchbook. She had one of them pressed flat at the bottom of her suitcase, which she would treasure forever.

She looked out of the scarred, dusty windscreen to the horizon where she could see the bell tower of a church rising from the surrounding huddle of terracotta roofs which shimmered in the heat haze. They were almost there.

Henri pulled the truck over to the side of the road and switched off the engine. Wordlessly, he drew her to him and held her close. When he kissed her it was filled with emotion, and their tears mingled as they pressed their cheeks together.

'I'll always love you, my Belle,' he said hoarsely. 'And when this war is over, we'll be married and never have to be apart again.'

Annabelle clung to him, the silver and garnet ring on her finger now a constant reminder of the promises they'd made one another. 'I love you so much,' she breathed. 'Please don't let anything happen to you. I couldn't bear it.'

He kissed away her tears with such tenderness that she thought her heart would break. And then he was drawing away from her, turning the key in the ignition and steering the truck back onto the road. The real world lay just on the horizon, where someone would be waiting to take Henri back to the fighting, and she would be returned to Santa Rosa. Annabelle dried her tears and lit cigarettes for both of them, staring out of the window as the elegant buildings and ancient church tower came into clearer focus.

Belchite wasn't a big town, but the buildings were rather grand, many built with bricks made from the pale ochre earth that surrounded it. Its streets were narrow and cobbled, and the magnificent church stood regally at its boundary, the lovely stained-glass windows looking out on the deserted sweep of land that seemed to reach every horizon. They drove slowly through the town and found the hospital, which was a small building tucked away down a side street, but decided not to deliver the truck there, but to explore further as they had made better time than expected, and every moment they could be alone together was precious.

'It's been a while since breakfast,' said Henri as he parked the truck opposite a row of tall grey buildings with wrought-iron Juliet balconies gracing every window. 'I can see a bakery down there. How about I buy us some fresh bread and cheese, or some pastries for a picnic?'

'That would be lovely, and while you go to the bakery, I'll find some wine. I saw a place just as we turned the last corner.'

He kissed her lightly on the lips and then hurried away whistling, his satchel swinging from his shoulder. Annabelle dug her purse out of her bag and set off in the opposite direction in search of the *bodega* she'd spotted earlier.

It was dark and cool as she stepped inside, and as her eyes adjusted to the gloom, she saw that it had a whole wall devoted to bottles of wine, and on the counter was a tapped barrel which probably contained the rougher local wine. Her Spanish was good enough now to be able to ask the shopkeeper if she could taste the wine in the barrel before she purchased some.

As he poured some into a glass, they both became aware of a distant rumble. He shrugged and handed her the glass. 'It's very hot today,' he said. 'That's probably thunder. We've been expecting a storm for the last two weeks.'

Annabelle took the glass to the doorway and looked up at the cloudless sky as she sipped the rather pleasant wine. The rumble was still distant, yet she noticed how the birds seemed troubled, for they were flying in great swarms from their roosts in the rooftops and crying out in alarm.

She was aware of the shopkeeper coming to stand next to her, and they both stiffened as they realised the thunder was actually the roar of many planes. She exchanged a glance with him. 'Are they ours or theirs?' she asked.

He shrugged and shielded his eyes with his hand as he scoured the sky. 'The enemy has no reason to attack us,' he said. 'We're not important.'

Annabelle was about to reply when a Fiat fighter shrieked overhead, guns rattling as bullets thudded along the street and into the walls of the houses. She ducked instinctively, and as the red wine spilled from the glass onto the white-painted stone floor, another Fiat screamed overhead, to be closely followed by many more.

'Quick, quick! This way!' He grabbed her arm, yanked her from the doorway and into the deep gloom at the back of the shop, where he pressed her down beside him behind the solid wooden counter.

'I have to find Henri,' she yelled above the rattle of machine guns and the screeching plane engines.

'You must stay here,' he shouted back, his eyes wide with terror as bullets thudded into the roof and stitched a line along the front wall of his shop.

Annabelle cowered behind the counter, frantic with fear for

Henri. She had to get to him, but it would be suicidal to go out in this. All she could hope was that he too had found somewhere to hide.

The screech and whine of the Fiats was now drowned out by the sound of heavy bombers and the crump and crash of many explosions. The building shook and trembled and bottles began to fall from the shelves and shatter onto the floor. Bullets twanged and zipped against metal, stone and cobbles and the church bell rang out discordantly as it was repeatedly struck.

Then the earth shook with a mighty explosion that shattered the windows and sent lethal shards of glass winging through the air. Annabelle and the shopkeeper cringed and trembled at the onslaught, and they both cried out in alarm as they heard the loud, ominous groan of a nearby building that was about to collapse.

They waited, breathlessly and in dread, as slowly but surely the groan became louder and they heard the shatter of glass, the screams and snaps of wooden beams breaking under the pressure – and then, finally, the inevitable crash of falling masonry.

A great cloud of thick, choking dust swept in through the entrance and they covered their faces and stayed low behind the counter as it slowly settled over them. Distant booms and bangs and crumps continued to vibrate in the floor, and when Annabelle next dared to look up, she gasped in horror. A long, jagged crack had opened up in the wall behind them.

'We have to get out,' she yelled over the heavy-bellied roar of the enemy bombers. 'Or we'll be trapped when that wall comes down. Is there another way out?'

He shook his head, his face and hair grey with dust, his eyes wild with fear.

Annabelle realised he was frozen with terror, and although she was more frightened than she'd ever been, she knew it was up to her to get them out. 'Come on,' she urged, tugging at his arm. 'We have to move.'

He whimpered and curled into a tight ball as he tried to crawl between the shelves beneath the counter. 'No, no. It's not safe.'

Another explosion brought the front wall down and there was an ominous creaking coming from the roof as the jagged crack behind them began to spread and open. She grabbed his arm and in her fear, managed to find the strength to get him to his feet. 'The roof's about to—'

The rafter holding the roof snapped under the pressure and plaster rained down on them as terracotta tiles slid and smashed on the floor and the stone chimney breast began to crack and crumble. The fissure in the back wall had deepened and the whole thing was now terrifyingly unstable.

Annabelle kept a tight hold of the man's arm and dragged him over the rubble of his shopfront. She couldn't see anything in the thick clouds of dust, but she could smell burning and hear the thunder of the returning bombers. She hustled him over the unstable piles of debris that littered the street, her only focus on getting to the bakery.

As the explosions rocked the ground beneath their feet and the buildings around them began to disintegrate, the returning Fiats strafed with their guns and the bombers continued to drop their deadly cargo. Annabelle felt the wind of the whining bullets as they zipped past her and looked frantically for a place to hide.

She eventually spotted a steep flight of steps leading to somewhere dark, and without pausing to consider whether it was wise, she kept hold of the terrified man and plunged down them.

It proved to be the cellar of a house which had been completely demolished by a direct hit, and she cowered with the shopkeeper at the bottom of the steps as wave upon wave of enemy planes reduced the town of Belchite to rubble. There was nowhere to run, nowhere to hide. They were under siege, and Annabelle mewled in terror.

The raid seemed to last for hours, but when the last of the planes finally droned away into the distance, Annabelle realised it had been less than forty-five minutes. She held the shopkeeper's hand as they tentatively climbed the steps which were now littered with shards of terracotta and broken masonry, and dared to look out into the street.

It resembled a scene from Dante's *Inferno* for the devastation was total. The skeletal remains of buildings stood open to the skies, the pathetic remnants of people's lives on display as torn curtains fluttered from empty windows and dust-laden furniture teetered on the brink of shattered floors, whilst precious belongings lay in a jumble of burning wreckage on the street below.

The once graceful balconies now lay in twisted heaps across the cobbles and the church tower and roof were gone. The shattered remains of the walls revealed ancient frescoes destroyed beyond repair, and the empty arches of the once beautiful windows were stark against the bright blue sky. Intricately carved stonework was pitted with machine gun bullets, and the stench of burning came from the roiling, greasy black clouds that blotted out the sun and sent ash raining down to choke and stifle.

Annabelle put her handkerchief over her nose and mouth, while the shopkeeper could only stare in horror at the ruins of his business. Nothing remained but a burning pile of rubble. She squeezed his arm in sympathy and as he stumbled towards it, she picked her way over the debris that lay in great mounds across the narrow street.

'Henri!' she called, coughing on the smoke and ash that was clogging her throat. 'Henri, where are you?'

The screams of women trapped in the remains of their homes rose to meet the cry of children and shouts of men as those who'd survived the onslaught and were able to walk shook off their numbed disbelief and began to dig into the rubble to free them.

As Annabelle's search for Henri became more frantic, her light shoes slipped over the shifting tiles and bits of wood that lay in a jumble of twisted lead piping, electricity wires and the pathetic remnants of people's belongings. Disorientated and terrified, she tried to find some point of reference, but it was impossible.

'Henri!' she called. 'Henri, where are you?'

There was no reply amid the screams of the terrified and injured and she ploughed on, coughing and spluttering, the fear growing. She found the truck jammed beneath a thick mound of rubble, the roof caved in, the doors buckled and the windows gone but for jagged shards. Debris lay across the seat, and she could see her handbag lying on the floor.

Reaching in past the lethal stilettos of glass, she managed to pluck it out of the mess, and then forced the back doors open so she could get to her case. She didn't want to risk Henri's precious painting getting damaged or lost.

'Annabelle? Annabelle, where are you?'

She turned towards the sound of his voice, her spirits rising with joy and relief as she clambered onto the truck's bonnet to try to see him through the swirling smoke and dust. 'Henri! Henri, I'm over here!' she shouted back.

And there he was, herding a group of terrified women and children out of a cellar. Annabelle was overwhelmed with relief, and she almost fell from the bonnet in her eagerness to get him to see her. 'I'm here, Henri! I'm all right!'

He finally spotted her and waved, but his full attention was on the women and children as he helped them negotiate their way around a fiercely burning building.

Annabelle lost sight of him as the clouds of choking black smoke belched from the ruins. She clambered down from the truck, grabbed her case, and was about to struggle towards him when Etienne appeared from a side street. His face was streaked with soot, sweat and ash, and there was blood on his forehead.

'What are you doing here? Are you hurt? Let me see.'

He waved away her concern. 'I'm fine. I'm here to take Henri back to base. Where is he?'

'He's further down the road, leading some women and children to safety. I have to get to him, Etienne.'

'Thank God you're both alive,' he replied as he took her case and helped her over the debris of someone's home. 'It's a miracle anyone survived.'

Annabelle's eyes were stinging from the acrid smoke, and she could feel the oiliness of it on her skin and in the back of her throat as she slipped and slithered her way down the street towards the place she'd last seen Henri.

And then the unmistakable sound of enemy planes brought a second wave of destruction, their bombs and bullets tearing into the survivors and bringing down the few remaining walls of the buildings.

Etienne yanked her into the deep shadows of a broken pillar as the Fiats' machine guns rained down death. A bomb went off nearby, but Annabelle hardly flinched, for she was completely focused on Henri and the small group he was trying to shepherd into the lee of a building.

As the Fiat screamed through the canyon of the shattered town, its guns opened fire, and before anyone in the little group could escape, they were mown down.

'No!' she screamed. 'No, Henri!' She fought against Etienne's grip, but he was too strong and she couldn't get away. And as they watched in horror, the building from which Henri had been taking the group began to sway. Huge cracks opened up and masonry clattered onto the bodies beneath it, and then slowly, almost majestically, it sagged and crumbled with a resounding crash and a vast cloud of dust.

The bombers droned away, swiftly followed by their cohorts of Italian Fiats and Russian fighters, and a deathly silence fell. The crackle of burning wood and shifting rubble, and the clouds of smoke and bright orange flames lit the scene of carnage, and Annabelle could only stare in horror and disbelief at the place where she'd last seen Henri.

'Stay there and don't move,' ordered a grim-faced Etienne. 'I'll go and find him.'

She did as she was told for once, numb with terror and unable to move even if she'd wanted to. 'He can't be dead,' she muttered. 'He mustn't be dead. Please, please God, don't let him be dead.'

People once more emerged from their hiding-places and rushed to where Etienne was urging them to start digging. 'There are women and children under here,' he yelled. 'We have to get to them quickly.'

Annabelle stood in a trance as the frantic digging began. She saw men and women and even children tossing aside the debris and burrowing down, but when one of the women screamed and cradled the limp body of a child, Annabelle was galvanised into action.

She stumbled and tripped and slid to get to the site, and began to dig with her hands, desperate to find Henri.

Etienne dragged her away. 'There are only bodies under there,' he said grimly.

'You don't know that,' she screamed at him. 'He could be alive and fighting to get out. We have to keep digging.' She tore away from him and began to sling the debris aside, desperate for some sign that there was still life beneath it all.

They dug for over two hours and found the mangled bodies of two women and five children. They all bore the wounds of bullets, and had been crushed beneath the weight of the fallen building.

Annabelle continued to dig, the tears streaming down her face. 'Henri,' she sobbed. 'Henri, speak to me. Please, darling, be alive.'

She found the crushed and bloodied remains of two small children who were still holding hands as they'd been mown down by the machine guns, and it was too much. She collapsed onto the ground, her wails of despair mingling with those of the other women.

'I'm here, Annabelle,' said Etienne softly as he drew her to her feet and into his arms. He cradled her against his chest, his own tears coursing unheeded down his cheeks. 'It's over, Belle. He's gone from us.'

Annabelle knew in her heart that she would never see Henri again, but how could he be gone? How could such a vibrant, talented life be snuffed out so swiftly and completely, taking with it the hopes and dreams and plans they'd made for their future together?

The pain wracked her, the tears coming from a deep well of sorrow as she replayed the scene repeatedly in her head. She clung to Etienne, glad of his solid presence and his strong arms that kept her from falling to her knees, but they weren't Henri's arms – and she would never feel them around her again.

'Come, Belle. We must get you back to Santa Rosa where your friends can help you get over this.'

'I'll never get over it,' she rasped through her tears. 'Never, never.'

He said nothing as he retrieved her case and bag and began to steer her back over the debris.

Annabelle was in a world of pain as she clutched the case containing Henri's painting and allowed Etienne to lead her away, her legs moving automatically, her eyes blinded with tears and acrid smoke. She no longer cared what happened to her, or where she went, for without Henri her life meant nothing.

She didn't hear the blast of the unexploded bomb, but felt the heavy blow to her back which ripped her hand from Etienne's and sent her flying. She hit the ground with a bone-jarring thud and knew no more.

13

George had had to be rather firm with Felicity Jenkins, for she'd become overfamiliar and was beginning to make sheep's eyes at him, hinting that perhaps they might go out to the theatre or for a drink. He found such situations painfully difficult and had struggled to be tactful and carefully polite, whereas he would have preferred just to tell her straight that he wasn't at all interested. Yet he'd managed to get the message across that he was perfectly happy being on his own and had no intention of being anything other than her employer.

It had all been horribly awkward, and since then she'd been quite frosty, and he hoped it didn't mean she was about to hand in her notice, for she was an excellent and efficient secretary and the practice would be lost without her.

As August drifted into September and Felicity still remained at her desk, he had to assume that she'd forgiven him and perhaps placed her affections elsewhere, for which he was profoundly relieved. He hated awkward situations – especially when they involved young women – and anyway, all the while he was still haunted by memories of Annabelle he simply couldn't begin to consider another relationship. He knew it was ridiculous to feel so strongly about a girl who clearly didn't love him, but there it was, and there seemed to be absolutely nothing he could damned well do about it.

The late September sunshine was warm, and he was sitting outside on a rare afternoon off, enjoying the tranquillity of his garden as he sipped from a glass of very good Irish whiskey. He was feeling pleasantly tired after his game of golf and looking forward to meeting some of his friends this evening at the rugby club to discuss the next season's fixtures.

He lit his pipe, his thoughts – as always in these quiet moments – turning to Annabelle. He hadn't heard from her since July, and his deepest concern was that something might have happened to her. Silently cursing the unreliable Spanish postal system and the civil war in general, he took another sip of his whiskey and decided to remain positive. No news generally meant nothing of note had happened.

He was distracted by the sound of raised voices, and he turned to see Felicity hurrying towards him. 'Dr Ashton, I'm sorry but this woman insists upon—'

Caroline pushed past her. 'George. Thank goodness you're at home.'

One glance at her face told him everything and his pleasant mood was swept away in a great wave of dread. 'What is it, Caroline? What's happened?'

'Now, you're not to panic, George. Annabelle is alive and expected to make a full recovery.' She turned back to Felicity, who was still looking disgruntled. 'Would you mind giving us some privacy?'

Felicity stomped off and Caroline took George's arm. 'I know this must come as a terrible shock, but really and truly, George, Annabelle is on the mend.'

'What happened? Where is she?'

'Annabelle was hurt in a bombing raid. It was thanks to Etienne, who, despite his own injuries, managed to get her medical help, that she's still alive. She was taken to a field hospital in Logroño – where the Brigade has its HQ – and initially treated there before being transferred by hospital train to Toulouse and then a short while later on to Paris. Once she's deemed well enough, she'll go to Aline's and recuperate there.'

His heart was thudding. 'How badly was she hurt?'

Caroline lit a cigarette with an unsteady hand. 'She and Etienne were luckily some way from the unexploded bomb when it went off, but they suffered several broken bones, and some internal injuries. Annabelle has some scarring from the burns, but the doctors are hopeful that they'll fade as they were considered superficial.'

'And the internal injuries?'

'They had to remove her spleen and one of her kidneys,' she replied softly.

'I must go to her.' He took a step towards the house and she blocked his way.

'Before you go rushing off, there are a few other things you should know, George.'

He found that his legs simply wouldn't support him, so he sank into the chair. 'Then you'd better tell me – and don't prevaricate, Caroline, tell me everything and be truthful about it.'

Caroline's expression was serious as she carefully told him about Annabelle and Henri's romance, their short holiday together, and the ensuing tragedy that had befallen him. 'The town was completely flattened and the few survivors have abandoned it, so there's no news coming out of that area. But Etienne assured me that no one could possibly have been left alive beneath that rubble.'

George's stomach knotted at the thought that his beloved Annabelle had loved another so utterly that she'd given herself to him. He gripped the arms of the garden seat, his jaw clenched in the effort to remain calm and think things through their logical progression. Annabelle and Henri were in the midst of a war, and he could understand that in such times of great upheaval and strife senses and emotions could be heightened; that the excitement and danger inevitably led to the very human need for love and comfort. But the awful images of her lying in another man's arms almost broke him.

'I see,' he said, careful not to let Caroline see the emotions that were raging inside him. 'But you say she's recovering from her wounds, that the prognosis is positive?'

Caroline nodded. 'But she's grieving, George, and that won't help speed up her recovery. At least now she's in Paris, she has Aline to watch over her.'

George regarded Caroline and noticed for the first time that she had dark shadows beneath her eyes, and that her tanned face was drawn and lined. 'You didn't come back to England just to tell me about Annabelle, did you?'

She shook her head, and there was a hitch in her voice as she replied, 'I got leave to travel up to Paris to be with Annabelle, but I hadn't been there for more than a few days when word came through that Bertram had been killed.' She sniffed back her tears. 'With both my brothers gone, I had to come home. My poor parents are devastated, and I couldn't put them through any more worry.'

'Oh, Caroline,' he sighed. 'I'm so sorry.'

'Pa was right,' she said fiercely as she swept away the tears. 'War is vicious and cruel. But at least Annabelle and Etienne are still alive. They were incredibly lucky.'

George awkwardly patted her hand, unable to think of anything to say in the light of such raw pain. 'When do you think Annabelle will be well enough to come home?'

Caroline shrugged. 'It will depend on what future plans she has.' She chewed her bottom lip. 'There are certain deciding factors which will make it very difficult for her if she comes back here,' she said hesitantly. 'She certainly won't want to go home to Camille and Edwin; and although I'm sure they'd agree immediately, my parents are in no fit state to look after her.'

'She can come here. I'll take care of her.'

'Oh, George, that's very dear of you, but it wouldn't do at all, don't you see?'

'Nonsense,' he retorted. 'Do you think I care a fig about what the gossips might say? And what are these deciding factors you're talking about?'

Caroline's gaze dropped as she stubbed out her cigarette. 'Medical ones,' she said quietly.

'There you are then,' he said flatly. 'I'm clearly the best person to look after her, so I'll go to Paris and bring her home with me whether she likes it or not.'

'Oh, George,' she sighed. 'Please try and be tactful just for once and don't bully her into anything she doesn't want.'

'What sort of man do you think I am, Caroline? Of course I won't bully her. I shall simply point out that the best place for her is here in England with me, and that she'd be very foolish not to accept my help.'

Caroline chuckled. 'Best of luck with that, George. She can be as stubborn as you at times, and I'd like to be a fly on the wall when that conversation takes place.'

It was the second day in October and a fire was blazing in the hearth as Annabelle rested against the pillows that Aline had placed on the couch. It was good to be out of the hospital at last and the sight of the familiar clutter and jarring colours was strangely comforting after the pristine coolness of white walls and shiny bare floors.

'I've made tea the way you like it,' said Aline. 'And Miriam has brought you a slice of her delicious chocolate gateau as a little treat.'

'It's so good to see you home again,' said Miriam as she fussed over the cake and the china. 'You'll get better much quicker now, I'm sure.'

Annabelle's smile was wan, and she could feel the onset of

tears again. 'You've all been so kind,' she murmured. 'But please don't think you have to fuss over me. I know how busy you all are, and I want to do my share around the house.'

'Of course we must make a fuss,' said Aline as she plumped the pillows. 'You are our precious girl, and we have to take great care of you, especially now.'

Annabelle's fingers softly moved over her flat stomach. 'It's a miracle, isn't it?' she breathed.

'It certainly is, which is why you must be cossetted and spoilt,' said Aline. 'And I'll hear no more about you helping around the house. Goodness knows I avoid housework as much as possible. Life is too short to be worrying about cobwebs and a bit of dust.'

Annabelle felt the prick of tears as she thought of the tiny life that was growing inside her. Henri's last and most precious gift had defied the dire warnings of the surgeons and doctors and survived. This baby would be cherished and treasured, for it was the living proof of the love she and Henri had shared.

'Try not to be sad, Annabelle,' said Miriam in her heavily accented French. 'Henri lives on in your child, and when he or she is old enough to understand, you can talk of him and ensure that his memory never fades.'

'Thank you, Miriam. How is it that you're so wise?'

She shrugged. 'Malachi and I have lost many loved ones over the years, and we've been moved from place to place so often that we are like gypsies. Our home is where we are together, and our lost are never forgotten, for they are always in our hearts.'

Annabelle squeezed her hand in empathy and wondered what her own future held. She was safe and secure with Aline for the moment, but once the baby was born she couldn't expect her aunt to keep them both. It would be impossible to return to her parents, and equally impossible to foist herself on the Howdens after all they'd suffered. With the shadow of her father's spite still looming over any future employment in London, and with very little money to support herself, let alone a baby, she had run out of options.

'Mind the cat. *Ooh là là!*' screeched Napoleon.

Mignonette slunk past the cage and jumped lightly into Aline's lap where she curled up in a purring furry ball.

There was a sudden series of sharp raps on the door, and to Napoleon's shouts of 'Come in, come in. Mind the cat,' Aline carefully transposed Mignonette from her lap onto a cushion and went to answer it.

Annabelle tried her best to enjoy a few morsels of Miriam's cake, but she had little appetite still. She sipped from the cup of tea as Aline talked to someone at the front door, and was about to speculate on who it was when Aline returned looking flushed and rather animated.

'Annabelle, you have a visitor,' she said.

She frowned. 'I'm not really feeling bright enough to have visitors,' she replied. 'Who is it?'

'It's me.' A grim-faced, determined-looking George strode in.

She gasped in surprise, and felt more than a touch of trepidation, for he did look horribly serious and much too masculine for this cluttered, very feminine room. 'Good heavens,' she breathed as she tried to struggle off the sagging couch.

'Stay where you are,' he ordered as he hurried forward and pressed her back against the cushions. 'You shouldn't move about after such a serious operation.'

She saw how his gaze swept over her face to the ugly puckering of skin on her neck, cheek and wrist, and wondered what he was thinking.

'You're far too thin,' he said in a gentler tone, 'but those scars are only superficial and will fade eventually.'

'That's what the doctor told me,' she replied. 'It's lovely to see you, George, but what on earth are you doing here?'

He sat on the end of the couch and looked down at her, his blue eyes so intense that they made her feel uncomfortable. 'Caroline told me what had happened to you, so I've come to take you home.'

'I will make more tea,' murmured Aline. 'Miriam, perhaps you could come and help me?'

The two women left the room, but neither Annabelle nor George really noticed, so intent were they upon each other. Annabelle's hand fluttered nervously over her scarred cheek, sure that he must find it ugly.

'You don't have to hide that from me,' he said gruffly. 'You're still beautiful.'

Annabelle realised George was in a strange sort of mood, and if he wasn't to turn difficult about things, she'd have to handle him carefully. 'I look a complete fright,' she replied, 'but thanks for the compliment.'

'I went to the hospital before coming here, and spoke to one of the doctors who managed to understand my schoolboy

French. He said you were to rest as much as possible, but that you would soon be fit enough to travel back to England.'

'I can't go back there,' she replied firmly.

'Don't be ridiculous. England is your home and I'm suitably qualified to take over your care.'

'That you might be, but I'm not going back.'

His jaw tightened and his blue eyes became rather fierce. 'Caroline told me all about you and Henri and I realise you'll find it difficult to settle after all that's happened, but I'm here to offer practical help with your accommodation and finding work.'

'George, that's very kind, but—'

High spots of colour showed in his cheeks. 'I'm not doing this out of kindness, Annabelle. I'm here because I love you. Really, you are the most exasperating woman I've ever met.'

Annabelle bridled at this. 'Don't bully me, George, and if this is your roundabout way of making another proposal, then you'd be wise to stop right there.'

She watched him take a deep breath and knew he was struggling to keep his emotions under control. 'I'm not about to make a fool of myself by doing that again,' he said quietly. 'All I'm proposing is an offer of a home and a return to nursing.'

She reddened beneath his steady gaze. 'That's awfully good of you but—'

'Let me finish, Annabelle, for goodness' sake,' he interrupted. 'One of my lodgers has just bought into a London practice, and the other has returned to South Africa. The two empty rooms on the top floor can easily be converted into a small apartment where you'll have your privacy. As for work, I've already spoken to the Matron at the Dartford General and they have a vacancy for a theatre nurse.'

Annabelle stared at him, unable to halt the tears she could feel trickling down her face. He still loved her after everything that had happened, still cared enough to make things easier for her in England, and he had made the long journey here to be confronted by an ungrateful woman who had betrayed him by falling in love with someone else.

George drew a pristine handkerchief from his pocket. 'Don't cry, Annabelle, you know I hate seeing you upset.' He waited for her to settle again and then continued, 'Don't reject my offer out of hand because you think it could make for an awkward situation. I can deal with the gossips and you'll have all the privacy you need in those upstairs rooms – and I promise to behave like the perfect gentleman at all times.' He smiled then, his blue eyes warm and endearing. 'So, what do you say?'

Annabelle knew the time had come to reveal the real reason why she could never go home to England, but her heart ached at the thought of how much hurt it would cause him. 'That is the sweetest, kindest offer, George, but I don't deserve it. You see, there are things that you don't know – things that happened while I was in Spain, which you might find too difficult to accept once we're sharing the same house.'

'I know you're grieving over Henri, and that it will take time to come to terms with your loss. But please, Annabelle, don't judge me too harshly. I do accept what happened, and now I want to help you find your feet again.' Their eyes met and held. 'Do you wish to come back to England, Annabelle?'

She couldn't lie to him any longer, for she did want to go to England, even though her situation made it impossible. She nodded, unable to say the words that would dull the light in his eyes and probably turn him against her forever.

'Then why not accept my offer? What is it that's holding you back?'

'I . . . It's not as easy as that,' she began hesitantly. 'Of course I would love to go back to England and have a job and somewhere to live; but there are complications and I couldn't possibly expect you to shoulder the added responsibility.'

George frowned. 'Neither the doctor nor Caroline spoke of complications, but whatever they are I'm perfectly able to cope. After all, I am a doctor.'

Annabelle knotted her fingers tightly in her lap as she tried to think of a way to tell him. 'The complications aren't anything to do with my injuries.' She looked back at him then, her fingers fluttering protectively over her stomach. 'You see, George, that despite everything that's happened to me, I've been blessed with a miracle.'

He frowned, clearly unable to comprehend what she was trying to tell him, and then his gaze dropped to her fluttering hands and his sharp intake of breath told her that finally he understood. There was a long moment of deafening silence in which his gaze became even more penetrating.

'You're having a baby.' he said flatly. 'Did Caroline know this when she came to see me?'

Annabelle could see his hurt beneath that carefully non-committal expression, and knew he was struggling to keep it under control. 'She was at the hospital when the doctors told me, and I swore her to secrecy, so please don't be angry with her.'

He sat stiff and unapproachable at the end of the couch as a pulse flexed in his jaw.

'George,' she said softly as she sat up and reached for his hand. 'George, this makes it impossible for me to return to England, don't you see? Thank you for being such a good, loving friend after all the hurt I've caused you, and I want you to know that I hate what this is doing to you.'

His hand remained unresponsive within her grasp, his gaze fixed on his highly polished brogues.

'George, please say something.'

He raised his head and took a deep breath. 'I've always thought of myself as a sensible, intelligent man who is capable of dealing with most given circumstances, but when it comes to you, Annabelle, I'm lost.'

He looked at her then, his expression intense. 'I've loved you from the moment we met,' he said, his voice gruff with emotion, 'and although I've tried very hard not to love you, I've found it impossible.'

She was about to speak when he ploughed on. 'If you come back to England with me, I promise to take care of you – and your baby. If you wish to avoid the inevitable scandal, then I will gladly marry you; but it will be a marriage of convenience only and I will ask nothing of you but friendship. If you decide that you don't want to marry, then we can concoct some story that's close to the truth that will satisfy the gossips.'

Her eyes widened and she could feel her heart thudding. 'You'd do that for me after all that's happened?'

He nodded, his blue eyes suspiciously bright despite his determined chin and serious expression. 'I might appear gruff and rather overbearing at times, and I know I'm inclined to speak my mind and trample on people's feelings, but beneath all that is a man who simply wants to be with the girl he loves on any terms.'

His gaze was intense as he looked at her. 'Which is why I'm offering you the respectability of marriage, and a home for you and your baby. I realise you see me as someone who is a friend rather than a lover, and I promise you'll be free to live your life as you see fit. I would be content with that.'

She felt a great rush of warmth and love as she took his hand and nestled it against her cheek. He was sacrificing his chances of finding true happiness with someone who could love and cherish him, and she had so little to offer in return. 'Oh, George, it's far more than I deserve. Are you really sure?'

'I wouldn't have suggested it if I wasn't,' he replied stiffly.

Annabelle studied his face and saw that despite the clenched chin and solemn expression, George's eyes betrayed his true feelings. Perhaps her mother had been right all those months ago when she'd said that friendship was more important than heady romance in a marriage. And now, here was George, offering her his hand while appearing to understand and accept that friendship was all she could bring to this marriage of convenience.

'Then I accept,' she said quietly.

George cleared his throat and then kissed her lightly on the forehead. 'That's settled then,' he said. 'Now, you lie back and rest while I go and ask Aline to help with the arrangements. No doubt a wedding in France will be convoluted in the extreme – the French never can do things in a straightforward manner.'

Aline managed to pull a great many strings throughout her wide circle of acquaintances, and secured a date in late November for the wedding. George had had to return to his Dartford practice after his initial visit to Paris, and during his long absence, Annabelle tried very hard to match Aline's enthusiasm for all the arrangements.

A marriage of convenience was not the ideal way to begin a new life, and although she loved George for his kindness and friendship, she couldn't help but compare that love with the passion she'd felt for Henri. They had made such plans for their future together, and every time she thought about him, she would burst into tears.

Annabelle had written to her mother about the wedding plans, carefully leaving out any mention of the baby. Camille's reply had come almost immediately, and it was clear she was suspicious of the hasty arrangements, but she enclosed a short note of congratulations from Philippa Howden, and promised a wedding gift once the newly-weds returned to England. Her decision to keep the news from Edwin was probably wise, for he certainly wouldn't approve and was bound to cause trouble.

It was a late October day, the sun was shining brightly and Annabelle's scars had fully healed. She left the house on rue de l'Arbre, purchased a single rose from a nearby flower-seller and slowly walked down to the Pont Neuf for the last time.

She stood there remembering the day she'd met Henri, and how there had been an instant attraction between them which had grown into something far deeper than either of them had been able to resist. They'd made a promise to meet here after the war and make their engagement official, and the knowledge that fate had intervened and they would never meet again tore at her heart.

She kissed the red rose and let it fall into the water, where it was swiftly swept away. 'Goodbye, my love,' she whispered. 'I will think of you always.'

George returned to Paris the day before the wedding, and booked into a hotel. He was clearly on edge, concerned that Annabelle might change her mind at the last minute, and she'd done her best to reassure him despite being beset by doubts. Aline had bolstered his courage with wine and a good filling meal before sending him off with her lodgers to enjoy the delights of the city bars.

As the day of the wedding dawned, Aline went into Annabelle's room and found her staring disconsolately out of the window as she turned the little silver and garnet ring round and round on her finger. 'It's never a good thing to live in the past, Annabelle,' she said softly. 'Henri will always be in your heart, but now it's time to put that ring away and let him become a sweet memory so you may look to the future.'

'You don't think I'm being foolish by accepting George's proposal so soon after . . . after . . . ?

'No. I think you're very wise,' murmured Aline as she gathered her into her arms. 'There are times when the head must rule the heart, Annabelle, and George is a good man who loves you deeply. In time you may find you can love him back – perhaps not with the same passion that you had for Henri, but something more gentle and enduring.'

She stepped back and regarded Annabelle sadly. 'Passion is a wonderful, thrilling thing, but it doesn't last, Annabelle. A fire that burns too brightly quickly dies, and without the kindling of friendship and shared interests to shore it up, there is only the cold ash left.'

Annabelle's heart was heavy as she looked over Aline's shoulder to the cream lace dress and silk jacket Miriam had made for today. 'I feel as if I'm betraying both of them,' she murmured.

'Why? Because you think you cannot love George the way he wants? Pah, he loves enough for both of you. As for Henri, he wouldn't want his child to be branded a bastard.'

Annabelle flinched at the ugly word.

Aline held her chin and looked into her eyes. 'I'm sorry to be so crude, but it's the way of this world, Annabelle. Henri would approve of what you're doing, and in George you have found the right man to be at your side.' She patted her cheek. 'Now, no more tears. It's time to get ready.'

George was dressed in a new suit and waiting stoically on the steps of the town hall, certain now that Annabelle would change her mind and not come. He'd sailed through life on a deep belief that he couldn't fail, but this was different, for his future happiness didn't lie in his hands any more, but in Annabelle's who, he realised, must be having doubts as to the wisdom of marrying him in such haste.

He glanced at his pocket watch and saw that only a minute had passed since the last time he'd looked, so he paced back and forth on the steps that led down to the square in an effort to dispel this unusual and debilitating nervousness.

As the car pulled up at the kerb he let his breath out on a sigh of relief and made a concerted effort to appear calm. Aline looked magnificent in a striking hat of peacock blue and a chic suit of grey silk, but he hardly noticed the others as Annabelle stepped out of the car and smiled up at him.

Her dress was cream lace, and she wore a little silk jacket buttoned at her still slender waist and a straw hat perched fetchingly on her curls so it shadowed the faint scars on her face. She was carrying a small bouquet of cream roses nestled amongst fronds of fern and the delicate white froth of gypsophila.

'You look beautiful,' he said gruffly as he took her hand. 'I must be the luckiest man in the whole of France.'

She kissed him on the cheek. 'It's me who is lucky, George, and I promise you will never regret today.'

The civil ceremony was conducted by the Mayor, who was delighted to show off his ability to speak passable English so that George understood what was going on. When it was declared that they were now legally married, George and Annabelle hesitated for just a moment before they kissed, and this was greeted with a round of applause from their few guests.

As the Mayor handed them the *livret de famille*, which was a booklet containing a copy of their marriage certificate, he explained, with a knowing wink, that any future children's birth certificates would also be recorded in it.

There was to be no formal wedding breakfast as the newly-weds would be flying back to England later that afternoon, so they returned to the house on the rue de l'Arbre where Aline and Miriam had laid out a tremendous spread of delicious food and wine.

Annabelle could see the happiness on George's face, so she tried very hard to put the past behind her and join in the celebrations. She had mixed feelings about Etienne's absence, for it would have eased her conscience to have his blessing; and yet his presence would have served as another painful reminder of Henri. It was perhaps a good thing that he was still in Spain recuperating from his wounds.

When it was time to leave for the airport and everyone escorted them to the main road, she tearfully clung to Aline. 'We'll see each other again, Aline, I promise,' she whispered. 'And thank you for everything.'

'Just keep smiling, my darling, and be content. That is all I ask.'

The taxi was waiting and George was looking impatiently at his watch. She waved goodbye and climbed in beside him, and within moments they were speeding towards the airport and the new life that awaited them in Dartford.

As the small wedding party headed back to the rue de l'Arbre, none of them noticed Etienne, who was watching from the deep shadows of a nearby doorway. He leant heavily on the walking stick to ease the pain in his damaged leg as he watched the taxi drive away, his thoughts and emotions warring against one another.

His grief over losing Henri was still raw, and it enraged him to see Annabelle smiling and laughing on her wedding day. How could she do that so soon after losing Henri? Hadn't she cared for him at all? And who was that Englishman she'd married? If she'd been in need of comfort, then why hadn't she turned to him, Henri's best and closest friend? He could have consoled her because they had both loved Henri, and maybe, in the fullness of time, they could have found love together.

He turned away and slowly hobbled towards the Pont Neuf where it had all begun. Leaning on the parapet, he looked down the river, past the Louvre to the rooftops and spires of Paris, feeling more alone than ever before.

It had been two weeks since Annabelle's wedding, and Aline had already received a postcard from her saying that they had arrived safely, and that she was busy decorating and furnishing her set of rooms at the top of George's lovely house. She was well and surprisingly contented, and that morning she had felt the first fluttery quickening of her baby.

Aline shivered and wrapped the thick woollen cardigan around her as she went into the draughty hallway to collect the post from the doormat. The house was so cold that even the cats had hibernated to the kitchen where the range cooker provided the only heat.

Picking up the letters, she sifted through them with a sigh. They were mostly bills and she really didn't know where she'd find the money to pay them, for there was no planned exhibition and she hadn't had the chance to go south this year to paint.

The last letter made her frown, for it bore a Spanish post-mark, and the writing was unfamiliar. Turning it over and over in her hand, she felt a growing sense of unease. Who could be writing to her from Spain? Caroline had left there some time ago, and Etienne was now back in Paris, and she couldn't think of anyone else who would have known her address.

The uneasiness grew, and a strong sense of foreboding made her hesitate.

'Come on, Aline,' she muttered crossly. 'You can't stand here staring at the damned thing all day. Just open it.'

Her fingers were clumsy as she slit the envelope, pulled out the single sheet of lined paper and read the short note that had been penned by a nursing aide. '*Mon dieu,*' she gasped as the few words and their tragic consequences sank in. 'Oh, Henri,' she whispered through her tears, 'if only this had come earlier. But you're too late. Much too late.'

14

England, 1956

Annabelle leant into George's embrace as he softly kissed her cheek. He was such a very dear man, and although he too must be feeling the void left by their daughter, Eugenie, departing for Paris, he'd understood her need to wander alone for a while. 'I'll be back in time for evening surgery,' she promised. 'But I don't want you moping about in the meantime. Why don't you telephone Dr Harvey and arrange a few holes of golf?'

George grimaced. 'I don't really feel like it, to be honest. I think I'll just go home and potter about in the garden.'

'Don't be sad, darling,' she murmured as she touched his face. 'Eugenie will have the time of her life in Paris with Aline, and a year isn't so very long to wait until she's home again.'

He nodded. 'The house will seem awfully empty without her, though,' he said gruffly before he squeezed her hand. 'Enjoy your walk. I'll see you later.'

She watched him walk away, a sturdy figure in a well-cut suit, the width of his shoulders and energetic stride belying his forty-nine years. His dark, curly hair glinted with only a few threads of silver, the hectic practice schedule and rounds of golf kept his waistline fairly trim.

Annabelle smiled fondly, knotted her headscarf more firmly under her chin, and headed towards Westminster Bridge, her high heels rapping on the pavement. It was a beautiful sunny day in late August, and the River Thames was busy with tourist boats, barges, motor boats, and a few hardy souls pulling determinedly against the river's swift flow in rowing boats. The Houses of Parliament gleamed warmly in the sunshine, and the bridge was busy with pedestrians, black taxis, cars and red double-decker buses.

She turned her back on all of them and leant against the parapet to look down on the dark waters of the river that rushed beneath the arches of the bridge. How long ago it seemed that she'd stood on another bridge, in another city, and looked down at a river – so long, in fact, that that episode in her life now felt as if it had never belonged to her; that she'd dreamt it, or watched someone else play her part. Even the pain of losing Henri had faded, to be replaced by a sweet contentment that had come from her marriage to George.

Her doubts as to whether she'd acted in too much haste had soon been allayed, for George had been as good as his word and not expected anything but friendship from her. She'd settled happily in the upstairs apartment, coming down to help cook meals and keep the place tidy. During the evenings she would often sit with him in the comfortable drawing room to read or listen to the wireless, and they soon settled back into the easy companionship they'd known before.

Apart from her mother, Camille, being scandalised once she realised Annabelle must have been pregnant before she married, the only real difficulty had come from Felicity Jenkins, whose stiff dislike had made her feel most uncomfortable. It had been a relief when she'd handed in her notice and gone to work at another practice, and Annabelle had eagerly taken on the reception duties and fielded telephone calls and medical reps, and become adept at avoiding the awkward questions as it became obvious she was pregnant.

The change in their relationship had been so subtle that neither of them really noticed but the birth of Eugenie had been the defining moment. Annabelle smiled as she remembered the look of awe on George's face as he watched her breastfeeding her tiny baby, and how tears sparked in his eyes as he took Eugenie into his arms for the first time. His look of adoration tugged at her heart then, and did so now, and she could still hear the words he'd said that had finally bound them together as a proper family.

'Eugenie,' he'd breathed. 'A beautiful name for my own, beloved, beautiful daughter. I promise now that I will cherish, protect and guide you until my last breath, you precious, precious little girl.'

Annabelle blinked back her tears, feeling rather foolish at being so emotional after all these years. Yet from that moment on she and George had become closer, and once she was quite recovered from what had proved to be a difficult and exhausting delivery, it seemed the most natural thing in the world to share George's bed.

They'd had a gloriously happy year and a half together before the Second World War was declared and George was called up, and they had both hoped that she would fall pregnant again. Yet it wasn't to be, and it was a sadness that lay between them still.

A retired GP had come to take over the practice until George returned, and Annabelle had heeded the government warnings and taken Eugenie to Wales for the duration. They had lived in a rented bungalow which overlooked the sea, and Annabelle had helped out at the local cottage hospital whilst Eugenie went to a nearby nursery, where even at such an early age she began to show a great aptitude for painting and drawing.

Annabelle had decided very early on that it would be good for Eugenie to learn French, so when they were alone, it was the only language spoken between them. She also kept a photograph of George by Eugenie's bedside, and when she was old enough to understand, she talked about him every day and read out his letters so that Eugenie would feel she knew him when he returned.

It had been an anxious, harrowing time, for not only had Aline refused to escape occupied Paris, George was sent abroad to use his medical skills in some of the most dangerous theatres of the war – thereby earning several medals for bravery under fire, of which he was quite dismissive. Yet as proud as she was, she still fretted over him, for she hadn't seen him for almost the whole of the six-year duration. On his return he'd knelt down to introduce himself to the shy little girl who hid behind her mother's skirts, and Eugenie's eyes had widened in delight as she finally realised who he was and ran into his arms with a joyful cry of 'Daddy.'

Annabelle and Caroline had been in constant touch since she'd returned to England with George, and once war had been declared, Caroline had joined the WAAFs and was posted to a hospital somewhere on the south coast. She wrote often, always including a pretty card or present for her godchild, Eugenie, whom she adored.

Caroline's parents remained in Fulham, Robert busy in parliament, and Philippa occupied with her work for the Women's Voluntary Service. It was by sheer chance that they were both away from home when their house received a direct hit, but Edwin Blake had not been so lucky. He'd been killed by a V2 rocket that had exploded on contact with the roof of the tobacconist's shop where he'd gone to buy a newspaper.

Annabelle turned away from the view of the Thames and headed towards St Thomas' Hospital and the narrow streets beyond. Life could be strange, she mused, as she walked past the empty bomb sites which were still waiting to be cleared and built upon. Camille had moved down to live with her and Eugenie in Wales after Edwin's death, and had proved to be an excellent fundraiser and organiser of events, to the point where, at the end of the war, she'd received a medal for her services to the war effort.

Camille never returned to the house in Fulham, and after it was sold, she'd bought a small cottage in the Welsh village where she'd made so many friends. It wasn't long before she remarried, and now at sixty-five she was settled and happy with Dai Davies, who was a cheerful, generous man who let her run rings around him and spoilt her rotten because he was tickled pink to be married to a very chic Parisienne.

Annabelle strolled past the prefabricated houses which were beginning to show wear and tear after so long. They'd been put up as a temporary measure to house those who'd been bombed out, but it seemed there were still people living in them, even after all these years.

London continued to bear the scars of the war in the many bomb sites, the blackened masonry, the boarded-up shops and houses and the pitted walls, but there was a sense of optimism and purpose in the air now the restrictions and shortages were slowly coming to an end. New high-rise buildings were going up to replace the devastated slums of the East End, plans were being drawn up for thousands of new homes in the Barbican area, the marvellous Festival Hall had been opened to celebrate the Festival of Britain back in 1951, and modern office blocks were slowly rising from the ashes of the inner city.

The parks were returning to their verdant green now the allotments had been dug over and laid with fresh turf, and although there was still some rationing, the women had cast off the dour grey, navy and black of the utility clothing and were emerging like brightly coloured butterflies in their white high heels and full-skirted summer dresses which they wore over layers of organza petticoats.

Annabelle drifted back the way she had come and found a seat which overlooked the river. Smoothing her skirt and petticoats, she sat down and adjusted the cardigan over her shoulders before donning her sunglasses. The glare on the water was quite strong, but it was lovely to just sit here and watch the world go by after the chaos of preparing Eugenie for her journey, and the trauma of seeing her leave.

She would be in Paris now, she thought wistfully, and she wondered if she'd even pause by the Pont Neuf before finding her way to Aline's. There was no reason why she should, for she didn't know what significance it held, and Aline had been warned not to say anything about Henri or Etienne.

Annabelle sighed and dug in her handbag for a packet of cigarettes. Having lit one, she watched the boats chugging past and the mewling seabirds follow one of the barges as it made its slow way down the river to the dockyards. She'd realised she could never tell her daughter the truth on the day Eugenie had been born, and as she'd looked into George's eyes over the sleeping baby's head, they'd made a silent, tacit agreement that he was her father now.

As the years had gone by and Eugenie and George had formed a tight and loving bond, she'd known she'd made the right decision. Their adoration was mutual, and it would be immensely cruel to damage that. There was no reason for her to know about Henri, for he was long dead; Etienne never knew she was pregnant, and Aline would keep the secret for the rest of her life.

The lie had worried her a little over the years as she'd watched Eugenie grow into a bright, lively little girl, and then into a lovely, talented young woman. She had the look of Henri about her sometimes: in a fleeting expression, or the way she lifted a brow in question; but her eyes were the same blue as George's, her hair the same flaxen gold and honey mix as Annabelle's, so perhaps she was only imagining it. Eugenie had certainly inherited Henri's artistic talent, and when she'd asked where she'd got it from, it had been all too easy to say it must have missed a generation and come from her Tante Aline. They were lies told out of love, and the need to protect the strong family bond – and therefore acceptable.

Annabelle finished the cigarette and started to walk again towards Westminster Bridge. She had, of course, told Eugenie about her short time in Paris with Aline, and her journey into Spain which had ended with her being injured so badly she'd had to come back to England. It was necessarily an edited version of what had happened, but Eugenie's many questions had had to be answered.

Like George, Annabelle was extremely proud of their daughter, for Eugenie had been accepted at the Slade School of Fine Art in London when she was just seventeen, and on her eighteenth birthday in May, she'd been awarded a year's scholarship at the Ecole des Beaux-Arts in Paris. It had come as a bit of a shock to them, but it was an opportunity not to be missed despite her youth – and of course she could not only speak French fluently, but would have Aline to look after her.

Yet privately, Annabelle fretted over Eugenie being in Paris, for she would walk the same streets that she and Henri had walked, and visit the same places; and in a way she was a little jealous, for she would have loved to accompany her. She was being selfish and stupid, she thought crossly as she headed back across the bridge. There was nothing to gain by returning to old haunts and sad memories; better to let Eugenie have her adventure and discover her own Paris, and be satisfied with that.

15

Paris

Despite the passing of the years, he'd hoped that by some miracle he would see her there once more, so when she finally appeared, he wondered if it was the sheer force of his longing that had somehow conjured her up.

His breath caught and his pulse quickened as he sat forward in his wheelchair by the third-floor balcony windows, the glass of wine and cigarette forgotten as he tried to believe it was really her. Almost two decades had passed, and his eyes were not as reliable as they had once been. Could they be playing a cruel trick on him? Was his imagination running riot? Yet as she stood on the Pont Neuf and gazed down the swift-flowing Seine towards the distant Eiffel Tower and the rooftops of Paris, it was as if those years had been swept away and she had returned to him.

He eased further forward, confident that she couldn't see him in the rapidly darkening room, but still not trusting what his eyes were telling him. Her hair was longer than he remembered, flowing over her narrow shoulders in a tumble of silken curls, but her slender figure still retained the delicate grace that belied the fierce energy and determination she'd always possessed. And even in her relaxed state, there was an almost defiant tilt to her chin that he remembered so very well. Dressed in narrow slacks and a sweater, she carried a coat over her arm and there were suitcases and a portfolio at her feet.

'Belle?' he breathed. 'Can it really be you?'

As if she'd heard him, she turned from the river, her gaze sweeping beyond the bridge to the cobbled Quai de la Mégisserie, and the tall grey houses whose balconies and long windows overlooked the Seine.

His breath caught again as her face was illuminated by the nearby street lamp, and her eyes seemed to find his momentarily before she looked away. The disappointment was sharp. It wasn't Belle, couldn't possibly be Belle. Too many years had passed, and this girl was younger than Belle had been on that fateful day they'd met on the bridge. And yet there was something about her that held echoes of the past . . .

'Are you all right, Patron?'

The light was switched on, startling him, and he blinked in its sudden glare. 'Turn that off and come here,' he ordered the young man as he turned once more towards the window. 'See that girl? Go and find out who she is and where she's come from. Now, quickly, before she leaves the bridge.'

The look was quizzical, the smile wry. 'She's a bit young, even for you, isn't she, Patron?' he drawled.

His impatience made him sharp. 'Just do as I ask, Max,' he rasped. 'I'll explain later.'

As Max left the room, he turned once more towards the window. She was looking up now, her gaze drifting over the wrought-iron balconies, perhaps drawn by the sudden glare of light which had just as swiftly been extinguished. Her eyes seemed to hold him there for a second, and he could sense her unease as she broke the spell and hurriedly looked away.

He touched the glass in the window as if by doing so he could keep her there, but before Max had even reached the street, she'd picked up her cases, turned her back and was immediately lost amongst the stream of homeward-bound office workers and strolling tourists.

He slumped back into the chair, the moment lost, his pain raw. He closed his eyes to try to dispel some of his anguish, but all he could see was the young, vibrant Belle who had stood on the Pont Neuf so many years before, and the memories and deep regrets over what had happened to tear them apart now threatened to overwhelm him.

Eugenie had fallen in love with Paris from the moment she'd stepped outside the Gare de Lyon. There was a sense of energy in the smartly dressed pedestrians, and in the rumble of the traffic crossing over the cobbled streets. The sound of French voices, of church bells ringing out, and the sight of flowersellers and little pavement cafés all combined to welcome her to this city that her mother had talked about so fondly.

The long journey to get here had been a little daunting, because she'd never travelled on her own except to Ireland to stay with her grandparents, but any concern she might have had was instantly dismissed, for she felt right at home.

After consulting the map her mother had drawn, Eugenie had decided to walk along the embankment by the Seine to get her first real feel of the city. When she'd realised that the Louvre was just a bit further on from the turning she would eventually take to get to Aunt Aline's, she hadn't been able to resist the opportunity to see the marvellous Old Masters she knew were displayed there. With her suitcases and portfolio safely locked away in the luggage room, she'd spent the next two hours drinking in the magnificence of the building and the treasures within it.

Now, as she stood on the Pont Neuf and looked down the river to the rooftops, spires and turrets of Paris, she felt a sudden prickle of unease. It was close to dusk, and although there were plenty of people around her, she got the distinct impression she was being watched.

She looked away from the river, her gaze travelling along the tall row of grey houses, the windows of which were in deep shadow behind their wrought-iron balconies. Was there someone looking out from the third floor? Her eyesight was good and as she looked more intently the unease grew. There was definitely a figure seated there.

She hurriedly turned away just as a flash of light came from the building, but when she looked again it was all in darkness. Eugenie wondered if the long journey and the excitement at being in Paris had made her imagination run riot, for why should someone be watching her? She decided not to linger anyway, picked up her cases and portfolio and hurried off the bridge and across the cobbled street into the broad, busy boulevard.

It was almost dark now and the streetlights were quite dim, but she could still see the drawing her mother had made for her and read the instructions on how to get to the rue de l'Arbre. She found the narrow alleyway with the dog-leg bend in the middle, and stepped into the square to discover that everything was the same as her mother had described, but perhaps a little shabbier and more run-down. The gnarled tree at the end of the square was still there, but the blooms had long since died, leaving only glossy leaves behind.

Eugenie approached the house with the faded blue shutters and climbed the steps to the front door. She'd seen photographs of Tante Aline, and had heard her mother's stories about her chaotic house, the cats and the parrot, and hoped it hadn't changed too much, for it sounded like great fun. She rapped the brass knocker and waited nervously on the top step.

'Come in. Come in,' shouted a voice from inside the house.

Eugenie frowned and tentatively pushed the door, but it was tightly shut. She knocked again, and then heard slow footsteps approaching. She stepped back as the door was opened and a pair of wary brown eyes regarded her. 'Tante Aline?'

The door opened wider to reveal a tiny, thin woman with a great mop of snow-white hair that was held back by a strip of dark purple silk. Her dress was rusty black beneath a long flimsy wrap of dull grey and her only jewellery was a cheap bead necklace. She peered short-sightedly at Eugenie. 'Annabelle?'

Eugenie felt suddenly uncertain of her welcome and wondered if her aunt were deaf, or slightly deranged; she certainly looked rather odd and nothing like the woman in her mother's photographs. 'No, Aunt Aline,' she said loudly and clearly in French. 'I'm Annabelle's daughter, Eugenie.'

The broad smile lit up her thin face and her eyes sparkled as she fluttered her fingers. 'Well, of course you are. *Ooh là là*, how silly of me. It's these old eyes, you know, I don't see things as well as I did, and I hate wearing glasses – so unflattering.'

Eugenie hovered on the step, the weight of her cases and portfolio dragging on her arms. 'Mother and Father send their love, and I have some presents for you too – in my case,' she added as a strong hint.

Aline clapped her hands girlishly. 'How exciting. Don't stand about there, come in. Those cases look very heavy and you must be tired after your long journey.'

Eugenie followed her into the hall where bright pictures hung on the walls and a collection of coats, hats and shoes cluttered the clothes rack and floor beneath it. The stairs were plain brown wood, she noted with sharp disappointment, and there were no plaster cherubs or hanging baubles; the ceiling was a faded blue with no sign of clouds, and even the beaded curtain at the end of the hall had been replaced by an ugly wooden door.

'Put your things down there and come through. I expect you'd like a cup of tea – it was your mother's favourite.'

'Actually, if it's not too much trouble, could I have a cup of coffee?'

'Of course, of course. And don't take any notice of Napoleon's squawking. It's all nonsense.'

'He's still alive?'

'Oh, yes. And will probably outlive us all,' Aline replied with a wry smile.

As Eugenie followed her into the dusty, cluttered room, she sadly noted how the wallpaper was peeling, the furniture had been ravaged by time and misuse, and the couches sagged and bled springs and tufts of stuffing beneath the blankets, cushions and shawls that littered them. Instead of the beautiful chandelier her mother had described, there was a single bulb hanging from the ceiling where the dark stain of damp flaked off the plaster. Even Napoleon's feathers seemed faded, but his bright eyes had lost none of their wickedness as he regarded her slyly from behind the bars of his ornate cage.

'Your mother probably wouldn't recognise it now,' said Aline as she walked through the room. 'But it was lovely once.' She gave a sigh. 'I had to sell everything of value just to eat during the occupation, but at least I survived, which is more than so many of my friends did.'

'It must have been very hard for you to see all your lovely things go,' Eugenie murmured in sympathy.

'Not as hard as having the Boche in my home,' she retorted. 'Commandeered it, they did, and took over with their great boots, loud voices and constant demands. Oh, they could be charming when they wanted to be, but on the whole they had few manners.'

'Mother told me you had to take them in,' said Eugenie softly. 'I hope they treated you kindly.'

'They treated me better than they treated Miriam and Malachi,' she muttered as she went into the kitchen. 'The poor lambs had gone into hiding and someone betrayed them. The last anyone heard of them they'd been taken to one of the death camps.'

She put the coffee pot on the ancient stove and folded her arms. 'War is an ugly, inhuman thing, Eugenie, as I'm sure you've heard from your mother. But her experiences in Spain were no real preparation for Hitler's war; and here we are, with trouble in Aden. It seems we never learn.'

There was no real reply to this, so Eugenie stroked the old cat dozing on a kitchen chair, and was rewarded with a deep, rumbling purr. The kitchen was as shabby and ramshackle as the other room, and her heart was heavy at the thought of how hard Aline's war must have been.

She watched surreptitiously as Aline made the coffee and hunted out milk, sugar and cups. She looked much older than Grandmère Camille, and yet she was the younger sister by five years. The lines on her face told of hardship and sorrow, and her gnarled hands had surely lost the ability to hold a paintbrush. It was all so terribly sad, and in a way she wished she hadn't come, for the images and expectations she'd had from her mother's stories were in sharp contrast to the reality.

Aline seemed to sense her disappointment. 'Enough gloomy talk. Take this into the other room so we can chat about why you're here and how everyone is back in England. I hear my sister has seen some sense at last and married someone with less money and more kindness than that bully she'd tied herself to before.'

Eugenie bit down on a smile at the touch of acid in her aunt's voice. It was well known in the family that the sisters didn't get on, and it seemed nothing had changed. She took the tray and tried to find somewhere to place it, but every flat surface seemed to be covered in books, magazines, abandoned knitting or dirty dishes. In the end, she had to put the tray on the floor to clear a low table of magazines.

As Aline poured the coffee into the tiny cups, she told her the news from home and handed over the money order her father had given her that morning for her first three months of board and lodgings.

Aline's eyes widened as she read the amount, and then quickly placed it on the mantelpiece. 'I will put it in the bank first thing tomorrow,' she said. 'Such an amount is very generous – and I'm not ashamed to say, most welcome.'

'Daddy will send the same amount every three months. He and Mummy know how expensive things are here, and they're enormously grateful to you for putting me up.'

Aline returned to the couch and sipped her coffee. 'I'm glad your mother and father are well and happy together. And it's good to hear that Camille is finally settled with a man who truly appreciates her. Edwin was a terrible mistake, you know, and he made everyone's lives miserable. I can't say I was at all upset to hear he'd died, and I should think that Camille was extremely relieved to be free of him.'

'I never knew him,' Eugenie said quietly. 'He was killed when I was about five or six.'

Aline tilted her head, her eyes bright with interest. 'And what about you, Eugenie? I hear you're considered to be a rather talented artist.'

Eugenie blushed. 'I was awarded a year's scholarship to the School of Fine Arts here in Paris,' she said shyly. 'I'm told I'm one of the youngest students ever to be awarded such an honour, and I can't wait to get started.'

Aline's myopic eyes regarded her steadily over the rim of the chipped cup. 'It's a tough school and very demanding of its students,' she said. 'What are you specialising in?'

'Architecture and its history. I've always loved old buildings, and Paris seems to be stuffed with them. There's hardly any damage here, not like in London.'

'The Boche had the sense to realise that Paris is a city to be cherished, and therefore saw to it that it remained almost in one piece.' Aline sighed. 'I do envy you, Eugenie. How wonderful to spend a year immersing yourself in art.' She looked down at her crippled hands. 'I can no longer paint, you see. My right hand has never been the same since one of the Boche officers lost his temper over a burnt stew and smashed his rifle butt across my knuckles to teach me a lesson. And although I tried to work with my left hand, it proved to be impossible. Now the arthritis has set in, it's all I can do to hold a cup.'

Eugenie winced, not only at the brutality her aunt had suffered, but at the almost matter-of-fact way she mentioned it. 'Why didn't you come to England while you still could? I know Mother wrote to you many times, begging you to go to her.'

'This is my home. Paris is my city. I wasn't about to let the

Germans have it all their own way.' She gave a sniff of derision and tilted up her chin, her eyes sparking with defiance. 'I might have been forced to house them and cook and clean for them, but I heard things, saw things, and that information helped my friends to fight back.'

Eugenie's interest was immediately piqued. 'You were part of the Resistance?'

Aline shook her head. 'I had friends who were,' she said sadly. 'Friends who died and friends who survived to see our country returned to us in victory. I still see some of them, even now.' She smiled at Eugenie and changed the subject. 'You look very like your mother, but you have your father's eyes, I see.'

'Mine are a darker blue than Daddy's, but I admit I do wish they were like Mummy's. Her eyes are an amazing colour.' She giggled. 'Daddy said it was her eyes that made him fall instantly in love with her.'

Aline nodded thoughtfully. 'Yes, I can understand that,' she murmured. She sipped her coffee and seemed to shake off some hidden sadness. 'It will be quite like old times with you here, and I'm sure you'll get along with the other students who lodge with me, although they are somewhat older than you. Fleur and Jean-Michel are both in their final year at the School of Fine Arts, and Antoine and Pascal are studying music at the Conservatoire. I prefer having artistic people around me. I understand them, you see.'

Eugenie's spirits lightened. 'They sound fun. I look forward to meeting them.'

'They should be back soon for supper. They usually go to one of the coffee houses or bars after school to catch up on gossip and see if they can persuade someone important to become their patron.' Aline glanced at the cheap clock on the dusty mantelpiece. 'Let's get you settled before they come.'

Eugenie picked up her things from the hall and followed Aline's slow progress up the bare wooden stairs. She could see the pale traces of the frescoes on the walls and up here there were more landscape paintings on display. They were bright with colour and skilfully executed, which made Aline's inability to paint even more tragic.

'Here we are,' said Aline as she threw open the door at the end of the first-floor landing. 'This was your mother's room, right next to mine. I hope you like it.'

Eugenie looked at the plain blue walls and the faded frieze of cherry blossom someone had painted below the picture rail. There was a single landscape painting on the wall, the bed was a rather grand four-poster and the rest of the furniture was dark, solid mahogany.

'It's lovely,' she said truthfully, 'and from what Mummy told me, it hasn't changed all that much since she was here.'

'No, I managed to keep my room and this one pretty much as they were. I couldn't let the war destroy everything.'

Eugenie put her bags on the patchwork coverlet and crossed to the window, where she knelt on the padded seat and gazed out onto the rooftops and chimneys and the stars that twinkled so brightly above Paris. 'I can hardly believe I'm really here,' she breathed.

Aline came to stand behind her, her gnarled hand resting lightly on Eugenie's shoulder. 'Paris is a very special place,

Eugenie,' she said softly. 'And if you take time to explore and watch and listen, you'll find she will welcome you, just as she did your mother.'

Eugenie moved from the window seat and into Aline's warm embrace. Her aunt was thin and frail, but her spirit was still strong despite all she'd endured, and Eugenie knew she would be happy here. The many questions that had haunted her since she'd discovered the things hidden in the attic at home could wait for another day.

16

Max Preston wasn't a vain man, but he'd discovered soon after arriving in Paris that the girls seemed to like his height, as well as his bush hat, sturdy boots and moleskin trousers, and had decided that as they made him attractive to the opposite sex, he'd stick to wearing them. He was twenty-five, fair-haired, hazel-eyed and proudly Australian, but loved living in Paris, especially now he'd got the hang of the lingo and was under the patronage of Le Basque. His room in the large, riverside house that his patron owned was comfortable, the attic studio was full of light, and the three other artists he shared it with were a lively, talented bunch that he got on with very well.

Living in a vibrant, ancient city that was steeped in art, culture and history was very different to life on a remote cattle station in the Australian Northern Territory, and although he'd been in Paris for five years, he still found it fascinating and couldn't quite believe his luck. He dug his hands in his pockets, turned back down the boulevard and strolled towards the house where he knew his patron would be waiting impatiently for news of the girl. Quite why he was so keen to find her was a mystery, but no doubt he would explain it sooner or later.

Max went through the front door, bypassed the rickety lift which he found claustrophobic, and took the stairs two at a time. Two of the large rooms had been knocked into one on the third floor so the light poured in from both windows. This was his patron's studio, and where he spent most of every day. Cluttered with finished paintings and clean canvases, there were several easels – one of which held his latest painting – and a trestle table littered with tubes of paint, brushes, sketches and palettes.

A red velvet chaise longue had been placed along one wall, and displayed on the shelf above it was an interesting collection of mineral rocks, gnarled and twisted pieces of wood that had been sculptured by the elements, some beautiful coloured glass and a crystal bowl filled with seashells. A set of weights sat incongruously on a wooden chair, with a towel neatly folded beside them, and draped over the nearby hatstand was a collection of shawls, scarves, exotic Chinese silk robes and feather boas – useful props for the endless stream of models who traipsed in and out.

The older man was still sitting in his usual place by the uncurtained window in his wheelchair, his crippled legs covered with a light blanket. At forty-eight he was still handsome, his blue eyes bright and intelligent beneath his black brows, his dark hair showing only a glint of silver at the temples. He had a neat beard and moustache, and his sturdy torso was maintained by rigorous daily exercise to compensate for the frailty of his wasted legs.

He turned eagerly as Max entered the room. 'Well? Did you find her?'

'I'm sorry, Patron, but she disappeared amongst the crowds and I lost sight of her.' Max sat down in the chair next to him so he didn't have to keep looking up at him. 'From what I saw of her she was pretty enough, but not your usual type of model. What made you so keen to find her?'

His patron stared morosely out of the window to the darkness of the river and the twinkling lights on the Left Bank. 'She reminded me of someone I once knew,' he muttered. 'If you see her again, I want you to talk to her and find out who she is.'

Max stretched out his long legs and leant back in the comfortable chair. 'Paris is a big place,' he drawled, his Australian accent mingling strangely with the French. 'She might not come this way again.'

His patron regarded him with a smile. 'For an artist, you're very unobservant,' he gently chided. 'She was carrying a portfolio, which means she's an artist of some sort. Paris isn't that large; you'll see her again, I'm sure of it.'

Max grinned. 'If that's the case, then I probably will. But I only caught a glimpse of her, Patron. I might not recognise her again.'

'You will. You have an eye for a pretty girl,' he said dryly. His patron looked at Max thoughtfully. 'While we're on the subject of pretty girls, have you finished that painting for Monsieur Delacroix?'

'I think so. I was going to have a good look at it in the morning just to make sure it doesn't need a touch more here and there before he comes to view it.'

'Bring it down and let me see. Delacroix is a difficult man to please.'

Max left the room and ran up the two flights of stairs to the deserted attic studio, which was in its usual chaotic state. The portrait of Delacroix's young wife was on an easel, and he took a moment to study it before he carried it downstairs. Henri's faith in him had been a terrific boost to his career prospects and this was one of several commissioned paintings he'd had over the past year of his patronage.

He set the painting on an easel so the chandelier's light fell directly upon it, and then waited anxiously for the other man's critique, all too aware that his mentor's latest painting of the old Parisian flower seller was there to compare it with – and he couldn't hope to compete with such skill.

However, Sophia Delacroix was a beautiful woman in her early-thirties and he hoped that he'd captured the creamy skin, black hair and soulful eyes of her Italian heritage. She'd been delightful company during the hours she'd sat for him, and although she'd flirted openly, he'd been careful not to encourage her. Delacroix was a wealthy man who moved in the sort of circles that bought paintings and appreciated the finest things that money could buy, and as tempted as he was, he wasn't about to jeopardise his future.

His patron moved the wheelchair across the room and sat in silence as he thoughtfully stroked his moustache and beard and regarded the painting. 'She has the look of a woman who's been made love to quite thoroughly,' he muttered after a long moment. 'I hope you weren't the cause.' He turned his head, his bright blue eyes twinkling with humour.

'Not this time, Patron,' said Max with a rueful grin. 'Her husband is far too important, and she'd probably eat me alive anyway.'

He laughed. 'I'm glad you've learnt your lesson, my boy. There are plenty of single, willing women out there for you to bed without risking the wrath of a jealous husband.' He wheeled the chair back and forth, his gaze once more on the painting. 'You've captured the skin tones well, and I like the way the light on her face shows her fine bone structure.' He smiled and headed back to the window. 'Well done, Max. You're definitely improving.'

Max could feel the flush of pleasure infuse his face. Praise from Le Basque was rare and therefore to be cherished.

'Tomorrow, you might just do something about her index finger,' he said casually after he'd lit a cigarette. 'It's a little long, and perhaps the ring on it should reflect some of that light.'

'I might have known you'd find something wrong,' Max replied without rancour as he studied the painting and realised his patron's experienced eyes had seen what he'd missed.

'It's why I'm the master and you're the student,' his patron said mildly. He picked up the glass of red wine and took a sip. 'But you soon won't need me, Max. You're well on the way to being independent.' He pushed the carafe of wine towards him as he sat down. 'Have you had any more thoughts as to where you'll go?'

'Not back to Australia,' he replied as he poured the wine into a clean glass. 'If I'm to make my name, then I need to stay here in Europe. Although it would be good to see home again for a visit, and catch up with everyone.'

'Europe is the heart of our world, Max. You'd be wise to stay here.' He smoked his cigarette and stared out of the window. 'I wonder why she's in Paris,' he murmured. 'Do you think she could be studying at the School of Fine Arts across the river?'

It took a moment for Max to realise who he was talking about. 'If she is, then she must be extremely talented. It's a tough school, and they only take the very best.' He glanced across at the older man with a wry smile. 'I reckon the woman she reminds you of must have been pretty special,' he teased.

His patron sighed deeply, his expression wistful. 'Yes, she was.'

Max saw the sadness and it intrigued him. Le Basque liked women and they liked him, but he'd never married, and he wondered now if this mysterious woman from his past had been the reason why. 'D'you want to talk about her?'

He shook his head. 'It all happened so long ago, and I still find it painful. But that girl tonight . . .' He looked across at him, his eyes reflecting some secret sorrow. 'Find her, Max. Go to the art schools and see if she's a student; trawl Montmartre – they all end up there – and if you don't have any luck, try some of the boarding houses and look around in the bars and cafés.'

'This girl's important to you, isn't she?'

He shrugged. 'I'm probably being foolish – it's what happens when one is stuck in this thing day after day without much to occupy or stimulate the mind – but until I know who she is, I won't be able to rest.'

'Then I'll do my best to find her, I promise.'

*

Le Basque rarely slept well, and it was almost three in the morning when he left the deserted main salon and went into his bedroom. His widowed housekeeper had cooked a very good bouillabaisse, which he and his protégés had eaten with the traditional garlic, oil and herb bread, and although it would probably play havoc with his digestion, he hadn't been able to resist it.

He closed the door behind him and switched on the light, noting that Madame Doumer had drawn the curtains and turned down his bed. She was a marvellous woman and he counted himself lucky to have found her, for looking after him and the four young art students wasn't an easy task – which was why he'd happily agreed to her living in the basement apartment rent-free. He'd been warned by his doctor that there would come a time when his disability called for added help, but at the moment he was coping quite well and maintaining a fair degree of independence.

The house was a joy to him, for he'd only ever dreamt that he could buy such a place, but following a very successful exhibition in 1949, his star had risen and now his soubriquet was known all over the world. He smiled wryly. The Germans had called him 'Le Basque', and he'd decided to keep the name out of sheer bloody-mindedness and disdain. He'd certainly given the bastards a runaround, and for that he felt he'd earned the self-indulgence of pride.

As he prepared for bed, he looked repeatedly towards the cupboard he'd had built into the niche beside the chimney breast. The tiny key that unlocked it hung from his watch-chain and never left his side except when he slept. No one else had a key and he guarded the contents of the cupboard jealously from prying eyes, for hidden there were the most precious reminders of his youth.

He pulled on his dressing gown, used the specially adapted en-suite bathroom, and then wheeled across to the cupboard. Slotting in the key, Henri-Pascal Baptiste opened the two doors and sat back to look at the framed portrait of Annabelle.

He'd started it on that day he'd first met her on the Pont Neuf, and over the weeks, as he'd got to know her better, he'd spent long hours trying to capture the very essence of her. He gazed at it and wondered if his imagination *had* been playing tricks on him, for although the young girl he'd seen earlier had something of Annabelle about her, she certainly wasn't his Belle.

Henri lost all track of time as he gazed in reminiscence at the portrait, and then, realising that the sky was beginning to grow light, pressed a hidden button so that a secret drawer slid out from beneath the painting. Reaching into it, he drew out the sketchbook that had survived far better than he in the bombing of Belchite.

The drawings and watercolours he'd done of her during those magical ten days on the Spanish coast had been far more skilled, and ultimately more telling and personal than the portrait, for they'd been executed with so much love that it sang from every line of her beautiful face and each delicious curve of her body.

As he turned the pages and relived those few short, treasured days they'd spent together he wondered where she was and if she was happy, and whether she'd kept the painting he'd given her, or ever thought of him.

'But I'm dead to her,' he murmured sadly as he closed the book and returned it to its hiding-place. 'Dead and buried in the rubble of Belchite. But at least if she does remember me, it will be as a strong, fit, lusty young man with two working legs and no scars on my face.'

He stroked the beard, his sensitive fingers tracing the rough folds of discoloured skin he now kept hidden. It was probably for the best, he thought as he locked the cupboard and rolled the chair back to the bedside. Memories were easier to deal with than the reality of what war and age could do. She would be in her early forties now and was probably a plump matron with half a dozen children, lost in the domesticity of marriage. Not that it would make any difference to the way he felt about her, for his love was still strong enough to overcome time and change.

Henri tweaked open the curtains and then lay in bed and looked at the lightening sky. He'd fought so hard to stay alive for her; had endured the tortuous treatments and the hideous weeks when he thought he'd been blinded; and had refused to give in to self-pity and the awful temptation to just let go. Yet all the while he was going through that ordeal he didn't know if she'd survived the bombing. There had been no word from her or Etienne, and as far as he could make out, he, Henri, had been left for dead until he'd been miraculously found. It was only once he'd discovered that he wasn't going blind, or about to die, that he got one of the nursing aides to write to Aline.

'Too late,' he whispered. 'I left it too late.' The slow tears trickled down his face and soaked the pillow as her betrayal once more squeezed his heart. She couldn't have loved him – not in the way he'd loved her – for why else would she have married someone else so soon after his reported death?

Henri pulled at his useless legs until he could lie on his side and, drawing the pillow towards him, buried his face so that the waking house couldn't hear his sobs of despair.

Eugenie lay in the vast four-poster bed and watched the sky lighten over the rooftops. Despite the late night, she was already wide awake at five in the morning, her mind working continuously through all that had happened and what was to come, for in two days' time she would be going through the admissions process at the art school, and getting her first real feel of the place.

She'd read everything she could find on the school, which had been founded back in the seventeenth century, and had seen pictures of it. She had found them daunting, for the place seemed to be as huge as the Louvre, which stood directly across from it on the other side of the Seine. She wasn't worried about the fact that the school was extremely tough on its students, demanding an exceptional standard of work and a total commitment to the academic studies; in fact, she was looking forward to stretching herself and discovering just what she was capable of. Her main cause for concern had been the fact she didn't know anyone.

People were often sceptical when she told them she was quite shy, for outwardly she came across as sociable and self-assured; but only she knew the terror she felt when walking alone into a room full of strangers. Her fears on that score had been less-ened somewhat by Aunt Caroline, who'd told her to imagine everyone naked, to get her hostess to introduce her to people with a common interest, and to smile until it hurt. Nevertheless, Eugenie was missing her best friend Dianna and the small group she usually hung around with, and was secretly dreading that first day.

She'd had high hopes that Fleur and Michel would prove to be open and friendly when she met them last night, but they'd been dashed within minutes. Fleur was a bubbly little Parisian blonde in her second year, who clearly liked to be the centre of attention. She was studying different media to Eugenie, and made it plain that she didn't appreciate having the competition of another girl in the house, for she'd set her sights very firmly on the Swiss musician, Antoine. It hadn't helped that Antoine clearly thought he was God's gift to women and had flirted out-rageously with Eugenie throughout the evening, despite Fleur's dagger-like glares.

Michel, who was from Belgium, also studied at the school. Tall, gangling and rather dour, he wore tattered, baggy clothes, ate as if he was ravenous, and his conversation was mono-syllabic. It was only when he grudgingly showed her his port-folio of life drawings that Eugenie realised that he was not only painfully shy but extremely talented.

Pascal was a dark-eyed, quiet youth from a small village in the south of France and, like Antoine, was studying music at the Conservatoire. He played the Spanish guitar as well as the violin and piano, and Eugenie had been entranced when he'd rounded off the evening by playing a sadly sweet Spanish tune on his guitar.

Throughout the evening, Eugenie became aware that there was a certain rivalry between all three young men, but despite their obvious enthusiasm for wine and girls, it was clear that their art and music came first. Eugenie approved of that, for she knew and understood how fortunate they all were to have such an opportunity to learn from the masters.

Eugenie grew restless and clambered out of bed. Once she'd looked out of the window to make certain it all hadn't just been a dream, she washed and dressed and went downstairs.

The old cat, Bobo, stretched and yawned and insinuated herself around Eugenie's ankles until her saucer of food was put down. The house was quiet, for it was still very early, but Eugenie didn't mind that and set about making a pot of tea. She eyed the dirty dishes in the sink, the remnants of their supper strewn across the table, and the chaos in the sitting room, and decided that as she had nothing better to do, she'd make a start on tidying up.

Having washed the dishes and cleaned the table and floor, she drank two cups of coffee and then started on the sitting room. Once the magazines and books had been tidied away, the cushions plumped, ashtrays emptied, and the couches cleared of abandoned bits of clothing, old crusts of bread and the odd slipper, she spread the shawls and scarves over them artistically and stood back to admire the effect. There was a marvellous sense of satisfaction in a job well done, and like her father, she liked things to be neat.

The sun-bleached curtains had been drawn last night and she pulled them back with the tasselled ties which she slipped over the tarnished brass hooks. She opened the French windows to let in some fresh air and noted that the small garden was still in the shade. Yet she could see some decrepit furniture out there, a dry fountain with a broken cherub covered in lichen, and the faded, chipped remains of a mosaic fresco. Weeds pushed up through the rough paving slabs and the rows of terracotta pots held only the wizened remains of long-dead herbs. Eugenie regarded it with sadness, for her mother had painted a very different picture of how it had once been.

With her thoughts on all the things she could do to help her aunt, Eugenie hunted out a dustpan, broom, polish and duster and set to cleaning the sitting room. Napoleon squawked and rattled his cage from beneath the cover Aline had placed over him, but Eugenie decided he could wait until she'd finished. When it was done the room still looked shabby, but at least it was tidy and smelt a bit fresher.

She pulled the cover away from the cage, filled Napoleon's water dish and seed pot and then went into the kitchen to find some old newspapers and a cloth. It was still early and there was no sign of anyone moving about upstairs, so she would make a start on the windows.

'*Ooh là là*, you have been busy,' said a delighted Aline as she came into the kitchen some time later. 'Couldn't you sleep, my dear? Was the bed uncomfortable?'

Eugenie returned her kiss and shook her head. 'I'm too excited to sleep, so I thought I'd use up some of my energy by tidying up.' She suddenly realised that her aunt might think she was being very rude by doing such a thing. 'I hope you don't mind,' she added hurriedly.

Aline folded her red silk wrap around her thin figure and sat down at the neatly laid kitchen table with a smile. 'Of course I don't mind. In fact, it's a great pleasure to come down and find the place so neat. But you aren't here to do housework, Eugenie.'

She gently took her crippled hand. 'I'd like to do it, Aunt Aline. And it's time the others lent a hand as well. It's not fair to expect you to wait on them hand and foot.'

Aline chuckled. 'I hardly do that. But don't be too harsh on them, dear, they have busy lives – and so will you once you start at the school. Don't feel you have to do it if it gets too much, Eugenie. The dust will still be there long after we're gone.'

Eugenie poured her some coffee. 'I don't know what everyone has for breakfast,' she said. 'Would you like me to boil you an egg or something?'

Aline laughed. 'It's Saturday and I doubt any of them will be up before noon. I usually go to the bakery at the weekends for croissants and bread.'

'I'll go. Where is it?'

Aline told her and handed over her purse. She was still chuckling as Eugenie rushed out of the front door. *'Mon dieu*, Napoleon,' she muttered as she stroked his feathers, 'she has the energy of youth, not like us poor old things.'

She turned from the cage and went back to finish her coffee, but as she sat at the kitchen table her thoughts drifted back to when Annabelle had first written to ask if Eugenie could stay with her. Aline had been tempted to make some sort of excuse, and offer an alternative solution. Yet she'd known even then that she couldn't refuse to take in the girl – it would have thrown up too many questions and concerns, possibly even bringing Annabelle here, which wouldn't have done at all. She'd been trapped by the web of secrets and lies she'd woven to protect everyone, and had prayed fervently that Eugenie would prove to look nothing like either of her parents.

It had been a false hope, for as she'd watched Eugenie closely during the previous evening, her uneasiness at having her here had grown. The girl certainly had the look and manner of Annabelle about her, but there were also echoes of Henri in those eyes and in some of the expressions on her face. Would Henri recognise that if he saw her?

Aline shivered as a sense of foreboding swept through her. Eugenie would be crossing that bridge twice a day once she started at the school, and with Henri almost always sitting at his window it was inevitable he would see her. The secrets she'd kept from him and Annabelle were surely about to be revealed, and it seemed there was absolutely nothing she could do to prevent the inescapable heartache and retribution that would follow.

17

With her sketchbook tucked in her shoulder bag, Eugenie had spent most of the weekend walking through Paris. She'd paused to browse at the windows of the expensive shops in the Champs-Elysées, had taken the lift to the top of the Eiffel Tower and explored the narrow, winding streets of the artists' quarter on the Left Bank. The School of Fine Arts buildings proved to be as daunting as she'd expected, but Michel had kindly shown her round so that she knew where she'd have to go on the Monday morning.

On that Sunday, despite not being a Catholic, she'd slipped into a pew at the back of Notre-Dame Cathedral during the morning service and enjoyed the Latin Mass, which was accompanied by heady clouds of incense and the heavenly voices of the schoolboy choir. She'd eaten lunch at a pavement café after she'd climbed the many steep steps up to Montmartre, and had then wandered happily through the tiny squares and narrow lanes which seemed to be populated by hundreds of artists and tourists.

Each artist had set up an easel and some were painting scenes of Paris from memory to sell as souvenirs, while others were kept busy sketching rapid likenesses of the tourists. There were some very clever cartoonists, she noted, and although the sketches weren't particularly flattering, they were proving popular.

It was sunny, the skies above Paris clear and pale as she stood and looked out over the city that sprawled before her. There were the scents of garlic, herbs, olive oil and good coffee drifting in the air, and the bright scarlet geraniums that were blooming on every windowsill bobbed their heads in the warm breeze. An aged flower-seller had set down her baskets of roses and lavender on the steps of Sacré-Cœur, and was now sitting beside them, her nimble fingers twisting the lavender into fragrant bunches.

Eugenie watched her for a moment and then found a vacant chair at one of the cafés where she had a good view of the woman. Having ordered a cup of coffee, she opened her sketch-book and began to draw.

The woman's craggy face told of age and harsh experience, but her bright-black button eyes were lively and intelligent as she kept watch for a likely customer. Dressed all in black, she could have come from another time, for her skirts were long, her iron-grey hair was partially covered by a fringed scarf, and she had an embroidered shawl over her narrow shoulders.

She really is the most perfect subject, thought Eugenie as her pencil flew across the paper, *but how much better this would be if I'd brought my paints.* The contrasting colours of the flowers were quite startling against her rusty black clothes and the backdrop of the gleaming white arches of the basilica.

'She makes a good subject, doesn't she?'

Startled, Eugenie looked up to find a young man looming over her and blocking her view. His broad-brimmed hat shaded his features, and he seemed to be wearing boots and thick trousers which looked incongruous in this heat. 'She certainly does,' she replied, hoping he would move on.

He tipped the brim of his hat. 'Sorry if I startled you. Can I buy you another coffee?'

His accent was odd, so he clearly wasn't French, but if this was an attempt at a pick-up, he'd chosen the wrong girl. 'No thank you,' she said rather primly. 'Now, if you wouldn't mind, I'd like to finish my sketch, and you're in my line of sight.'

He didn't take the hint, but sat down in the vacant chair next to her, waved to the waiter and without so much as a by-your-leave, ordered them both coffee and glasses of Pernod.

Eugenie took a deep breath and would have got up and left if she hadn't been so keen to finish her sketch, so she tried to ignore him. Yet she was aware of him watching her, heard the waiter arrive with the drinks, and realised the only way to get rid of him was to walk away. She quickly finished her sketch and reached for her shoulder bag.

'You're very good,' he said. 'And strangely enough, my patron is painting a flower-seller at the moment; it could even be the same one.'

Eugenie closed the sketchbook with a snap and buried it in her bag. 'Look,' she said rather crossly, 'I don't know what you're up to, but I'm not interested.'

'Don't go,' he said hastily. 'I've been trying to find you since Friday, and if I lose you again, my patron won't be at all pleased.'

She felt a prickle of unease. 'Have you been following me?'

He shook his head. 'I came up here as a last resort, and it was just a matter of luck that I saw you.' He sat forward in his chair and tipped back his hat. 'Look, can we start again? The name's Max Preston and I'm from Australia.'

Eugenie bit down on a smile. 'That would explain it,' she replied.

He frowned and his hazel eyes narrowed. 'Explain what?'

'Your atrocious French accent and those ridiculous clothes,' she retorted in English.

'Fair go, miss. I was only trying to be nice.' His handsome face split into a wide grin. 'So, you're English, eh? What are you doing here in Paris?'

'I'm going to art school.' Eugenie still wasn't at all sure what he was up to, and therefore reluctant to tell him anything much. 'So, what's an Australian doing all the way over here – other than bothering girls in cafés?'

He crossed his booted feet at the ankles and leant back in the chair that looked too small for his large frame. 'I came here to go to art school five years ago. I got the chance through an exchange programme the academy in Sydney was running.' He looked fondly around at the bustle in the square. 'I spent a lot of time up here trying to earn enough to eat and pay the rent, but it was worth it in the end.'

Despite her wariness of him, she was intrigued. 'Why, what happened?'

He grinned. 'I got me a patron. And not just any old patron – Le Basque.'

Eugenie gasped and her eyes widened. 'Not *the* Le Basque? The one whose paintings are exhibiting at the Tate, and whose drawings and paintings from the Spanish Civil War are now part of every art student's curriculum?'

'The one and the same, I reckon,' he drawled, his eyes still twinkling. 'I was a lucky bloke to be in the right place at the right time. I was painting down by the river and he happened to come by. He looked at my work, told me I needed to learn to paint properly and took me on. It's through him that I'm starting to make my own name.'

She regarded him thoughtfully, still suspicious. 'Indeed, you were extremely lucky. I heard he'd become almost a recluse.'

Max's expression became solemn. 'He still lectures and visits the coffee houses, cafés and bars where the artists meet, but mostly he's in his studio. He can't get about much now, but that doesn't mean to say he's lost interest in what's happening. Who's new in town; who's got a commission or an exhibition; who's showing great promise . . . it's all grist to his mill, as they say.'

'Goodness,' she breathed. 'I would love to meet him. Do you think it would be possible?'

His smile was broad. 'I reckon that could be arranged,' he said. 'But there's plenty of time for that, and you haven't touched your drinks. Why don't we get to know one another a bit first?'

She regarded him squarely. 'Is this a come-on? Because if it is, you're wasting your time.'

He blew out his cheeks. 'Strewth. What's a bloke gotta do to convince you I'm not here to seduce you? Hen . . . My patron asked me to find you. That's the only reason I'm talking to you.'

Despite her own dismissal of him, Eugenie was slightly miffed that he was only talking to her because of his patron, but as he seemed to be genuine, she was cautiously prepared to listen to what he had to say. 'So, how does he know I'm here and why should he want you to find me?'

'His house overlooks the river, and he saw you on the Pont Neuf late Friday afternoon.' He finished the cup of coffee and poured water into the two glasses of Pernod. 'I know it doesn't make much sense, but it appears you remind him of someone he knew years ago, and he's interested in finding out who you are.'

Eugenie sipped at the Pernod, her thoughts skittering wildly. 'I knew someone was watching me that evening,' she murmured. 'I could feel it.' She felt a tingle run up her spine. 'It's all a bit creepy, really, isn't it?'

'I don't think he has any dark designs on you,' he drawled as he rolled a cigarette. 'He's just interested in who you are and where you've come from. If you tell me about yourself, then I can tell him and you wouldn't even have to meet him if you didn't want to.' He eyed her over the flame of his lighter. 'But I reckon you're still sceptical.'

'Tell me about yourself first,' she countered. 'And then I'll think about it.'

She listened as he told her about the cattle station his family had owned for three generations, and how his parents had been part of the huge wartime cattle drove from Winton across the Outback to Brisbane. He talked about his siblings, his time at the art academy in Sydney, and the difficulty he'd had in learning to speak French. As he went on to talk about his patron and the house he shared with his protégés, and the commissions that Henri had arranged for them all, she began to relax.

He was a bit older than her, probably mid-twenties, but good-looking in a raw, rangy sort of way, and although she couldn't think how he'd fit in amongst the social elite in their salons and exhibition halls, she *could* imagine him on horseback in the Australian outback. The clothes he wore suited him, though combined with his height and the breadth of his shoulders they certainly made him stand out. But perhaps that was deliberate – artists wanted to be noticed, and it was always good to have something that made them different.

He fell silent and looked across at her. 'Your turn,' he said. 'And it would be nice if you could tell me your name.'

She reddened. 'It's Eugenie Ashton.'

'Good to meet you, Eugenie Ashton.' His great paw swamped her fingers as they shook hands. 'How come you've got a French name – I take it your dad is English?'

'He's Irish, actually,' she replied and then smiled. 'My grand-mother is French, and my mother lived in Paris for a while with my aunt, Aline Fournier, which is where I'm staying at the moment.'

His eyes widened. 'Aline? Really?' At her puzzled nod, he gave a low whistle. 'Strewth, it's a small world and no mistake,' he drawled. 'Aline and my patron have known each other for years and I've been to her house for supper a couple of times.'

He dropped his gaze. 'I was seeing a girl who was lodging with her, but she's gone back to America now.'

Eugenie realised she had little to fear from this man, for he might be rather brash, but he seemed to be open and honest. She told him about her parents, and about their comfortable home in Dartford where her father shared his practice with another young doctor while her mother was the local district nurse. She continued to talk of her time at the Slade before she'd been given the amazing opportunity to study at the School of Fine Arts across the Seine.

'The letter arrived in May and it was the most wonderful eighteenth birthday present I could ever have imagined,' she finished happily.

His eyes narrowed as he regarded her through the cigarette smoke. 'Not many people get that privilege, so you must be very good. What are you specialising in?'

'Architecture and its history.'

He grinned. 'Well, you've come to the right place. Paris is fair stuffed with magnificent buildings, as you can see.' He waved his arm towards the view of the city below them.

'And what do you paint?'

'Portraits mostly, but I also like doing still life and figure drawing.'

'Le Basque is the master of portraiture,' she murmured. 'You really have fallen on your feet, haven't you?'

'Yeah, I know how lucky I am, Eugenie, and I reckon he'd be delighted to meet you.' He grinned as she sat forward eagerly. 'Give me time to talk to him first – he's a bit wary of visitors calling unannounced – and once I've arranged things, I'll get in touch with you at Aline's.'

'Really? You're not spinning me a line?'

'I wouldn't do that, Eugenie. I can see how important your art is to you.' He finished his cigarette. 'It might be an idea to bring your portfolio along. You never know, he might like what he sees and decide to sponsor you.'

Eugenie gasped. 'Do you think he might?' she asked breathlessly.

'Aw, well, I'm not promising anything,' he said hurriedly. 'But I reckon he might at least give you some advice and help if he thinks you're worth it.'

Eugenie couldn't speak for excitement.

He grinned and finished the Pernod. 'I've got to go.' He stood and tipped his hat. 'It's been nice meeting you, Eugenie. See you later.'

Eugenie watched him stride away, a tall, well-built young man with a slight roll and swagger to his step, who cut a swathe through the tourists as he ignored the admiring glances of the girls. The whole situation was odd, and she knew she should think this through thoroughly before making any hasty decisions. Yet her pulse was racing and the adrenalin was coursing through her at the thought that Le Basque had noticed her and wanted to meet her. How exciting it would be if he asked to look through her portfolio. She gathered up her bag and hurried out of the square. She couldn't wait to tell Aline.

Aline had been delighted to see her come rushing in all excited and flushed from her day in the sunshine, but as the girl poured out her extraordinary tale, her pleasure was swept away in the

295

bitter realisation that all her fears had been justified. And so soon.

'I shouldn't take too much notice of Max,' she said airily. 'He's apt to get overenthusiastic about things. Le Basque probably thought you'd make a good model, and once he knows you're living here, he won't want to take things any further.'

'But I'd love to meet him and show him my work,' Eugenie said breathlessly. 'Oh, Aunt Aline, this could be the start of something really special if he likes what I do.'

It would be a disaster, thought Aline frantically. She made a concerted effort to appear calm, but her heart was racing and she felt light-headed. 'The art school you're about to go to is considered one of the finest in the world; you'll get all you need from the tutors there without pinning your hopes on an artist who's little more than a recluse these days.'

Aline could see the stars in her eyes, knew she hadn't convinced her, and changed tack. 'It sounds as if you and Max had a very long chat. I know how charming he can be, and how easy it is to talk to him, but I'm a little concerned that you may have told him rather too much about yourself. I usually find it's wise to hold back on certain things until I know the person better.'

Eugenie blushed and looked down at her clasped hands. 'I did get a bit carried away, to be honest,' she admitted. 'I told him about the family, and how Mummy came to stay here for a while before she went to nurse in Spain. And how I came to Paris to go to the school and stay with you.'

Dear God. Aline slumped into the couch and shakily lit a cigarette. Henri would definitely want to see her once Max had relayed that all-too revealing conversation. He would probably question her closely and, in her youthful innocence and excitement at having such an important man taking an interest in her, Eugenie would tell him everything. Henri was far from stupid, and it wouldn't take him long to work out the truth. This had to be nipped in the bud – and quickly.

'You don't seem very excited about it, Aunt Aline,' said Eugenie dolefully. 'In fact, you almost look disapproving. Have you and Le Basque had some sort of falling-out?'

Aline thought fast. She had to be careful what she said, for it could come back to haunt her later. She decided to stick closely to the truth. 'Le Basque has a reputation for being a lothario,' she said. 'He might be confined to a wheelchair, but that hasn't stopped him being quite outrageous with his models. There have been many scandals over the years – reports of affairs with other men's wives, that sort of thing. Not that it's frowned upon too much here. Affairs are all a part of life in Paris. But with four lusty young men living in that house and their patron condoning their risqué behaviour, it would be best if you didn't go there. After all, you're very young, and your mother would expect me to guard your reputation.'

Eugenie giggled. 'I'm sure I could outrun a wheelchair if the need arose. And I do know how to take care of myself, Aunt Aline.'

'I'm sure you do, my dear, but you've allowed yourself to be persuaded by Max that Le Basque might sponsor you. He had no right to do that, and I suspect he was just trying to impress you.' She rested her crippled hand on Eugenie's knee. 'You'd be better off staying away from Max – he shares the same reputation as his mentor, and I doubt you could outrun him.'

Eugenie's shoulders slumped and all the joy of the day drained away. 'Oh, Aunt Aline, I've been very foolish, haven't I? I suspected Max was trying to impress me, but I so wanted it all to be true that I didn't stop and really think it through.'

'It's Max's favourite chat-up line, as you youngsters call it,' said Aline. 'My advice is to forget about the pair of them and keep what happened today to yourself. There's no point in writing to your mother about it, it would only worry her.'

Eugenie smiled ruefully. 'Yes, it would. And after all those lectures she gave me, warning me about the men in Paris, she wouldn't be at all happy with me.' She rose from the couch and kissed Aline's cheek. 'I'll make some tea and then start on supper. You look tired.'

Aline felt the weight of fear heavy on her heart despite the girl's agreement. 'It's the heat,' she sighed, 'and even with the doors open, it's uncomfortable in here.'

'Then why don't I tidy the garden so you can sit out there? I'm sure I saw an umbrella tucked away under the stairs the other day.'

'Just make the tea, dear. I'll be fine, really I will.'

As Eugenie hurried away, Aline sank back into the cushions, her heart thudding painfully. She suspected that Eugenie's pride had been hurt somewhat today, so it was unlikely she'd mention anything about it in her letters to Annabelle. But what to do about Henri?

From what the girl had said, Henri would know that she was Annabelle's daughter – which in itself wouldn't come as much of a surprise to him, for he knew the family connection to her, and it would be natural for the girl to stay here. But if they met and he discovered her age, it would take him mere seconds to realise he'd been lied to for years. '*Mon dieu*,' she breathed. 'It's a tangled web, and I'm caught right in the middle of it.'

Henri knew Max had found her the moment he came tearing up the stairs and crashed, unannounced, into the studio, his face alight. He carefully kept his expression blank, asking only a few questions to keep Max focused as he recounted their meeting.

Yet his pulse was racing at the thought of Annabelle's daughter being here in Paris; at the idea that she was staying with Aline and had been accepted at the School of Fine Arts. As Annabelle didn't have an artistic bone in her body, the girl must have inherited her talent from Aline's side of the family. He had to meet her, to talk to her and see her work; but of course it must be done with tact, for it was clear that she had not been told of his relationship with her mother.

'She gave me the runaround for a bit,' admitted Max, helping himself to a large glass of wine from the carafe that always stood on the table. 'No doubt her mother told her to be careful of strange men trying to pick her up. But the minute I told her about you, she relaxed and the rest was easy.'

Henri watched as Max sprawled across the chaise longue with a grin of satisfaction on his face. The arrogance and self-belief of youth never failed to astonish him, but then he'd once been young and arrogant too, so he could hardly reproach the boy.

'You did very well,' he murmured as he wheeled away from the painting he'd been working on and regarded it critically. The flower-seller had an interesting face full of character, and he thought he'd captured that well, but it was far from finished. 'You say she was drawing the woman on the steps of the Sacré-Cœur?'

'Quite a coincidence, eh?' Max beamed at him, totally unaware of the chaos in Henri's heart and thoughts. 'Making a good job of it too. I can see why they wanted her over the river.'

'It would be interesting to meet her,' he said casually, 'and see for myself.'

'Now that I've found her, has it laid a few of your ghosts to rest, Patron?'

On the contrary, it had stirred them up and unsettled him, and in a way he wished he hadn't started all this. But that was something he would never admit to Max. 'It was a bit rash of you to suggest that I might sponsor her, Max. It wasn't your place to do such a thing.'

He had the grace to look penitent. 'Yes, I know, and I'm sorry about that. I got a bit carried away.'

'You always do when there's a pretty girl involved,' he replied with a sigh. 'But I'd appreciate it if you left this particular one alone.'

He saw Max look at him questioningly and knew he had to justify his reason without telling him anything important. 'If she's as talented as we suspect, then she'll need her wits about her to succeed at the school, and the sort of distractions you probably have in mind won't help her at all.'

'She's really not that sort of girl, Henri. I doubt that even I could charm her into bed. Besides, she's a bit young for me. I prefer my women to be more mature and knowing.'

'Just how young is she?'

Max shrugged. 'She turned eighteen in May.' He finished the wine in one gulp and rose from the couch. 'I'm starving. I think I'll go and raid the kitchen.'

Henri barely heard him and was unaware that he'd even left the room as he sat very still in the wheelchair. His heart was hammering against his ribs as he tried to absorb the shock. Mathematics was not his forte but even he could work out that Annabelle must have fallen pregnant during their idyllic stay on the Spanish coast.

'She's my child,' he breathed in wonder. He closed his eyes and recalled those blissful days in the small cottage on the beach, when passion had overruled common sense and they'd taken no precautions. She couldn't have known then that their child was growing inside her, or indeed when the air raid had flattened Belchite and effectively shattered their dreams of a future together. And yet she and the baby had survived. It was a miracle so great he could scarcely believe it.

He wheeled the chair over to the window and stared out at the scarlet and orange of the sunset. He could still clearly remember every word of that letter from Aline, in which she'd told him they'd all thought he was dead, that Annabelle and Etienne had barely survived the air raid, but she'd now married and gone home to England. It had been a short letter, written with great feeling and sympathy, and on his return to Paris he'd gone to see Aline to thank her for the gentle way she'd tried to convey this bombshell.

'But it was all a ruse,' he rasped as he clenched his fists on the arm of the wheelchair. 'A cruel and wilful ruse to hide things from me. And all because I took too long to let them know I'd come through.' He dipped his chin to his chest, the tears streaming unheeded down his face as his heart ached for all the lost years he could have shared with Annabelle and their daughter.

It was after nine when the telephone rang in the hall, and Aline left the lively debate amongst her lodgers to go and see who was calling so late.

'It's me, Henri.'

Her heart skipped a beat and she quickly closed the door between her and the others. 'Hello, Henri,' she said nervously. 'How are you?'

'Max told me about Eugenie,' he said without preamble. 'I want to meet her.'

'That probably isn't wise,' she said hastily. 'It would take only a slip of the tongue or a thoughtless reminiscence to make her curious. One question would lead to another, and ultimately it could cause Annabelle great pain and do no good for anyone.'

'You mean it will expose you as a liar,' he said harshly. 'I know who she is, Aline. I worked it out from her age and the month of her birth.'

Aline closed her eyes and had to lean against the wall for support. Eugenie had clearly said far more than she'd admitted earlier. 'She must never know, Henri.'

'She has a right to know. And as I've been denied all knowledge of her since her birth, I too have the right to be with her.'

Aline gripped the receiver. 'It's a selfish, dangerous game you're playing, Henri,' she said fiercely, 'And I won't allow you to do this.'

'You have no say in what I can and cannot do,' he snapped back. 'Your meddling has caused enough trouble as it is.'

Aline was incensed by him describing her act of kindness and love as meddling. 'You've been dead to Annabelle for eighteen years, Henri,' she said coldly. 'The girl adores the man who's been her father for all that time and I will not let you destroy that. She knows you only because of your fame in the art world. Leave it that way, Henri, or you'll wreck everything Annabelle has done for her.'

There was a long silence at the other end and as Aline listened intently, she thought she could hear the sound of weeping. 'I'm truly sorry, Henri,' she said quietly, 'but I didn't know what else to do. We thought you were dead. Annabelle discovered she was pregnant, and George offered her a marriage of convenience so she could raise her child in respectability. How could I in all fairness tell you about Eugenie – or tell Annabelle that you'd survived when it was all far too late?'

'You say it was a marriage of convenience. She didn't love him then?'

Aline heard the break in his voice and it twisted her heart. 'She was still in mourning for you, still in love with you – even on her wedding day,' she said gently. 'But now she's found a different kind of love, and her marriage to George is strong.'

'It all makes a terrible sort of sense now you've explained it,' he said sadly. 'But it doesn't alter the fact that Eugenie's mine and I want – no, need – to get to know her. I promise to say nothing to her about me and her mother.'

'She's bound to tell Annabelle that she's caught the interest of one of the most famous artists of our era,' she replied. 'Does she know your real name?'

'Max assured me he hadn't told her that, and I believe him.'

'Then you'd better make certain it stays that way,' she retorted. 'If you meet, she'll write to her mother about it. Luckily, Annabelle doesn't know the first thing about art and artists; is unaware of what you did during the war, and therefore unlikely to know you paint under the name the Germans gave you.'

'I'll give it some serious thought,' he said after a long moment of silence. 'Would you tell her I called, and ask her to come here tomorrow with her portfolio?'

'It's a little soon, Henri. Can't you wait for a while and—'

'I've waited eighteen years,' he interrupted bitterly, 'and that's enough.'

Aline closed her eyes and took a deep breath. 'Then I will come with her,' she said finally. 'That way, I can be certain you keep your word and don't start talking to her of things she has no need to know.'

'You're always welcome in my home, Aline,' he said softly.

'And I'm sorry if I was unkind and rude to you earlier. But this has all come as a terrible shock.'

'For me too,' she admitted. 'I'll see you tomorrow after she's gone through the admissions tests, filled in all their wretched forms and done the guided tour. We should be there at around four.'

She replaced the receiver and grasped the newel post to keep her balance. Her heart had not functioned well since the deprivations and brutalities of wartime had weakened it, and now it was painfully and irregularly thudding against the wall of her chest, making her feel light-headed and unsteady on her feet.

She glanced towards the door, hearing the youngsters talking on the other side and laughing at something Antoine had said. For once she had no appetite for their silly, youthful chatter, and felt no urge to stay up long into the night. She needed the comfort of her bed and the peace of her own company.

Eugenie realised that Aline had been gone a long time since she'd left to answer the telephone, so she went out into the hall. As there was no sign of her, she quietly went up the stairs and stood outside the bedroom door. She could hear drawers opening and shutting, and her aunt muttering to herself, so assumed she was all right and had simply decided to have an early night for a change.

Once she gauged that the others were thinking about retiring, she suggested they help her to clear up the mess they'd made of Aline's kitchen and sitting room. This was met with a surly look from Fleur and a half-hearted shrug from the boys. She pressed the point and chivvied them into clearing the kitchen table while she began on the washing-up.

'If we all lent a hand each day, Aline wouldn't have so much to do,' she said firmly. 'And it's unfair of us to take advantage of her soft heart.' She tempered her words with a smile. 'It only takes a few minutes, but it would make such a difference.'

Fleur sniffed and dumped the dirty glasses on the drainer. 'You'll be writing out a rota next,' she said sourly. 'Just because she's your aunt, it doesn't give you the right to boss us about.'

Eugenie was about to reply, but Fleur had already flounced out of the room. She glanced at the boys, who had the decency to look rather ashamed.

'Don't let Fleur get under your skin,' said Michel quietly. 'She's just a spoilt brat who's never had to lift a finger before.' He began to dry the dishes as Antoine finished tidying the sitting room and Pascal swept the kitchen floor.

Within minutes the rooms were tidy, and after Eugenie had covered Napoleon's cage, she followed the others up the stairs. It had been a strange day, she thought as she wrestled with the French plumbing in the small bathroom. Her emotions had swung from high to low, and it was really quite exhausting.

She went into her bedroom and closed the shutters against the open window to keep the bugs out. Aunt Aline had clearly not approved of her getting involved with Max's patron, but how on earth could she possibly deny herself the chance to have someone so august critique her work? It was almost as if her aunt disapproved of Le Basque; and yet according to Max, they'd known each other for years. Perhaps she knew things about him that she considered too risqué to reveal to someone of her age? Either way, she was determined to meet him.

Having prepared for bed, she climbed between the covers and tried to settle. The day had been strange and exciting, and tomorrow would be even more so, so it was important that she got a good night's sleep. However, she lay there for a long while, her mind churning over all the questions she wanted to ask Aline about her mother's time in Paris. Le Basque could have been living here then, and if so, was probably a frequent visitor to this house. Had her mother met him? Did she know that he was now a famous artist?

She snuggled down and closed her eyes. Le Basque was obviously not his real name. She must remember tomorrow morning to ask Aline what it was.

Annabelle snuggled into George's embrace as they sat on the couch and listened to the music concert on the wireless. 'I could get used to having you to myself,' she murmured, 'although I do miss not having Eugenie and all her friends about the place.'

He rested his cheek on the top of her head. 'I miss her too, but it's rather nice not to have their awful music blaring out. I can't think why they want to listen to Little Richard – such a stupid name – whose voice goes right through my head. Elvis can certainly sing, but all that wriggling about isn't at all decent.'

Annabelle giggled and poked him in his ribs. 'You're getting to be an old fuddy-duddy,' she teased. 'Elvis is considered to be a real heart-throb, and I must say that the pictures of him in those magazines Eugenie buys certainly bear that out.'

He tightened his grip on her and kissed her hair. 'Rosemary Clooney gets my heart racing,' he teased. 'Now there's a girl – and what a voice.'

She prodded him again and nestled closer as the string quartet reached the final, stirring movement of the piece.

George wasn't really listening to the music, he was too absorbed in the scent and feel of Annabelle, who fitted so perfectly into his side, and whose love had refined his hard edges and made him whole. He understood that she was missing Eugenie, just as he was, and suspected that, deep down, she might even be envying their daughter.

He'd considered taking Annabelle to Paris one day, but had realised it wouldn't be wise to try to make their own memories of the place. Paris meant only one thing to Annabelle – Henri – and he couldn't hope to change that.

In the early days of their marriage she'd talked about him rarely and now not at all, and he understood that her memories of that time were private. As he had no wish to pry, he hadn't encouraged her to reminisce beyond her experiences with Aline or the hardships she'd encountered in Spain. Yet he knew instinctively that now their daughter was in Paris, Annabelle's thoughts had returned to the past.

He held her close as the music rose to a crescendo and then ended on a lingering, rather haunting note which seemed to resonate with his deepest fears. Henri might be long dead, but he could still feel his shadow between them even though Annabelle would strongly deny it. How could he fight a ghost, a memory?

As Annabelle went across the room to turn off the wireless, George decided he was overtired and therefore becoming foolishly sentimental. Their marriage was strong: they'd come to terms with the past and together would withstand anything the future might have in store for them.

18

Eugenie had slept well and risen early so she could dress carefully for this most special of days. Having chosen a full red skirt with bars of music embroidered on the hem – a design she'd copied from one of Aunt Caroline's American fashion magazines – she'd pulled it on over the froth of a pale pink organza petticoat. A white blouse, broad black belt and flat black pumps had completed the look, and she'd pulled back her thick, tawny curls from her face with a strip of red ribbon which she tied in a bow just above her right ear. Adding some bright plastic bangles and a pair of red earrings to match her lipstick, she'd regarded herself critically in the mirror and decided she'd achieved the look she'd been aiming for.

She'd been down to the bakery to collect the bread, and had made the coffee by the time the rest of the household came downstairs. She looked up from the kitchen table and felt immediate concern as a rather pale Aline came in. 'Are you all right, Aunt Aline?'

'A little tired.' She sat down and smiled at her. 'You look lovely, this morning, dear. I see you've inherited my love of colour.'

'You don't think it's too much?' she asked, suddenly doubtful.

'It's perfect,' she replied softly. 'You look every inch the modern young art student and will fit in just right.'

Michel and Pascal fussed around Aline, pouring the milky, sweet coffee and making sure she had the softest bit of the baton to dip into it, while Fleur and Antoine argued over who'd put the butter knife into the jam.

'Are you excited about today?' Aline asked as she dipped her bread into the large cup of milky coffee, 'or just nervous?'

'Both,' Eugenie admitted, 'but I can hardly wait to get started. It's going to feel like hours before it's time to go and register, so I thought I'd go for a walk after breakfast.'

Aline eyed her sharply. 'Try the park at the end of the street. There's a lovely pond and a sweet little gazebo all covered in passion flowers and rambling roses.'

'Yes, I might just do that,' she replied, though she had been planning on going down to the Quai de la Mégisserie to have a look at Le Basque's house and see if he was watching at his window. She didn't know quite what she'd do if he was – probably just smile and wave and beat a hasty retreat.

'What time was it when you finished your registration day, Fleur?' asked Aline.

The girl shrugged. 'About four, I think. But it was a year ago, so I can't be sure.' She looked from Aline to Eugenie and back again. 'You aren't thinking of going with her, are you? It would hardly be appropriate – unless poor little Eugenie needs a hand to hold,' she added spitefully.

Aline looked across the table, her brown eyes unwavering, her expression cool. 'You might consider yourself to be pretty, Fleur, but your manners are certainly not at all attractive.'

Fleur blushed as the boys tittered. 'Sorry,' she muttered. 'I didn't mean to be rude.'

'Oh, I think you did,' she murmured, 'and I'll have no more of it. This is my home, and you are to respect it and the people who live here.' Aline carefully picked up the cup in both hands and sipped from it, her gaze still fixed on Fleur.

Eugenie began to feel rather sorry for the girl, and would have tried to catch her eye and give her a reassuring look if she thought it might help. Yet Fleur had been very rude and didn't seem at all contrite, so it was probably best just to ignore her.

Breakfast was swiftly finished in an awkward silence and once the others had left with a clatter and slammed the door behind them, Aline visibly relaxed. 'She's just jealous, Eugenie. Take no notice of her.'

'I don't see why she should be. I've no interest in Antoine; in fact, I think he's a bit of a show-off.'

Aline smiled. 'He reminds me a bit of Etienne,' she murmured. 'He was always flirting and talking himself up.' She blinked and gathered her thoughts. 'Sorry, Eugenie, I was remembering someone I knew many years ago. Now, I have something important to tell you.'

Eugenie frowned. Aline was sounding very serious.

'I've made arrangements for us this afternoon, so I'll be waiting for you outside the school in the little café on the corner.'

'What arrangements?'

'You'll see,' Aline said mysteriously. 'But don't get overexcited about it, it will probably prove to be very boring.'

Eugenie giggled. 'I doubt anything could be boring if you're involved. But why the secrecy?'

Aline shrugged. 'I'm an old woman. I have these fancies now and then.' She stood up from the table and slowly went into the sitting room to pull back the curtains. 'I think I might sit out there this morning while it's still cool. But I don't trust those chairs. Could you bring out one of those from the kitchen and find me an umbrella?'

Eugenie hunted out both and went into the garden. She hadn't had time to do anything about the weeds and the pots of dead plants, but perhaps she could make a start on it this evening. Gardening was something she enjoyed, and she'd often helped her father, working in quiet harmony with him, their minds drifting as they weeded and hoed and planned the planting for the next season. This sudden reminder of home brought a wave of nostalgia, and she wondered what her parents were doing now and how they were coping with an empty house.

Once Aline was settled comfortably beneath the umbrella with another cup of coffee and her newspaper, Eugenie kissed her goodbye. 'I'm too tense to relax,' she said. 'A walk will do me good.'

'Good luck, my dear. I'll see you this afternoon.'

Eugenie picked up her portfolio and shoulder bag and clicked the front door shut behind her. She stood on the top step and then decided she would walk in the park first and then go down to the river. That way she wouldn't have to lie to Aline if she asked where she'd gone.

The park wasn't very large, but the flower beds were bright with colour, the grass was springy and green, and the little gazebo was a delight. She sat there for a moment, breathing in the scent of the white roses that fought for purchase on the trellis amongst the yellow-hearted purple passion flowers, and watched the swans and ducks on the pond. Then, still restless and nervous about the forthcoming interview, she found a way out of the park and headed towards the river.

The Seine was flowing swiftly beneath the bridges, and the bronze statue of Henry IV riding boldly upon his horse stood out against the clear blue of the sky. Eugenie walked along the cobbled quay, her gaze trawling the tall houses with their iron balconies and French windows. Le Basque lived in one of them, but she had no idea which, so she looked closely at the names above the doorbells as she passed.

Most, she soon realised, were divided into apartments, for there were several names listed, but as she came to the last but one, she saw there were no names, merely a number depicted in the stained-glass above the door. Her pulse began to race as she stared at the shiny black door and the highly polished brass knocker. Did she dare to rap that knocker and introduce herself?

The sound of footsteps approaching from behind the door made up her mind, and she quickly darted away and went to stand on the bridge. A plump woman in a voluminous apron appeared on the step and began to polish the dolphin-shaped brass knocker, and Eugenie wondered if she was Le Basque's wife, or his housekeeper. She knew so little about the man other than his paintings, and, she suddenly realised she'd forgotten to ask Aline his real name.

Feeling rather cross with herself, she watched the woman for a moment and then caught a glimpse of movement from a window three storeys up. She narrowed her eyes and looked hard, her heart thudding madly as she realised he had drawn his wheelchair closer and was looking straight at her.

It was difficult to tell his age, for he had a beard and moustache which hid most of his face; but he had to be old, probably older than her father, which meant he was at least fifty, and therefore positively ancient. Yet the breadth of his shoulders and torso was that of a much younger man, and his hair and beard seemed still to be very dark.

She saw him raise his hand and smile, and she tentatively raised her own and smiled nervously back. And then she heard the church clock strike the quarter hour and realised that if she didn't get a move on, she'd be late. With a quick wave, she turned and ran across the bridge to the Left Bank.

The School of Fine Arts sprawled at the heart of the area known as Saint-Germain-des-Prés in the sixth arrondissement. The main entrance was an imposing wall topped by decorative railings and finely wrought iron gates.

Eugenie hurried into the main cobbled square and, because she was out of breath, came to an abrupt halt by the tall plinth at its centre, on top of which was the bronze statue of the school's founder, Cardinal Mazarin, who regarded his creation from on high. As she fought to catch her breath and find some calm, she looked around her with the same awe she'd felt when Michel had brought her here two days before.

The original building from 1648 had been added to by the architect Félix Duban between 1830 and 1861, and these additions spread along three sides of the square, their elegant arched windows and doorways adding a sense of stately beauty and solid permanence. There was little doubt that this was the beating heart of the artistic side of Paris, for Eugenie knew she was walking in the footsteps of the masters who been students here – masters such as Degas, Monet, Renoir and Moreau. It was a daunting path to follow, and she could only pray she was good enough to tiptoe in their long shadows.

She realised she was wasting time, so she quickly tucked her blouse back into the broad belt, smoothed any imagined creases from her full skirt and hitched her bag over her shoulder. With the leather portfolio case her parents had given her on her birthday tightly grasped in her hand, she nervously walked through the archway into the echoing marble reception hall.

Once she'd been directed to the appropriate room, she hesitated at the door, remembering her mother's story about her own nursing examination all those years before. That had ended in failure because her French hadn't been good enough, but Eugenie had no fears in that quarter, for she'd had a French tutor during her last year at school and had insisted she learnt everything she'd need to know should she ever make it to Paris. It had been a long-held dream, encouraged by her mother's stories, and now she was actually here, she was so nervous she could barely breathe.

'You look as terrified as I feel.'

Eugenie looked over her shoulder to find a tall, dark-haired girl standing close by, whose brown eyes seemed huge in her pale face. 'It's scary, isn't it? Shall we go in together?' Eugenie offered.

The other girl nodded. 'If you wouldn't mind. I'm Ellie, by the way.'

Eugenie introduced herself, and as they talked, she discovered that Ellie was twenty-three, also from England, and, in fact, had just graduated from a three-year course at the Slade. Feeling a little more relaxed now they were together, they both took a deep breath for courage and went into the room.

Aline walked down to the Pont Neuf, taking her time so she could enjoy the light breeze that drifted up from the river. It had its own dank, dark smell, and the timeless, eternal flow of the water was swift beneath the arches of the many bridges, reminding her that some things in Paris would never change.

She paused at the centre of the bridge, the breeze blowing in her hair and gently ruffling the hems of her long, orange silk coat and bright purple dress. She'd decided she would wear colour again after seeing Eugenie looking so bright and pretty this morning, for she'd been in black ever since Paris had fallen – mourning not only the loss of her city, but the part of her which was her art, and the youthful vitality with which she'd once faced the troubles of the world head-on.

Her choice of colour had also come from an almost defiant pride which she'd thought she'd lost. Black was dowdy; black screamed old and forgotten; and most importantly, black made her look sallow, and far from chic. Just because she was in her seventieth year and troubled with her heart didn't mean that the embers of her inner fire could not be coaxed into a flame again – and time was running out.

She experienced a prickle of something that told her he was there, watching her, and she turned slowly towards the houses on the *quai*. Dipping her head in silent acknowledgement as he raised his hand, she turned away and continued across the bridge, heading for rue Bonaparte and the café on the corner. They would meet soon enough, and although she believed he would keep his word, she was still rather tense at the thought of him and Eugenie being in the same room as one another.

The clocks had struck the hour some time ago, but Aline was happily ensconced at the small table on the pavement, shaded from the bright sun by a blue-and-white striped awning. She sipped the glass of very good red wine and listened in with amusement to the chatter and gossip of the youngsters around her, wondering why she didn't do this sort of thing more often.

She had once been a regular at the cafés and bars, enjoying the company of other artists, and becoming enthralled by the tutors and masters from the colleges who sat with their students and discussed techniques and argued about the latest art forms. It had been a lively, interesting world before the war, and this new generation was clearly just as enthused and opinionated, and as argumentative and exciting to listen to as those who'd come before.

She was snapped from her thoughts by the sight of Eugenie coming through the ornate gateway with another girl. They were chattering away like sparrows, dawdling and gesticulating as if they'd known each other for years. Aline smiled. It seemed Eugenie had made a friend and that her first day hadn't been as terrifying as she'd thought.

'This is Ellie, Aunt Aline. And would you believe it, her mother's French, her father's Irish, and she's from London.'

Aline smiled and shook the girl's hand. 'I can see you've both had an exciting day, so why don't I treat you to a glass of wine while you tell me all about it?' She signalled to the waiter, raised her glass and three fingers.

The wine arrived as Eugenie was excitedly describing the large hall where, despite having passed the French language exams in England, they'd had to resit them before going through a lengthy oral test. And as they stopped long enough to take appreciative sips of the wine, they took it in turns to describe the vast lecture halls, the magnificent studios, the amazing work being done by the other students, and the glorious architecture of the school.

Aline sat back and smiled at their youthful enthusiasm, glad to be a small part of it, and delighted that Eugenie had made such a lovely friend. She regarded Ellie's dark, flashing eyes and creamy skin, the long black hair she'd tied back in the modern ponytail with a bright blue ribbon, and the elegant length of her legs and arms. She reminded her a little of Amélie, Henri's erstwhile model, for there was a ripe voluptuousness about her.

'So, Aunt Aline, what's your surprise?'

She gathered her thoughts and glanced at her watch. 'Goodness, it's very late. I'm sorry, Ellie, but we must leave.'

'Can't Ellie come too?'

'Not today, my dear. Perhaps another time.' She smiled at the girl as she gathered up her gloves and handbag. 'You're welcome at my home any time you wish. And please don't feel you need a special invitation, my door is always open.'

Ellie said goodbye and wandered off to her lodgings which were in a house situated off the rue Bonaparte. 'She's nice, isn't she?' said Eugenie as she took Aline's arm. 'And she's studying the same subject as me, so we'll be in the same classes.'

'I'm glad for you both,' said Aline as they headed towards the Pont Neuf. 'You must be missing your friends from home.'

'Where are we going, Aunt?'

'To meet someone in that house over there,' she replied.

Eugenie came to a halt, her eyes wide with surprise, her face flushed with excitement. 'We're going to visit Le Basque? Really? But how did you . . . ? When . . . ?'

'He telephoned last night,' she replied shortly. 'Come on, it's very late and he gets tired towards the end of the day.'

'I can't call him Le Basque,' said Eugenie as they began walking again. 'What's his real name?'

'That's something he never likes revealing,' she replied firmly. 'He prefers Patron these days, so I'd stick to that if I were you.'

'But Max told me you've known him for years – even before he became famous. You must know what it is,' she persisted. 'Come on, Aunt Aline, tell me.'

Now it was Aline's turn to come to a halt. 'You will call him

Patron and be done with it, Eugenie,' she said sternly. 'Is that clear?'

Eugenie blushed and dipped her chin. 'Yes, of course. I'm sorry if I've caused offence.'

Aline nodded in acceptance and headed for the glossy black door. Rapping the knocker, she soon heard the heavy footfall of someone coming down the hall. It was Max who opened the door.

'Hello. I didn't realise it was you coming today,' he said cheerfully. 'But it does explain why Patron has been fussing about and chivvying Madame to tidy up.' He stepped aside so they could enter. 'Good to see you again, Eugenie.'

Aline waited for him to slide back the sturdy metal gate on the small lift that stood in the centre of the hall, and then stepped inside. 'You come with me, Eugenie,' she ordered. 'I hate this thing.'

Once Max had closed the gate and the outer glass doors, Aline pulled the lever and the lift shuddered and squeaked and slowly groaned its way upwards. Max ran up the stairs and pulled faces at them as they reached each landing, and was there to open the doors when they arrived on the third floor.

'I'll leave you to it,' he said cheerfully. 'I have a pressing appointment in a local bar.'

Aline actually didn't mind the lift at all, but she hadn't wanted Eugenie racing up the stairs with Max and meeting Henri before she got there. She patted the rows of coloured beads hanging round her neck, tucked her handbag under her arm and stepped out of the lift with all the deliberate, imperious calm of a duchess.

Henri was sitting in the doorway to greet them, his wasted legs covered with a light blanket as usual. He looked well, she noticed, and had clearly made an effort to dress for the occasion, for he was in a suit, there was a silk kerchief showing in his breast pocket and his beard and moustache had been trimmed.

Aline could see that his gaze was on Eugenie, but she stepped forward and kissed him on both cheeks. 'It's good to see you looking so robust, Patron,' she murmured.

'And you, Aline,' he said distractedly. He tore his gaze from Eugenie. 'I see you've decided to come out of your mourning black at last. Colour suits you, but then it always did.' His gaze returned immediately to Eugenie.

'This is my niece, Eugenie Ashton,' she said as she nudged the tongue-tied, starry-eyed girl forward. 'You'll have to forgive her shyness, I think she's rather overwhelmed by being in your presence,' she added lightly.

'*Enchanté*, Eugenie,' he said as he took her hand and kissed the air above her knuckles.

'It's such an honour to meet you, Patron,' she stuttered. 'I love your work, and have seen the paintings that are being exhibited in the Tate,' she gabbled breathlessly, 'and of course I know your civil war sketches from our classes at school and—'

Henri chuckled. 'I think that before you run out of breath entirely, you'd better come into my studio. We have the rest of the day to get to know one another, so why try and say it all in five minutes?'

Eugenie blushed furiously and Aline quietly followed the pair of them into the vast sunlit room that acted as both studio and sitting room. It seemed she'd been forgotten, but she didn't mind as long as Henri didn't get carried away and say things he would live to regret.

Henri indicated that Eugenie should sit in the chair by the window so the light fell on her face, but not in her eyes, and that Aline should take the other chair beside him. He poured wine into glasses and watched in amusement as Eugenie gazed round the room in undisguised admiration.

'It's the flower-seller,' she breathed as her gaze settled on his unfinished painting. 'The same one I was drawing yesterday. But you've captured the character in her face so well, and the sparrow-bright light in her eyes . . .' She fell silent and blushed again. 'Sorry, Patron. I didn't mean to babble on.'

'It's all right, Eugenie, I have no problem with any critique, wherever it may come from. It's the lifeblood of creativity, and although sometimes it might hurt, it is never wasted as long as you use it to your advantage, and don't get precious about your work.'

He smiled and sipped his wine. 'Ultimately, each work of art is something you either understand, or don't; it's down to personal taste really. Even the critics have certain styles and subjects they favour. They have been frequently known to fulsomely praise a new work that is actually incomprehensible, and not very well executed, because they think it will make them appear more astute and discerning than the rest of us mere mortals. The art world can be very pompous.'

'I have so much to learn,' she sighed.

'Let me be the judge of that,' he replied. 'Would you care to show me your portfolio and your sketchbook?'

Eugenie wriggled in the chair, her expression a tortured mixture of excitement and dread. 'I'm not very good, and lots of that stuff is quite old,' she stammered.

Henri laughed. 'There's no place in our world for modesty, Eugenie. Show me what you can do, and always, always remember to be proud of it.'

Eugenie unzipped the portfolio while Henri pulled a small table over for her to rest it upon.

As Eugenie clasped and twisted her hands in her lap and chewed her bottom lip, Henri slowly and methodically went through the work that had won her the year's scholarship to one of the most highly regarded art schools in the world.

Aline sat quietly watching and noted the unmistakable likeness between them. It was in the eyes, without question, and in the bone structure of their faces. Even their hands were alike, with the long, tapering fingers and narrow palms, and although Eugenie had inherited her mother's colouring, there was absolutely no doubt that she was Henri's daughter.

She regarded Henri as he leant over the portfolio and slowly perused each painting and drawing with studious care. He must be finding this incredibly difficult, for he'd found a daughter he'd had no idea existed until yesterday; and yet he could never acknowledge her as such, never be a father to her.

Henri closed the portfolio and reached for the sketchbook. He pursed his lips as he went through the many sketches she'd done during her walks through Paris, and then regarded the one she'd done of the flower-seller. 'How long did it take you to do this, Eugenie?' he asked after a long moment of silence.

'About half an hour, I suppose. I wasn't really keeping an eye on the time.'

'It's clearly a quick study, as all the work is in this book, but you've captured the essence of her perfectly.' He closed the book and took a sip of wine. 'You're a talented young woman, Eugenie Ashton, and I'm not at all surprised you've been accepted by the School of Fine Arts, but you have a long way to go yet.'

Eugenie nodded, the light of hope in her eyes warring with the frown of worry.

'Are you prepared to work hard at the little things, the boring things, the things that you find the most difficult?'

'I'll work as hard as possible, Patron. I do realise what a privilege it is to be at the school – and to be here with you.' She dipped her chin, the colour rising once more in her cheeks. 'Do you think I stand a chance of really achieving something?'

'Indeed I do,' he said firmly. 'But it won't happen for a while yet.' He smiled at her. 'Don't lose heart, Eugenie, these things take time and a great deal of effort.'

She regarded him in mute anxiety.

'You'll have to gain more experience of life, become even more aware of the world around you, and see things not just with your eyes, but with your heart. Then you might just – just, mind you – achieve success.'

'Do you really think so?' she asked breathlessly.

'The art world is notoriously difficult to break into successfully,' he said gently. 'There are many very talented artists, actors, playwrights and poets out there who eke out a living and never fulfil their potential. Which is very sad, but that is the way of things: we don't always get the things we crave – or the things that we think are ours by right.'

He smiled to take the sting out of his words. 'But at least you've been given the very best chance right at the start, and that is an achievement on its own.'

'Yes,' she said softly. 'I know how lucky I am.'

He cleared his throat and took another sip of wine. 'Luck does sometimes play a part in it, but you'll discover when you are older and more worldly-wise that ambition is not enough – it's only *real* talent that counts.'

His smile was warm as she frowned in puzzlement. 'Real talent means that your art is a living, breathing part of you that will not be denied. It's the fire in your belly and your absolute belief that this is something you were born to do. You will suffer rejections and bad reviews; have to struggle to earn enough to keep a roof over your head while you battle to be recognised . . . but it will be worth it, Eugenie.'

She regarded him with absolute solemnity as she nodded in agreement.

'Rodin applied to the school on three occasions and was turned down,' Henri continued, 'but the fire was in him, Eugenie – the unbreakable faith in his talent never diminishing – and look how he proved to the world how right he was to believe in himself and not be defeated by those who didn't share that faith.'

'And what if that faith is misguided? What if I'm only fooling myself into thinking I could have a career with my art?'

'Ah, the worms of doubt,' he sighed. 'They live with all of

us – even at my great age. But beware, Eugenie, those doubts can grow and take over and all you have achieved will come to nothing.' He raised his glass to her. 'Have no fear, Eugenie, you show tremendous promise, and when you have your first exhibition, I expect to receive an invitation.'

Eugenie's smile was brilliant and, as they toasted each other, Aline had to blink away her tears. It was a lovely moment between father and daughter, a moment which Annabelle should have been able to witness had fate not dealt such a cruel and tragic blow.

Eugenie felt as if she were walking on air as they left the house, and she looked up at the window with a smile and a wave before she hurried after her aunt. 'Isn't he wonderful?' she exclaimed. 'He was so patient and wise, and I do so hope I didn't tire him with all my questions.'

'I doubt it,' murmured Aline. 'He enjoys talking about art, and to have such an enthralled audience must have really made his day.'

'It was such an honour to have his undivided attention for over two hours,' breathed Eugenie. 'I wouldn't mind betting that the other students would give their eye teeth for such an experience.'

'Well, it's probably not wise to go on about it,' Aline warned. 'It could make the others jealous, and you'd be inundated by requests to come with you next time.'

'You really think there will be a next time?'

'I suspect he's interested enough in you to ask you there again.'

Aline came to a halt by the front steps to her house. 'I realise you're excited and want to share the experience, but the Patron is a very private man – especially since he's been confined to a wheelchair – and he wouldn't appreciate you taking advantage of this rare kindness by asking all and sundry to go with you.'

'I wouldn't do that, Aunt Aline,' Eugenie replied firmly. 'But do you *really* think I might be permitted to visit him again?'

'Maybe. But only if he issues an invitation, Eugenie. You mustn't think you can just go round there whenever you want.'

'Of course not,' she agreed. 'But it would be nice to talk with him again. I felt so comfortable with him – as if I already knew him.' She smiled at Aline and opened the front door. 'He's younger than I thought, and really quite handsome under that beard and moustache. I wonder why he hides his face like that.'

'He was injured many years ago,' Aline replied as she stepped into the hall, 'and his face was badly scarred.'

'Was that when he was crippled?'

Aline kicked off her shoes and padded into the sitting room. 'No, that happened much later.'

Napoleon welcomed them in his usual raucous way, and once Aline had fussed over him and replenished his seed tray, she stroked the ancient cat and carried her into the kitchen where she gave her a saucer of milk. 'I don't know about you, but I could do with a cup of coffee before we make a start on supper.'

'I'll make it.' Eugenie quickly spooned the coffee into the percolator, added water and set it on the gas ring. There were so many questions going round in her head that she didn't know where to start, but as Aline seemed to be in a mellow mood and the house was deserted, it felt like a good time to ask some of them. 'Did Mother meet the Patron when she was living here?' she asked casually.

There was a long silence and Eugenie turned to find that her aunt was lighting a cigarette and looking a little disconcerted. 'I really couldn't say,' she replied eventually. 'There were always people in and out of the house back then.'

Eugenie regarded her thoughtfully, suspecting she wasn't being entirely truthful, but was then distracted by the coffee percolator.

'Mother told me about her trip down into Spain, but she was never very clear about who she travelled with,' she continued as she set the pot and cups on the table. 'She just said she went with some people from the Basque region, and ended up having to ride a horse. The Patron wouldn't have been one of those who travelled with her, would he?'

'There were a lot of Basque people living in Paris at that time,' hedged Aline. 'In fact, there were trainloads of volunteers from all over the world making their way down to Spain as I recall. Now, enough questions, Eugenie, I'm tired, and it's been a long day.'

Eugenie could see the weariness in her and was immediately contrite. But as she poured the coffee her mind was troubled with all the other questions she had yet to ask, for there were things that puzzled her – things that didn't add up – and it seemed that Aline was either ignorant of the answers or unwilling to divulge them. Perhaps, if she was given the honour of talking to the Patron again, she would ask him if he'd met her mother all those years ago.

As the others returned home and supper was eaten around the kitchen table, Eugenie found it almost impossible to keep silent about her afternoon visit. And yet she realised that Aline had been wise to caution her against speaking out, for Fleur was decidedly frosty already, and any jealousy she might be feeling would only be stoked by such a revelation.

Eugenie was exhausted by all the excitement of the day, and it was still early when she said goodnight to everyone and went up to her room. Sitting on the window seat, she gazed out to the dark, star-filled sky above the rooftops and thought over all that had happened.

The Patron's studio had been a magical place, and she'd been in awe of the half-finished canvas, the jars of brushes and palette knives, the preliminary sketches, the palettes and numerous tubes of paint. The smell of turpentine and oils, of cigars and good red wine had permeated the room where the light flooded in on both sides and sparkled on the magnificent chandeliers.

His eyes had been quite mesmerising in their blue intensity, and she'd found herself drawn to him almost immediately, his soft voice lulling her out of her nervous tension and putting her at ease. He'd answered all her questions, had given his advice and seemed to really care about her dreams and ambitions. But most of all, he'd understood the urgent need within her to fulfil them.

It had been an experience that she was unable to keep to herself, and so she reached for her writing pad and began to pen a letter to her parents. They knew very little about the world of art and artists, regarding it as rather louche and bohemian, but perhaps they might find the time to go to the Tate and see the patron's paintings before they were sent back to New York at the end of September. If they did, then they'd know and be assured that she wasn't in the thrall of someone unreliable, but one of the most highly respected artists of his era.

Henri had remained at the window long after they'd left the house. He'd stared out at the river and the bridge where it had all begun, and tried to accept the position he now found himself in. Of course he had regrets that he'd acted in haste and brought the girl here to satisfy his own curiosity – and now he had to live with the consequences.

There was no doubt that Eugenie had inherited her mother's elegance and that wonderful hair as well as her zest and determined sense of purpose. Yet, as he'd looked into her blue eyes it was as if he were looking into a mirror, and he'd quickly noted how their hands were shaped alike, with long, slender fingers and narrow palms, the nails short and neat. Her still raw, artistic talent was in no doubt – and neither was her burning ambition – if she took full advantage of the opportunities that were open to her, then she would go far.

Henri felt a swell of pride course through him. His daughter was everything he could have dreamt of, her youth and vitality bringing new interest into his life as well as recalling the past happiness he'd once known. And yet, and yet . . .

He gave a deep sigh of distress. She could never know him as her father; could never learn of the love he'd shared with Annabelle and the cruel way in which they'd been separated.

She was Annabelle – but not Annabelle. She was the legacy of their united past, and yet could never be acknowledged as such.

He finally wheeled the chair away from the window and went into his bedroom. Closing the door behind him, he turned the key in the cupboard and gazed lovingly at Annabelle's portrait.

'She's a beautiful, talented girl, our daughter,' he murmured as his eyes hazed with tears. 'I will guide and protect her,' he said softly. 'And do all I can to see that she fulfils her potential. But as much as it pains me, I swear to you, Annabelle, that I will respect the love and care you and George have given our child and will never betray our secret.'

19

Annabelle was in the garden enjoying the early September sun-shine on a rare morning off from her district nursing duties. She was becoming a little concerned that she hadn't heard from Eugenie for a couple of weeks, but that probably meant she was busy settling in to her school and making new friends. She remembered how lax she'd been with her own letter writing once she'd arrived in France, so she supposed she really couldn't blame Eugenie for letting the excitement of her new life take over. After all, it was bound to be far more interesting than the daily round here.

She adjusted her sunglasses and lifted her face to the sun, contented and happy that her recent annual visit to the Harley Street specialist had confirmed that she was in quite rude health considering she had no spleen and only one kidney. It seemed she'd been incredibly lucky when so many people had died that day.

At the thought of Henri it felt as if a shadow had moved across the sun, and she swiftly turned her mind to other things.

The house had suffered only minor damage during the war,

and the whole area was going through a phase of regeneration. New houses and blocks of flats were being built along with more schools and better leisure facilities. There was an indoor swimming pool, a bowling alley and even an ice rink, and the youngsters gathered in the coffee bars that were springing up all over town. The practice had grown to the point where George had had to take on another partner to join him and Dr Goodall, and her own round as district nurse now encompassed the new housing estate. They had busy lives, but they were fulfilled.

'We've finally got another letter from Eugenie,' called George as he crossed the lawn, his handsome face wreathed in smiles. 'I thought she'd forgotten all about us.'

'What does she say? How is she?'

'You'd better read it for yourself,' he replied as he plumped down in a chair beside her. 'It's quite long, and obviously written over a number of days, but it seems she's having a thrilling time.'

Annabelle pulled the brim of her sunhat down to shade her eyes from the glare as she pulled out the wad of airmail paper from the thin envelope and read almost greedily.

Eugenie had been in Paris for almost a month, and it seemed she was being kept very busy indeed. The art school was much stricter and more formal than the Slade, insisting that students achieved a high standard in figurative drawing before they were allowed to go on to their particular specialities or even put paint to canvas, and it was clear that Eugenie was getting impatient and frustrated.

'I'm so glad she's making friends,' she murmured. 'This Elspeth Grey sounds a lovely girl, and it seems Eugenie's also caught the eye of some famous artist who's offered to coach and guide her.' She put down the letter. 'I do worry about her, you know, George. Paris can be very distracting, and by the sound of it, this artist has taken a real shine to her. I hope he hasn't got designs on her.'

'I wouldn't fret too much,' he murmured. 'She's quite mature for her age, and of course Aline will be keeping a close eye on her too. I'm sure that if there was anything suspicious going on, she'd soon put a stop to it.'

'You're probably right,' she sighed, before returning to the letter. 'But she does seem terribly impressed: there are positively pages and pages about him. I do hope she's not neglecting her studies by spending so much time in his company.'

George lit his pipe and stretched out his legs. 'If he's as famous as Eugenie says, then it can only be to the good,' he said comfortably. 'If you read on, you'll see that the man has some of his paintings in the Tate. Why don't you go and have a look at them? They may put your mind at rest.'

Annabelle finished reading the letter. 'I wonder why he calls himself Le Basque? It's a bit pretentious, isn't it? Why not use his real name?'

'It's probably Fred Smith, or the equivalent in French,' he said around his pipe stem. 'You know how the French like to romanticise everything.'

'Mmm.' Annabelle swiftly read through the letter again before returning it to the envelope. She glanced at her watch. 'It's still early, so I think I will go and have a look in the Tate,' she said. 'Why don't you come with me?'

'I have the antenatal group this afternoon followed by evening surgery. Dr Goodall has been called out to one of his patients who's not expected to live for much longer, and Dr Jones is dealing with the factory health session, so I can't just abandon everything here.' He smiled at her. 'You go and enjoy yourself at the gallery, and treat yourself to a new hat or something. It's time you had some fun after all the hard work you do.'

'It would be more fun if you could come too,' she said with a sigh. 'But then, as a doctor's wife, I should be used to doing things on my own.'

He took her hand just as the telephone began to ring. 'I'd escape if I could,' he said, 'but I promise to treat you to a show and dinner at the weekend.'

'That would be lovely.' She kissed his cheek and went into the house as his middle-aged secretary came out to find him with the news he was needed for a house call.

Annabelle decided to take the train because driving in London was becoming a bit of a nightmare and there was rarely anywhere to park. She changed into a clean dress and lightweight jacket, low-heeled shoes and a broad-brimmed hat, then repaired her make-up, pulled on a pair of white gloves, and tucked her handbag under her arm. Returning downstairs, she discovered that George had already left, so she strolled happily in the sunshine to the station.

The Tate was quite busy, but there was a large noticeboard outside advertising the exhibition of the famous French painter she'd never heard of before today. Eugenie had tried to educate her in the world of art as it became apparent that she'd inherited

Henri's talent, but even though she'd done her best to show interest, she'd found that it all reminded her too much of Henri, and had closed her mind to it.

She followed the signs to the large echoing hall where an elderly man was sitting by the door. 'Is this the right room for Le Basque's exhibition?'

'Yes, madam. And you're lucky to have caught it, because most of the paintings and drawing are on loan, and will be sent back to New York in another week.'

Annabelle thanked him and stepped into the room where the ornate chandeliers glittered from the high ceiling; people spoke in hushed tones while others sat on the long leather couches and gazed in admiration at the paintings.

They are certainly beautiful, she thought as she regarded the exquisite way in which the sunlight fell on the children who were playing in a rock pool. She could almost hear the gulls and the lull of the waves breaking gently on the shore as the salty wind ruffled the children's hair.

She read the card next to the painting: *Rock Pool Adventure painted in the South of France, 1950.*

Annabelle moved on, noting the same lightness of touch in the way the sun reflected on his subjects. They reminded her of something she'd seen before, but she simply couldn't think where or when, and decided it must have been in some magazine Caroline had lent her.

She read the note at the side and learnt that this young farm girl had been painted in Spain in 1949. It seemed that Le Basque was a master at capturing the essence of his models, for she could almost smell the warmth of the sunshine on the girl's olive skin as she leant on her pitchfork and surveyed the cart laden with hay.

As she went from one glorious painting to another, Annabelle's admiration for the artist grew. If Eugenie was learning from this man, then she was indeed very fortunate. And then she wandered across the room and came face to face with a portrait she had seen before.

Her heart thudded and she thought for a moment she would faint, so she stumbled to a nearby couch and sank down, her gaze fixed on Amélie's beautiful face. Supine and sensuous, Henri's model slept in her hammock as the dappled sunlight fell on her from the overhanging trees, and her book and sun hat lay forgotten amid the wild violets in the grass.

Annabelle could hardly breathe, and she looked wildly to the next painting – and the one after that. They were all of Amélie, all paintings she'd seen in Henri's studio so many years ago. But it couldn't be. It couldn't possibly be.

She found the strength to leave the couch and walk back along the display. The notes beside the paintings told her they'd been painted in the late thirties, and that the model was Amélie. She looked back at the children playing in the rock pool and the farm girl leaning on her pitchfork. They'd been painted long after the war and her head swirled with the knowledge. She felt sick as she stumbled to a chair and plumped down.

'It can't be,' she breathed. 'It's impossible. Just impossible.'

And yet, on lifting her head she saw that she was sitting next to a wall of framed drawings, drawings that Henri had done during the Spanish Civil War, drawings that he'd shown her during their blissful few days on the coast.

Tears streamed down her face as she fought the terrible urge to cry out in anguish. Henri had lived – and she'd never known.

'Are you all right, madam?'

She looked up through her tears at the old curator's concerned face. 'Le Basque is Henri-Pascal Baptiste, isn't he?' she rasped.

'It's not something that is generally known,' he admitted as he produced a large pristine handkerchief from his jacket pocket and offered it to her. 'Please, madam, don't be upset by the subject matter of those drawings. They are emotive and very powerful, I can see that, and I'm sorry they have affected you so. May I suggest you go and have a cup of tea in our café?'

He was only being kind, but she didn't want to talk to him, let alone have a cup of damned tea. 'I'll be fine,' she said, making a concerted effort to dry her tears and find calm. 'Thank you for the handkerchief. I'll return it another day.'

She went to stand up and found that her legs simply refused to support her. 'Oh dear,' she said shakily as she sank back onto the couch. 'This has all come as rather a shock.'

He sat beside her, his face creased with concern. 'May I ask how you know about Le Basque?' he asked once she'd pulled herself together.

'I met him a long time ago,' she replied, her gaze once more settling on those stark drawings of scenes from the Civil War. 'I thought he'd been killed at Belchite.'

His eyes sparkled with interest. 'You obviously knew him well,' he murmured. 'But contrary to rumour, he survived Belchite and lived on to join the Resistance and fight the Nazis in occupied France – hence the name "Le Basque". It was what the Nazis called him.'

'And he's still alive today,' she said flatly.

'Oh, yes. He's living in Paris.'

She could see that he had a lot more to tell her, but she didn't want to hear it. All she knew was that he was alive and tutoring their daughter in Paris – and that she'd been lied to for years. 'I'm sorry, but I must go,' she said as she gathered up her handbag, gloves and sunglasses. 'Thank you so much for your concern, but I'm fine now, really.'

She couldn't get out of the Tate fast enough, and positively flew down the steps to hail a taxi. Ordering the driver to take her to the station, she realised it was an extravagance, but she needed to get home and gather her thoughts before George returned from his clinic.

Eugenie sat beside the wheelchair on a bench, her whole focus on the structure of the Louvre as she tried to replicate it in watercolour. They were in the sunlit square which overlooked the Tuileries and eventually led to the Place de la Concorde where the obelisk towered from the centre of the conjoining streets. The pale sandstone of the gallery was mellow in the sunlight and the shadows in the deep windows were dark and beginning to spread their fingers across the cobbles.

Henri watched as she worked, and smiled as she stuck her tongue into the corner of her mouth in concentration. Annabelle used to do that when she was writing her letters, he remembered.

They had been meeting nearly every day since that first time, and although he suspected Aline knew nothing about it, he hadn't found the courage to tell her. She would only put a stop to it, and now he was finally really getting to know the girl, it was impossible to think that she wouldn't continue to be a part of his life even after her year in Paris was at an end. Their time together would necessarily be short – a year could disappear in the blink of an eye and she'd be leaving to return to the Slade – so every moment was precious, and he'd begun to resent the hours she had to spend away from him at the school.

There were many questions he wanted to ask her, and he had the feeling that she too was seeking answers to something that had been bothering her, but for now he was simply content to be in her company.

He watched her for a while longer, approving of the way she was capturing the different colours and textures of the sunlit building, and then lit a cigarette, the low brim of his black fedora shielding him from the curious eyes of passing pedestrians. It was good to be out of the studio and in the sunlight and fresh air. He spent too long indoors these days and was in danger of becoming a real recluse. Perhaps when Eugenie returned to England he would go down to the south of France and stay in the house he'd rented after the war. He'd done some good work there, had found the peace he'd craved, and thereby eased the terrible pain of losing Annabelle to another man.

Eugenie washed out her brushes and eyed her efforts critically. 'The perspective is a bit out on that corner and the shadows are moving so quickly the tones are constantly changing, but it's not bad. What do you think, Patron?'

'You're right about the perspective, and you've been a bit careless with those top windows, but on the whole, it's an improvement on the last one.'

She put away her paints and brushes in her shoulder bag and after carefully lifting away her painting, folded up the small wooden easel. 'Why don't we go to a café and have some Pernod? I've developed quite a taste for it.'

Henri immediately felt uncomfortable. Cafés were full of people and he was bound to be recognised, which might make it awkward for Eugenie. So far, she'd kept their rendezvous secret from everyone but her friend Elspeth; if they were seen together by the other art students, it could provoke jealousy and some unpleasantness.

'I have a better idea,' he said. 'We can go to the tea room in the orangery. You're too young to be drinking Pernod anyway.'

She grinned and tested her painting to check it was dry before she closed it between the pages of her sketchbook. 'You sound as disapproving as my father,' she teased. 'But if it's tea you want, then it's tea we shall have.' She tucked the book in her bag, kicked the brake on the wheelchair and slowly pushed it along the cobbles and down the path to the orangery.

Once they were settled at a table with the tea ordered, Henri broached the subject that had always intrigued him. 'Tell me about your father, Eugenie. Is he a kind, loving man to you and your mother?'

'He can be a bit brusque at times, but he's lovely and I adore him,' she replied with a happy smile. 'He's a doctor, you know, and we live in a big house in a town called Dartford.'

As Eugenie talked about her parents and her home, Henri felt a knot tighten in his stomach. It all sounded idyllic and it was clear that the family was happy, but if things had been different, he and Annabelle would have raised their daughter together. Would they have been happy? Or would the passion they'd shared have burnt out by now? He had no way of knowing, he realised sadly, so there was little point in this self-serving speculation.

The pot of tea arrived, accompanied by a plate of sandwiches and another of cakes. 'You see,' he said teasingly, 'it's not only the English who enjoy a proper afternoon tea.'

'Have you ever been to England, Patron?'

'Once only,' he replied. 'But I don't travel much, not since . . .' He patted his withered legs beneath the blanket.

Eugenie selected a tiny egg sandwich and munched thoughtfully. 'There's something I've been wanting to ask you for ages, and although I've sort of mentioned it to Aline, she's not been very forthcoming.'

He eyed her with amusement as she selected a second sandwich, glad that her youthful appetite was making inroads into the food that held little appeal for him. 'And what is it you want to ask? Mind you, there's no guarantee that I will answer you if it's too personal,' he teased.

'Did you ever meet my mother when she was living with Aunt Aline back in the late thirties?'

His pulse picked up a beat and he took a moment to sip his tea. 'Paris is a big place,' he said carefully, 'and Aline's house was always full of people.'

'Yes, that's what Aline said. But you would have remembered her if you did meet her,' she continued. 'Her name is Annabelle, and she has the most fascinating violet-blue eyes.'

Henri knew he had to be very careful. 'I would certainly have remembered such eyes,' he murmured. 'Perhaps it is possible, but it was a long time ago, and my memory isn't as good as it was.' He cocked his head and regarded her warily. 'Why do you ask, Eugenie?'

She finished a third sandwich and leant forward. 'I suspect she fell in love with someone here in Paris,' she softly confided. 'And I was wondering if you might have an idea of who it was.'

'Everyone falls in love in Paris,' he said lightly to cover his alarm. 'I doubt it was anything serious.'

Eugenie slowly shook her head. 'There are things that I discovered just before I came here, and although I haven't told anyone about them, they've been worrying me,' she confessed.

'Do you want to tell me? Or are they too private?' he asked carefully.

She seemed to come to a decision and leant closer. 'When I was much younger, Mummy told me about her time here and her journey over the mountains into Spain. She described the hospitals she worked in and the friends she made, and even talked a little about the shelling of that isolated town which nearly killed her. She rarely mentions any of it now, but when she does speak of Paris and Spain there's a softening in her expression and a sadness in her eyes. I can't help thinking that she loved and lost someone during that time, and the memory still haunts her.'

'Fond memories often make one nostalgic,' he said gruffly. 'I think you're letting your imagination run away with you, Eugenie.'

'No,' she murmured thoughtfully. 'I don't think it's my imagination at all. I'm positive that something happened back then, and there were consequences,' she added darkly.

Henri deliberately kept his expression bland, but his heart was thudding so loudly he was surprised she couldn't hear it. 'Consequences?' he managed.

She nodded. 'And I think I was the consequence which led to her marrying Daddy just six months before I was born.'

A cold prickle of sweat began to crawl down his spine. 'Many couples marry in haste when a child is on the way,' he said quietly. 'I think you're making too much of this, Eugenie.'

She edged forward in her seat, her expression earnest, her eyes holding him captive with their intensity. 'But I have proof, Patron,' she said firmly. 'You see, I was looking for a suitcase in the attic when I found an old hatbox with a rusting lock. Ever curious, I broke the lock and found a necklace of shells, a garnet ring, and a faded painting of my mother which must have been done when she was still in her twenties. There was a sensuality in her face, a languorous, sleepy look of love, and I suspect that it was done by the man she'd met here in Paris.'

She'd kept the painting, he thought distractedly. And yes, it had been languorous and intensely sensual, for he'd painted it as she'd rested after a long afternoon of lovemaking.

He became aware of her watching him closely, and in that moment wondered if she'd guessed, if she'd recognised his hand in that painting and was waiting for him to confirm it. He cleared his throat of the lump that was forming there. 'A painting is just a souvenir, and could have been done anywhere – not necessarily here in Paris. If she'd hidden it away, then it couldn't have been important to her.'

Her gaze lingered for another long moment and he thought he saw disappointment in her eyes before she looked away. 'It wasn't the only thing in the hatbox,' she persisted. 'I also found the *livret de famille* which Mother and Father were given on their wedding day.'

Henri shrugged and tried his hardest to appear nonchalant. 'Of course, it's the way things are done here.'

Her blue eyes regarded him almost accusingly. 'But Mummy was already pregnant with me, and she'd only just recovered from the injuries she sustained in that Spanish bombing. Daddy had never been to Paris before he came over just before the wedding.' Her gaze never faltered. 'So you see, Patron, he couldn't possibly be my father.'

Henri could only stare at her in mute distress. His heart was thudding, and he could see the anguish over her uncertainty in her face. He wished he could make it better for her, but no matter how desperately he wanted to tell her the truth, he'd sworn he never would.

He realised she was waiting for him to speak, and had to dredge up some sort of courage to continue to prevaricate. 'Perhaps he came much earlier than you thought,' he said with studied calm. 'He might even have travelled down to Spain to be with her after she was rescued from that attack on Belchite.'

She shook her head impatiently. 'He couldn't have done. I checked his appointment books for that year and he was very definitely living and working in Dartford for the whole time Mum was in Paris and Spain. Apart from that, the dates don't add up at all.'

'Oh, my dear, I can see this is worrying you, but surely it doesn't really matter?'

'Of course it matters,' she hissed. 'My father can't possibly be my father, and my mother and aunt have lied to me. In fact, they've all lied to me throughout my life, and now I don't know what to do.'

He could see that she was on the brink of tears, was waiting for him to confirm her suspicions, but didn't quite have the courage to ask the question that was clearly burning within her. He would have given anything to be able to put his arms around her and comfort her with the truth. Yet it wouldn't be a comfort; it would be breaking the vow he'd made, and would bring only anguish to everyone involved.

'Oh, my dear girl,' he sighed. 'You have every right to be distraught and angry and confused.' He covered her hand with his. 'But when you told me about your father it was clear that you adore him, and that the feeling is mutual. Your parents have given you their unquestioning love and now it's up to you to hold it close and treasure it without casting doubt.'

His heart ached for her and his own tears were threatening to choke him as he gave a long, trembling sigh. 'The past is somewhere no one should be forced to return to, for there is always sadness there, secrets we must keep to ourselves so they don't hurt others. And why would you want to hurt those you love by exposing their long-hidden intimacies and trampling on the way they've cherished you?'

She sniffed back her tears and nodded. 'You're very wise,' she muttered. 'But it all came as a terrible shock, and I still don't know what to do about it.'

'My advice is to do nothing. Why cause such trouble when none is needed? If you're suspicions are right, then so be it. The man who fathered you hasn't figured in your life, but the man who took on the role of father deserves to be honoured with your love and trust. Don't destroy everything he's done for you, Eugenie.'

'I couldn't bear to hurt him,' she admitted quietly. 'He's been such a wonderful father.' She looked back at Henri, her blue eyes swimming with tears. 'But there's a part of me that's missing – a piece of the puzzle that I want to find to make me feel whole again. Do you think that if I asked Aunt Aline, she might help me to find this man?'

'I think she'd give you the same advice,' he said hastily. 'Aline doesn't necessarily know anything anyway, and it could stir up all sorts of problems.'

Eugenie nodded and consoled herself with a slice of cake. She munched her way through it and then licked the chocolate icing from her fingers. Her sunny nature seemed to be restored, for she smiled. 'I should just be thankful that my parents love me and have done their very best for me, shouldn't I, and not go tilting at windmills like Don Quixote?'

Henri nodded as the familiar lines of Cervantes' story came into his thoughts:

'Let them eat the lie and swallow it with their bread. Whether the two were lovers or no, they'll have accounted to God for it by now . . .'

He'd certainly swallowed the lie, and by the sound of it, so had Annabelle, George and Aline. Now they were all in danger of having to account for their past sins. He cleared his throat and pushed back his chair. 'I'm feeling a little tired now, Eugenie. It's time to go home before Aline starts to worry about where you are.'

Annabelle's head was aching with all the scattered thoughts and emotions that were overwhelming her. Her first thought on her return home had been to telephone Aline and demand an explanation as to why and how she'd permitted Eugenie to go anywhere near Henri. However, she'd turned away from the telephone, knowing that she was too distraught to be coherent and calm, and would only make things worse.

She'd tried to relax and think straight by taking a long soak in the bath, but that hadn't worked, so she prepared the evening meal and then sat in the still quiet of her drawing room and waited for George to finish his surgery. She would have to tell him, but she dreaded the hurt it would cause; hated the thought of seeing it in his eyes and knowing how deeply he'd be affected. Henri was a subject that was rarely broached after she'd confessed to him that she was pregnant, and once he'd made it clear that he wanted to put the past behind them and build their own family together with Eugenie, she'd accepted that it was for the best.

The subterfuge had worked all the while she'd thought Henri was dead, but the shock and overwhelming joy of discovering that he hadn't been killed was tempered by the fact he was now in Paris, in the company of their daughter. Her emotions were all over the place, torn between elation that he'd survived, anger at Aline for keeping this from her, and worry over the hurt this revelation might cause Eugenie and George.

How could Aline have kept this from her? She must have known that Henri was alive. But when had she found out? How long had she been keeping this most devastating of secrets?

As the room darkened, Annabelle lit the candles on the mantelpiece and then lit a cigarette. She opened the windows to the soft night air, noting distractedly how quiet it was, with only the occasional contented croon from a roosting bird to disturb the stillness of sleepy suburbia. And yet she could picture that awful day in Belchite so clearly, it was almost as if she could hear the roar and thunder of the enemy planes and the crump and crash of their exploding bombs.

'Hello, darling, what on earth are you doing sitting in the dark?'

Annabelle lifted her face for his kiss. 'It's a lovely evening,' she replied, 'so I thought I'd open the windows and take full advantage of it in the candlelight.'

He poured them both a glass of their customary evening gin and tonic and sat down on the couch beside her. 'It's been a long day,' he groaned. 'Could we eat supper a little later tonight? Only I need to relax first.'

'It's only salad, so it'll keep.'

He sipped his drink and sighed with pleasure. 'That's better. So, did you go to the Tate this afternoon? I don't see any evidence of a shopping spree.'

'I decided not to go shopping . . . and yes, I went to the Tate.'

There must have been something in her voice that alerted him to her inner turmoil, for he sat forward, his expression concerned. 'What is it, Annabelle?'

'I found out about Le Basque,' she began hesitantly. 'And I'm afraid you aren't going to like what I've discovered.' She silenced his protest by talking over it. 'My darling, there's something very important and rather urgent that I have to tell you, so please hear me out before you say anything.'

Annabelle watched his expression change as she talked. She saw the pain in his eyes and could do nothing to ease it.

His emotions were clearly running amok as he absorbed her words, and when she'd finished, his face set as if hewn from granite. 'But how did he survive?' he asked hoarsely. 'You said you saw him with that group of women and children who were strafed and then buried beneath that building. Surely no one could have survived that?'

'I don't know. All I can guess is that it was a miracle – the same sort of miracle that kept Eugenie alive inside me during all that had happened. But the fact that he is still alive and is now befriending Eugenie is something that has to be dealt with – and swiftly.'

'You want to go to Paris,' he stated flatly.

She nodded. 'I must, George, don't you see? I have to find out if he's already guessed who Eugenie is, and if Aline has been complicit in all this. The fact that she's lied to me for years certainly points to that, and I need to be certain that if Henri is aware that Eugenie is his daughter, he has absolutely no intention of telling her anything.'

'But she wouldn't know to ask the right questions, surely? As far as she's concerned, he's just a famous artist who's interested in her work.' He grasped Annabelle's hand. 'If you go to Paris, Eugenie will become suspicious,' he warned. 'And from her letters, it seems that she hasn't the least idea of any of this.'

'I can tell her I was missing her and wanted to visit Aline,' she replied. 'I need to go there, George, for my own peace of mind.'

He slowly released her hand, his blue eyes suddenly cold. 'Are you sure that's the only reason? It isn't the thought of seeing Henri again that makes it so urgent you get to Paris?'

'Oh, George, no,' she cried in distress. She slid along the couch and held him tightly. 'I love you so much, darling, that I would do anything not to hurt you.'

'Then don't go to Paris,' he replied, his body unyielding in her tight embrace.

'But I have to, don't you see. I need to talk to Aline, face to face, and discover exactly what happened to bring him into Eugenie's life. And to reassure myself that the secret we all hold remains between us.'

'You could do that on the telephone,' he retorted.

She could feel the tension in him, could see how firmly he was set against her going to Paris. 'A telephone call can hide things,' she said softly. 'I can't see her eyes or watch the expressions on her face, and I desperately need to know she's telling me the truth when I confront her.'

'I see.' His tone was flat, his expression unreadable as he took a drink from his glass and set it down purposefully. 'In that case I shall come with you.'

She regarded him in silence, her thoughts skittering madly. If he came, then she would have to be mindful of his feelings as well as deal with whatever Aline would tell her – and she didn't know if she had the mental strength to cope with that. However, if he stayed here, she would worry about him even more. 'Are you sure that's wise?' she asked softly.

'You're my wife and Eugenie is my daughter,' he said firmly. 'If this man's friendship with Eugenie is in any way threatening my family, then I have a right to be there.'

'But what about the surgery, and all your commitments here?'

'I'll get a locum in to cover my absence and will sort the rest out with the other partners. It's Friday now, give me until Monday night to make the arrangements and then we'll fly over on Tuesday.'

20

George had been living in his own hell over the past few days, and although he completed his day-to-day tasks with the efficiency of long-held experience, his mind wasn't really on them at all.

Whilst Annabelle had got the other district nurse to cover her absence, and coaxed George's secretary into accepting all these last-minute changes, he'd managed to find a locum at short notice and had arranged for the other doctors in the practice to cover any gaps whilst he was away. The airline tickets had been purchased on the Monday afternoon and he'd returned home to discover that Annabelle had packed him a small case and even managed to get his suit dry-cleaned that morning.

Annabelle was in a quiet, contemplative mood, and yet he could tell that she too was worried about what they might find in Paris. As they sat at the kitchen table that evening and picked at their food they could find nothing to say to one another, and as they lay in bed that night before their flight, each knew the other couldn't sleep, but made no move to console or comfort.

George had never imagined that something like this would

come between them; that the future he'd seen so clearly only weeks ago was dwindling to nothing in the uncertainty of what awaited them in Paris. He knew she was as worried as he about Eugenie, but as he'd watched her dither over which clothes to wear for the journey that morning, he'd noted the colour in her cheeks and the brightness in her eyes and recognised it as excitement. And as she fussed over her hat, gloves and handbag and checked the seams in her stockings, he realised it would take every ounce of his will to stay silent and deal with this in the only way he knew how.

She was taking a great deal of care over her appearance – even more than usual. Was it because she was planning to go and see Henri as soon as they arrived? He hoped not. He didn't want to meet the man; had no curiosity about him at all now he'd wheedled his way into Eugenie's life and caused so much trouble.

Eugenie is my *daughter*, he thought determinedly as they sat in the aeroplane and waited for it to take off. It hadn't been Henri who'd held her minutes after her birth; hadn't been Henri who'd put money from the Tooth Fairy under her pillow, or read her endless fairy stories even though she'd been too young to understand them. It hadn't been Henri who'd held her hand as she'd taken her first steps, or who'd sat proudly at the prize-giving ceremonies at her school – or Henri who'd helped her celebrate the scholarship to Paris.

If only that damned scholarship had never been awarded, he thought as he stared stonily through the aeroplane window, then none of this would have happened. But it had, and now he had to face the consequences.

The flight didn't take long and soon they were landing in Paris. As the other passengers quickly gathered up bags and coats and excitedly queued to disembark, George came to a decision. Whatever happened next, he would keep faith in their marriage and all they'd shared over the years, and do his best to be supportive and understanding.

It was late Tuesday afternoon and although Eugenie was helping Elspeth to put the final touches to Aline's garden, her thoughts were centred on Le Basque and the conversation they'd had the other day. It had been worrying her ever since, and snatches of past conversations had slowly come together to make a sort of strange and rather terrifying sense.

Max had said that his patron had seen her on the bridge and been reminded of someone he'd once known. Max had also said he suspected that whoever the woman was, she'd been the love of Le Basque's life, for he'd never married.

Eugenie sat back on her heels in the sunlit garden remembering Le Basque's intense interest in her when they first met. It was as if he were searching for something in her face and recognising what he sought. And then there was the conversation they'd had in the orangery. He'd become quite emotional, and at one point she'd thought she'd seen the sheen of tears in his eyes. It was clear that she'd touched a raw nerve in him; that he knew far more than he was telling her. But then he'd made a mistake in mentioning Belchite. If he hadn't known her mother, how on earth had he known she'd been injured there?

'Hey, daydreamer. I could do with a bit of a hand here,' said Elspeth.

'Sorry, Ellie. I was miles away.'

She determinedly tried to dispel the suspicions that had been growing for days, and helped her friend lift the stone cherub back onto the top of the fountain. But as they stood back to admire the effect, Eugenie knew that she would have to see Le Basque this evening and find the courage ask the question that had lain like a dark shadow between them since the other afternoon.

As Paris was basking in the heat of an Indian summer, the girls had decided to sort out Aline's courtyard garden once and for all, and as they stood admiring their work, they felt a terrific sense of satisfaction. They had placed a large sheet of hardboard over the outside of the downstairs windows for the past two days so that their progress couldn't be spied upon, and Aline had been warned not to take a sneaky look until it was finished.

'You've done a fine job restoring that mosaic,' said Eugenie. 'I don't know if I'd have had the patience to glue all those tiny pieces of tile to the wall.'

Ellie pushed back the strands of dark hair which were sticking to her hot face. 'I enjoyed doing it, and you've worked wonders on those old metal chairs.'

'I found them in a *brocante* nearby, but now they're rubbed down and repainted, they do look nice, don't they?' Eugenie shifted a terracotta pot an inch to the left and cast a critical eye over the numerous tubs and pots she'd planted and placed strategically around the small space. They'd scrubbed the paving to get rid of the moss and mould and reset some of the slabs so they lay flat again; they'd even managed to repair the broken wing on the stone cherub and now the fountain was clean and working, water trickling down from the stone shell he was holding. With the white wrought-iron furniture, purple umbrella and bright plants set against the blue and silver mosaic on the wall, the scene pleased her artistic eye.

Elspeth fetched the small pot of petunias she'd brought with her earlier and placed it in the centre of the table. Their deep purple blooms matched the seat pads she'd sewn and finished off the garden perfectly. 'There. It's done. I do hope she likes it.'

They shifted back the hardboard and hurried through the closed curtains to find Aline and the boys in the kitchen. 'We're ready for the grand opening of your garden, Aunt Aline,' said Eugenie. 'Close your eyes and don't open them until we tell you.'

Aline clapped her hands in excited anticipation and willingly closed her eyes to let the girls lead her towards the sitting room doors. As they pulled back the curtains with a flourish, she opened her eyes and gave a gasp of delight. 'But it's beautiful,' she breathed. 'So much more than it ever was.'

She turned to both girls with tears in her eyes. 'Thank you so very much. I don't deserve to have such a wonderful gift.'

'It's all a lot of fuss over nothing,' grumbled Fleur as she came through from the hall to join them. 'Anyone can do a bit of gardening and painting.'

'That's not fair,' retorted Elspeth. 'I haven't seen you getting your hands dirty or spending any time helping Aline in any way.'

'I'm an artist, not a gardener,' spat Fleur, 'and I don't pay rent here to ruin my hands and nails with menial work.'

'You're spoiling my surprise,' said Aline crossly. 'If you can't be pleasant then I suggest you keep quiet.'

'You mean like Eugenie's been quiet about her secret rendez-vous with a certain artist?' Fleur said slyly.

Eugenie felt the colour drain from her face as Aline's questioning gaze fell upon her.

'Have you been meeting Max?' she asked. 'Is that why you've been coming home so late these past weeks and spending half the weekends out of the house? He's a little old for you, Eugenie, and I don't think—'

Elspeth broke in, 'It's me who's seeing Max,' she admitted. 'We were hoping to keep it quiet, but of course we didn't count on nosy parker here sticking her oar in.'

'It's not Max I'm talking about,' snapped Fleur. Her cold blue gaze settled spitefully on Eugenie. 'Eugenie has much older, richer and bigger fish to fry.'

Eugenie glared back at her, but couldn't think of anything to say in her defence.

Aline's frown deepened. 'You've been visiting the Patron,' she breathed. 'Oh, Eugenie, no.'

'Yes.' Eugenie lifted her chin defiantly, glad that the subterfuge was at an end. 'Le Basque invited me to visit each day after school, and sometimes we spend the weekend afternoons together. He's teaching me how to paint in different media and helping me with perspective.'

'Oh, I just bet he is,' sneered Fleur. 'You're a selfish bitch for keeping him to yourself when you knew that Michel and I could benefit from such tuition. But then, of course, I shouldn't be surprised – you're obviously a spoilt brat and used to getting your own way.'

'It takes one to know one,' said a furious Eugenie. 'Put a sock in it, Fleur, before I land one on that pert nose of yours.'

'That's enough,' snapped Aline as she stood between them. 'You have ruined my pleasure. Fleur, with your spiteful tongue . . . and you, Eugenie, with your deceit. I'm disappointed in both of you.'

They stood in awkward silence as she stepped through the open doorway and went to sit in her lovely garden.

'There, see what you've done,' hissed a furious Elspeth. 'You've ruined days of very hard work and upset Aline into the bargain. If you had any decency, you'd go and apologise to her.'

Fleur folded her arms and lifted her chin, her blue eyes blazing. 'Why should I? I only told the truth, which is more than you both have. You knew all along that Eugenie was going to see Le Basque, didn't you?'

'So what if she did?' stormed Eugenie. 'It's none of your damned business.'

'It is when a student gets an unfair advantage,' Fleur retorted. 'I wonder what the school would say about your private lessons? If that's what they really are,' she added nastily. 'Le Basque has a reputation with women and he's old enough to be your father – hardly an appropriate liaison, would you say?'

'You've got a dirty mind,' Eugenie replied heatedly, 'and shouldn't judge everyone by your own low moral standards.'

The three boys made a tacit agreement and slunk out of the room. Eugenie and Elspeth turned their backs on Fleur and went out into the garden to try to pacify Aline.

'This isn't the last of it,' shouted Fleur. 'I'll make sure the tutors know what you've been up to.' She turned on her heel and slammed her way out into the hall and through the front door.

Eugenie shivered despite the warm September sunshine. 'Can she really make trouble for me, Aunt Aline?'

'Not over something like that. Le Basque is a very important man and one of the school's prime fundraisers and supporters. He has a reputation, yes, but I doubt he's ever been anything more than a tutor to you.'

Aline gave a deep sigh. 'That was an unpleasant scene with Fleur. She's clearly in possession of a vicious tongue, and I suspect is out for revenge. You'll have to watch your back, Eugenie.'

'I've met girls like her before,' Eugenie said lightly. 'She can't hurt me, because I have nothing to be ashamed of.'

'But why didn't you tell me you were going to see him every day? I could have come with you – after all, I have little else to occupy me.'

'I didn't think you'd approve,' she admitted. 'And although it was lovely of you to introduce him to me, I'm a bit old to be chaperoned, Aunt Aline.' She perched on the chair beside her and gently took her hand. 'He's teaching me so much,' she said quietly, 'and we get along so well. Please don't bar me from seeing him.'

Aline's thoughts were whirling. She certainly couldn't force the girl to end the friendship, and Henri was the best tutor for anyone seeking a patron. 'Of course I won't do that,' she said distractedly. 'Do you talk much together, or is it really all about the art?'

'We talk about art and technique and we go out and sit somewhere so we can draw or paint together. He's a quiet man, a wise man, and although we don't actually say very much, we seem to understand one another.'

Aline was about to question her further when there was a knock on the front door.

'I'll go,' said Elspeth as she retrieved her shoulder bag. 'I'm due to meet Max in ten minutes anyway.'

'Thank you, Ellie. The mosaic has been restored wonderfully well, and my sweet little cherub is whole again. I do so appreciate all your hard work.'

'It was a pleasure.' She kissed Aline's cheek, grinned at Eugenie and dashed indoors just as there was another knock on the door and Napoleon started screeching.

'I'm not expecting anyone,' said Aline. 'Let's hope they get fed up and go away.' She settled more comfortably into the cushion. 'How long has Ellie been seeing Max?'

'About two weeks or so. He met her when we were in a coffee bar with some other students, and we could all tell it was an instant attraction between them.'

'Then let's hope it lasts longer than all his other attractions,' said Aline with a twinkle in her eyes. 'He's a rogue, that Australian, but very likeable. I can see why girls fall for him.'

The front door slammed. 'Eugenie? Eugenie, where are you?'

Shocked to hear Annabelle's voice, Aline froze while Eugenie rose from the chair. 'Mummy!'

'Yes, darling, it's me. And Daddy too,' she said as she stepped through the glass doors and opened her arms.

As Eugenie hugged them both, Aline's crippled hands knotted in her lap. They knew about Henri – it was the only explanation. But how? She tentatively met Annabelle's cool gaze over the girl's shoulder and shivered as if stormy clouds had suddenly blocked out the sun. Their unexpected arrival did not bode well.

'This is a wonderful surprise,' said Eugenie in delight, 'but what made you come? I've only been away for a month.'

'The house felt too empty and I wanted to see you,' said Annabelle, her gaze warming as it turned from Aline to her daughter. 'I also thought it was time to visit Aline – it's been too many years.'

'Well, I'm thrilled to see you both. It's a miracle you managed to get Daddy out of his surgery, but I'm so glad you did. How long are you planning to stay? Will you have time to see something of Paris and visit the art school while you're here?'

Aline felt the coldness of Annabelle's gaze settle on her again.

'We can't stay away from the practice too long,' she said, 'so we're only here for a couple of days at the most.' She glanced at George. 'We could both do with a cup of tea, do you think you . . . ?'

'Of course,' Eugenie said. 'Sit down and I'll go and make it.'

The three of them watched her dash back into the house, and Annabelle closed the French doors so they wouldn't be over-heard. Her eyes lacked any warmth as they settled on Aline. 'You know why we're here, don't you?'

Aline's heart was thudding and she was finding it hard to

breathe. 'He's said nothing to her, and he promised he never would,' she stuttered.

'He knows who she is?'

Aline nodded and placed her crippled hand over her racing heart.

'How does he know?' Annabelle perched on the edge of the garden bench next to George. 'Did you tell him?'

Aline shook her head so vigorously it made her feel slightly giddy. 'He saw her on the bridge and thought it was you at first,' she managed. 'He got one of his students to track her down and find out who she was. Max discovered enough about her for Henri to put two and two together, and then demanded that I take her to meet him.'

'You were with them all the time at this meeting?'

'Yes. Nothing untoward was said. They talked about her scholarship and her painting and he looked at her portfolio. But I could see he was drawn to her, even then. The likeness between them is quite evident if you know where to look.'

Annabelle's pale face looked as if it were etched from marble. 'And since then? She's been seeing him on her own, hasn't she?'

'I didn't know that,' Aline replied hastily, 'not until this afternoon. But she hasn't said anything that has given me cause for alarm, so I have to believe that Henri has kept his word.'

'When did you know he was still alive?'

Aline felt as if she were being interrogated, and it brought back awful memories of the time when her home had been invaded by the enemy and her life had changed irreparably. She had found the courage to stand up to them then, and she would do so again now with Annabelle.

She lifted her chin and met Annabelle's gaze squarely. 'A letter arrived about two weeks or so after you and George were married. He was in hospital recovering from the wounds he'd sustained in Belchite, and they'd been so severe that he hadn't been able to write any earlier.'

Annabelle dipped her chin and her shoulders sagged. 'I wish you'd told me,' she said after a moment of silence. 'If you had, then we wouldn't be in this mess today.'

George went to open the door so Eugenie could carry the tray of tea things into the garden. 'You're all looking far too serious,' she said jokingly. 'It's a lovely day in Paris, and we're finally all together, so for goodness' sake cheer up.' She gave them all an encouraging smile and then dashed back into the house to fetch the milk.

'We'll talk later tonight,' said Annabelle. 'And I want to know everything, Aline. This is no time for lies and half-truths.'

'I did what I did out of love,' she replied tearfully. 'Just as you've done for Eugenie. Perhaps we should all be honest with each other and let fate decide what is best for us.'

'I'll decide what's best for my family,' said George firmly.

Aline regarded him sadly. This trip to Paris must be the hardest thing he'd ever done, and who knew what the future held for any of them? She could only pray that Annabelle's love for him was strong enough to withstand any meeting she might have with Henri – and there was absolutely no doubt that they would meet at some point.

*

Eugenie was trying to understand why everyone was being so stiff and gloomy on such a lovely occasion. She could see that her parents were trying very hard to make a show of enjoying their surprise visit, but it was falling flat. And Aunt Aline looked suddenly much more frail and elderly.

As she poured the tea and handed round the biscuits, she surreptitiously watched her father. It was strange to know that he wasn't her real father, for he was the dearest, most loving one she could ever have wished for. And yet she could sense an unusual tension in him and in her mother, and wondered exactly why they'd really come to Paris so unexpectedly. Something was going on here that she couldn't understand, but rather than ask outright what it was, she decided to wait and see what was said, and try to make sense of it.

Everyone seemed to relax a little as she prattled on about the school and her friend Ellie, and the work they'd done to restore Aline's little garden. Yet it was when she mentioned her time with Le Basque that she noted wariness creep into her mother's eyes, and was intrigued by it.

'Do you spend a lot of time with him?' asked Annabelle casually.

'I go to his house after school each day, and spend some of the weekend with him. He doesn't get out much, but I think he enjoys our little trips to the park or the museums and galleries.'

'You should be spending more time with friends of your own age,' replied Annabelle. 'What about the others here? From your letters, they sound a lively bunch.'

'Fleur is certainly lively, but not someone I want to be friends with; and the boys are always sitting in bars ogling the girls. Ellie and I go out together sometimes, but now she's with Max, I feel a bit out of it. I actually prefer being with Le Basque, because he seems to understand the passion I have, and I learn so much from him.'

'I went to see his paintings at the Tate. They're certainly very beautiful, but those drawings from the Spanish Civil War are quite brutal. Does he ever talk about his past?'

Eugenie shook her head. 'He said the past was somewhere that should never be revisited because it can bring unhappiness and sad memories. We talk about what's happening now, and about our art.'

She regarded her parents evenly. 'If my friendship with Le Basque is your reason for coming all this way, then you have nothing to fear. He's a good man – a very talented man – who's only interested in my work. He has no designs on me, if that's what's concerning you. It's all very respectable.'

'I should hope so,' hissed Annabelle, as she set the cup on the tray with a clatter.

'I did ask him once if you and he had ever met when you were here before,' Eugenie said, watching for a reaction and finding it in a spark of something in her mother's eyes. 'But he said it was a very long time ago, his memory wasn't good and there had been many women in his life since those days.'

'I see.' Annabelle dipped her chin and hunted in her handbag for her cigarettes. 'Well, it's only to be expected, I suppose. Artists are notorious for their women and shady lifestyles.'

'Thanks, Mummy,' Eugenie said dryly. 'I'll bear that in mind.'

'You know what I mean,' she replied a little sharply.

Eugenie decided to pursue the previous conversation, for she was intrigued. 'So you don't remember meeting an artist with dark hair and blue eyes back then? He's from the Basque region and of course he was a volunteer in the Civil War in Spain.'

'I wouldn't know, darling,' she said as she lit a cigarette. 'I didn't really move in those artistic circles.'

'But you stayed here,' said Eugenie quietly. 'And Aline's house was full of artists, poets and musicians at the time – as it is today. He and Aline were friends back then and he was a frequent visitor. You must have met him.'

'I said I didn't,' said Annabelle firmly. 'For goodness' sake, Eugenie, you're giving me a headache with all your questions.'

Eugenie watched as her mother nervously flicked ash onto the freshly scrubbed paving, and began to drum her fingers on the arm of the seat. She saw that Aline's eyes were wary and that her father was looking decidedly frosty. 'I think you'd better tell me the real reason you're here,' she said quietly.

'To see you and Aline, of course,' Annabelle replied too quickly.

Eugenie knew then that she was lying, and she felt a stab of disappointment. 'If you were so keen on seeing Aline, then why no kiss and hug for her? You didn't even say hello, or remark upon her poor crippled hands.'

'Of course I spoke to her,' she said crossly. 'We greeted each other when you went to fetch the tea.'

Eugenie regarded her mother with a mixture of sadness and frustration. 'But neither of us are the reason you're here, are we?'

Annabelle wouldn't look her in the eye and continued tapping her fingers while she smoked her cigarette.

'I think I know the real reason,' Eugenie continued remorselessly.

'Enough of this, Eugenie,' snapped George. 'You're upsetting your mother.'

'I'm sorry, Daddy, but there are things going on here that I need to understand. If you and Mother refuse to be truthful with me, then it's up to me to demand an explanation. And I want the truth, Daddy. I *must* have the truth this time.'

She saw how her mother glanced with quick concern at her father, and knew she had to continue this before she lost her nerve. 'When I was packing to come here I went into the attic,' she began, 'and found your marriage certificate and a painting.'

Annabelle stared back at her like a frightened rabbit.

'It was a beautiful painting, and now I've seen others like it, I can recognise the technique and guess who did it.'

There was a complete stillness in the garden as the three of them froze in anticipation and dread.

'Is Le Basque my father?'

'I'm your father,' said George.

Eugenie's heart ached with love for him as she saw the way his jaw clenched. 'Yes,' she said softly as she reached for his hand. 'You're my father – the daddy I adore and the man I will always look up to as the one who loves and protects me. But you weren't with Mummy when I was conceived, were you?'

George clasped her hand tightly. 'I love your mother more than life itself,' he said gruffly. 'When I heard she'd been injured at Belchite and had been transferred to Paris I came straight here. She told me she was expecting you, and of course I wanted to do what was right for her.' He looked at her then, his blue eyes unwavering. 'But from the moment you were born you were *my* precious girl – and you always will be.'

'Oh, Daddy, I'm so sorry. This must be awful for you,' she sobbed as she put her arms around his neck and wept against his cheek. 'And I know you did what you did because you love me and wanted to protect me. But I do wish you'd both told me the truth right from the start.'

'I wanted to at first,' said Annabelle, her voice rough with emotion. 'But your father and I were happy together and you were our little miracle. And with Henri dead, there seemed little point in dredging up the past and allowing it to overshadow all our futures.'

'Henri?'

'Henri-Pascal Baptiste. Le Basque.'

Eugenie wiped away her tears as she regarded all three of them, noting that although they were distressed, they seemed more relaxed now the truth was finally out. 'How did you meet him?'

Annabelle's expression softened, and her voice was so low Eugenie had to strain to hear her. 'I was standing on the Pont Neuf on my first day in Paris. I'd walked past the turning to Aline's and was feeling a bit lost. Henri and his friend Etienne offered to help me find the house because they knew Aline very well.'

Eugenie now understood the significance of the house that overlooked the bridge, and Le Basque's habit of always sitting by the window. He must have loved her mother very much to still be pining for her – and perhaps that explained why he'd been so determined to track her down after seeing her on that same bridge. The likeness between her and her mother had often been a cause for comment.

She listened without interrupting as Annabelle grasped George's hand and talked about those heady weeks in Paris and the terrifying journey into Spain. Her mother's descriptions were so vivid that she could imagine the devastating scene of the bombing of Belchite, and could understand why everyone had thought Henri had been killed there.

'I was in hospital in Spain for a while and then got transferred here to a specialist unit. Caroline managed to come with me for a few days before she got the awful news about her brother, and of course Aline was a stalwart help.' Annabelle reached for Aline's hand.

'I'm sorry I was so harsh with you earlier, but I was frightened and cross and my emotions were all over the place.'

Aline shrugged. 'It's to be expected. None of this is easy for any of us.'

'Especially for Daddy,' said Eugenie softly.

George straightened in the chair. 'We were wrong to keep the truth from you, I can see that now, and whatever you decide to do from now on, we'll support you.' He glanced at Annabelle who nodded back. 'You see, you'll always be our Eugenie, and we'll never stop loving you.'

Despite being eighteen and all grown up, Eugenie nestled into his side and rested her cheek against his chest, careless of the fact that her tears were soaking through his best shirt. 'I'll always love you too,' she said as the tears slowly ebbed. 'And as I don't want to cause either of you any more anguish, I'll stop going to see him.'

'No, Eugenie,' he said as he firmly held her away from him. 'You must do what you feel is right and not think about us. He obviously knows who you are, and it's only fair that you should get to know one another.' His smile was tender as he tucked a fair curl behind her ear. 'After all, Eugenie, he can teach you far more about art than I ever could.'

'So, you wouldn't mind if I went to see him this evening? You see, I suspected who he was some time ago, and I think he ought to know how I feel about everything.'

'Yes, you go, Eugenie,' said Annabelle. 'We'll wait for you here.'

Henri was sitting in his usual place by the window, the glass of wine on the table beside him, a cigarette burning in the ashtray. The house was silent, with the boys out in the city for the evening, and so he was alone and feeling rather sorry for himself. He'd missed not seeing Eugenie for her usual late afternoon visit, but she'd promised to come this evening if she finished the garden and could get away. He glanced at the clock on the mantel. It was getting late, and he doubted she would come now.

His thoughts meandered over the times he'd spent with her and the conversations they'd had, and he had realised imme-diately that it had been a mistake to mention Belchite in the context of Annabelle. He suspected that Eugenie was very close to the truth – perhaps had already worked everything out for herself – and he wondered how she felt about him being her father. Would she resent his absence during all those years she was growing up – even though he'd never known of her existence until she'd come to Paris? Would she be able to understand why everyone had lied to her? And would she find it in her generous little heart to forgive them all?

He gave a deep sigh and picked up the wine glass. Taking a sip, he idly watched the young lovers strolling along the bridge as the lights twinkled from the buildings and street lamps. It had all happened so long ago, but the memories lingered with a clarity that had never faded.

The sound of footsteps running up the stairs lightened his heart. Eugenie had come after all. He put down the glass and turned the wheelchair to face the door.

Eugenie was out of breath, her face flushed and animated as she came into the room and took his hands. 'Patron, I have something to tell you,' she said softly.

He smiled into her sweet face, noting how, in her excitement, her eyes had taken on almost the same violet hue as her mother's. 'What's happened, Eugenie?' he asked fondly.

She perched on the low stool, maintaining her hold on his hands as she looked up at him. 'I found out who you really are,' she breathed. 'You're Henri-Pascal Baptiste – and you're my father.'

He gazed down at her, his heart so full he couldn't speak.

'I know what happened, and why you never played any part in my life,' she continued, 'and although it saddens me that so many lies have been told, I can't resent them now I know how much love was behind them.'

'Oh, my dear child,' he murmured as he touched her hair and traced the curve of her cheek with a trembling finger. 'I so wanted to tell you, but I'd made promises that I had to keep.'

'I realised that when we talked in the orangery. You see, I was waiting for you to say something as I didn't have the courage to ask you outright.'

'It was my mention of Belchite that confirmed it for you, wasn't it?'

She nodded. 'That was a Freudian slip if ever there was one,' she replied with a wry smile. 'But today I had the confirmation I was really seeking.' She must have seen his frown of puzzlement, for she continued, 'Mummy and Daddy arrived in Paris and they told me everything.'

Thrills of pleasure and shock coursed through him. 'Your mother's in Paris?'

'She came because I'd written about you in my letters, and told her about your exhibition in London. She went to see your paintings – and knew immediately who'd done them.'

Henri nodded and dipped his chin, almost ashamed of the tears that clouded his eyes. 'She would have recognised Amélie in three of them. They were in my studio the day she came to visit.'

'You loved her very much, didn't you?'

'Yes,' he said gruffly. 'And I still do. Your mother is an extraordinary woman, and I've never met another who can match her.'

'That painting I found . . . It was obvious she was in love with the artist, and although I know she adores Daddy and is very happy, I've never seen her look at him like that.'

Henri was saddened by her words, for he'd hoped that she'd discovered the same passion with her husband that they had once shared. But then he'd never done so, and in a way it was a testament to the strength of that first, overwhelming love.

'There's something I'd like you to see,' he said. 'Come on. It's in the other room.'

He wheeled the chair out into the hall and through into his bedroom. Extracting the small key from his waistcoat pocket, he inserted it into the lock of the cupboard. 'What I'm about to show you is something I did on the evening I first met your mother. It's rough and rather raw compared to what I do now, but I think you'll see her the way I did on that day.'

As he opened the doors and switched on the light, he heard Eugenie gasp.

'She's beautiful, and so young,' she breathed, 'and it's as if her eyes are watching us.'

'We were both young then, and thought we'd live forever,' he replied, sadness in his tone. 'She was beautiful and full of determination to achieve her rightful place in the world, and I was whole and healthy and full of my own importance.'

He watched Eugenie as she studied the painting of her mother. He could hardly bear the thought of Annabelle being here in Paris. He would have loved to see her again, to feast his eyes on her face and look into those violet eyes that had once held him in thrall; to hear her voice and her laughter and reminisce about the time they'd spent together and learn about all the years that had come between them. His gaze fell to the blanket over his wasted legs and his spirits were dashed by the reality.

'I don't want her to see me like this,' he said as he closed the doors and turned the key in the lock. 'Better she keeps the memories of how I once was. I couldn't bear to see pity in her eyes.'

'But she's bound to want to come. How can I stop her?'

'Tell her I've left Paris. Tell her I'm not well. Tell her anything you like, but please, please don't bring her here.'

'Then I won't,' she said as she placed her hand softly on his shoulder. 'But aren't you just a little curious about her? Don't you think that after all these years she might also be unwilling to let you see how she's changed?'

He was desperate to see her – to look once more into those glorious eyes – to hear her voice and breathe in her scent. Yet he couldn't bear the thought of her seeing him as the pathetic cripple he'd become.

'Take some photographs and show me once she's gone,' he said brusquely as he wheeled the chair back into the studio drawing room. He knew he was probably being unreasonable, but he couldn't help it.

He lit a fresh cigarette and then gulped down some wine. 'Will you still come here now you know I'm your father?'

'Of course.' She sat opposite him, the lights from the street lanterns casting shadows on her face. 'I want to get to know you properly, and learn all I can from you. But you must understand that I love George very much and will always think of him as my father.'

'Can we be friends, do you think?'

'Oh, yes,' she breathed. 'The very best of friends who understand each other without words, and who share the same passions and interests. I wouldn't want to lose that for the world.'

'Do you think you might stay on in Paris and complete a second or third year at the school?' he asked hopefully.

'Maybe. It's too soon to decide anything much. But I will certainly visit you every day all the while I'm here.' She glanced at the clock. 'I have to go, Patron . . .' She giggled. 'I can't call you that, not now. But what should I call you?'

'Papa Henri,' he said, and returned her smile. 'I'd be proud of that, and not at all afraid that it might damage my reputation.' His smile became a grin. 'After all, I've managed to ruin my reputation quite well enough over the years, so one more scandal is unlikely to change things.'

She kissed his cheek. 'You're a rogue, and with that twinkle in your eye it's hardly surprising that women fall all over you. Goodnight, Papa Henri. I'll see you again when my parents leave for England.'

Henri heard her clatter down the stairs and the front door slam. He wheeled the chair to the window and looked down. She was on the embankment, looking up at him with her bright smile and cheerful wave.

His eyes filled with tears as he waved back and watched her disappear from sight. Eugenie had given him a second chance, and this time he wouldn't fail her.

21

They heard the door close after Eugenie left the house and sat in an awkward silence. Annabelle hadn't missed the fleeting look of anguish in George's eyes that he'd tried so hard to hide as he'd watched his daughter rush off to be with Henri, and all she could do was hold his hand and silently pray that they would all come through this without too much heartache.

'I think I'll go and have a bath, if you wouldn't mind, Aline,' he said. 'It's been a long, rather exhausting day, and I suspect you and Annabelle need time to talk things over.'

'We have nothing to say that excludes you, darling,' said Annabelle. 'Please don't feel you need to go.'

'I'm sure not, but I'm tired and feel grubby. A bath will sort me out, and then perhaps, once Eugenie comes back, I could treat us all to supper at Aline's favourite restaurant.'

'It's not there any more,' said Aline, her French slow so that George could understand her. 'The Germans took it over as an armoury and the Resistance blew it up. There's another little bistro just around the corner. We could go there.'

George looked at his watch. 'I know how late you like to eat here, so let's say about nine, then, shall we?'

'I have yet to prepare a room for you, but use Eugenie's for the moment. Annabelle and I can sort out something later.'

Aline watched as George went indoors, and waited until his heavy tread faded as he reached the top of the stairs. Turning to Annabelle, she regarded her evenly. 'Will you go to see Henri while you're here?'

'I want to,' she admitted. 'But it would hurt George so, and I couldn't bear to do that to him. This journey has been hard enough, although he's made a sterling effort not to show it.'

'Did George ever see that painting of Henri's which you'd hidden away?'

She shook her head. 'I doubt it, for if he had he would have mentioned it.' She shot Aline a sad smile. 'George is a very honest, upright man, and it's not in his nature to keep secrets.'

'He managed to keep yours.'

'Because he loves me; and because from the moment Eugenie was born she was his.' She lit a cigarette and watched the smoke spiral into the soft air of the Paris evening. 'How did Henri survive Belchite, Aline?'

She gave a shallow sigh. 'He said he'd been knocked out cold, and when he finally came to, he discovered he was in total, smothering darkness. He could hear faint sounds from above him, and soon worked out that he was in a cellar, but that he was buried beneath a mountain of debris. He also realised that although he was clearly badly injured, he'd been incredibly lucky, for as the blast had knocked him off his feet, he'd been flung into a corner of the cellar and actually had space to move and breathe.

'He passed in and out of consciousness, not really knowing anything very much. It was as black as night down there and utterly silent, and he feared he would die before anyone found him. And yet again, fate had been kind. His satchel was still hanging across his chest, and there was a small flask of water in there. He rationed it, drip by drip, and when they found him, unconscious, blind, badly wounded and dehydrated, the bottle was empty. He heard later that he'd been down there for seven days, and had only been found because grieving parents were determined to shift the rubble of that collapsed building to get to their dead children.'

'God, how awful.' Annabelle blinked away the tears. 'They were so young, some just babies in arms. Etienne and I helped try to rescue them, but none were left alive, and it seemed futile to carry on. But he was still alive, waiting for us to find him.'

Aline put her hand on Annabelle's shoulder. 'You weren't to know,' she murmured. 'War does so many cruel things, and it was tragic that those women and children died, but at least Henri survived to tell the tale.'

'But by then it was too late, I was married to George.' Annabelle dashed away the tears. 'Not that I'll ever regret that,' she said fiercely. 'George has been my rock, my friend and my lover – and the very best father any child could have wished for.'

'It's a shame you couldn't have had more children,' murmured Aline.

'It wasn't to be, and although it took some time, we eventually

came to terms with that and poured all our love into Eugenie.'
She smiled ruefully. 'We could have spoilt her, but she seems to
have grown into a very level-headed girl who definitely knows
her own mind.'

Aline poured some wine from the carafe Eugenie had brought
out before she'd left the house. 'And you? Are you fulfilled at
last, Annabelle?'

'I am, yes. I'm still doing my nursing and thoroughly enjoying
being a part of the community. I've made some good friends and
learnt to play golf – very badly I must confess – and enjoy just
being at home with George.'

She took a sip of the dark red wine. 'Caroline makes a flying
visit now and again from her very grand penthouse apartment
in New York. She and her husband have two strapping sons and
they're named after the brothers she lost. Her parents are quite
elderly, and now Robert is retired from politics, they're thinking
of moving to America to be close to her and their grandchildren.'

'I hear from Camille now and again,' said Aline. 'My sister
has certainly fallen on her feet at last, but I doubt she'll ever
return to France.'

'And you, Aline? Your letters over the years told me very little
– especially during the war years. Was it very bad?'

Aline looked down at her hands. 'They took my city, my home
and my ability to paint,' she said quietly. 'I had to sell my treasures to eat, but at least I never had to sell my body like some.
And I survived. What more can I say?'

Annabelle realised that her aunt was becoming distressed, so
quickly changed the subject. 'I know you told me that Etienne

had survived Belchite, albeit with some damage to his hip and leg. Does he still live here? Or has he made his name as a poet or a journalist and is now living the high life in America?'

Aline stared at her in distress. 'I'm sorry, Annabelle. I thought you knew. He was killed by the Nazis while he was on a raid with the Resistance.'

Annabelle covered her mouth with her hand, reeling from yet another awful shock. 'What happened?' she asked.

'It was at the very end of the war, and the Germans were already on the run from the advancing Allies. The Resistance successfully cut the power lines to the headquarters in La Rochelle, and sabotaged the tanks and military vehicles to delay the Nazi attack on the Americans who were expected to arrive within days.'

Aline sipped her wine and lit a cigarette, her hand not quite steady. 'One of his comrades was hit in the barrage of rifle fire coming from a hidden group of Germans, and realising he was still alive, Etienne went back for him. They shot him and the man he went to rescue was taken to the Gestapo for questioning.'

The anguish Annabelle felt was overpowering, for Etienne had died a hero, trying to save a comrade – just as he'd saved her at Belchite. 'Poor Etienne,' she said tremulously. 'I remember his swagger and his talk and the way he'd flirt with every girl he met. That is so very sad.'

'He was awarded a posthumous croix de guerre,' murmured Aline. 'But the man he went to rescue wasn't so fortunate as to be shot dead. He was tortured by the Gestapo. You see, he was quite a famous Resistance fighter – a man whom the Germans had been hunting since Paris had fallen. He was the instigator of many daring exploits during the war and the Germans lost countless weapons, men and machinery because of him. They called him Le Basque.'

Annabelle felt as if she'd been punched. 'Henri? Henri was in the Resistance? Oh God, Aline, what did they do to him? How did he survive?'

'He survived because the advancing Allies attacked the prison where they were keeping him and took him and the other surviving prisoners to their field hospital. He doesn't speak of what happened – none who survived the Gestapo ever do. Needless to say, he is now confined to a wheelchair.'

'But they didn't damage his hands. He can obviously still paint.'

Aline nodded and looked at her own crippled fingers. 'They didn't know he was an artist,' she murmured, 'otherwise they'd have done to him what that bastard did to me.' She took a deep breath and let it out on a sigh. 'We all bear the scars of war in one way or another. Now it's time to forget, to look to a brighter, more peaceful future. Our young have never known war, and I just pray to God they never will.'

Annabelle's thoughts were on the boys she had once known who'd been killed in Spain; and on Etienne who'd been so brave; and finally on Henri who'd led a secret life in the Resistance and paid a terrible price for his courage. 'I must see him, Aline,' she said quietly.

'Of course you must,' she replied. 'He will know you're here and be very hurt if you don't. The circle needs to be closed,

Annabelle. And you can only do that if you make your peace with the man you once loved so passionately.'

'What about George? How can I explain to him without hurting him?'

'You'll only hurt him if you let your emotions lead you astray – and I don't think that's likely, do you, Annabelle?'

'You're right, Aline. I shall be honest with George and tell him I'm going to see Henri – and the reasons why. It may hurt for a while, but not long enough to do any real harm to our marriage.'

Eugenie returned to Aline's shortly after George had come downstairs from his bath. He kissed her and gave her a hug and asked her what she'd decided to do in the future.

'It's too soon to decide anything yet,' she replied. 'But if at all possible, I'd like to apply for a second year here. Paris and London are the centres of art, and I'd be foolish to let such an opportunity slip through my fingers.'

'And Henri?' he asked carefully.

'I will get to know him properly and learn to treasure any part he wishes to play in my life. In time, you might even decide to meet him. I think you'd both get along rather well.'

'Maybe,' he murmured. 'But, as you say, it's rather too soon to make lasting decisions.'

'I've decided to go and see him tomorrow morning,' said Annabelle as she pinned on her hat. 'It would be heartless of me not to go now he knows I'm here.'

'He was afraid you'd want to do that,' said Eugenie fretfully. 'Look, I'm sorry, Mummy, but he really doesn't want to see you.'

Annabelle felt a sharp pang of shock and disappointment. 'But why? What's he afraid of?'

'He isn't the same as he was, and he's afraid to meet you because he doesn't want you to pity him.'

'I know about the wheelchair, and how he ended up like that,' said Annabelle, now more determined than ever to see him. 'I'm not going to pity him, although it's ghastly what those people did to him; I simply want to see him again and resolve this whole thing with some dignity. He's clearly going to be a part of your life from now on, and I think we're all adult enough to be able to deal with that.'

'What if he refuses to see you?'

'I'll cross that bridge when I come to it,' she said firmly.

The evening was surprisingly pleasant after the trauma of the day, and once Eugenie had been settled on the couch in the sitting room and Annabelle had closed the bedroom door, she slipped into bed beside George.

'I know these past few days have been a torture for you, but it will soon be over, and then we can go home.' She slipped her arm across his chest and nuzzled his cheek. 'Make love to me, George,' she whispered.

George turned his head on the pillow and in the moonlight that poured in through the window she could see his love for her shining in his eyes. And as he softly kissed her lips and drew her close, she knew that this was the man she would love for the rest of her life.

*

It was early morning and Henri was waiting eagerly at the window hoping to see Eugenie as she went to school. And there she was, looking bright and pretty in a blue skirt and a frothy white petticoat, with a white cardigan and a ribbon in her curls.

She turned on the bridge and waved to him, and once he'd waved back, she blew him a kiss and broke into a run. She was late for class again, he thought with amusement, but she'd soon have to get out of that habit. Being an artist wasn't all about late nights, drinking and being late for things; it was about discipline and keeping a sharp mind.

He turned away from the window and sipped the milky coffee his housekeeper had brought him earlier. It was growing a little cold, but he was used to that, for he often forgot to drink whilst he worked. He regarded his painting of the flower-seller with a critical eye and then raised the cup in salute.

'You're finished, madame, and soon you will be sitting not on the steps of the Sacré-Cœur, but on the walls of some of the most prestigious galleries in the world. *Félicitations!*'

He wheeled himself back to the table by the window to fetch a cigar to help him celebrate, glancing as he did out to the Pont Neuf. His heart skipped a beat and then began to race. Annabelle was standing there, just as he'd remembered her, her hair lightly ruffled by the wind, her slender body still retaining a youthful vigour as her gaze trawled the windows and balconies of his building.

He pushed the chair back, suddenly afraid she might see him. How lovely she was – and he wished with all his heart that he could look into her eyes and reassure himself that she was contented in her life. But it wasn't possible – he couldn't allow her to see him like this.

He watched her lean against the parapet as she looked upriver towards Notre-Dame Cathedral. From this distance he could see no sign of the years that had passed since they'd last met, and yet he knew they must be there. His breath was shallow and swift as he drank in the sight of her, and then he groaned in anguish as he realised she was about to leave the bridge.

'Don't go, my love. Stay just a while longer.'

He leant forward, thrusting open the windows so he could see down into the street below, but the balcony was too narrow for his wheelchair and he couldn't see beyond the railings. Where had she gone?

The answer came with the determined rap of the knocker on the door, and in a panic, he tried to turn his chair from the window and get to the door so he could call down to his housekeeper not to let her in. But the rubber wheel got caught in the leg of the small table and everything crashed to the floor. 'Don't let her in,' he yelled in frustration and fear. 'Don't you *dare* open that door.'

He wrestled with the chair and the debris of broken china, glass and a tangle of books and drawings, the sweat beading on his forehead and trickling down his back making him shiver with apprehension. He heard the murmur of voices coming from the stairwell, the light patter of feet running up the stairs. He was trapped.

Henri had just managed to get the blanket back over his wasted legs when she appeared in the doorway. He could only stare at her, his thoughts and his ability to speak lost in the reality of her being there.

Annabelle's heart was drumming as she entered the room and took in the scene at a glance. Henri looked so trapped in that wheelchair, his poor legs only partially covered by a blanket as he sat surrounded by the debris from the fallen table. And yet his eyes burnt as fiercely blue as they had done in his youth, and despite the facial hair, he still retained the dark, magnetic good looks and sturdy torso that she remembered.

'Hello, Henri,' she said as she walked towards him. 'I hear you've been getting to know our girl.'

He was clearly having some difficulty in talking, for she saw him swallow and his tone was gruff when he said her name. 'Belle,' he rasped. 'Belle, I've waited so long to see you . . . and now you're here, I can hardly believe it.'

She experienced the old, delicious tingle as he gazed into her eyes, and wondered if he'd felt the same.

'Your eyes always remind me of the wild violets I once picked in the countryside,' he murmured. 'You're still so lovely, Belle. It's as if no time has passed at all.'

She was feeling increasingly awkward as she stood there under his penetrating gaze. 'Aren't you going to invite me to sit down?' she said reproachfully.

'Of course, of course,' he muttered. 'But this blessed chair is entangled in all this mess I've made and . . .'

'Don't worry about all that,' she said. 'I can easily sort it out.'

He went red with embarrassment as she bent to clear the clutter and free the wheels on his chair. 'The damned thing's always getting stuck in things,' he muttered.

She righted the table and dumped everything back on it before sitting down opposite him. In the light that poured through the window she could see the lines around his eyes and shadows of the scars beneath his beard, and her heart ached for him.

She could see the yearning in his expression as his gaze travelled over her face and hair and down to her hands that were clasped loosely in her lap, and remembered how it had once felt to have his fingers running over her skin and through her hair, and how his lips had softly brushed her eyelids and mouth. His magnetism was drawing her in even after all these years and she understood how dangerous that was.

'Eugenie said you didn't want me to come,' she said rather firmly to cover her raging emotions. 'But I couldn't leave Paris without seeing you – not after all we meant to each other.'

'The years have been kinder to you than me,' he replied lightly. 'As you can see, I'm stuck in this damned thing.'

'Aline told me what happened, Henri,' she said softly, 'and you can have no idea of how very proud I am of how brave you were.' Her gaze shifted from his face to his hands, which were clasping the arms of the wheelchair. 'And your paintings are still beautiful, and I'm so glad you found the recognition you deserved.' She smiled. 'I always knew you'd be famous one day, and although I'm sad that you didn't find someone else to share your life, it seems you've found the solitude and peace so necessary to concentrate and be truly creative.'

He shrugged away her praise, but couldn't hide the gleam of pleasure in his eyes.

Annabelle decided to try to lighten the heavy atmosphere. 'I went to the Tate and saw Amélie. Is she still beautiful and sexy and all the things an artist's model should be?'

He chuckled and shook his head. 'She's a middle-aged frump living with some rich farmer in the south. I see her once a year when they come to Paris for Christmas.'

She giggled. 'Well, I'm sort of glad she isn't as gorgeous – it would be too unfair to the rest of us, wouldn't it?'

'But you're still beautiful, Belle. I can still see that girl in you – just as she's in Eugenie.'

'There are lines on my face and silver strands in my hair, and there's an artifice to the way I have to dress now to hide the lumps and bumps of middle age. But I'm content, Henri. George has given me more than I ever could have hoped for.'

'Oh, Belle,' he sighed as he reached for her hand. 'If only I could have told you sooner . . . If only things had been different . . .'

She felt the electricity in his touch, and knew she had to be careful of what she said as she looked into his eyes. 'What we had was a precious gift of love and we didn't waste it, Henri. We lived each moment of it, and now we have Eugenie to watch over. We will never know if that bright, shining passion could have withstood the years because fate intervened. But we can cherish the memory of what we once had. Now it's time to put it away deep in our hearts where it can slowly fade.'

'I don't want it to fade.'

'It must, Henri. We can't live our lives always looking behind us; we have to keep our eyes on the future – on Eugenie – on all the years we still have ahead of us. I loved you once, and somewhere deep inside there is a part of me that always will. But it's over, Henri.'

He nodded and she could see he was battling to keep the tears at bay. 'Then I wish you every happiness, my sweet Belle. And I promise to do all I can to help our daughter succeed. And she will, you know. She's exceptionally talented.'

Annabelle slowly withdrew her hand from his grasp and stood up. She bent forward and for a breathless moment he was surrounded by her perfume and felt the soft brush of her hair against his cheek as her lips lightly touched his. 'Goodbye, my dearest Henri,' she murmured.

And then she was gone, her light footsteps hurrying across the landing and running down the stairs.

Henri's tears blinded him as he turned his wheelchair towards the open window. The front door slammed and then she was walking swiftly across the bridge to meet the man who waited for her on the Left Bank. His heart ached as George put his hand on her shoulder and they talked earnestly for a moment before they walked away soon to be lost in the maze of streets beyond the bridge.

'Goodbye, my darling, most precious Belle,' he whispered. 'You may leave me here and walk into the future, but I know there's a tiny part of your heart which will always belong to me – and to Paris.'

AUTHOR'S NOTE

The idea for *Echoes From Afar* came when I was in Paris at the invitation of my French publisher, L'Archipel. I had spent a delightful evening with a group of enthusiastic fans and bloggers in a restaurant, and my host, Jerome Pescheux, suggested that as it was a balmy evening my husband and I should take the path alongsidpe the Seine to get back to our hotel. The lights of Paris were reflected in the Seine as it rushed beneath the Pont Neuf, and like the other couples, we strolled hand in hand along the pathway enjoying our last evening in this most romantic of cities. As we stood on the Pont Neuf I looked across the cobbled street to the line of tall elegant grey stone houses that were so distinctly French. Five storeys high, each window opened onto a wrought-iron balcony, and behind some of the gauzy curtains were the tantalising glimpses of lights and movement. Being an author and a natural nosy parker, I began to imagine the people who lived beyond those windows, and as I stood there I saw in my mind's eye a figure sitting at the third-floor window. He was a solitary man, with an aura of sadness about him, who gazed steadily towards the bridge. Who was he? What was his history and why did he gaze with such longing at the Pont Neuf? And then suddenly I knew, and his story began to flow as swiftly as the Seine. By the time I'd arrived back at our hotel the story was complete and I wrote it all down. Some ideas come swiftly only to leave the same way, but this one remained with me, and I knew I had to tell it for him.

ACKNOWLEDGEMENTS

I would like to thank Jean-Daniel Belfond, Jerome Pescheux and the wonderful team at L'Archipel for their generous hospitality. The whole experience was great fun, but of course a stay in Paris was the icing on the cake! So thank you all for giving me the opportunity and the inspiration to write *Echoes From Afar*. Thanks go also to my editor at Quercus, Kathryn Taussig, who is always a delight to work with. None of this would have been possible if I didn't have the sterling support from my brilliant agent, Teresa Chris, and I hope she knows just how much I appreciate all her efforts in helping me attain my goals. Last, but never least, I thank my husband, Oliver, who holds my hand, makes coffee and generally keeps me sane!

EXCLUSIVE EXTRACT FROM

Savannah Winds

PROLOGUE: GULF SAVANNAH

1951

Annie Somerville gathered up her little daughter, Lily, and set-tled her firmly on her hip. Nothing much frightened Annie any more – life in the Australian Gulf Country demanded courage and tenacity – but this morning was different, and she couldn't shake off the deep-seated dread that had been with her since waking.

The roar of the Spitfire shattered the dawn's silence as it raced along the dirt runway and lifted into the sky. Shielding their eyes from the ensuing dust, Annie and her two-year-old daughter followed the Spitfire's path until it was lost in the great dark heart of the enormous cloud that had come at dawn. This was the legendary Morning Glory, and it lay between the north and south horizons, overshadowing the vast savannah plains as it rolled in on itself, like an eternal, never-breaking wave, its crest glittering and shimmering with the crystal drops of ice it had captured on its progress across the Gulf of Carpentaria.

It was terrible in its beauty, and Annie tightened her grip on the child as she searched that roiling behemoth for sight of the plane, her prayers silent, her pulse racing as the fear grew.

And there it was, a tiny speck, riding that wave, diving, twisting and turning like a toy, racing along the crest, careless of the dangers.

Annie's imagination took her into the cockpit where she could see her husband laughing with the sheer joy of having achieved a long-held dream. How could he possibly understand how fearful she was – how helpless? The battle-scarred Spitfire and the brave, foolhardy man who flew her were as chaff in the wind to the mighty Morning Glory.

The Spitfire banked sharply and swooped back into the cloud. Annie waited breathlessly for it to re-emerge – but the cloud was fading now, leaving only a shimmering reminder on the far horizon, and a silent, empty sky.

1

Brisbane, 2000

Fleur had taken extra care with dinner that night – she'd known Greg would come home from the hospital tired and hungry after yet another long, busy day in theatre. Yet the lovingly prepared meal was wasted on her: she was too tense, and had no appetite. She abandoned her plate, sipped the chilled Chardonnay and took pleasure in watching him eat.

At thirty-nine, Greg Mackenzie had an athletic physique, and looked more like a rock star than a much-respected paediatric surgeon. His shoulders were wide, his belly taut, his shock of fair hair curling over his ears before sweeping back from his handsome face. But it was his eyes that had drawn her to him three years ago. They were the green of a summer ocean, fringed by long, thick lashes, and conveyed an undeniable and dangerous sensuality that had swiftly ensnared her.

He'd surprised her when he'd asked her to move in with him: they'd been dating for almost a year and she'd almost given up hope that they might have a future together. Greg had previously held fiercely to his independence – he was driven with the ambition to make a difference in the fraught, sometimes heart-breaking, world of paediatric surgery and there was little space in his life for other commitments. They had now been together for almost three years, and although life with Greg wasn't always easy, due to the nature of his work and his reluctance to discuss her growing need to start a family, her love for him was stronger than ever.

Greg caught her watching him, then noticed she hadn't touched her meal. 'Oh, Fleur.' He sighed. 'You're not still fretting about your job, are you?'

She nodded, letting her long dark hair drift over her face so he couldn't see the tears that had come so unexpectedly.

He reached across the table and took her hand. 'I'm sure everything will turn out just fine,' he said firmly. 'Oz Architects is a big company with a good reputation. They won't go under, you'll see.'

Fleur wished she shared his optimism, but the mood in the office had changed of late, and there was a sense of gloom that nothing could dispel. The rumours had been rife for months, growing in their intensity as projects were put on hold, staff left, and previously loyal clients decamped to rival companies. She wanly returned his smile and took another sip of wine as he once more tucked into his steak.

'I could apply for another job, I suppose,' she murmured, as she plucked at her table napkin, 'but the company has nurtured me since I finished uni, and I've done very well with them. It would feel disloyal to leave on the strength of the rumours, and I still can't quite believe it's about to implode.'

Greg pushed away his empty plate and rested his warm hand over her restless fingers. 'There's little point in getting stressed about it, Fleur,' he said softly. 'Any decision regarding the company is out of your hands. And even if it does go to the wall, you're a brilliant architect and I can almost guarantee that you won't be out of work for long.'

She couldn't help but smile at his unswerving faith in her abilities. 'At thirty-four, I'm a bit long in the tooth to be on the dole,' she said wryly.

Greg pushed back his chair and went round the table to gather her up in a warm embrace. 'Now you're just feeling sorry for yourself,' he murmured against her cheek.

She silently admitted she was feeling down in the dumps as she nestled into him. But the steady beat of his heart was reassuring as she breathed in his clean, crisp scent and drew from his strength. Greg was her rock, her soulmate, and no matter how rough the seas of life became, he would always be there to anchor her.

'I knew I could rely on you to make me feel better about things,' she murmured against his lips.

He kissed her deeply, held her in a tight hug, then patted her backside. 'That's my girl.' His smile was broad as he looked down at her. 'Things will work out, Fleur, they always do – and who knows? This could be a turning point that leads to even bigger and better things.'

Fleur watched as he began to clear the dishes. 'I'm not so sure I really want anything bigger and better,' she said hesitantly. 'I love what I do, but my priorities have changed since I started out, and the thought of trying to succeed in what can be a fiercely competitive business no longer has the same appeal.'

Greg dumped the plates on the stainless-steel draining board and turned to look at her with a frown. 'But you've worked so hard to get where you are,' he said. 'Surely you're not thinking about giving it all up?'

Fleur could feel her pulse beating wildly as she faced him, for this was rocky terrain they'd covered before. If she wasn't careful they would end up having yet another argument. 'I just thought,' she said quietly, 'that if it doesn't go well tomorrow, I might take a few months off to re-evaluate things.'

Greg folded his arms, his gaze steady as he leant against the granite worktop. 'What things?' he asked warily.

Fleur took a deep breath. 'I'm thirty-four, Greg,' she said softly. 'You know exactly what I mean.'

He dipped his chin as his shoulders sagged. 'Not that again, Fleur,' he said, with a sigh. 'We've discussed the subject of babies too many times already, and I don't want to fight with you.'

'I don't want to fight with you either,' she replied, as she took a step towards him and tentatively placed her hand on his arm. 'But time is slipping away so fast, Greg, and I'm frightened that soon it will be too late to start a family.'

'We're too busy to have babies,' he said. 'Especially now I'm head of Surgery, and you'll be either looking for a job, or totally immersed in some new building project.'

'I don't *have* to find a job – not for a while at any rate – and even when I do, I could go part-time and find a good crèche nearby,'

'Having kids is a full-time job, Fleur. You can't just dump them with strangers when they become inconvenient.' He shrugged off her hand and went to open the large glass doors that led onto the penthouse terrace.

A curl of uncertainty began to unravel inside her. 'Then I won't work at all,' she said quietly. 'We can afford to live on your salary if we move to somewhere smaller.'

'I like it here,' he muttered, staring out to the panorama of the Brisbane city lights twelve storeys below. He stepped into the balmy warmth of the early summer's evening and went to contemplate the view from the far side of the terrace.

Fleur followed him, glancing only momentarily at the glittering sweep of the city below them. 'I like it too,' she said, 'but if I'm made redundant we won't really be able to afford it – and it's not exactly a family home, is it?'

'It was never meant to be.' His expression softened as he turned to face her. He snaked an arm over her shoulders, drawing her close until he could gently rest his chin on the top of her head. 'We live here because it's in the heart of the city where we have a good social life – and, besides, it's convenient for the hospital. I can easily afford to keep us going until you find another job, Fleur.'

She looked up, her fingers running lightly over his bristled chin. 'I have no doubt of it,' she said, 'and of course I appreciate the wonderful life we have here. But it's time for us to think further ahead, my darling, and to discuss this block you seem to have when it comes to having a family.'

Greg's expression hardened again as he took a step back from her. 'I'm sorry, Fleur, I thought I'd made it plain when we first moved in together that babies were never part of the plan.'

'I know that's what you said at the beginning,' she admitted, 'but I thought you'd change your mind once you realised how good we are together, and what a loving home we can give to our baby.'

'I've never given you reason to think that I'd ever change my mind,' he said flatly.

Fleur could have sworn the apartment building shifted beneath her as her heart lurched and she fought back the tears. 'But I hoped you would,' she said, her voice breaking. 'And I really believed you might come round to the idea once we were settled.'

He took a deep breath and let it out on a sigh as he ran his fingers distractedly through his hair. 'I love you, Fleur. I love being with you, and waking up beside you every morning, but I don't want a kid. It would spoil everything.'

She moved away from him. 'But a child is a gift, the very proof of our love and commitment to each other. It will bind us even closer, and give us far more than all this.' She took in the apartment and the view with a sweep of her hand.

His eyes darkened as he rammed his hands into his trouser pockets. 'Easy for you to say when you've never known how tough it is without all the luxuries. A kid needs two parents to look after it, guide and protect it. It will wear you out, divide and separate us with its demands – it'll tie you down and change you.'

The tears were blinding her, but she was damned if she'd let them fall. 'Of course it won't,' she managed. 'Just because you have no family and mine isn't exactly the Waltons – that doesn't mean we can't be good and loving parents. A baby will bring us even closer,' she persisted, desperate now to convince him.

He was clearly making an effort to keep control of the situation, but a pulse beat in his jaw, his tone was sharp-edged, and his eyes sparked with determination. 'It won't, believe me,' he said grimly. 'And it's no good you trying to persuade me otherwise. There will be no babies, Fleur.'

The world seemed to rock on its axis. 'No babies?' she whispered. 'Not ever?'

He shook his head, his expression hinting at a regret that wasn't mirrored in his resolute eyes. 'I know you're disappointed right now,' he said tightly, 'but you'll thank me in years to come when your career takes off and your building designs are winning awards.'

Shocked by the sheer audacity of his argument, she began to tremble. 'You're denying me the only thing I've ever asked of you,' she breathed. 'Don't you *dare* tell me I'll be grateful.'

'I'm sorry. That probably didn't come out right,' he blustered. 'But surely you can see how impractical it would be for us to have a child?' He ruffled his hair again, clearly battling to find the words to placate her. 'I'm at the hospital all hours. You'll soon be busy with new building projects, and away on site. You can't have it all, Fleur.'

'I'm not asking to have it all,' she said, through the tears which were now streaming, unheeded, down her face.

He took her into his arms and held her as she sobbed. 'Oh, Fleur, I'm so sorry. I hate hurting you like this, but I thought you'd accepted things the way they are.'

She pulled away from him and saw the anguish in his expression that must surely mirror her own heartbreak. 'But this isn't the first time we've discussed this – you knew how I felt about having a baby.'

'And you knew that I didn't want any.' He gave a ragged sigh. 'Admit it, Fleur, you chose to ignore what I was telling you, and kept on hoping. Now it has led to this. I'm truly sorry that you're so hurt, but I won't change my mind.'

'I don't understand,' she said. 'You say you love me and that you're sorry you're hurting me, but with every word you're hurting me more.'

'Oh, Fleur . . . I don't know how to put things right between us.'

She looked up at him. 'You could start by explaining the real reason behind your determination not to have children. And don't tell me it's because we're too busy or that this apartment isn't right or we'd make lousy parents, because I think all that is a smokescreen for something far deeper.'

He dipped his chin. 'We're both too emotional to talk sensibly tonight,' he murmured. He held out his hand to her. 'Let's leave it for now, and go to bed.'

She ignored the hand and walked back into the vast open space of the main room, which served as kitchen, dining room and lounge. The thought of lying next to him, of feeling his arms about her, their bodies entwined, was too much to bear.

'I need time to think things over,' she replied, 'so I'll sleep in the spare room tonight.'

He grasped her hand, stopping her before she could reach the bedroom door. 'Don't do this, Fleur. Please, my darling.'

'I'm sorry, Greg. I can't talk any more tonight, please don't make this any harder than it already is.' She saw his stricken expression in the moment before she closed the door, and knew there would be little sleep for either of them that night.

The dirty dishes had been stacked in the dishwasher, the table cleared, but there was no sign of Greg, who must have left early for the hospital – no doubt to avoid any further confrontation. In a way, it was a relief, for Fleur was wrung out after a restless night of tormented thoughts and emotions, and the last thing she wanted for either of them was a continuation of an argument that appeared to be unsolvable.

She showered and dressed for the day, taking extra care with her makeup to hide the ravages of the night before going back into the kitchen to make a pot of strong coffee. Greg's note was leaning against the percolator.

Darling Fleur, a thousand sorries for the pain I've caused you. We'll talk tonight, and then perhaps you'll come to understand why I feel so strongly – and hopefully forgive me. I love you, Greg. PS. Good luck on the job front.

Tears threatened again and she hurriedly blinked them away as she made the coffee and tried to focus on the morning's meeting, which suddenly didn't seem important at all. They could talk things through, certainly, but it was clear that one of them would have to change their mind if they were to continue in this relationship. He was asking her to make a terrible sacrifice, but if he was unwilling to bend, then she had some very serious decisions to make.

The anguished thoughts went round and round in her head as she drank the strong black coffee and stared out of the plate-glass windows to the distant horizon where Mount Coot-tha shimmered in the early-morning sunlight.

The vista was impressive, but the spacious, silent apartment seemed to close in around her. She finished the coffee and hurried down to the underground car park, climbed into her Mazda roadster and drove, at speed, into the city.

She parked in the designated space behind the offices of Oz Architects, gathered up her handbag, briefcase and laptop, and took a long, deep breath before she climbed reluctantly out of the car.

'G'day, Fleur. How ya going?' Jason Delaney, dressed in sweat pants, cut-away singlet, running shoes and black bandanna, was out of breath.

Fleur smiled up at her colleague. 'Not too good,' she said, the gold bangles jangling on her delicate wrist as she flicked back her hair and adjusted the collar of her suit jacket. 'I'm worried about today's meeting.'

Jason stopped jogging on the spot, his handsome face immediately doleful. 'Aren't we all? What do you reckon, Fleur? Are we for the chop?'

'I hope not,' she muttered, her high-heels ringing on the paving as she headed for the office block. 'Greg and I have a huge mortgage to pay, and thirty-four isn't a good age to be out of work.'

'But I thought Greg had just been promoted to consultant surgeon. Surely he's earning enough to keep you going for a while.'

Fleur wasn't about to discuss her financial situation with him. He might be well-meaning – and her best friend at work – but he was a gossip. She tapped in the security code, pushed through the door and headed for the ground-floor office suite. Walking into the great white space that was cluttered with desks, drawing boards and filing cabinets, she switched on the banks of lights, then dumped her bulging briefcase and heavy laptop on her desk.

'There's no point in speculating until we know the facts,' she said quietly. 'Oz Architects is a big company, and we have to hope it can weather this latest storm.'

Jason took off the bandanna, stuffed it into a pocket and folded his muscled arms against his toned chest. 'Well, I've already applied for a couple of posts, just in case. There's no way I can expect Enrique to keep me in luxurious idleness, however much I might enjoy it.' He glanced at the showy watch on his wrist. 'I'd better get a wiggle on and make myself beautiful before the powers-that-be descend.'

Fleur smiled as he strolled out of the office on his way to the cloakrooms. Jason could always lift her spirits, no matter how low she was, but the memory of the lonely, restless night she'd spent in the spare bedroom, her thoughts and emotions in turmoil, couldn't be vanquished even by Jason's cheerfulness.

She slipped off her jacket and plumped down in her leather chair, the rather heavy silence of the deserted office engulfing her. It didn't alleviate the uncertainties of the day, and it was with some relief that she heard the other members of staff arriving. Tying her hair back from her face, she did her best to greet them brightly as they poured in, their noise and clatter shattering the ominous silence. The only topic of conversation was the forthcoming meeting and, as ten o'clock approached, the chatter lessened and the tension mounted.

'Why don't you come to the bar and drown your sorrows with the rest of us, Fleur?'

She shook her head. 'I just want to go home, Jason,' she said as, under the watchful eye of the bailiff's guard, she packed the last of her personal belongings into a cardboard box, then slipped on her jacket.

'But Greg will still be at the hospital,' he pointed out. 'It's not good to be on your own at a time like this.' He glanced swiftly at the burly guard, lurking nearby, and nodded as the man tapped his watch. 'Come on, Fleur,' he coaxed.

She resisted his attempts to get her out of the office, for she needed a quiet moment to take everything in. 'I've been with this company for ten years,' she murmured, as she sat at her desk for the last time. 'I got chartered here, and was promoted only a few months ago. How could they do such a thing?'

'Greed,' replied Jason, tartly. 'They got caught giving backhanders to developers and politicians, and exacerbated the situation by fiddling the books. No wonder we're all out of a job.'

'But they were such a big company. Why did they need to do that?'

He reached for her cardboard box and placed it on top of his own. 'Who knows? And we're out of work, without a cat's chance in hell of getting redundancy. I for one would like to shoot the bastards.'

She giggled despite everything, and got to her feet. They walked past the hurriedly cleared desks, the filing cabinets that spewed reams of paper, the discarded drawing boards, charts and scale models of projects that now would never be finished. The once cutting-edge architects' office had already taken on the aura of abandonment.

The bailiff's man opened the door and locked it firmly behind them.

She deposited the cardboard box in the roadster's boot and Jason gave her a hug. 'Are you sure you don't want to come to the bar? I'm buying.'

She drew back from his embrace. 'Greg and I have plans for tonight, Jason, but thanks for the offer.'

'Oh, it's like that, is it?' He raised a mocking brow.

She knew what he meant, but didn't put him straight. He was the best girlfriend a woman could have and she would miss not seeing him every day, but some things were far too private to share. She stood on tiptoe and lightly kissed the smooth cheek that was scented with Paco Rabanne. 'Stay in touch, Jason,' she murmured, 'and let me know if you hear of any good jobs going.'

Fleur drove towards the Brisbane River and the penthouse apartment that overlooked it. Losing her job so soon after her devastating argument with Greg was like another small death, and she felt numb, isolated and uncertain about everything she'd once thought was set in stone.

The hot, needle-sharp shower went some way to restoring her spirits and, by the time she'd applied fresh makeup and changed into a cool, button-through summer dress, she was feeling more positive. She had proved her worth at Oz Architects, and would soon find another position – perhaps in a smaller, well-established company that would appreciate what she had to offer.

She ran the brush through her hair as she thought about going through the interviewing process, the settling-in period, the new colleagues. The prospect of starting again didn't excite her as it might have done only a few days before: no career could fulfil her deepest yearning.

With a sigh, she put down the brush and went into the third bedroom, which she'd turned into a home office. It was no good thinking like that, she scolded herself silently. Far better to focus on preparing her CV and putting her portfolio together, rather than dwelling on things she couldn't change.

The drawing boards stood by the floor-to-ceiling windows that overlooked the terrace, each covered with intricate plans that were now obsolete. Rolls of plans and scale models of past and future projects filled every shelf, and research books were stacked precariously on the desk beside the computer. A large photocopier stood against the far wall, its lid open to reveal the ground-plans of a project she and her colleagues had been preparing for tender. Pencils, rulers and all the paraphernalia of her trade were stuffed into pots, and forgotten coffee mugs festered on top of the filing cabinet. But the walls were covered with bright, beautiful pictures of the buildings she'd helped to design, and the crystal butterflies and birds that hung before the windows shot rainbows of colour about the room as they moved imperceptibly in the air-conditioning.

The silence was too profound, so she turned on the portable radio and tuned it into a classical music station, setting the volume low. As the beautiful nocturne drifted into the room, she sat at her desk and stared out of the window to the distant, hazy outline of Mount Coot-tha and the ribbon of the Brisbane River, which ran beneath the elegant bridges and through the heart of the city. Was Greg feeling just as confused and hurt – or was he as determined as ever to keep things as they were? Did he even realise how damaging all this could be – and what could he possibly say to her that would make her change her mind?

Weary with the thoughts that ran endlessly through her head, she checked that her portfolio was up to date, then trawled the architectural website to see what posts were on offer. She book-marked the ones that sparked any interest into her Favourites folder and then began to sort through the paperwork she'd need at interview. There were some certificates missing, but she was fairly certain Greg had filed them in his own home office.

Greg's office was neat to the point of sparse. The filing cabi-nets were lined up like soldiers; the desk was bare of paperwork; there were no pictures on the wall, no crystals dangling at the window or plants to alleviate the blandness. The only personal items in the room were Greg's beloved guitars, neatly propped in their stands.

Fleur went to the desk and hunted for the keys to the filing cabinets, most of which held copies of medical records, scholarly tomes on all things to do with paediatrics and endless back issues of the *Lancet*. Fleur had no interest in any of these, and went straight to the cabinet that held their certificates, passports and other documents.

She found her birth and graduation certificates neatly filed in a folder marked 'Fleur', but there was no sign of her chartered architect's certificate, and the drawer seemed to be stuck. She gave it a tug, but still it refused to budge, so she reached in and scrabbled about until her fingers found the offending folder that had become jammed in the mechanism.

She wrestled it free, then tried to smooth out the creases and return the spilling papers to some kind of order. It was unusual for Greg to be so careless with his files – some of the papers, including her certificate, had torn edges now. He must have been in a hurry when he put it away.

Her hand stilled as she caught sight of the familiar heading on the writing paper, and before she knew what she was doing, she'd read the short, concise letter. 'What on earth?' she breathed, as she read it again. 'But this makes no sense – especially after what happened last night. Why, Greg?'

She stared at the letter for several more minutes, trying to work out Greg's reasoning, then lost patience, stuffed it back into the folder and slammed the drawer. She wished she'd never read it, for now she had no choice but to question him about it.

Greg came home at lunchtime, his handsome face bearing lines of weariness and unhappiness as he entered the apartment, armed with an enormous bunch of roses. 'I managed to offload my theatre list so I could have the rest of the day off,' he said. 'I know the roses are a bit of a cliché, but I wanted to give you something to show that I've been thinking about you.'

Fleur was sorely tempted to fly into his arms and hold him tight, to kiss away those lines and tell him they could survive this. But she couldn't – not after the hurt he'd caused. She took them from him and breathed in their scent. 'They're beautiful,' she replied, then kissed him lightly on the cheek.

'I'm guessing the meeting didn't go well as you're home early,' he said, as he shed his jacket and shoes.

'I'm out of work and there's no redundancy pay,' she replied, as she placed the roses in a vase and set them on the glass dining-table. 'But there are other jobs out there.'

Greg seemed to realise she was tense and needed to keep her distance, so he didn't embrace her. He poured a glass of juice from the fridge and perched on the arm of the cream leather couch. 'I'm sorry it didn't work out,' he said, 'and for the hurt I've caused you. We've both had a hellish twenty-four hours.'

Fleur sat down on the bar stool by the kitchen counter, determined to put space between them and stay calm. 'You said in your note that you'd explain everything,' she replied. 'I'm ready to listen, Greg.'

He twisted the tumbler in his hands, his expressive face showing his inner turmoil. 'I love you, Fleur, and I want us to get married and share the rest of our lives together.'

'But marriage isn't the answer, Greg – not if there are to be no children.'

'But our life can be perfect – just the two of us. And—'

'Not for me, it wouldn't,' she interrupted. 'Marriage is about raising a family together, not living as we do now.'

'But I thought you were happy with the way things are.'

Fleur was holding tightly to her emotions. 'I was before you told me there wouldn't ever be any children,' she said, her voice betraying the tears that were gathering.

Greg scrubbed his face with his hands. 'I'm sorry, Fleur, but I'm not going to change my mind on that.'

'You made that very clear last night,' she managed, through the lump in her throat. 'But you don't seem to understand how much damage this is doing to us, Greg – or to me. Surely I should have some say in such an important decision.'

He stood up and began to pace the room. 'It's not a decision I've taken lightly, Fleur, believe me.'

She watched him and knew he spoke the truth. 'But why make it at all? I don't understand.'

He stopped pacing and came to stand on the other side of the counter. 'We have a good life, and without children we'll have the freedom to live it to the full,' he said in a rush. 'We work long hours as it is – and it would be far worse if we had children.' He took a deep breath, clearly struggling to keep his own emotions in check. 'I've seen what it does to my colleagues and, believe me, Fleur, the divorce rate at the hospital is as high as the stress levels.'

He put out his hand towards her, hesitated and withdrew it again. 'I love you, Fleur, but I don't want our lives turned upside down just because your hormones are raging.'

'My hormones?' she gasped. 'This isn't about my hormones, Greg – it's all about *you*, and what *you* want.'

'No, it isn't,' he insisted, with a frown. 'I love you, Fleur, and I've always had your best interests at heart. I really think you should—'

She was breathing hard, struggling to keep the anger at bay. 'I already know what you think,' she said sharply, 'and *none* of it is in my best interests.' She was trembling now. 'And don't keep blaming all this on me and telling me you love me because I don't believe you.'

'Fleur—'

She ignored his outstretched hand. 'If you really loved me, like you keep saying you do, you'd at least think about having a baby with me.'

His jaw set in a stubborn line as his eyes hardened to ice. 'That's emotional blackmail, Fleur, and absolutely beneath you.'

'I know, and I don't like myself for it – but it's the only weapon I have.'

He seemed to have no answer to this for he turned away from her and began to fiddle with the coffee machine.

'You said you'd explain,' she said. 'But so far, you've said very little to convince me that you have a valid reason for laying down such a draconian law.'

'I've explained as much as I feel I have to,' he replied, 'and you getting over-emotional about it isn't helping.' He cut off any further exchange by turning on the coffee grinder.

Fleur glared at him in fury and frustration as the noise filled the open-plan room and made her head throb. She moved to the other side of the granite counter, determined to discover what really lay behind his decision.

Greg refused to look at her and, as the loud grating came to a sudden end, the silence was heavy with tension.

'Talk to me, Greg,' she pleaded. 'Let's not fight.'

He plugged in the espresso machine, laid out the tiny cups and saucers, then leant against the granite counter, bare feet crossed, arms folded over his chest as if to ward off further confrontation. 'Okay, let's get down to the absolute basics, Fleur,' he said. 'How do you know you're even capable of having children?'

'I had all the tests done two months ago,' she replied evenly. 'I'm ovulating up a storm, and the doctor reckons there's no reason why I shouldn't conceive.'

He raised a fair eyebrow. 'And what if I'm firing blanks?'

She met his gaze. 'We both know you're not.'

He slowly straightened, his eyes almost feline as they bored into her. 'What makes you so sure of that, Fleur?' His voice was soft, but laced with anger.

Her gaze didn't waver, but her heart was banging against her ribs. 'I've seen your latest medical test.'

The green of his eyes was now Arctic. 'How?'

Her mouth was dry and she was finding it hard to swallow. 'I was looking for my certificates, and your folder had come loose. It was jamming the drawer. All the papers spilt out – and there it was.'

The tic in his jaw beat faster as he narrowed his eyes. 'When was this?'

She'd never seen him so angry before, and it made her nervous. 'This morning.'

'How *dare* you pry into things that are none of your business?' he hissed.

'We share this apartment and a bed – of course it's my business,' she retorted. 'And it's a good thing I did find it, Greg, because you obviously weren't going to tell me about that medical, were you?'

'It was just a routine annual check-up,' he said, his gaze sliding away before he turned and poured the thick dark coffee into the tiny cups.

'If it was so *routine*, then why did it include a sperm test?'

The silence stretched and the tension in the room was almost tangible as he still refused to look at her. Then he abandoned the coffee neither of them wanted and stood with his back to her, his head bowed. 'I asked for it.'

Fleur could barely breathe. 'Why?'

He still couldn't look at her. 'I was considering a vasectomy.'

She felt as if he'd punched her and staggered back to the stool, numb with shock.

'But I didn't have it done, Fleur,' he said. 'I was just curious,' he raced on. 'I thought that if I was firing blanks, you'd be able to come off the pill – and, if not, that a vasectomy would make things easier for both . . .' He tailed off.

'You bastard,' she rasped. 'You absolute bastard. How could you even contemplate such a thing without discussing it with me?'

He folded his arms defensively again. 'It was just a thought – no need to make a drama out of it.'

She stared at him, seeing not the man she loved but a cold, distant, unfeeling stranger. 'You really, *really* don't want children, do you?' she breathed. 'That's why you insist upon using condoms when I'm already on the pill.' She gave a harsh bark of humourless laughter. 'Talk about belt and braces. How stupid was I not to realise?'

'The pill doesn't always work,' he muttered defensively. 'And I wasn't sure I could trust you to take it. You've been acting very strangely lately.'

Fury, anguish and pain galvanised her and she flew at him. 'Bastard!' she screamed, as she tried to claw his face and beat his chest. 'Selfish, arrogant bastard!'

He dodged her nails and grabbed her wrists. 'Calm down, for God's sake, Fleur. You'll make yourself ill.'

'I don't care,' she sobbed, wrestling against him.

'Well, I do.' He half carried her to the couch and pushed her down into the soft leather. 'Stop it, Fleur. Nothing can be resolved if you carry on like this.'

Fleur curled into her pain, unable to believe how deeply he'd betrayed her. 'But there's nothing to resolve, is there?' she moaned. 'You've already decided.'

Greg snatched up the car keys and shoved his feet into his loafers as he scooped his mobile and pager from the worktop. 'I can't talk to you when you're like this,' he muttered.

'Where are you going?' she asked in panic.

'Out.'

'But you can't. Not now. Not like this.' She clambered off the couch and stumbled towards him. 'Please, Greg, don't leave me.'

'You need time to calm down and think things through. It's better if I go now before either of us says things we'll regret.'

The door closed behind him, thereby enforcing his absolute determination to bring closure to the argument.

She sank back into the couch. He didn't love her – and at that very moment she hated him. He'd destroyed everything they'd had together.

Greg discovered he was trembling as he stood in the echoing silence of the private underground car park. He abhorred confrontation and had clearly learnt nothing about women in his thirty-nine years, for he'd handled the whole episode very badly. Fleur was distraught, hurt to the point where she probably – and with good reason – hated him right now. And he didn't have the first idea of how to put things right between them without compromising on the one thing he'd vowed never to do.

His loafers made little noise as he crossed the concrete and headed for the Porsche, but the very silence of the place made him want to bellow with anger and frustration – to punch something and give vent to the troubling emotions he'd always been so careful to control. He hadn't meant for her ever to know about those tests – but now she did, she'd made him feel cornered and vulnerable, which had resulted in him retaliating in the only way he knew how: coldly, clinically, logically.

His reined-in emotions and enforced coolness were the defences he used when faced with situations that overwhelmed him – but he knew that, although they might succeed in his work at the hospital, they could be fatal to his relationship with Fleur.

'You're a bloody coward, Greg Mackenzie,' he muttered, as he unlocked the car. 'You should have made it absolutely plain right from the start.'

He slid into the luxurious leather seat and slammed the door. His regrets were legion, but he knew that to return to the apartment right now would only cause Fleur more hurt – perhaps even give her hope. And that was the last thing he wanted.

The sensuous aroma and feel of new leather should have cocooned and soothed him, but today it merely stifled him as he leant back and closed his eyes. The Carrera had been a gift to himself once his promotion had been confirmed. She was a beautiful car, a long-cherished dream, with shiny black bodywork, alloy wheels and a three-litre engine. It was the perfect symbol of his hard-won success – a real boy's toy – and certainly not suitable for car-seats and all the paraphernalia small children demanded.

He glanced into the next parking bay at Fleur's Mazda MX5. Scarlet and sleek, it was also entirely unsuitable for ferrying kids about. His lip curled. It had been yet another extravagant gift from her father, who seemed to think that expensive presents could make up for his complete lack of parenting skills.

He pushed aside all thoughts of Don Franklin and gave a sigh of deep regret. He didn't want to lose Fleur – couldn't bear the thought of life without her – which was why he'd prayed this day would never come. But it had, and now he was afraid that his future was heading down the same torturous road as his past.

In his foolishness, he'd thought she was happy as they were – thought that her childhood experiences had cured her of ever wanting children, and that her nieces and nephews had been enough to satisfy any maternal stirrings. He hadn't missed the occasional reference to children, or the way she watched babies in prams, but had fooled himself into thinking it was just a momentary lapse, idle wistfulness that would soon be forgotten in the excitement of their busy and fulfilling lives. How very wrong he'd been. How blind to Fleur's real and urgent needs, which he'd refused to acknowledge. Now their future together was uncertain. He bowed his head and closed his eyes as the terror of losing her grew ever stronger.

He was in the wrong. He should have explained to her how afraid he was of having children. The responsibility of raising them, of guiding them safely through the quicksands of life was something he didn't dare take on – the chance of failure was too high.

He could almost hear his father's sneering voice – the barrage of words that had dripped like poison throughout his boyhood and remained with him still. It had been so hard to overcome them, to disbelieve them when they'd been so firmly instilled. But he'd proved he was worth something – proved he could rise above the old man's tangible hatred and stand tall, confident in his skills, at ease with himself and the life he'd chosen. In short, he'd escaped from hell and had no intention of ever visiting it again.

He'd been careful to tell Fleur as little as possible about those years, saying only that his parents were dead and he didn't like talking about them. But there was so much more he should have trusted her with because the legacy of pain, isolation and anger that lay just below the surface haunted him still, and now threatened to destroy everything he held dear.

The tap on the window made him jump and he stared stupidly at his neighbour and colleague John Watkins before recognising him.

'You all right, mate?' the older man asked, once the window had slid down. 'If you don't mind my saying so, you look a bit crook.'

Greg quickly blew his nose. 'Just a touch of hay fever,' he said, trying to gather his wits. 'Forgot to take my antihistamine.'

John's craggy face showed little sign of conviction, but he didn't probe further. He squared his broad shoulders and patted his trim waist – he was almost sixty but in excellent shape. 'I was off to see if I could persuade someone to play squash,' he said, hitching up his large sports bag. 'Care to take up the challenge?'

Greg could think of no better way to release all the pent-up emotions than to hit a little ball against concrete walls. 'My kit's at the club. I'll meet you there.'

He turned the key and the Porsche roared into life, the throaty pulse echoing in the silent concrete garage. He buckled up, then eased the car out of the narrow space and followed John's

Subaru up the ramp. Fleur would have to be faced, and soon – but he prayed he could find the courage to tell her why he never wanted children, and why it was so important that she understood and accepted the fact.

Fleur had stood beneath the powerful shower jets, her sobs drowned by the sound of the water until she was drained of all emotion. She dragged a towel around her and slowly traipsed across the sunlit bedroom. Her world was shattered. Hope had died, and there was no joy any more in the beautiful room she'd furnished with such love and care.

She slumped on to the bed and dragged the towel from her head so that her long hair fell wetly over her shoulders, dripping down her back and breasts. Staring at her reflection in the mirrored closets that lined one wall, she had to accept that things could never be the same again. She couldn't force him to give her a baby – and although she might have been tempted to resort to sticking pins in condoms or secretly stop taking the pill she knew that was not the answer. A child had to be born from love, not deceit.

'Can we ever get over this?' she asked her reflection. 'Do I love him enough after today to stay and put aside all the dreams I've cherished?'

She couldn't answer that, for at this moment she was bereft of love and numb with pain. There were so many difficult, heart-searching questions she didn't know how to answer, and she longed for the comfort and advice of her mother. But she was long dead, an ethereal figure whose name was never mentioned, and whose face she couldn't remember.

There was always her half-sister, Beth, who'd taken her into under her wing during those early years even though she herself was only a teenager. But they had drifted apart over the past three years, and she didn't feel she could run to her for advice after such a long time. As for their father, Don Franklin was not a man to turn to in times of trouble – he was neither loving nor caring.

She eyed the sunlit room and the rumpled bed. Greg was an enigma, and although they'd been together for three years, she realized now that she didn't know him at all. His childhood was a closed book, and she'd always suspected it had been unhappy, but he'd become a successful and skilled surgeon – a man who worked tirelessly to erase suffering, a man whose gentle voice and even gentler hands could comfort the little ones in his care.

She'd seen him distraught when his skills couldn't save them, and jubilant when his tiny patients were returned fit and well to their anxious parents. How could he possibly not want one of his own when he so clearly had the skills to nurture?

Flopping back against the pillows, she soon became restless. Her thoughts were whirling and her emotions in turmoil. She swung off the bed, rubbed her hair dry and got dressed. Shoving her feet into sandals, she went into the kitchen and eyed the mess.

The bar stool was still on its side where it had fallen as she'd attacked him, and the tiny cups of espresso coffee had shattered, spilling their viscous contents over the granite worktop and down the stainless-steel cupboard doors.

Housework busied her hands, but her mind refused to be still, and once the kitchen was gleaming again, she took a moment to regard the apartment they had bought with such excitement only two years before. After the morning's revelations, she discovered she could regard it with the cool detachment of someone who didn't care.

The huge open-plan space was awash with the sunlight that streamed in through the picture-windows. Cream leather, chrome and glass dominated it, relieved only by splashes of orange, green and scarlet from the bird-of-paradise flowers standing in the tall earthenware pot in the corner, and the vast abstract oil painting on the wall. It was achingly modern and cutting-edge – a designer's dream without clutter, warmth or personality. No child would feel at home here. And now neither did she.

She plucked a carton of iced coffee from the fridge and scooped up the day's post on her way out to the terrace. Brisbane was sweltering, the rooftops and glass towers shimmering in the heat-haze, the river running almost sluggishly through the city towards the green and gold of the surrounding countryside.

Fleur opened the large parasol over the white wrought-iron table and chairs and sat down to sip the coffee and stare at the vista before her. Life was continuing out there, the day unfolding as it always did, and there was no one to really care that she'd lost her job, the chance to have babies and that her relationship with Greg was in ruins. This apartment was a symbol of the having-it-all generation – but now it meant nothing: it had proved to be as fragile and transient as a house of cards.

She put on her sunglasses and turned determinedly to the latest edition of the *Architectural Times*. It was time to stop feeling sorry for herself and concentrate on finding a job. At least if she had work she wouldn't have time to think.

Greg slid down the cool, solid wall of the squash court and tried to catch his breath. 'You play a demon game, mate. Where the hell do you get the energy?'

John squatted beside him, his rugged face creasing like a bloodhound's as he grinned. 'Not bad for an old bloke, eh? I warned you, Greg, youth is no match for experience. Up for another?'

'Not bloody likely,' he grunted. 'I already owe you a hundred bucks as it is.'

John got to his feet. 'C'mon, mate. The beers are on you.'

After a long, hot shower to ease his aching muscles, Greg headed for the bar. The sports club was fairly new, and on this late Thursday afternoon there were few seats available by the vast windows that overlooked the riverside gardens. But John had managed to snag a couple and waved him over as he returned from the bar laden with a schooner of beer, a pint of orange juice and a plate of sandwiches.

Greg had taken his first sip of the ice-cold juice when his mobile and pager burst into life. 'Dammit,' he muttered, looking longingly at the sandwiches – he hadn't eaten since the previous evening and was ravenous.

The pager told him he was wanted in A and E. Quickly answering the mobile, he listened to the precise voice at the other end. 'I'll be there in ten,' he said. Looking at John with a wry smile, he shrugged. 'That's the end of my afternoon off.'

'Serious?'

'Serious enough. Shane Philips has been a patient before, and I've warned the authorities time and again to get him away from his father – but they never listen.'

'Makes me glad I chose obstetrics,' John replied, taking a huge bite of his sandwich. 'Good luck, mate.'

Greg downed the juice, wrapped his share of the sandwiches in a paper napkin and, with a nod, left the club and headed for his car. The hospital was only a short drive away, but he suspected he would be several hours in theatre and would be too tired to want to walk back for it.

Having parked in his allocated space, he keyed in his home number on the car phone. It was dead – so the answering machine wasn't working either. Fleur's mobile was similarly unavailable, and he suspected she'd switched it off, determined not to talk to him.

With a groan of frustration he climbed out of the car, his stomach clenching at the thought of what awaited him at the hospital. As an experienced surgeon, he'd witnessed a great deal of suffering, but it never got any easier – and the knowledge that sometimes he could do very little to protect his small, vulnerable patients from the people who were supposed to love and care for them made him exceedingly angry. He'd done battle with the bureaucracy of the social service agencies and had too often vented his frustration on the poor overworked social workers who were only trying to do their best – but it was a battle worth fighting, and he felt he was beginning to make some headway.

Greg hurried into the hospital, aware he was improperly dressed but not really caring – it didn't matter in the scheme of things. He tried to reach Fleur again, but the line was still dead and he switched off his mobile. Taking a deep breath, he followed the duty doctor to the curtained-off cubicle and braced himself for what lay behind it.

Greg was still wearing hospital scrubs. He'd been in theatre for four hours, had sat through a long interview with the police, social worker, psychiatrist and hospital manager, and was now exhausted. In the silence that followed the end of the meeting, he slumped in the leather chair and shared a moment of quiet contemplation with the woman on the other side of the board-room table.

Carla Fioretti was the antithesis of what anyone would expect of a consultant psychiatrist and counsellor. In her late thirties, with black hair and eyes, a flawless olive skin and the innate Italian ability to dress with panache, she wore a cream silk blouse, tight black skirt and high-heeled shoes. Her arrival at the hospital had turned heads, and caused excited speculation even among the most staid male staff, who suddenly made a point of smartening themselves up in the forlorn hope she might notice them.

Carla sashayed through the hospital corridors seemingly unaware of the admiring glances that followed her every move. Her private life was a mystery, and there was no outward sign that she was married, engaged or batted for the other side. She didn't flirt, and steered clear of forming any relationships at the hospital unless they concerned her work. She had proved to be tough and focused on her job, and when she got her teeth into something, she had all the tenacity of a Jack Russell.

Greg dredged up a smile as they regarded one another. She was a stunning woman, and he'd have had to be made of stone to be immune to her charms, but there it ended, for he was very much in love with Fleur.

'Thanks for being so supportive, Carla,' he said, through a vast yawn. 'I feel a lot better now something positive is being done.'

'The mother's totally inadequate,' she replied, in the seductive, husky voice that made lesser men tingle. 'With the father in prison, she simply won't be able to cope.' She sat back in her chair, raking her long red nails through her hair. 'I'll do my best to persuade social services to get Shane into a reliable foster home, but you know how few places there are at the moment.'

'He's going to be in hospital for a few weeks yet,' Greg muttered, as he dragged himself out of the chair. 'Keep trying, Carla. I don't want him ending up in some children's home.'

'Sometimes they're the best short-term solution for a child his age,' she replied, pushing back from the table.

'I disagree,' he said shortly, reaching for the door handle. 'Kids need a proper home, and at five years old, fostering is the only solution in cases like this. Shane needs to know what it's like to live with a proper family who will care for him, not be left to get on with it as one of a horde of other damaged, scared kids.'

She touched his arm, halting his progress out into the corridor. 'You speak as if you have experience of such things,' she murmured. 'Want to talk about it?'

Her perfume was musky and enticing, her dark eyes mesmerizing, but he could see the concern in her expression and shied from it. 'There's nothing to discuss,' he replied coolly. 'Keep your counselling skills for those who need them, Carla.'

He left her standing in the doorway, his easy stride whispering through the empty corridor, his emotions tightly under control. He did need to talk – needed to get a great many things off his chest. But certainly not to Carla – and not tonight. He was far too fragile even to face Fleur. With a deep sigh, he dredged up the last of his energy and went to check on his young patient.

TAMARA
McKINLEY

Ocean Child

1920

Lulu Pearson is a young and talented Tasmanian sculptress.
The future is looking bright until Lulu learns she has inherited a
racing colt called Ocean Child from a mysterious benefactor,
and she must return to her homeland to claim him.

*

Baffled by the news, Lulu boards a ship to uncover the
truth, but it seems a welcome return is more than she can hope for.
Unbeknownst to Lulu, more than a few fortunes ride on Ocean Child's
ccess – it seems everyone from her estranged mother to the stable hands
has a part to play, and an interest in keeping the family secrets buried.

TAMARA
McKINLEY

Undercurrents

1894

The SS Arcadia sets sail from Liverpool, carrying Eva and Frederick Hamilton – a young married couple determined to make a new start in an exciting new frontier: Australia. But as the ship nears its destination, it goes down in an unexpected storm.

*

Years later, Olivia Hamilton makes the same journey, hoping to learn more about her mysterious origins. As Olivia draws closer to discovering the truth about her past, she realises that, like Eva Hamilton all those years ago, this could be a journey with unexpected consequences.